CoreFires

Colin Cantwell

Book Design by
www.Createbook.org

PROLOGUE

FROM MOTHEREARTH, HUMANKIND's civilization had spread throughout the galaxy until only the CoreFires remained untamed — their
last frontier.

Or so they believed — unaware of the intergalactic portal deep in the
CoreFires, unaware of the Rad:na, master sailors of energy winds and
gatekeepers to all the galaxies, even unaware of their own origin from
a galactic "seeding". That a superior technology could have created
the CoreFires and powered its strange physics by interconnecting the
galaxies was beyond their wildest dreams.

This prosperous civilization, intent on daily details of commerce,
organization, and order, pretty much ignored its frontier, and so it
was left to a few motley outcasts to determine Humankind's entry
into the family of all the galaxies.

———————————————

Chapter *1*

PASSING THE INTREPID
— GAP NEAR DUTCHMAN'S

BARELY A HALF mile wide, the glowing plasma-walled tunnel wound deeper into the CoreFires.

"Hailing space freighter," a rusty voice called on the comm channel, "Gap tug Aries, out of Dutchman's, is overtaking you from behind. Captain Junker calling."

"'Evening, Aries. The Intrepid here, from Space End. I'm Captain Holliger," came the reply. "Appreciate the warning. No surprises at this speed, eh? We see you on rear screens now. Moving right along, aren't you?"

Only by carefully threading the Gaps, as these interconnected tunnels of normal space were called, could Humankind's spaceships venture into the vast plasma firestorm surrounding the galaxy's mysterious core. One mistake, one moment within the quantum chaos of the CoreFires, and a spacecraft engine became a miniature sun.

Accelerating round a bend, the two ships balanced speed against danger as both cut the corner, close — but not too close — to the fiery blue Gap-walls where slowly roiling whirlpools of incandescent gas waited to claim the unwary. With the space tug close behind, the big supply ship was already setting up for the next curve as Junker again spoke into the comm. "No moss growing on your ship, either," he observed with a smile. "Urgent cargo?"

"Top priority, and a bonus if we're on time. Brings out the best in us. We'll be much slower than you, though, in that twisty section coming up — why don't you pass us here?"

In the slightly cockeyed pilot house of the Aries, Junker peered through windows rimmed with scrap-sculptures and stained glass. His grizzled head nodded. "Much obliged. Looks like a good spot. You'll need all the tunnel width you can get, so I'll pass below or above. What's your druthers?"

"You take the high road, Aries."

"And I'll be in Dutchman's afore ye," Junker added with a chuckle. "Commencing pass."

Carefully eyeing the seething tunnel walls and the triple-engined stern of the huge freighter, Junker spun the spokes of the wheel for the next bend, then pulled the yoke back. In response the fast-moving tug rose upward until the glowing blue tunnel vault was flying by close overhead.

Communication was short-range within the CoreFires. Cut off from the calls of the starry worlds, the ships threading the Gaps were on their own, with only occasional ramshackle space-villages, like Dutchman's, as havens along the way. To the spaceship crews, their isolation was at least inconvenient, sometimes dangerous. Only those galactic misfits, the hardy Gappers, counted it a blessing.

Once he had a clear view over the top of the Intrepid's exhaust plumes, Junker inched the throttles forward, his salt-and-pepper beard curving in a broad smile at the Aries' answering surge of power. "Atta girl," he murmured. "Now that we can see where we're going, let's show them what a patched together Gap tub can do."

While the two ships wound through a series of bends, the tug steadily overhauled the freighter, first passing over the big engines, then moving forward above the long hull housing its enormous cargo bays. Curving gracefully around the turns, the battered old Gap craft arced back and forth across the full width of the supply ship, gaining a little advantage on each bend by cutting the corners close to the CoreFires walls. "About to pass over your bridge, Intrepid," Junker reported into the comm. "Let me know when I'm far enough ahead to get a little further from this flaming ceiling."

"We see you. That's some engine, Aries. Looks like you could snag our urgent cargo business in no time."

"A scrapped freighter engine, Captain. Not to worry though — no place on board to stow cargo, urgent or otherwise. This is the ship to call, however, if you need a tow."

"Not planning on it, thanks. You're far enough ahead now to drop down to our level, Aries. When you arrive at Dutchman's, tell their sparks that we'll be coming through as close on your heels as we can, will you?"

"Will do, and much obliged for the pass. Aries clear."

Both ships slowed as the fiery tunnel narrowed, the jaunty Gap tug now leading the way. Ahead lay a sinuous defile where the CoreFires was glowing in shades of deep ultramarine. Although the gloomy passageway was wide enough for the Intrepid to proceed without the aid of a local pilot, the big ship had to navigate each bend with caution, and shortly the Aries was out of sight, leaving the freighter to grope its careful way between the tall darkly glimmering walls alone.

Soon after, when the freighter was halfway around an especially tight bend to starboard, a small heavily-armed pirate ship dropped from a fiery hollow high in the roof of the CoreFires tunnel. Descending like a lamprey onto a fish, it landed quietly and undetected atop the hull of the moving freighter. Immediately grappling the metal surface with powerful magnets, the intruder disgorged a dozen men in black spacesuits.

The first of these — fitted with magnetic shoes and hand magnets to keep from sliding off the hull around the turns — scuttled crabwise on all fours to a small hatch, paying out a safety line as he went. As soon as it was secured, the others clipped themselves to the line. Whenever the movements of the Intrepid permitted, they dashed one or two at a time to the hatch where they waited with weapons at the ready. The last to join them was their leader, who knelt beside the hatchway, tapping out an entry code.

———————————————

Chapter 2

[RAD:NA] HINT OF EVIL — PAWN PUSHING PAWN

NEARBY, WITHIN THE CoreFires itself, an alien, Questor-Joss of the Rad:na, shivered inside her spacesuit. Oblivious to the energy storm raging all about, oblivious to the spaceship deck bucking beneath her feet, she was suddenly attuned to something more ominous than the storm.

"I felt you," she thought. "For just a moment." A ninth generation Keeper, Joss was instantly alert. "You may think yourself undetected, Owd," she whispered, "but I felt your ancient presence."

Her delicate gloved fingers wrapped tightly around two Finder figures set into the railing. In answer the elaborately carved figures glowed moonlight bright, amplifying her probing senses. Shutting her eyes she focused on all she could intuit — seeking, lightly touching the shape of Unfolding Now. Touching, discarding, seeking far and wide until she found something she could not touch. Not a void, but a black cloaking fog.

Grasping the glowing figures still more tightly, she resisted the temptation to try to pierce that fog. "No, if you think your evil presence is unknown to this Rad:na," she whispered, "let it be so." Instead, she spoke a mantra that took her into a receptive trance.

Her mind became two thoughts only. The first: "I seek not." The second: "I am open to all." Over and over her mind re-iterated the two, dwelling ever more on the latter. Finally, with her focus at the very edge of the dark cloud, her mind became perfectly still. "I am open."

And suddenly, she saw! Somewhere, hiding within Humankind's galaxy, an Owd's ancient clawed hand pushing a pawn. The pawn's

4

hand in turn pushed a pawn on another chessboard. That pawn's hand also pushed another pawn. On chessboard after chessboard, pawn pushed pawn pushed pawn! She cried out as she felt the final pawn move toward her!

"What is it!" First-Mate-Norr's comm called from the pitching deck below. "Are you unwell?"

Questor-Joss staggered back from the railing of the navigator's platform, the vision fading as she released the glowing Finder figures. Regaining her senses she called back, "No, I'm well. I was probing afar. Our immediate path is clear in any event." Resuming her normal stance grasping the Finders, she checked the ship's course. "Steady as she goes until we come about at the Gap-wall."

"Aye, Honored One," the mate acknowledged. "Steady as she goes until the Gap-wall."

Ship's gravity was anchored to the galactic plane, and Joss had to plant her feet firmly on the steeply slanting deck. Although Joss and her crew-mates looked much like tall thin versions of human beings, the alien ship underfoot could hardly have been more different from Humankind's vessels. Propelled by straining energy sails instead of engines, she heeled hard over as she drove through the streaming CoreFires.

Utilizing an ancient technology invented by the Rad:na, the gate-keepers of all the galactic cores, her hull was embedded in the nebula's planar field. With all their skill the crew fought to balance the two forces powering her and threatening to tear her asunder. Aloft, the ionic gale bent her masts as it howled through her myriad energy sails. Below, in mid-space, her keel cleaved the resistance of the planar field, carving spacetime into a chaos of incandescent singularities, spewing a wide wake of short-lived infinitesimal stars.

The longer the trail of blue-white embers and the wider the swath of far-flung star-foam, the more her crew exulted in their wild ride through the stormy nebula.

At the navigator's station, Questor-Joss's keen eyes scanned the turbulent blue glow ahead for the first signs of the Gap-wall while she puzzled over her disturbing vision. "An Owd! Hiding somewhere within

Humankind's galaxy! Yet," she reasoned, "the portal's been guarded since its creation. What if the Owd had guessed that this would become a nursery galaxy, and hid one of their kind before the seeding? Hiding, waiting millions of years for the new species to emerge? Why?"

Amplified by the two carved figures, her other senses ranged beyond the reach of her eyes.

"Be alert," she cautioned herself, and shivered again. "There's something strange in the wind."

————————————

Chapter 3

SEIZED BY PIRATES — CHAIN HIM UP

"ANY VALUABLE CARGO, Captain? Something special aboard that you wish to declare? Come, come, Captain Holliger! I'm not known for my patience." The voice as it came over ship's comm was disguised by a distorting audio circuit. The source was the all-black pirate ship now hovering near the bridge of the stationary Intrepid with its armament trained on the freighter.

Glaring through the bridge windows, Holliger clenched his fists. Three helmeted figures in black spacesuits surrounding him immediately raised their hand weapons to fire. Holliger growled, "You have the advantage, Captain...? I don't believe we've been properly introduced, this time."

"This time, Captain?" The menace was clear, even though the voice was distorted.

"Your voice is disguised. There must be a reason."

"Observant of you," the voice hissed. "But I'll not satisfy your curiosity. Now, one last time! Any valuable cargo aboard?"

"No! What's the fate of my crew?"

"Wrong answer, Captain!" the voice snapped back, then it took on an icy gloating tone. "Your crew is aboard my ship — more you need not know. As to your reply, it's truer than you think. For instance, 7 crates formerly located at W-94 in the aft cargo bay are now on board my ship, as is the chest that was sequestered in your quarters."

"Chain him to the wheel!"

Holliger leaped to wrest the weapon from his nearest captor, but was immediately overwhelmed and dragged struggling to the big ship's

7

wheel as the voice continued to taunt him over the comm. "Overly impulsive! You, sir, are a rank amateur at violence, while my men are skilled professionals, experts in their field."

With his arms and body chained to the wooden spokes of the wheel, Holliger tried to kick with his legs. In moments even that was impossible. As he was futilely testing the strength of his iron bonds, one of the spacesuited trio passed a final loop of chain around his neck from behind. "Not too tight," the voice from the pirate ship cautioned, "he's to remain conscious at all times."

"Kill me and get it over with!" Holliger shouted.

"Nothing so quick, my dear Captain, or should I say, my dear captive? Yes, make it the latter, with the emphasis on `my'. Especially since your ship will no longer answer to your command. We have a final scene to play out, in which you will star. Men! Switch one of his rear-view screens to a picture showing the cargo bay! Run the Crystal and be at the hatch in one minute!"

With that, the all-black pirate ship rose out of sight. While one of the pirates switched the big monitor, another raced to the ship's command station, inserting a Crystal into the reader. As soon as the readout showed Running, the trio fled from the bridge.

Try as he might, Holliger was unable to move. As he continued to struggle against his bonds, he was startled to see rows of flickering colored lights coming alive on the ship's consoles, showing some sort of automatic sequence initiating. On the monitor screen he could see that the cargo bay, was empty. Cursing, he took as deep a breath as the chains across his chest would permit, then concentrated on trying to twist his left hand free.

———————————————

Chapter *4*

DESTROYING THE CRYSTALS — BON VOYAGE, CAPTAIN

TWO MINUTES LATER, the black ship halted a hundred yards from the freighter's cargo bay, facing the freighter. The distorted voice on the comm channel chuckled. "Too bad," it said. The pirate ship then wheeled, moving down the Gap ahead of the stationary freighter until it was part way around the next bend, where it spun and hovered, waiting expectantly.

The reason soon became apparent. The Intrepid's engines fired under automatic control, and the big supply ship began to accelerate down the tunnel. Unmindful of the deadly CoreFires walls, it was proceeding faster and faster on a perfectly straight course, heading for the Gap-wall at the next bend.

Through the bridge windows the figure of its captain could be seen, still chained to the wheel, now with one arm free. As the engines thrusted, the massive freighter steadily picked up speed, moving past the swirling blue fires on each side, boring on toward the glowing whirlpools ahead. Down the gloomy passageway it accelerated, the violet exhaust plumes of its engines flaring brightly. Soon only two hundred yards remained, then a hundred, fifty.

A mocking voice called over the comm channel, "Bon voyage, Captain!"

Moments later the freighter's prow disappeared into the Core-Fires as a powerful explosion ripped the bridge to tumbling shreds. A succession of blasts erupted along the length of the Intrepid's hull, tearing open the cargo bays, but the engines drove on still, propelling the wreckage into the Gap-wall. Last to go was the engine room. As it became engulfed in the swirling plasma the powerful fields so carefully captured in the triple-engines encountered the quantum chaos of the CoreFires.

Three small regions of spacetime collapsed to singularities, flooding the gloomy indigo defile with the brilliance of a hundred suns.

————————————

Chapter 5

[RAD:NA] NEAR DISASTER — FLYING WRECKAGE

ON THE RAD:NA side of the Gap-walls, the energy winds born at the heart of the galactic Core drove indigo CoreFires eddies in an endless stampede. Humpbacked gusts of phosphorescent sapphire raced from afar, roiling and weaving as they jostled each other in their headlong flight, separating at the last moment to flow around the stable Gap-wall fields. Unmindful of the interruption, the fiery plasmas again closed ranks as they tumbled on into the distance, intent upon fulfilling their destiny, to birth new stars.

At first the only hint of the Rad:na was a glimmer of gold among the boiling blue clouds, but a sudden gust soon parted the cloaking veil wide, revealing a wondrous alien ship riding the winds of stars to be.

Tall masts wreathed in blue sparks leaned in the streaming plasma, supporting a host of billowing energy sails, their surfaces straining taut, afire with flickering golden traceries of captive lightning. Her dark hull ignited a broad wake of blue-white embers in mid-space as it plowed through the resistance of the invisible planar field. The gale drove the brilliant golden sails, the tall masts heeled over, and the dazzling ship careened on toward the cliff-like barrier of the Gap-wall as the alien crew swarmed on her decks, preparing to come-about.

On the navigator's platform, Questor-Joss, famed Navigatrix of the Rad:na, harkened to an especially high-pitched keening of the energy winds in her ear-comm. Her eyes flicked upward to the huge taut energy sails where the flashing captive lightning suddenly redoubled under the force of the gust.

Underfoot the ship heeled even further, and she could feel it accelerate as the keel below ignited great gouts of star-foam. Hands firmly on the Finder figures, she carefully gauged their speed and the distance remaining as the ship bore down on the Gap-wall. "Prepare to come about," she called.

"Aye," replied First-Mate-Norr, "Preparing to come about." Then in a voice that carried easily above the howling gale he shouted to his crew, "Be ready, beings! Do you see that great wall of whirlpools hungry to claim our fair ship?"

"Aye! Aye, we do," they called back.

"And would you have her end our voyage by slipping through that wall into the void beyond?"

"Nay! No! We would not!"

"Then stand ready and able to bring her about!"

"Aye, ready to bring her about! Ready!"

From her high platform, Questor-Joss eyed the looming wall of slowly rotating fire-forms, any one of which dwarfed the alien ship. At the last moment she called out in a clear voice, "Come about!"

First-Mate-Norr thundered, "Bring her about, beings! With a will!"

As the sails swiveled, the tall ship came upright and began to heel to the other side. The starry wake began to curve. The waiting wall was close at hand as the mighty ship heeled hard, its keel almost buried in star-foam as it flew. The masts leaned far over, the topmost of its myriad lightning-sails almost touching the Gap-wall.

Just as it looked as if she was clear of the Gap-wall cliff, Questor-Joss felt a momentary sense of foreboding. Rebuking herself for attending too much to the ship and the storm, she gave her intuition full rein, immediately feeling a hint of evil greed somewhere close at hand, cruel and triumphant, then something more specific. Reacting instantly, she shouted, "Norr! Have them protect their eyes! Now!"

Norr bellowed, "Shut your eyes! Cover them! Everyone!"

In the next second the ship was simultaneously enveloped by a blinding flash and shaken by the fierce quake of a spacetime singularity.

"Keep them covered!" Norr roared. "Steady, beings, steady as she goes 'til we can see again!"

The great ship staggered in the plasma wind, the captive lightning of the energy sails crackling loud as they snapped taut, but held. Recovering, she plunged on, spreading great swaths of star-foam as she bucked and rolled.

"That's the way, beings! Keep her steady." Even with his lids shut tight and his hand covering his eyes, Norr's vision was awash with red. It seemed forever before the brilliance diminished enough for him to risk squinting through slitted lids. All about him the deck and crew were etched in blazing white. "Those who first can see, sing out!"

"Ahead!" someone called, "Coming through the Gap-wall! Beware!"

As glare subsided and vision returned many raised their voices in consternation, for great pieces of tumbling metal wreckage, some red hot, were piercing the Gap-wall in spreading trajectories.

Questor-Joss, holding tight to the Finder figures set in the navigator's platform railing probed with senses other than her eyes. Gasping, she perceived imminent doom. "Hard aport!" she shouted. "Pull, beings, for our lives!"

"You heard her," the first mate roared, "Hard aport! Pull!"

"Hard aport!" they answered. "Pull! Pull!"

From the Gap-wall, huge pieces of the Intrepid emerged on a collision course with the Rad:na vessel.

Heeling far over, the ship spun ninety degrees in half its length. Several of the crew slid down the steeply sloping deck, saved at the last moment as they piled into the rail. The masts leaned far, closer to horizontal than vertical, and for a while it appeared she was doomed to go over.

"Keep her there!" Norr thundered. "Hold her!"

Slowly she began righting herself. The violent maneuver had turned the ship aside as suddenly as a toreador executing a pass before the charging bull, and the crew watched in agonized suspense as massive pieces of wreckage hurtled by close across her bows. Although she had escaped the worst, many minor projectiles were still striking amid her rigging, snapping spars wreathed in blue sparks, dropping golden sails to flap futilely, partially adrift in the ionic gale.

"Look sharp above you!" cautioned the voice.

"Beware, the bow!" called another, and all hands saw one last red-hot piece of the dismembered hulk spinning directly towards the bow, almost at deck level.

Desperately the deck hands fled as it approached, most getting clear, a few trapped in its path.

"Drop low!" a voice called. "Drop to the deck!"

Above, Joss dove over the railing of the navigator's platform, somersaulting to the deck and dropping flat just as the huge piece of metal passed like a glowing scythe, clipping off part of the railing and mowing the rigging as it flew. Rolling on her back, she felt the heat of it's passage on her face and saw it smash her platform to fragments before carrying it away over the side.

Slowly the crew rose, marveling at their good fortune, and assessing the damage about them.

"Turn to, beings," First-Mate-Norr called out. "We're favored this night, thanks to our honored Questor! Turn to! Let's set our fair ship aright! You three, rig a temporary navigator's platform! You, fetch the spare Finders! The rest, tend to that rigging. Any that's beyond repair, cut it free. Quickly now!"

As soon as the hands were ascending the tangled rigging, Norr strode across the deck, as quickly as he could without appearing to hurry. He expelled an explosive sigh of relief as he saw his Navigatrix rise from the deck and begin calmly picking hot debris off her skintight spacesuit. Coming to her side, he spoke in a low voice. "I thought you were doomed."

"I thought we all were," she replied in kind, then aloud. "No leaks, nothing broken." She flexed a bruised shoulder. "No damage that a day or two won't fix. And our ship and crew?"

Norr laughed in spite of himself. "Much the same, all hands and the ship as well — no damage that a day or two won't fix. We'll have a temporary station rigged for you in no time. Whereaway?"

"Excellent, Norr! Keep her off the wind 'til that rigging's repaired, and give my compliments to all hands."

The first mate bellowed out, "Keep her as she heads. A ship is only as good as her crew, and this one has earned compliments to all hands! From Questor-Joss!" His announcement was answered by a rousing cheer from the rigging. "Look lively now — there's work to be done before we're ship-shape again."

Turning again to his Navigatrix, Norr spoke quietly. "You anticipated the flash and the wreckage coming through. Otherwise we'd have never made the turn in time."

"Aye, Norr," she muttered grimly. "We were lucky this time." Dropping her voice even further, she continued, "Between the two of us, we must remain alert at all times. Something evil is afoot." She turned to the first mate, placing a hand on his shoulder. "We're the only ship in this region. It may come to us alone to fulfill the obligations of the Rad:na."

Norr returned the Questor's gaze. "Joss, whatever's required of us, you choose the course and I'll give you the finest ship and crew that sails. I hear your warning." He kicked a piece glowing debris off the deck into the embers of star-foam. "If I seem to forget, give me a big boot in the back-side!"

Questor-Joss looked up into the rigging where new lines were being reeved through the blocks even as the tangle was being cut away. She laughed. "Do the same for me, Norr, lest we be caught unawares. I was too lax, and we barely made it. Only fools count on being lucky twice!"

"Aye, Questor. When that wreckage hit your platform, I thought... Well, let's say I'd not like to shave it any closer." Looking aloft Norr saw some detail above that wasn't to his liking. "Alert is the watchword!" he agreed as he swarmed up into the rigging to supervise at close hand, bellowing, "Avast there! The upper yard first or we'll have a rat's nest below! That's it! Cut all that away!"

The glimmering ship sailed on, making half speed in the CoreFires storm. Behind, she left flickering remnants of torn energy sails, broken spars, and tangled scraps of rigging drifting in her evanescent wake of microscopic blue-white stars.

Also left behind was the great ragged remnant of the Intrepid's hull, tumbling on and glowing red, except for the few entangled fragments of the Rad:na navigator's platform and the two Finder figures, glowing as softly white as moonlight.

The fierce plasma gale continued to buffet the scattered wreckage, and the small force it transmitted gradually began to take effect, steadily sweeping the widespread debris back toward the Gap-wall from which it came.

Slowly the tortured tributes to violence drifted, tumbling one by one back to Humankind's side of the wall.

Eventually, the CoreFires were clean again.

————————————

Chapter 6

INTREPID'S HULK AT THE RING
— LAST OF A GRIM JOB

JUNKER'S RING. GHOSTLY it loomed in the green glow of the perpetual plasma mists drifting through this Gap-cavern.

Junker's Ring. A million tons of massed space-scrap orbiting a hovering junk-sculpture castle. The ultimate scrap-yard in the sky.

Like the countless shattered asteroids orbiting Saturn in Human-kind's original solar system, countless pieces of Gap junk circled round the tug captain's lair.

Wrecked hulks and derelicts by the hundreds, dismembered sections of spaceships by the thousands, all orbited endlessly about Junker's castle amid a two mile wide disc of obsolete devices and discarded debris. To the Gappers, junk was everything, and everything was here, serenely circling in space. Often Junker's customers circled as well, searching among the orbiting flotsam for some urgently needed component vital to their precarious existence.

The castle was almost completely wrapped in Glowmist, but the near side of the Ring was clear as Junker's battered tug maneuvered carefully above the flotilla of wrecked ships. The Aries stayed just high enough to be able to thrust without disrupting any of the orbits below. On the other end of her long tow-cable the last section of the Intrepid's remains was settling in toward an upcoming vacant spot in the Ring.

At the wheel, Junker called into the comm, "How are we doing, Mr. Garms?"

Second Mate Garms, a space suited figure standing on a neighboring derelict in the Ring, gave a thumbs up, replying, "Looking good, Captain. Coming in nicely."

Again Junker called on the comm, this time to his first mate who was standing on the now cooled piece of the Intrepid where the tow cable was attached. "Lyard, when Garms gives the signal I'll start a low power thrust to kill your momentum. The moment your speed exactly matches the orbits around you, knock the cable latch free. I'll stop thrusting when I feel the cable come loose. Agreed?"

"My hammer's at the ready, Cap'n," came the reply.

"Getting close," reported Garms.

"Say when," Junker called, his hand on the throttle.

Garms watched the new arrival nestle in among its neighbors. "Thrust, Captain!"

"Thrusting."

Lyard, a sledge upraised in his hands, carefully judged the relative speeds, then swung a mighty blow at the big steel latch on the end of the tow cable, triggering its release mechanism. As the freed cable slowly recoiled toward the stern of the Aries, Junker cut the power. "Perfect!" Lyard reported.

Within minutes the tug was standing off a short distance from the Ring with the tow cable re-stowed. All three crew members, helmets off, were looking thoughtfully out the pilot house windows at the orbiting stream of wreckage, especially the remains of the Intrepid.

"Pretty grim," muttered Junker, stroking his beard.

"That's the last of it, anyway," said Garms with a sigh. "A labor I'm glad to have behind us."

"Aye to that!" affirmed Lyard. "Pirates for sure, casting their evil shadow over this Gap, may they slip into the CoreFires! I wonder how they got on board her."

"Very strange," Junker agreed, "more puzzles than answers." Squaring his shoulders, Junker reached for the throttles. "As Mr. Garms has so wisely noted, we'd best put these last few days labor behind us. Anyone willing to accompany me into town? I'd wager there are three seats waiting for us at the tavern."

"More than willing, Cap'n," answered Lyard with a twinkle in his eye. "In fact, if the Aries, bless her, isn't up to it, you have but to break out the oars and Mr. Garms and I will put our backs into it until we are delivered to the inn."

"Not to disagree, Captain," interjected the smiling Garms, "but if it's all the same to you, I'd ask the Aries first, just in case she might be interested in moseying in that direction anyway, without the need for us to be laboring so on the way."

Junker hit the throttle, the mighty engine fired, and he wheeled the tug away from the grim new additions orbiting in the Ring. "Seems as though she has a mind to head for the POSH," he chuckled. "Ship your oars, gentleman, it appears we're in luck."

———————————————

Chapter 7

WOMB OF FIRE — THE COREFIRE'S RESTLESS

THE SPACE FREIGHTER Steadfast floated in the darkness above Dutchman's, one metallic form suspended in a vast womb of blue flame. At her stern the captain and first mate inspected the supply ship's engines from a small open space-dinghy.

Two miles below, still well within the womb's fiery walls, the dark hovels and spidery gangways of the dilapidated village that served this section of the Gap also floated in mid-space, the village called Dutchman's.

In all that scene, only the village, the freighter, and the dinghy were motionless — the glowing nebula walls were alive with slowly swirling whirlpools and mysterious upwellings of indigo plasmas.

"The CoreFires's restless tonight," Captain Baldwin observed.

"Aye, everywhere you look, the walls are stirring," replied the mate.

"We'd best get her underway soon," the captain said, "I can feel it in my bones."

—————————————

Chapter 8

THEY'RE NOT COMING DOWN
— WHAT IF THEY HAD TO?

FAR BELOW IN the village, a small figure ran along the network of dark gangways, dashing around corners, pounding down the straightaways, two knapsacks bouncing on his back. "Hang on, Marneen," he whispered breathlessly as he ran, "I've got 'em." Sticking out his arm as he went by, he grabbed hold of a pipe on a run-down metal shed and whipped himself around a bend. "Almost there," he puffed, "almost there!" Rounding the last corner, he nearly collided with another small figure.

"Mutch!"

"I've got 'em! Are they coming down yet?"

Marneen looked up into the blue-walled void, picking out the distant freighter and the tiny flashing light that marked the ship's dinghy. "They're not coming."

"They what!"

"They're not coming down. I heard Salty talking. There wasn't any cargo on board for Dutchman's."

Mutch's shoulders sagged, and he dispiritedly dumped the knapsacks on the gangway. "Oh, great!" he moaned, plopping himself down on one of the knapsacks. "At this rate we'll never get to be stowaways!" Then he brightened. "Wait! What about the local pilot? Couldn't we get towed up by the pilot's cruiser?"

"Way too fast — we'd get killed for sure! No, what we need is for them to come down in the dinghy."

"Right!" Mutch exclaimed, making a sour face. "I can just see Salty sending the message now, `Please come down in the dinghy 'cause there's two kids down here that need a tow.' Fat chance! Salty'd kick us right out of the comm shack!"

Marneen hung onto a post and swung way out over the edge of the gangway, totally oblivious to the empty void below, her eyes still on the ship and dinghy. "Yeah, he would," she muttered thoughtfully. "What if they had to come down anyway, Mutch?"

Mutch looked up at the distant winking light. "Why would they have to come down anyway?"

"That's just what I've been thinking." She swung all the way around the post, feet flying over empty space before alighting again on the worn metal gangway. "The go-boards are hidden under the gangway. Take the knapsacks down and get the stuff ready. I'll be back in a few minutes." With that, she disappeared around the corner.

Puzzled but hopeful, Mutch picked up the knapsacks and carried them to the brink of the gangway. Before scrambling off the edge to make his way into the gridwork underneath, he paused for one more look at the freighter so far above.

———————————————

Chapter *9*

ENGINE CHECK — WE'LL TELL 'EM OURSELVES

JUST OFF THE Steadfast's stern, the tiny ship's dinghy moved toward the huge starboard engine. Its two occupants were suited up for space, with the mate seated in the stern of the dinghy — actually more of a space-sled, but the old name survived — and Captain Baldwin standing erect in the bow. All about, the deadly nebula walls roiled and churned in ceaseless slow-motion tumult, only three to five miles distant.

Baldwin remembered a phrase from the heroic poem, "Lifelines":
Dark Leviathans threading through shifting cathedrals, Coursing the caverns of frozen fire.

"Almost frozen fire," he thought, his practiced eye scanning the cloud-slow turbulence in the Gap-walls. As always, he was trying to sense the violent order that lay beneath that incandescent surface, trying to foretell a flare or a coming quiescence. He had brought the Steadfast on another of her many voyages deep into the CoreFires, carrying cargo from the worlds of the starry skies, and like all good Core-captains he relied on a mix of experience and intuition to guide his ship safely through CoreFires's dangerous beauty. At the moment, his intuition was prowling like a caged tiger.

"We'll finish this inspection and get moving as quickly as possible," he announced.

"Aye, sir. But won't we have to wait for the pilot to come up from Dutchman's?" asked the mate.

"Perhaps not. With a little luck, we may be able to save some time."

Amused as well as frustrated by the image of his ship as a whale suspended motionless in mid-cathedral — specially the motionless part — he turned his attention toward the next challenge awaiting them, a narrow vertical cleft in the womb-walls through which the Steadfast must soon pass.

"Dutchman's Gorge," the mate muttered, following his captain's gaze. "Wouldn't take but a few turns of the screw to squeeze those walls together like a vise."

Baldwin studied the luminescent Gap dead ahead. With each journey through those twisting curves the shapes were a little different. But as narrow as it was, its walls had never closed since Humankind's first ships had entered here, exploring the mysterious tunnels that led into the CoreFires. Arteries, the Gaps had become, the only access to the worlds discovered within the Core-caves, and the supply ships were the corpuscles bearing the necessities of life.

The Gorge was far too narrow, Baldwin knew, for a freighter the size of the Steadfast to attempt without the aid of a local pilot, and he saw no sign of the pilot's vessel.

"If the bosun's made contact," he instructed the mate, "have him tell the pilot to make directly for us if he's agreeable. We'll take his craft aboard 'til we reach Littlebend and make it worth his while to save us some time."

"Aye, sir."

While the mate was uncapping a shielded comm-tap on the big ship's stern, Baldwin peered intently into the dark exhaust bell of the starboard engine. As his eyes became adjusted he saw a swarm of faint blue sparks writhing deep in its interior, confirming a suspicion that did nothing to improve his mood.

"I thought so!" he muttered.

"Captain?"

"Field leakage on number three. Better have it looked at soon. What's the word from the bosun?"

"Bad night for comm, sir. Lots of static. No range. Bosun says Dutchman's station is the only chance, but their last report was no contact either. Now their local docking comm is out so even if they can contact the pilot, we can't raise them at all."

"Very well", the captain replied evenly, although his face belied the words. "We'll go down and tell them ourselves."

The mate turned again to the comm. "Note in the log that we'll check engine number three at the next port with suitable facilities. We're going down to tell Dutchman's in person. Mind the store."

Baldwin observed the mate's manner as he recapped the comm-port. "We're all uneasy," he thought. "You, me, even our `whale' is all itchy and twitchy to get through the Gorge. Past time to get under way."

The mate swung the dinghy away from it's mother-ship, and with a few rapid pokes at the control panel, began the descent to the village of Dutchman's.

———————————————

Chapter 10

GOING DOWN — GAP VILLAGES

GAP VILLAGES. COLLECTIONS of ramshackle huts and dilapidated structures floating in mid-space, some tied together with spidery gangways, some hovering off at a distance, reachable only by small craft.

Among Gap villages, size was a measure of their circumstance. A few were larger; most were tiny. Cut off from all normal commerce and communication with the rest of the Galaxy, they were scattered along the Gaps, serving the ships that in turn served them.

Some, located at the junction of two or more heavily traveled arteries, were relatively prosperous. Most were small monuments to some minor need and Humankind's propensity for adapting to almost anything, for settling almost anywhere. The smallest were little more than temporary experiments, pitting the rigors of Gap life against the adaptability of their wildly assorted inhabitants.

So it was with Dutchman's. Located between two tricky sections of the chain of Gap-caverns, it served mostly for temporary repairs, the taking on and dropping off of pilots, and scavenging what was left of any ships that failed to navigate the tricky sections. Still the village hung on and became a Place, and its resident Gappers were certainly more adaptable and wildly assorted than most. Eventually the village came to resemble its inhabitants.

"Dutchman's!" the mate exclaimed with a snort, peering at the motley assemblage far below. "As if they've ever sighted the Dutchman in this hole! I've seen a lot of poor Gap stations in the CoreFires, but this one looks like it was built out of rejects from a junkyard."

"It probably was," replied the captain. "Originally it was named for the Gorge, but eventually it just got shortened to Dutchman's. The local tale has it that the Flying Dutchman was seen in the Gorge, but whether there's any substance to it I couldn't say."

"Not likely! There're too many ramshackle dumps whose only claim to fame is that they've seen the Dutchman. If one in a hundred of the tales were true, he'd have been so busy flying from place to place we'd all have gotten a good look at him by now." Although largely unaware of it, the mate had come to view anything disorderly or makeshift as dangerous — if and when an emergency struck, as dangerous as a snake under foot. What he saw below looked as appealing as a nest of vipers. "Look, even the marker lights aren't working right!"

Baldwin saw that it was so. Even on the village pier and the big antenna, each strobe would flash a few times, then quit for a while, so that the total effect was of some weird form of syncopation. "Looks rather appropriate, I'd say," he replied, "besides, nothing works quite right for long when it's that close to the Gap-walls."

When big supply ships hove to, they did so in mid-channel, constantly monitoring their position to stay a safe distance from the disruptive energies of the CoreFires. The villages, however, were located much closer to the fiery walls, anchored — more or less — in a favorable configuration of the CoreFires flux fields. Sea-anchored might be a better term, since as the walls shifted and warped in response to the complex tides within the Core-clouds, the entire village moved with them.

The ideal sea-anchors had proven to be old cold engines that had "gone singular", trapping part of the planar field in a point space. Relative to the CoreFires, burnt out motors tended to stay where they were, and supply a local pseudo-gravity as well.

As a result every structure in Dutchman's was perched atop a massive piece of defunct space-junk, a big step toward achieving the dilapidated appearance that so rankled the mate.

"Get it over with, and get on our way," he thought, giving a few more pokes to the dinghy control panel.

Chapter 11

ARIES AT THE PIER
— POWER OF THE WRITTEN WORD

NOW I'VE SEEN it all!" the mate grumbled as he guided the Steadfast's dinghy toward Dutchman's pier.

Captain Baldwin, however, was convulsed by another belly-laugh, hugely enjoying the sight that so offended the mate. "That does take the cake!" he agreed weakly, lapsing into another round of laughter.

The object of their attention was tied up at the pier — the Aries.

"Obviously a space-tug," managed the captain, noting the bumpers and the large cable spools set amidships like paddlewheels, "and a rather powerful tug, at that!" Powerful was an understatement. Fully the aft third of the vessel was taken up by a somewhat discolored and totally outsized engine that had once propelled a large freighter.

Quelling a laugh, Baldwin pointed toward the bow, where the pilot house looked more like an exceptionally tall outhouse set with elaborate stained-glass windows. It was also several degrees out of plumb, which made it seem to be peering intently over the port bow.

Try as they might, neither the mate nor Captain Baldwin could long keep their eyes from what lay abaft of the pilot house. To the mate it brought a pained grimace. To the captain, it never failed to administer the coup de grace to his composure, sending him into another round of helpless merriment.

There, surmounting machinery of mixed origin and unknown purpose, the normal superstructure of the tug had been modified into four large metal-sculptures.

First, every inch of the tall comm-mast had been embellished with multitudes of welded gears and bearings, old fittings and pulleys of every description, curly-cues of connecting rods, rosettes of rivets, and gargoyles of butterfly valves and flanges. The mast had been extended right through the bottom of the tug, where it curved forward in a profusely filigreed semicircle.

Behind that, the winch motor exhausts had been extended upward in a large U-shape, also lavishly decorated with ex-machinery, as was the winch truss itself, which had grown an extra leg.

Finally, the tug's crane-mast and booms atop the giant engine had received similar rococo treatment, and were positioned to make the whole much greater than the sum of its parts: the four tall sculptures formed the letters J U N K, with the J piercing right through the middle of the tug and coming out the bottom.

Still chuckling as he debarked, Baldwin exclaimed, "J-U-N-K! Superb! Best laugh I've had in ages. Shows the inspiring power of the written word!"

Another rumbling laugh broke free as the captain strode along the pier, looking up at the ornate letters. "Splendid!" he guffawed, shaking his head.

Turning toward the inn, neither he nor the mate noticed a handlight flash three times from under the gangway.

————————————————

Chapter *12*

INSIDE POSH — DUTCHMAN'S FINEST

OTITIUS, AS USUAL, had one ear cocked to the ebb and flow of overlapping conversations rippling through the room. By nature, he was more a listener than a talker, an excellent trait for a "keep".

Also as usual, he was polishing his pride and joy, the rich fullerium surface of the bar, a long hull plate set on two dented ore trommels. It's dark iridescent sheen spoke of long exposure to the emanations of CoreFires, and Otitius knew and loved every inch of it, every dent and gouge, although he could only muse on what adventures and misadventures might have created them. Carefully looking at the reflections — but seeing only the surface — he traversed the length of the bar, banishing every spot and spill, wiping and buffing his way to perfection. Finally, he stepped back, tilted his head this way and that, and smiled with satisfaction.

Looking up he checked around the room, and finding, as usual, nothing that required his attention, Otitis contentedly resumed polishing his two-ton bar.

The decor was consistently early scrap-yard. Hanging by chains overhead, a metal sign with welded letters proclaimed, "Port Out, Starboard Home", then added "Dutchman's Finest". (It could as truthfully have said "Dutchman's Only".) To the right, a smaller sign admonished, "If it's dark, it's night." Gap folks had a fierce pride in their difficult existence, and both signs were subtle gibes at the well-paid supply ship crews that had opposite definitions of "out" and "home", and sometimes went by Universal Galactic Time which had little meaning within the CoreFires.

The voluptuous Li-Tharm, ever popular "tender" of the POSH, leaned against the end of the bar, talking to two men in the shadows, one apparently dressed in tatters. Like most Gappers, she almost always wore her Mono-mol suit so that she could step outside or inside without thinking about it, even though outside was the hard vacuum of empty space. In spite of its name, the suit was actually several molecules thick, a bio-technical wonder that made Gap life possible. Except for the occasional bulges of some of its components, a Mono-mol suit fit the body it contained like a stretchy coat of paint, shiny or otherwise, which in Li-Tharm's case was a spectacular benefit that she enjoyed as much as anyone. Her "paint" was shiny.

The other locals lounging around the POSH were similarly dressed in rainbow colored bio-suits. Their helmets, of a more rigid Mono-mol, varied in size and shape as a matter of individual expression. The face was open "indoors", and appeared nearly so "outdoors", where it was protected from the vacuum by a nearly invisible molecular barrier called a field bubble. A similar bubble protected the "open" door of the POSH.

————————————————

Chapter 13

THE SPARKS' CONCERN
— A BAD NIGHT FOR COMM

THERE WAS A double audible pop as the captain and mate of the Steadfast entered the inn and the fields of their face bubbles — finding themselves in air once again — dutifully collapsed. The uniform white of their bio-suits identified them to the locals as transport line crew-members, and the insignia told their rank.

"Where's your sparks?" asked the captain.

Otitius gestured toward the door to the right and behind the bar. "Comm shack's there, and you can call him Salty. Can I get you anything?"

"No thanks."

The mate, who was looking down the bar in the direction of Li-Tharm, was obviously pleased when the captain said, "I'll handle the comm business — you relax for a bit."

A slight smile played on the captain's lips as he walked toward the door of the comm shack hearing Li-Tharm's cheery voice behind him hailing the mate. "Hi, stranger, what'll you have?"

--- --- --- --- --- ---

Chapter 14

COMM SHACK CAUTION
— WORDS TO THE WISE

SALTY'S COMM SHACK was as makeshift as everything they'd seen so far at Dutchman's, and Baldwin was relieved that he didn't have to worry about his mate offending the sparks. "Any word yet from the pilot?"

"Nothing yet. It's a bad night for comm."

"So I've heard", the captain replied dryly. "I'd like you to give him a message as soon as you can raise him."

As Salty and Baldwin sat down in front of the comm station, neither noticed the small figure of Marneen edge out from underneath the transmitter behind them, and silently dart out the door.

"Who's taking you through?" Salty asked.

"Pasquil. He's due from Littlebend."

At Salty's laugh, Captain Baldwin hoisted a questioning eyebrow.

Salty raised his hands in a reassuring gesture. "Pasquil the Magician. He's OK. He's good, real good." He chuckled again, and added, "He'll pull your leg 'til you can only stand upright on a slanting deck, but don't be put off. He's real good. If he's due, he'll be here soon. His vessel's fast, and he never misses a contract."

"That speed could be helpful. As soon as you contact him, direct him to make straight for the Steadfast rather than putting in here. We'll take his vessel aboard and drop him back at Littlebend, and make it worth his while."

"He'll like that," Salty smiled, "but you might as well wait and tell him yourself. When he gets in range, you'll still have enough time to beat him back to your ship. What's your cargo, that they're in such an all-fired hurry for?"

"A bonus cargo, if we're on schedule. The usual, plus a few tons of updates to replace all that stuff that was lost…" The captain's voice trailed off, and a shadow passed over his face, a momentary darkness at the memory of someone now gone.

Salty, too, was quiet, internally debating over whether to speak further. Coming to a decision, he spoke again. "Excuse me, Captain, for sticking my nose in where it's none of my business, but may I speak confidentially?"

"Please." The captain leaned forward.

Hesitantly, Salty continued in a lowered voice, "It sounds improbable, but there's been some talk of pirates. Do you have any kind of protection?"

The captain in turn hesitated, judging the character of the man before him. "I appreciate your warning. We've heard a few wild rumors and some speculation. Nothing more." Again he looked into Salty's eyes, then added, "The Core Patrol's been notified, the cargo's keyed to me, and even I don't know what the key is until we reach port. There's not much else that we can do, but I'd be obliged if you wouldn't mention the bonus cargo."

"You have my word on it, Captain." The two men exchanged a firm handshake, and Salty once more bent over his equipment. "I'll try to raise Pasquil."

He quickly configured the comm, getting a rewarding rush of static, but then repeated the next sequence three or four times with no apparent result. Shrugging his shoulders, he apologized, "Sorry, Captain, the local docking comm is back up, but now we have a glitch in the main antenna. I'll have to fix it before we can continue. Sit still — it'll only take a minute or two."

As the flustered sparks bustled out the door, Baldwin was doubly glad he'd left the mate in the other room.

———————————————

Chapter 15

EYES IN THE BACK OF HER HEAD
— COLLARING MARNEEN

WITH ONE HAND clutching a brew and the other casually working its way down the bar to test the waters in Li-Tharm's direction, the mate was growing expansive — most likely under the influence of having such a sensational listener, since he had a copious capacity for brew. She was leaning on the end of the bar, looking attentively up into his face, and the mate began hoping that of all the men at the tavern, she might only have eyes for him.

Among the regulars, however, Li-Tharm had a formidable reputation for also having eyes in the back of her head. They were sure of it when they saw her suddenly reach one hand underneath the bar and collar Marneen, who was sneaking by on hands and knees. Without once shifting her gaze from the mate or interrupting his story, she held Marneen up for all to see just as Salty poked his head out of the comm shack door at the far end of the bar, asking the room in general, "Anyone seen Marneen?"

Before anyone could answer, Marneen, in midair, cried out sincerely, "I didn't do it!" From the roar of laughter that followed, it seemed few were willing to bet on it.

Marneen did little to help her case by cringing at Salty's "There you are!"

Even as she lowered Marneen to the floor, Li-Tharm continued to give the mate her rapt attention, but he was so distracted he forgot what story he'd been telling.

At that point Salty further confused the issue, as well as Marneen the Guilty, by saying, "Of course you didn't do it."

Seeing a faint possibility that she might not even be Marneen the Accused, the girl decided to check her standing. "I didn't do what?" she asked.

That brought down the house, and there was much hubbub, repeating, and back slapping while Salty explained that the main antenna field was out, and that he needed Marneen's help to fix it.

Once this was generally understood, all the locals followed Salty and the still dubious Marneen out the front door. Since even Otitius and Li-Tharm were joining the exodus, the mystified mate gave up any hope of resuming his yarn and decided he might as well find out what was going on. Over her shoulder, Li-Tharm reminded him that if he didn't leave his brew inside, it would instantly vaporize all over him.

———————————————

Chapter 16

G-THROW — GRAVITY PINBALL

UNDER THE GANGWAY, an electrified Mutch, hearing steps and commotion, risked poking his head up. He immediately retracted it, turtle-wise. That glimpse had shown him Marneen being led out onto the gangway by Salty and three others. Rolling his eyes upwards in disgust, then closing them, he contemplated the benefits of a full confession. Briefly.

"Dumb, dumb, dumb, and stupid," he murmured, rejecting the idea. "Don't be hasty. Maybe it's not as bad as it looks."

Cautiously he worked his way toward a pile of junk that might give him cover for another peek, wishing the bio-comm in his suit was somehow adjustable so he could overhear their conversation. Unfortunately for him, the ideal communication range for people working together "outside" — in space — had long ago been found to be just what they were used to "inside". Crossing his fingers, Mutch crawled out from under the gangway and up behind the junkpile. Like a moonrise behind a mountain, his helmet slowly rose above the scrapheap.

"It's worse! It's a lynch mob!"

Just about everybody was out on the gangway, some pointing toward the big antenna at the end of the village, and Salty and Marneen were coming directly toward him! Marneen was even pointing at him! How could she?

Ducking down, Mutch was frozen. He couldn't get back under the gangway, and they were getting close. Now he could hear their voices.

"I don't know," Marneen was saying, fairly calmly he thought, "the compressor house was shifted yesterday. It'll take me a few tries."

Mutch almost fainted with relief. "If the antenna field collapsed and they want her to..." he thought. Too tense to wait, he risked a quick peek at the antenna, and instead of a giant glowing green umbrella, he saw the dark naked spokes futilely facing the Gorge. She hadn't been pointing at him — they were coming for the junk! "Now, if only they don't see me!" Mutch hunkered down behind the debris, trying to make himself small.

The mate was taking his cue from the locals as they lined the gangway in front of the POSH. Unable to get close enough to question Li-Tharm, he contented himself with an occasional glance in her direction while wondering what sort of an event in village life he was about to witness. Soon the sparks and the girl they called Marneen returned, each carrying several pieces of junk, which they deposited in a pile in front of the door.

"I'll start with something small," said Marneen, examining several pieces in turn. Finding one to her satisfaction, she stepped to the edge of the gangway and leaned out, carefully surveying the water tank about a hundred feet distant, the compressor house some distance beyond, and the village powerplant a good hundred yards further away, each perched on its anchor, a long-dead engine floating in mid-space. All eyes were on her.

Slowly she stepped back, hefting the piece of junk in her hand, her eyes darting back and forth between the water tank and the compressor house, a picture of total concentration. Her arm drew back, and her eyes fastened on the water tank. Nobody moved.

She threw. Launched into the void, the metal part spun end over end, arcing toward the distant water tank, then whipping beneath it in a classic gravity-sling rising in the direction of the compressor house. Feeling the tug of a new field, it dove under that structure, barely missing the anchor beneath and whipping upward beyond. But the cheer that greeted its arc in the direction of the village powerplant faded to a moan when its momentum died, and it gradually fell back to glue itself under the compressor house.

For the second attempt, she corrected her aim slightly, and was rewarded as it soared past the water tank and the compressor house all the way to the powerplant where the projectile whipped around and spun on out into the void.

From the crowd's disappointment the mate knew that wasn't the desired outcome, and he began to speculate on what the goal might be. Looking in the direction one of the locals was pointing, he finally saw that the e-field had collapsed on the big antenna at the end of the village, leaving it dark and bare. Still he couldn't bring himself to believe that anyone could reach it with a hand-thrown piece of junk, no matter how clever the gravity-sling.

Marneen was bent on proving otherwise. She considered her course corrections, then hurled an old hydraulic piston in a beautiful trajectory. This time the arc was low and fast as it spun toward the distant power plant and disappeared only to emerge beyond in a breathtaking ascent toward the far end of town. Higher and higher it flew, flashing faintly as it spun end over end.

All eyes were judging its course as it began to descend, all hopes were high as it neared the goal, all mouths lost a mighty cheer as it squarely hit the transmitter at the center of the antenna, jarring it into action! The glowing green e-field sparked into being, then swiftly expanded, stretching out over the spidery spokes until the luminous umbrella facing the Gorge was once again complete.

Surrounded by well-wishers, Marneen the Gravity-Slinger had to duck her head as she was carried through the door on Salty's shoulders.

Following the crowd, and particularly Li-Tharm, back into the POSH, the mate was disappointed to find his view of her stern blocked by the intervening form of the Gapper in tatters, although on closer inspection he seemed to be wearing several layers of Mono-mol, with the top layer so shredded as to be mostly holes revealing the next layer of a different color, and so on. The mate had never seen a rip in Mono-mol, and didn't even know it was possible, let alone how it could be joined and layered. He sighed. Somehow, it struck him as the ultimate example of the slipshod and make-do that permeated village existence.

"I'll bet they haven't fixed the antenna," he thought, "just so they can have the fun of bopping it one when it fails."

————————————————

Chapter *17*

JUNKER'S CHAIR — A SIT-ME-DOWN

INSIDE, THE POSH was awash with excited babble. Freshly charged with hours worth of new conversational fuel, the Gappers were milling about, forming and dissolving duos and trios, establishing who had seen what, and gradually sorting themselves into compatible groups ready to begin some Serious Chatting.

Setting Marneen down, Salty hurried back into his comm shack, while she became the center of brief recruiting efforts on the part of three competing clusters. They were soon abandoned, however, because Marneen kept edging toward the door, more nervous than conversational. Besides, she'd have been a handicap as well as a centerpiece, since in her absence all opinions about her performance — no matter how outrageous — had equal merit and would have to be thoroughly discussed before arriving at a consensus.

Many also tried to recruit Li-Tharm, but she handled them easily as she glided around the room, tray over her head, asking, "What can I get you?" and "Where are you going to sit?"

Retrieving his brew, the mate observed the activity — Otitius pouring, Li-Tharm serving, Gappers settling down — with a view toward figuring out where he himself was going to sit. Several groups were already convening with much scraping of chairs when he noticed a desirable area in the center of the room, as yet unoccupied.

Approaching, he saw that one of the chairs was quite different from the others. As they were nondescript, this one was grandiose, at least in the style of the POSH Inn decor. Swiveling on a base of scores of welded plumbing fixtures, its commodious seat leaned back in indolent invitation, a sort of opulent junk-sculpture throne.

With a new-found if resigned tolerance, the mate allowed that it had a certain frayed majesty, and even looked like it might be comfortable. Just as he was about to try it out, Li-Tharm's voice in his ear commanded his complete and instant attention. Turning, he saw her bright eyes very close to his.

"Looks like you're ready for another."

He thought her voice might be a little lower than he remembered, and hoped it wasn't just due to her proximity.

"Or," she continued, "would you like me to bring you the Specialty of the House? I think you'd like it."

After nodding his ascent he remained transfixed, watching her slip away toward the bar. Coming to himself again, he was about to sit down when he was taken aback to find the chair already occupied by the sprawling form of the local in multicolored tatters.

"Excuse me, sir," said the mate, "I was about to sit there."

The face looking up at him had obviously seen some mileage, with a graying mustache and beard and intense grey-blue eyes peering from beneath bushy eyebrows. The lanky figure made no move to get up, but exchanged a leisurely glance with another bearded man seated beside him before replying in a rusty voice, "And who might you be, sir?"

The mate was so close to the elaborate chair that he couldn't see how its occupant had managed to slip in unobserved. Although he was too close for comfortable conversation, he decided against backing off. "I'm First Mate of the supply ship Steadfast," he replied, drawing himself up proudly.

"I saw your vessel arrive," said the other, "you should have the number three engine looked at soon."

The mate reddened at the accuracy of the self-assured response.

Hoisting his mug in mock toast, the seated figure continued, "As to this chair, I believe I out-rank you in two regards. First, I am captain of the Aries, and second, this is my chair."

Incredulous at the idea of such a ragamuffin being captain of anything, the mate countered, "To your health, Captain, but I don't recall having seen your vessel."

"To yours, Mate," came the answer, whereupon both drained their mugs. "You must have failed to notice it as you passed by on the pier."

The mate almost choked as it all came together — the outrageous space-tug, the flamboyant rags, the junk-sculpture throne! "I should have known," he groaned.

"They call me Junker, Captain Junker," the seated Gapper added, "and while your vessel far exceeds mine, sir, if we can ever be of service, such as that matter of that number three engine, or a tow, don't hesitate to call on us." Junker and his bearded companion rose. "Since we've finished our drinks, we'll depart. I see you understand, sir, that I meant no offense in the matter of the chair. It is, simply, my chair," he finished, easily giving it a spin in spite of its mass.

"Obviously," replied the mate, standing aside and touching his helmet in the slightest of salutes. "Good evening, Captain Junker." Fortunately for his mood, Li-Tharm returned, trading his empty mug for another containing the "Specialty of the House", but even so, he couldn't help feeling that somehow he'd come out second in the exchange with Captain Junker.

Looking about the room, the mate saw that most eyes were on him. "Is there someone else who's next in line to sit in this chair?" he asked.

"Hup sits in it all the time," one voice offered.

"When Junker ain't here," snorted another.

"Who's Hup?" asked the mate.

"Hup ain't here. He could have piloted you all the way from The Maze to Littlebend, but he's aboard an outbound to Grand Jetty."

"So Hup's not here," said the mate, swiveling the baroque seat around to face him. "Is there anyone else?" Scanning their faces, he was met by silence and shaking heads, but no contenders for the prestigious chair.

Nodding to all, and taking a healthy draught from his mug, the mate announced, "In that case, I do believe I'll have me a sit-me-down."

Challenging each face for disagreement and finding none, the mate sank into the welded throne — and crashed right on to the floor as it separated into a dozen pieces that fell about him!

A great peal of laughter shook the tavern as the mate, doused from head to foot with the Specialty of the House, realized that this wasn't the first time something like this had happened. "You set yourself up, boy," he said to himself, "good and proper."

Li-Tharm gave him a hand up amid the foot-stomping gales of merriment, saying, "I'll buy you another."

Dripping wet, the mate raised both hands for silence, his gaze sweeping the faces of the locals. "Keep," he shouted to Otitius, "one round on me for all hands!"

"Make that two," added Captain Baldwin, emerging from the comm shack.

All else was drowned in a rousing cheer.

————————————

Chapter *18*

STOWAWAYS TO THE PIER
— HOOKING TO THE DINGHY

BENEATH THE GANGWAY, Marneen and Mutch sat cross-legged on their respective go-boards.

"Is your knapsack lashed down real tight?" asked Marneen in a whisper. "You don't want it to jerk you off!"

That hadn't occurred to Mutch, who began to reconsider the hazards of stowing-away. Still, it did seem pretty exciting, and a chance to see Littlebend before they stowed-back was too much to resist. "Stowing-back" didn't sound right, but neither could he see how you could stow-away when you were no longer heading away. He decided to wait and see how somebody else said it. Scrunching hard against the knapsack, he tested the lashings for give. "It's good," he whispered.

Both were carefully coiling long towlines on the boards in front of their feet.

"No tangles!" Marneen warned, and Mutch screwed up his face to show her he knew better.

When they finished, they cast off silently, staying under the gridwork as they made for the pier.

"See! Junker's gone, and their dinghy's all by itself," Marneen whispered, "I already checked, and there's two eyebolts in the stern that are perfect for the tow-hooks. You take the port, and I'll take the starboard."

"Do we stretch them tight, or just leave them slack when they're starting?" Mutch asked, a little too loudly for his companion.

"Shhh! I thought of that. We have to stretch them out under the pier, and keep them taut until they start up. Otherwise, they might feel our weight when the slack runs out. Besides, what if the jerk loosened our hooks?"

"Oh, great!" thought Mutch, picturing her starting off on a great adventure while he was left stuck under the pier on the end of a loose tow line. "Why don't we just tie the lines to the eyebolts?"

"Shhhhhh! We can't! When we get to their ship, we're going to have to follow far enough behind so they don't see us, but close enough to get in before they close the hatch. When they get close, they'll slow down, right?"

"Right," Mutch agreed.

"That'll slack the lines, and all we have to do is sort of snap the whip, and the hooks'll pop out. I've practiced and it's real easy."

"Great," thought Mutch again, seeing the opportunities for failure multiplying before his eyes. "You've practiced, but I haven't." Still, he had to admit, it did sound easy. And even if someone heard the hooks coming out, by the time they looked back there'd be nothing to see with the two of them way back in the dark.

It took only a moment to rig the hooks, but paying out the line as they backed their boards way under the pier took several anxious minutes. Finally, they were ready, waiting side by side for their quarry, carefully keeping the lines to the dinghy taut and steady.

From time to time they looked at each other in the darkness under the pier, trying to suppress giggles of excitement.

"Stow-aways!" thought Mutch. "Wow!"

———————————————————

Chapter *19*

CIRRA DESCENDS — FOREBODINGS, A BLESSING

SALTY CAME HURRYING out of his comm shack and found Captain Baldwin and his first mate in the main room of the POSH. They were seated at a large round table swapping tales with several of the locals, and Salty was trying to decide whether to interrupt when the captain saw him and nodded.

Excusing himself, Baldwin left the group as the current storyteller was in mid-yarn, elaborately setting the scene in which someone who had talked to someone who knew a close friend of his had maybe seen the Dutchman.

Joining Salty in the shadows at the end of the bar, the captain was delighted to hear his news.

"I've made contact with Pasquil, and as soon as he exits Dutchman's Gorge he'll make directly for your ship. His vessel is the Slick Trick, and he's agreeable to your taking it aboard for the trip back to Littlebend."

"Excellent! Is your docking comm still up?"

Salty hastened to assure him it was. "Not a hint of trouble since it went back on. Do you want to send a message to your ship?"

"Yes, if you'll raise them." The captain accompanied Salty back into the comm shack, and waited while the sparks made the connection.

"Steadfast? Captain Baldwin here."

"Aye, sir." In spite of considerable static the voice of the bosun was fairly clear.

"The pilot has been contacted, and he'll be clearing Dutchman's Gorge soon, whereupon he'll make directly for you. Be prepared to take his vessel on board."

"Aye, Captain." acknowledged the bosun.

"The mate and I will depart Dutchman's immediately. When we get within range, patch the ship's main comm through to the dinghy so that we can give the pilot final instructions as he approaches the Steadfast. He should be arriving close on our heels. Is everything ready to get under way?"

"All is in readiness, Captain. We can move as soon as you're on board."

"Very good, Bosun. Baldwin clear."

Salty disabled the connection, and walked the captain to the comm shack door.

"It's been a pleasure, Captain."

"Thanks for your help, Salty, and for your discretion."

The two men shook hands, and as he turned back to his equipment, Salty added, "Safe journey, Captain, and take care."

Pausing in the shadows, Captain Baldwin looked across the warm dilapidated tavern with Salty's farewell words echoing in his mind. In the center of the room, a hanging forest of mismatched lamps bathed the equally mismatched Gappers in a pool of friendly light, their animated conversations merging into a single sound that spoke of a rich camaraderie. "I almost envy them," Baldwin thought.

Looking across the room, now almost unseeing, the captain was casting about in his mind trying to identify the source of his disquiet when the hairs on the back of his neck rose. Opposite him, in the darkness of the far wall, a dim ghostly wraith seemed to be manifesting as it floated down from the blackness above.

So incongruous was the vision, it was some time before he realized that he was seeing the form of a woman descending a darkened staircase that he hadn't noticed. The more she emerged into the light, the more amazing was her appearance in the context of her surroundings.

Unlike the others, she wasn't dressed for space, but clad in a flowing full length gown of gossamer white. Only her bare feet, appearing each in turn, showed that she was gracefully stepping, not floating, down the stairs. She was tall, and her long hair — reddish with hints of gray — must have been freshly brushed, for it hung about her in a loose cloud that stirred and lifted in the air that parted at her descent. Still a step or two above the floor, she paused.

The captain felt goose bumps on his arms.

"Cirra!" someone said. "Come join us!"

Her expression seemed to be a cross between serenity and distraction, as if she were listening to something far away. "Has anyone seen Marneen and Mutch?" she asked.

"Marneen was here a little while ago," someone volunteered, "She was just fine."

"I saw Mutch earlier," another voice offered. "He was OK, too."

Cirra didn't seem reassured by their answers. The captain was reminded of his dog, ears cocked, sniffing the wind for something beyond his master's ken. "And so it is with you," he mused, looking at the woman, wishing that he too could sniff the wind this day. "Those sounds too faint for human ears, the scents too subtle for us to track, they speak to you, don't they, as the CoreFires almost speaks to me."

Cirra, still apparently searching for something, stepped down into the crowd, and was lost to the captain's gaze. Moving on, he tried to shake off his philosophic mood while wending his way to alert the Mate to their departure. As he rejoined the table another tale had just concluded and the mate rose to meet him. After a round of farewells, the pair made their way toward the front door of the POSH, where the almost invisible field-bubble divided "inside" from the vacuum of space.

When they turned to the exit Captain Baldwin was startled to see Cirra's gossamer clad form silhouetted against the glowing ferocity of the CoreFires, as she stood barefoot just inside the open doorway to the void. The blue light of the incandescent fireforms outlined her figure within the fragile fabric of the gown. Her breasts moved with her breathing, and her hair stirred to some zephyr he didn't feel. Her lips were parted, her eyes on his. Her eyes, he saw, were almost purple, and the pupils, exceptionally large.

For a long moment, he looked into her face, her hair blowing softly in front of the Galactic violence of the CoreFires. Then he looked into her eyes. How long it was before she spoke, he had no idea.

"Captain Baldwin." Her voice was low. "My blessings go with you."

Without waiting for reply, she stepped aside, melting back into the darkness of the room.

The captain looked out at the deep indigo void awaiting them, then turned to the mate.

"Let's go," he said, and they stepped through the door.

———————————

Chapter 20

FREE RIDE — OFF WE GO!

THIS TIME THERE were no giggles under the village pier.

Hearing the heavy tread of approaching footsteps with the aid of their bio-suit sensors, Marneen and Mutch tried to stay absolutely still. Carefully keeping their towlines taut, they peered tensely into the darkness, trying to make out the stern of the dinghy.

The ringing of footsteps on the metal pier passed overhead, grew fainter, then stopped, to be replaced by confusing shuffling noises.

Hunched forward on their go-boards, the two would-be stowaways strained to make out what was happening. "If only they'd talk," Mutch thought. The comm channel remained silent, and — unable to hear in the vacuum of space — Mutch pressed one of the sensors more firmly against a pier support, hoping it might help. Marneen did the same.

There were a few more clicks and clangs before the loud impact of two pairs of feet jumping into the dinghy.

They could dimly see the mate's hands working with the motor controls until he turned away. Then one arm reached back for the tiller.

Marneen and Mutch looked at each other at the same moment.

Silently, Marneen mouthed, "Hang on."

Mutch nodded, and both looked ahead, concentrating on their towlines.

"Don't come out, hook!" Mutch muttered. Seeing the warning glow of the dinghy motor as it throttled up, he released his hand hold on the pier support, ready for anything, or so he thought.

"Oh, wow oh wow!" he exclaimed under his breath as the rapid acceleration far exceeded anything he expected, pressing his back hard into the knapsack. The lashings held. With the underside of the pier now flying by at a terrifying speed, Mutch thought of all the obstacles he should be avoiding. "I can't even see them, and it's too fast to steer! Gotta stay lucky," he told himself, "stay lucky..." He gritted his teeth and hung on for dear life. Grabbing the board and the towline even tighter, he risked a glance to the side.

There was Marneen, hanging on to her board with all her strength. Even in the dim light, she looked pretty grim-faced. The sight of the pier supports flashing by between them made him so dizzy he quickly looked ahead, trying to control his vertigo.

In a few more moments, he saw the end of the pier approaching, and it was hardly more than the blink of an eye before they were safely out in the blue void, where the sensation of speed instantly ceased, like awakening to a sudden quiet from a frenzied dream.

Ahead, the dark dinghy pulled steadily on the towlines as it began its climb. The go-boards, of course, could never make it on their own, and Mutch knew the dinghy would have to be under power all the way up to the big ship to overcome the combined fields of the village and all its gear.

As Mutch was trying to make out the two figures standing in the dinghy it became unexpectedly easy — the mate had turned on the bright yellow marker strobe at the top of the dinghy's comm-mast. At one flash per second, as regular as clockwork, it began marking off the time of their great adventure.

Looking to the side, Mutch could see the dark form of Marneen on her board, outlined against the blue of the CoreFires. Once per second, the faintest wash of yellow light showed on her face.

As she turned toward him, he thought he saw her smile. By the light of the next flashes, he saw the glint of her eyes, and he was sure she gave him a big thumb up.

"Wow!" he thought. "A free ride! We're doing it!"

———————————————

Just ahead, on the dinghy, the captain frowned. They were entering a patch of e-fog, visible only by its effect on their craft and the increasing static in their bio-comms. Almost the entire craft was limned in scintillating white sparkles. The comm-mast fairly crackled with energy, and the engine looked like it had sprouted a forest of tiny dancing lightning trees.

"Spooky," said the mate, keeping a steady hand on the helm.

———————————————

Some distance behind them, consternation reigned. Marneen edged her board closer to Mutch so she could whisper. "Look! The boards are crawling with sparks. Even the towlines have some. If they turn around, they're bound to see us! What can we do?"

"Nothing I know of," Mutch answered in an agonized tone. "Just hope they don't turn around 'til we get through this, I guess."

Marneen kept one hand on her towline, just in case, but on the other hand, she crossed her fingers. She didn't know if that helped, but soon the electrical display passed without giving them away.

———————————————

Chapter *21*

IT HAD BEEN a long climb, but the Steadfast now loomed large ahead.

"Just a few more minutes," said the captain with considerable anticipation. A faint flicker on the periphery of his vision caused Baldwin to shift his gaze. It was several seconds before he was sure of what he was seeing. "There," he indicated to the mate, "coming out of Dutchman's Gorge, a light."

The mate studied the glowing cleft for some time. "I see it! It's the pilot, all right. I wonder if the second's made him out."

As if in answer, a burst of static came through the dinghy's comm channel, followed closely by the faint but readable voice of the second mate.

"I've raised the pilot," reported the second, "and I'm patching ship's comm directly through to you, Captain."

"Very good, Second," the captain replied. "This is Captain Baldwin of the Steadfast, patching over ship's comm. Can you read me?"

The link was getting stronger, and the pilot's voice came through clearly. "Clear as bells, Captain Bald One. Tonight's your lucky day! Introducing me, the Pasquil, also known as the Magician! Before your very eyes, presto, I'll slip your ship through this Dutchman's Gorge so slick! Satisfaction guaranteed. Congratulations!"

The captain and mate exchanged glances. "Do you have us in sight?"

"Captain Bald One, as plain as the days on my face! I'm making straight for your ship."

"Steadfast to pilot, can you do a running start if we make way?"

"Can I? I, who can produce four aces every time? You want a

53

grown woman to disappear? Unequal-qualified, that's the Pasquil! You gotta net?"

With some misgivings the captain answered, "Yes, we'll rig the net, rated three g's, forty feet."

He winced when the voice replied, "She'll take four, I'll be so gentle!" Once again, the captain and mate exchanged glances. The voice of the pilot continued, "Which hatch you want?"

"Port cargo hatch, and our net's three, that's three g's!"

"Port hatch, my good Captain Bald One. Guaranteed! I'll be so gentle!" If he said more, it was swallowed in a crescendo of static.

Once again the comm-mast was crawling with sparks as the dinghy encountered more e-fog, and the intensity was increasing rapidly. The captain decided that although the pilot gave him some concern, the e-fog required immediate action. "Captain Baldwin to pilot. If you can hear us, we're experiencing heavy interference. We'll contact you again as you approach our ship. Baldwin clear."

"Come on," said the captain to the mate. "Let's get out of this."

"Anything you say, Captain," replied the mate, looking at the comm-mast, "but full throttle might attract a strike.

A quick look at the ever increasing buildup on the engine convinced Baldwin. "Full throttle, Mate. It looks like we'll get a strike anyway. Let's see if we can put it behind us!"

"Aye, sir! You're on. If it keeps building like this, we haven't got much time."

The entire dinghy was now enveloped in a pulsing blue glow, and they appeared to be speeding through a swarm of electrical fireflies. The glow grew brighter.

"Hang on, Mate. Fortune doesn't favor the timid!"

The strike was a great blinding bolt that exploded in the blue glow just behind them! The dinghy bucked, then seemed to leap ahead. Fortunately, both the captain and mate had been looking forward. Even so, for several seconds no matter where they looked they could only see the negative afterimage of the dinghy's prow on their overloaded retinas.

Gradually vision returned, and the mate realized the dinghy was still responding to the tiller, and the engine was running smoothly. Throttling back, he slowly straightened, then looked at the captain.

Captain Baldwin's voice was steady. "Well done, Mate."

Laughing, the mate replied, "I've got to hand it to you, Captain, you surely know when to make your move!" Locating the Steadfast again, the mate adjusted their course, then stood still with his head cocked. When Baldwin gave him an inquiring look, he said, "I thought I heard voices."

"I'd sure be surprised if we had company here," the captain laughed.

———————————————

Chapter *22*

Cut Loose — A Running Start

Disoriented and forgetting to whisper, Mutch had cried out, "My line's slack!"

"Mine too!" Marneen answered. "Either the hooks jumped out or the strike parted both lines!"

Suddenly remembering to keep his voice down, Mutch pointed at the dinghy. "Look, they're pulling ahead."

"Yes, and if we don't have enough momentum to make the ship, we'll start falling back toward Dutchman's."

"Oh boy oh boy!" Mutch whispered. "We'd better hope we reach the field of the ship!"

Marneen crossed her fingers, both hands, watching the dinghy gradually pulling ahead. "We're slowing down," she whispered to herself, "we're slowing down."

In the dinghy, Captain Baldwin had raised the Steadfast on the comm. "Bosun, open the port cargo hatch, and be ready to take us aboard. You'll have very little time to get the dinghy stowed and raise the net. Be sure to get all hands clear before the pilot comes aboard. Second, as we come aboard, I'll advise you when to begin a running start. Captain clear."

"Aye, sir. Bosun clear."

"Understood, Second Mate clear."

Just after he left the comm, the captain was startled to hear the pilot's voice. "Slick Trick to Steadfast, your good Captain Bald One awaits the Pasquil's arrival with a running start. That hatch better be open when I get there."

"That joker," muttered the captain. "I hope he's as good as Salty said he is."

————————————————

Mutch and Marneen were slowing to a stop.

Tantalizingly close to the Steadfast, Marneen knew they must be almost at the point where the ship's field would begin to pull them forward. She also knew that if they failed to reach that point, they would inevitably begin the long fall back toward Dutchman's, and if that happened... Her mind drew back, concentrating on the problem at hand. It felt like they weren't going to make it.

"Turn on your go-board," she said to Mutch — the dinghy was now so far ahead that they no longer needed to whisper. "It's not much, but at least it's something."

"OK," he replied bravely, looking at her. "Cross your fingers!"

She showed him her hands. "You, too, Mutch."

"Look, the hatch is wide open. If only we were there."

Marneen tried to encourage him. "We're still moving toward the ship."

"Yeah, but so slow! Are we speeding up?"

"Maybe," she said. "Yes! I think we are!"

Ahead, they could see the dinghy entering the docking bay.

Mutch pointed to the left. "Here comes the pilot! Keep heading for the hatch! We've got to get in before they close it!"

"What are they doing, Mutch? There, inside the hatch?"

"Oh, no! It's a net. They're rigging a net!"

"Why? What's it mean? Oh, I wish we could go faster!"

"It means they're going to do a running start. The big ship will have already started moving when the pilot steers his craft right into the hatch. The net's to slow him down and stop him. Listen, we've got to aim forward of where the hatch is now, 'cause the ship's going to be moving before we get there.

"Oh, Mutch, can we do it?"

"It's gonna be close, real close, but we've got to. We've just got to!"

They were picking up speed, aiming for where they hoped the open hatch would be when they arrived.

"See?" Mutch called out. "It's starting to move."

Toward the big freighter's stern they could see a pulsing violet glow blooming behind the massive engines. Ahead, the side of the ship seemed to be moving so slowly it looked as if they would arrive too soon, but with each passing second it was picking up speed, sliding by faster and faster.

Marneen pointed toward the bow, where the pilot's vessel was approaching rapidly. It was so close that they even heard Pasquil's docking channel coming through on their bio-comms. "Ahoy, Steadfast," he was saying, "I arrive! You are privileged to watch the Pasquil, the Magician! Guaranteed! So gentle! Before your very eyes!"

As Mutch and Marneen were accelerating toward the side of the ship, the open hatch was accelerating forward to meet them.

"We might make it!" yelled Mutch.

Just as it looked as if they would, the pilot's craft arrived, wheeling toward the hatch with a powerful burst from its motors, the backblast sending the go-boards and their riders tumbling back away from the Steadfast. Continuing his spin and firing his engines heavily, Pasquil aligned his vessel perfectly with the open hatch, and entered the docking bay dead backwards, slowing to rest on the deck without even touching the net.

As the cargo hatch was sliding shut, Pasquil's voice spoke over the comm. "Presto! Guaranteed! So gentle!"

Mutch and Marneen were now tumbling back away from the rapidly accelerating side of the Steadfast. Mutch looked toward the stern, seeing the great violet exhaust plumes coming their way. He had no idea whether they'd be clear when the stern passed by. A short distance away he spied Marneen, still clinging to her board.

Before he could help himself, his eyes filled with tears. "Marneen!" he cried.

"Mutch!" she answered. "Mutch!"

———————————————

On the docking channel, the calm voice of Captain Baldwin spoke. "Steadfast to Dutchman's. Thanks for the hospitality. We have the pilot on board, and we're making for Dutchman's Gorge. Steadfast clear."

"Glad you could stop by," came Salty's reply. "Safe journey. Dutchman's clear."

————————————————

When the mighty engines passed by, the small figures of Marneen and Mutch were just out of reach.

The triple violet plumes surged on toward the glowing cleft of the Gorge, soon becoming three tiny points of flickering light.

Alone in the vast womb of blue fire, two tiny figures drew closer together as they began a long fall.

"Mutch, I'm sorry!"

"Me too, Marneen."

Two miles below, in the dilapidated village called Dutchman's, Cirra asked, "has anyone seen Marneen and Mutch?"

————————————————

Chapter *23*

FAREWELL TO STARRY WORLDS — VIEW AT SPACE END

LOOKING LIKE TWO perfectly synchronized human athletes, except that they were metal, a pair of robots pedaled the loveseat-pedicab up the steep grade oblivious to the weight of its two flesh and blood passengers. As they crested the summit, their tireless silver legs circled in the same rapid cadence with which they'd begun the long climb from the city below.

"This will do, thanks," said Shanni.

"By the overlook?" asked one of the "bots", as humans had come to call the ubiquitous general-purpose robots. At Shanni's nod, the bots turned the pedicab off the network of bike roads, stopping near a heavy metal park bench.

Shanni and Stamford stood up and stretched.

"Which view do you prefer?" the bot asked. When Shanni pointed to the east, the metal pair quickly dismounted, each lifting — one handed — an end of the six-hundred-pound bench and repositioning it facing the desired direction. "And shall we wait? inquired the bot.

Stamford was about to say yes when Shanni said no, at which the bots remounted and pedaled rapidly down the hill toward their next call.

The cliff dropped away to the city far below, where sparkling lights spread in undiminished profusion to the far horizon, looking more numerous than the stars. To the west, all three of Space End's moons were visible as thin crescents — a notable view, but one that paled in comparison with the panorama to the east, where a broad reach of the starry sky was blotted out by the indigo immensity of the CoreFires.

Appropriate to Shanni's last night on the planet, the glowing blue nebula had risen high above the structures of the huge spaceport from which the planet took its name. Few were the planets that served as ports for the specialized ships supplying worlds within the CoreFires, and Space End was proud of its role.

"Isn't it beautiful!" exclaimed Shanni.

"Beautiful, and wonderful," replied Stamford. "And we're only seeing a little of it. Just think, a whole world devoted to one city, with all those billions of people living harmoniously, productively, their lives enriched, their needs provided for, secure and happy. We take it for granted, but it's pretty wonderful when you stop and think about it."

Shanni wrinkled up her nose. "I meant the CoreFires. Isn't it beautiful?"

"Beautiful? Well, perhaps. Maybe awesome. Almost terrible, when you think of the dangers. I don't see why you have to go there, Shanni."

Ignoring his remark, she continued, "I love the Firedawn so much more than sunrise — each time a new surprise, not knowing what the colors will be. It's so wonderful that the CoreFires has its own version of day and night. I just now realized for the first time that I won't be seeing Firedawn this way, from the outside, for a while. I'll miss it. I wonder what causes it."

"The answer lies hidden somewhere in the middle of that...," he reached for a word, then just gestured at the firecloud. "Even your ship can't get close to the core. At least no Gap's ever been found leading into that region. All we know, is that it happens."

"I know. Still," she sighed wistfully, "it's so lovely that I sometimes imagine that there might be something magnificent in there where it's born. Isn't it poetic that it happens once a day?"

"Approximately once a day," he corrected, "speaking of which..." He spoke into the Omnicomm on his wrist, asking, "What is the current prediction for Firedawn?"

Without perceptible pause, the Voice of Utility answered, "A sixty-three percent chance that it will be twenty-four minutes from now.

If you watch it for about twelve minutes, Shanni will probably be late arriving at her spaceship."

"Stamford!" Shanni burst out angrily. "I don't want to know!" She was shaking with frustration. "You of all people should know by now that I'd rather just experience it!" Her voice was indignant as she glared at the Omnicomm on her own wrist. "The way Utility is always tracking these, always looking at where we've been and what we've done, always trying to anticipate what we're going to do, I just don't like it! It's fine for you, but it's totally wrong for me!"

"You don't have to wear your Omnicomm; you don't have to use it."

"So you say, but it's impossible to get anything done unless you do. I just don't like it. It's inhuman!"

"Shanni, Shanni, you're being irrational. Your aversion to Utility's keeping track of us doesn't make any sense at all. How else is it going to provide what we need, keep the entire planet running smoothly, keep us from bumping into each other all the time? It's a blessing! Even our privacy on this hilltop comes from it. Utility knows where we all are, and when someone else wants to see the view Utility routes the bots so as not to disturb anyone, and we aren't even aware of it. Besides, you don't want to miss your ship, so it would be irrational to ignore the information."

"Oh, Stamford, don't! Let's not get into this again, especially now! Let's just watch the Firedawn, and be together while we can."

"That's fine by me, but the Firedawn will be too late for..."

"Stamford, you don't know that it's going to be too late. I'm going to watch it, and if you want to watch it with me, I'd like that. Now, just be quiet and put your arm around me. Let's taste what's on our plate."

Shanni, eager for her first voyage, was already wearing her new Mono-mol suit — white for the transport line, and devoid of insignia showing her low rank of trainee. Her hair was blowing free in the warm wind rising up the cliff. The glow of the city lights was upon her face, and as always he was fascinated by the animated play of expression he saw there, made so forceful by her near-beautiful features and her dark eyebrows.

"Hear the wind in the grass!" Shanni said, her anger forgotten. "I shall miss the grass and the wind." As she raised her eyes again to the CoreFires, she smiled with deep joy. "Look," she whispered, "the prediction was wrong — it's beginning! We just had to have enough faith to be here to see it."

Stamford was moved enough by her expression that he thought better of arguing the logic of her words. Then he, too, looked up at the CoreFires.

It was beautiful, and certainly awesome. The vast nebula, wrought in fire-forms of dark ultramarine, now showed a hint of purple in its deepest recesses. Majestically, the purple brought forth red, the red of darkest velvet, which began to spread. From the deep crevices and convolutions, it emerged, inexorably driving the midnight blue before it.

"It looks like it's going to be a Fireday," Shanni whispered, tightening her grip on Stamford's arm.

And so it was, for a progression of fire-colors welled from within the CoreFires, brighter reds, soon laced with hints of rust, then bronze. Now the blues retreated, ceding the surface to the colors of the far end of the spectrum, and the reds and coppers ranged far and wide. Shanni gasped at the first flood of oranges, hot as lava flowing from a volcano.

Stamford looked again at her face, now lit by the colors of the CoreFires. As much as he was used to seeing her almost boyish figure in all manner of circumstances, he found the sight of her body in the white — now firelit — spacesuit as exotic and arousing as if he had never seen her before. "In a way," he thought, "perhaps I haven't," and he vaguely regretted being dressed in his normal business clothes. He continued watching her as the light swelled to brilliant gold, echoed by two tiny flecks of CoreFires in her eager eyes. Almost breathless with emotion, he wondered if he could interest her in romance, one last time. "Of course not, her ship is waiting," his logical mind concluded, but he didn't want to listen to the answer.

Shanni rose, standing on tiptoes, face raised to the golden light.

"Shanni, why do you have to go? There's danger out there, and worse. Communication is impossible in the CoreFires. Except for the supply ships everyone is cut off, and the people are the outcasts of the Galaxy, without supervision and beyond the reach of authority.

The horrors that the civilized worlds have buried in the past can arise there at any time. People can do deliberate evil without fear of retribution. Anything could happen to you!" Desperately wanting Shanni to change her mind, he rose beside her. "There's even talk of pirates preying on ships like yours."

"My ship is named the Reliant III," she replied with a giggle. "What more could you ask?"

"What happened to Reliant I and Reliant II?" he countered.

They both laughed at that, he a little ruefully as he saw her face so obviously alight with the zest for new adventure.

"Stamford, you know I have to go. The very things that keep you here are the ones that make me go." She kissed him quickly, and embraced him.

"Shanni," he cried, inflamed again at the touch of her body, "don't go. You're the most exciting thing that's happened in my life!"

"Stamford," she laughed, "that's your own fault! If that's true a year from now, you have only yourself to blame!" She ran a few steps, then twirled and blew him a kiss. Smiling, she spoke into her Omnicomm, "I'm going to run down the path toward the spaceport. I need a pedicab to get me to my spaceship in time, and the bot's going to have to find me without this." Then she stripped the communicator off her wrist and threw it off the cliff with all her might, watching it fall toward the city below.

Incredulous and laughing, Stamford called, "Shanni, that won't do any good! The Omnicomm always knows where it is! To the nearest inch! Utility will just send a bot to pick it up! Why did you do it?"

"Because, dear Stamford, it felt wonderful! Goodbye!"

"I'll never understand you, Shanni!"

"Maybe someday you will." She turned and ran down the trail toward the spaceport and the golden CoreFires, her legs flashing in the light of Firedawn.

Sighing, Stamford turned away, and was about to speak into his Omnicomm when he saw that Utility had already anticipated his departure — a perfectly timed pedicab was arriving from the city below. As the bot politely pedaled up and waited for him to be seated, Stamford didn't even think about how Utility had known that only a single-seater would be required.

————————————————

Chapter 24

FALLING TOWARD DUTCHMAN'S
— DESPERATE MEASURES

SHE'S JUST GOT to be here somewhere!" Mutch told himself for the twentieth time. With his go-board back under control he'd been scanning the blue of the CoreFires two miles above Dutchman's, searching for Marneen's dark silhouette. "Looks like it's gonna be a Fireday — sure hope we live to see it!" When he finally spotted her she was almost above him and quite close, still tumbling rapidly from the backblast of the pilot's vessel that had so suddenly defeated their stowaway attempt.

"Hang on Marneen!" he yelled, "I'm coming!"

Maneuvering his board close to hers he timed his move carefully, then lunged, grabbing her spinning board and hanging on tightly. Now they were both rotating head over heels, but their motion was slow enough so that they were soon able to stabilize both boards.

"Oh boy, Mutch, am I glad to see you! Am I ever dizzy!"

"Yeah. At first I couldn't find you. But we're OK now."

"No, Mutch. No we're not. We're in big trouble!"

Mutch was silent for a moment. "Yeah, I know Marneen. If there was a ship real close by it could maybe save us, but..." He looked about them. Ahead, the Steadfast had disappeared into twisting passages of the Gorge, and far below lay the village. They were very much alone.

"You can hardly tell yet," Marneen continued urgently, "but we're already falling faster and faster. We've got to act quickly and I havn't got much of this figured out. Mutch, I'm sorry I got us into this, OK? and I'm just going to have to go by guess and by gosh to do anything that might help get us out of it."

"Hey, Marneen, gravity's your specialty. Go for it. Besides, you have to — it's our only chance."

"That's for sure. If we don't do something, in a few minutes we're going to splat right into Dutchman's so fast we'll be nothing but a coat of paint. We've got to use up the go-boards to try and miss the village, and they won't last long. One of us might have a better chance if we don't stick together."

"No way!" Mutch countered. "We stick together no matter what!"

They could hear each other easily over the comms in their bio-suits, but the bio-comms were also picking up a new sound that ominously underscored the urgency of their plight — a faint low moan, like wind sounding through the chimney of a tall house. Already that wavering moan was rising in pitch, telling of their ever faster descent through the stray particles and fields that permeated space within the Gap.

Handing Mutch a long strap from her pack, Marneen told him, "Tie the boards together tight, but with a knot we can jerk loose fast. We've got to get rid of any extra weight now, like the knapsacks. Untie the stuff, but hang onto it 'til I check the direction." Peering below at the pier and the antenna, she quickly estimated their orientation relative to Dutchman's. Already the village looked closer. "Everything ready?"

"Yep," Mutch replied, handing her one of the packs.

"OK, when I count three, throw it away from us in that direction as hard as you can. Ready?" When Mutch nodded she shouted, "One, two, three!"

The knapsacks went spinning away into the darkness.

Marneen had to raise her voice to make it heard over the rising moan in their ears, now almost a howl.

"Just the hand-light."

"Throw it in the same direction as hard as you can."

"OK if I turn it on?"

Even in their circumstance, Marneen had to laugh. "Sure." As soon as Mutch had hurled the hand-light into the void they hunkered down side by side on the two go-boards. "Set your power to max. We've got to start at the same time, and keep 'em headed right there," Marneen said, pointing at a little swirl in the CoreFires. "Ready?"

"Ready!"

"Full power!" Both boards started at the same instant. "Did you have a fresh charge on your board when we started?"

It seemed like another lifetime to Mutch, back when they were both hiding under the gangway in front of the POSH. "Yeah, but it can't have much left after trying to make it to the freighter and getting us under control afterwards." True words! After two minutes his board died, and Marneen immediately cut power on hers. Over the keening wind-sound in their bio-comms she shouted, "Roll over onto mine and jerk that knot loose, then hang on tight."

"Done! Go!" he yelled.

In less than five seconds they were back at full throttle on the remaining go-board. "Come on, board," Mutch shouted, "you can do it." Then, to Marneen, "Why full power? Wouldn't it last longer throttled down?"

"Yeah, but a bigger burn earlier gets you the most distance, and we'll need everything we've got to clear the village."

"Marneen, what happens if we miss the village?"

She looked ahead, fighting to ignore the wailing howl in her ears, fighting to control her voice. After a pause, her answer came out in a half-croak, "We'll do a gravity sling under it, and it'll pitch us into the CoreFires."

"Oh. Yeah." Mutch took a deep breath. "I guess I knew that." He concentrated on keeping the board aimed in the right direction, but soon it began to sputter. There was a brief surge, then another. "Come on board, don't give up! Just a little more!" he cried through clenched teeth, but it was clear that they were just coasting, falling.

"OK," she shouted, placing her head close to his, "I'm going to tie us together. Now, we'll push the board away from us, back that way. On three."

"Right. On three. You count."

"We'll both count."

"One!" they shouted. "Two!" even louder. "Three!"

As the board tumbled away into the semi-darkness, they could clearly see how quickly they were falling toward the village.

"Has anyone ever come back from out of the CoreFires?" Mutch asked, trying to keep his voice casual.

"Not that I've ever heard of," she yelled back.

—————————————

The warm light spilling out the front door of the POSH made a big bright square on the worn gangway. Into the square a shadow loomed, followed by Li-Tharm stepping out through the bubble for a short break. Reflected streaks of gold from the tavern and blue from the CoreFires rippled across her silvery suit as she stretched luxuriously, like a big cat. Leaning out into the void while hanging onto a gangway post, she swung lazily back and forth, looking up at the magnificent nebula walls.

From the base of her spine all the way up to her neck she slowly arched her back in an especially satisfying stretch. Head back, she murmured to herself, "Yum. Looks like it's going to be a Fireday."

—————————————

Hurtling through space, Marneen and Mutch had to keep their heads together and shout over the tumult of the hurricane shriek in their bio-comms.

"Boy, it won't be long now!" Mutch could make out the pier and the gangway, and was trying to see exactly where they were headed when a flash of light caught his eye. "Hey! Way over there, it's our hand light!" The tiny light, winking regularly, looked like a distant lighthouse, except that it too was plunging rapidly toward Dutchman's. "I don't know if we can miss the village, but I betcha that light's gonna squash dead center! Hey, if we do miss it, will the gravity sling hurt us?"

"Not unless we're too close — it'll just whip us in a new direction."

"How long after that before we go into the CoreFires?" he asked.

"Real soon after!"

"You know," Mutch yelled, "we might be OK in the CoreFires for awhile — I don't know if the face-bubbles can handle this speed, but the suit's all biotech, so it might be OK."

"Then how come no one's come back?"

"Well," he shouted back, "they're almost always in a ship that gets all torn up. Even little motors like the go-boards and tiny machines that aren't biotech get destroyed really big-time, like blooie! Dead junk's OK, e-fields and biotech are OK, but motors and bots and stuff are `goodbye Charley'!"

"Mutch, even if our suits are OK, we've had it. We can't get back!"

"Can't we fall back out? Maybe we could miss the village again and somebody could rescue us."

"No, once we're in the CoreFires the flux'll be all messed up, we'll be cut off from the village's field. We'll just keep going in deeper, whichever way the flux takes us."

"Well, looks like we won't have to worry about it — have you been watching where we're heading? Like right into the end of the pier?"

"Yeah, but we should curve a little. Maybe we'll miss it."

Mutch could barely make himself heard over the shrill scream of their passage. "Hang onto my hands, Marneen, we're sure gonna find out!"

———————————————

Chapter 25

Two into the Corefire
— Pack on the Gangway

Li-Tharm was still looking dreamily up at the CoreFires when she saw the tiny light winking regularly as it streaked downward. "I've never seen anything like that before," she muttered.

Poised as she was, at the very edge of the gangway, she almost lost her footing when the whole structure bucked with a mighty thump from an impact less than fifty feet away. Curious, she went to investigate. There, in the middle of the gangway, lay the crumpled form of Mutch's knapsack. Mystified, she picked it up and looked both ways down the walkway, but no one was in sight. "I wonder what those kids are up to now," she thought.

———————————

The whine of the wind-sound intensified to a steady roar as the pair plunged in a curving arc just beneath the structures of the village.

"Wow, Marneen!" Mutch shouted "Was that ever close! Look behind us — the village is already way back there!"

"Look ahead, Mutch. What's that black thing?"

Looking ahead, Mutch saw that they were approaching the Core-Fires swiftly, heading straight for a bright whirlpool of blue. Then he saw it, between them and the CoreFires, a small tumbling shape. "It's the go-board. We'll sure be able to tell when we're going in!"

Larger and larger the gaseous whirlpool loomed as they followed the dark spinning speck of the go-board. Hanging on to each other they winced as that speck exploded in a blinding flare of white, scattering a fireworks sphere of incandescent shards. Swiftly the two figures, still tied together, plunged through the center of the go-board's pyre, and on, into the swirling blue glow of the CoreFires.

————————————

Chapter 26

STEADFAST'S REMAINS
— GRIM SIGHT NEAR LITTLEBEND

"ARIES TO LITTLEBEND. Junker here."

The CoreFires was blood-red a short distance past Littlebend, and two reflected images smoldered in Junker's eyes. To starboard, to port, again and again his gaze locked on some aspect of the scene beyond his Pilot-house windows, then shifted and locked anew. The two fires burning beneath his bushy eyebrows seemed to intensify as his expression darkened like a thundercloud.

"Littlebend" Polly replied. "What's up, Junker? You don't sound happy."

Spinning the wheel a few spokes clockwise he turned his Gap tug a few points to starboard, easing it past a piece of debris twisting slowly in mid-space. Beyond the stained glass windows the beauty of the Firedawn was marred by blackened forms of drifting wreckage. "Sorry, Polliwog, next time I see you I'll kiss your pretty neck, but for now, I've got to abuse your ears. " Guiding the powerful tug as he talked, Junker maneuvered his vessel through the cloud of flotsam, proceeding at dead slow. Again he spun the wheel as the remains of a great bulkhead passed close aport, turning slowly as if skewered on a giant spit.

"Go ahead, Junker. Give it to me and I'll pass it on. What're you looking at?"

"Very large ugly, Wog, makes me want to puke. Used to be a fine ship, the Steadfast. Her engines pulled right out of her. Big pieces all over the Gap. Blown bots. Very large ugly, Polly. Is Pasquil safely down there?

"Yes, or rather he was. He's already on his way back to Dutchman's. They dropped off Pasquil's cruiser just before they went on. He brought them through the Gorge smooth and easy. They were right on schedule."

Junker side-slipped the tug past a big piece of wrecked machinery, still glowing red hot. As it slid abaft he could feel the radiated heat move from his face to his cheek, and then on around to the back of his head before it diminished. "Polliwog, I won't say much now, but this stinks. That ship had an appointment with the Grim Reaper, right on time. Most of the bridge is here, and there's no one on it. No suits. No sign of human crew."

"Pasquil said something about an engine..."

"Number three. I knew about that, and I've checked it. All three engines were perfect right to the end. They've all gone singular now, of course. I've gone through all the wreckage and Lyard and Garms are out in the dinghies going through it again. No survivors. No bodies. Something stinks in a high vacuum!"

"What happened, you think?"

"Looks like she was driven right through CoreFires."

"Cutting a bend? I don't believe it! They couldn't have been in that much of a hurry."

"Too wide and easy here, and the captain was an old hand. Wog, you recording this?"

"Standard procedure, Junker. Nobody's within range. Talk to me, old-timer, something's stuck in your craw."

"You know how to wipe a Crystal?"

"You know how to spell J U N K?"

"OK, love, but see that this recording gets erased when we're done. I don't want you squashed, or me either. That ship was raped real bad, and for some reason the crew was taken off."

"And you're thinking it wasn't the first?"

"Wog, something ugly and brutal is slithering through this Gap. So brutal it doesn't even notice us unless we're part of what it wants.

It stinks of greed, Wog, big greed.

"Pirates, Junker?"

"Doing the dirty work, maybe, but there's something more behind them, something or someone after more than ships or cargoes, Pollikins. I think they're trying to rape a Core-planet, and if I'm right, they'll squash us if they see us. Now go wipe that Crystal, cover your shapely ass, and call me back."

"You're incurable, you horny old bastard, but you're all talk. Littlebend out."

Having completed another sweep through the carnage, Junker brought the tug about and rendezvoused with the two dinghies. As they came along side, Junker queried his crew. "Lyard, what'd you see?"

"All the same Cap'n. All the same."

"Garms?"

"Pulled her apart, Captain. CoreFires for sure, where CoreFires's no threat. She was a good ship, rest her soul, but she's junk now. Someone's going into the fire for this."

"Crew?" Junker asked.

"None."

"Lyard?"

"Not a soul nor their remains. Cap'n, it's crazy! Like she went to her grave unmanned — I'd swear it! Look at those pitiful scraps o' her tumbling all over the Gap. There's nowt missing save part o' her keel where the red-hot power feeds come through, and that's sealed off from crew and bots. Twice we've been through every last scrap, and they're all the same. Deserted. I'd swear there wasn't a soul on board when she drove through that bend behind us!"

"Listen carefully, you two. Zip your lips when we get back. Belay all talk about what you think might have happened here, or we're all going into the fire. Follow me?"

"Aye, Cap'n. Mum's the word."

The dinghies cast off as Junker returned to the pilot house, just in time to hear the ship's comm come back to life.

"Littlebend to Junker, sorry about that interruption. We're back on the air. Anything new?"

"Junker here. No survivors, no bodies, no unburnt bots."

"You want to file?"

"I want to puke, but yes, I'll file for salvage. We'll post the pieces before we leave. I'll tow them to the Ring during the next few days. Let folks know it's there if they want something. The engines will take a little longer — they have to cool."

"Somebody's got to do it, Junker, and it might as well be you."

"Thanks, Wog, I think. Sorry for this rottenness."

"Comes with the station, Aries. I'll pass the word to the next vessels coming through, and they'll carry it up and down the Gap. Littlebend clear."

"Junker clear."

———————————————

Chapter 27

NEW HAND ON BOARD
— REPORTING TO THE BOSUN

SHANNI'S RAPID FOOTSTEPS rang on the metal deck-plates, filling the long passageway with swarms of reverberating echoes as she strode along, swinging her helmet in one hand and a small bag of personal belongings in the other.

Occasionally, she passed groups of pipes or conduits that came up through fittings in the deck, traveling along beside her in orderly array. Up the metal walls they went, like military snakes, turning column right, column left, until they merged with a host of their brethren in the rush-hour freeway of plumbing that jammed the upper reaches of the passage.

"At least they seem to know where they're going," Shanni thought.

The steady clang, clang, clang seemed to be the only sign of any progress until the sound suddenly changed as the deck-plates ended and some gratings began. She found herself standing at the intersection of two passageways, listening to the echoes dying away in the distance.

Peering left and right down the somewhat narrower cross-passage, she had difficulty believing that Core-freighters like the Reliant III were not especially large as starships go. "More than big enough to get lost in," she murmured.

The passageway ahead looked a little wider, which she considered a plus, but appeared to soon go through a bulkhead and bend to the left, which she decided was a minus. "If I were the aft port cargo bay, where would I be?" Lost in thought she glanced down at her feet, only to drop her helmet and bag in a flood of adrenalin as she jumped back from the abyss below!

For a moment, nothing made sense. A few of the smaller belongings from her bag were falling into the depths, bouncing and tinkling off unknown machinery far below, only to drop further still. But the helmet and bag, along with the rest of her gear, weren't falling at all!

Shanni burst out laughing in sudden relief, and stepped gingerly forward onto the floor grating to retrieve her remaining belongings. The grate was quite transparent, having more holes than metal, and it gave her the shivers to be looking straight down thirty or forty feet to the machinery she had glimpsed below. Rising to her feet again, she realized that the entire cross-passage was floored in a similar fashion. "That settles it," she said, "Straight ahead it is."

And straight ahead it was. As she passed from the open airlock into her destination, the cargo bay, she stopped, awe-struck by its size, amazed by the level of activity that greeted her wherever she looked.

Bots were everywhere, carrying crates of cargo, stacking them in piles, hurrying back for more. Elsewhere, pairs of bots working in perfect synchronization were lifting heavier crates between them and carrying them off, only to be replaced by additional duos in turn. Just in front of her, four bots converged simultaneously, lifted the corners of a huge container and swiftly carried it out of sight, only to have the space immediately occupied by rapidly growing stacks of boxes delivered by the most incredibly coordinated bucket brigade she had ever seen. Swiveling in unison, the bots caught, turned, and tossed the boxes in a flowing stream that raised a wall of boxes before her eyes, at least seven feet tall and twice as wide, in half a minute. As quickly as it had formed, the bucket brigade split into several groups bustling off to different tasks.

To Shanni it seemed that collisions were imminent as squads of bots crisscrossed the open spaces of the cargo bay and poured into and out of the narrow aisles between stacks of crates, but no matter how disastrous things looked, there always turned out to be a fraction of a second to spare. Now three groups of bots formed a single line in front of her wall of boxes, and each stooped in turn, picking up and balancing an entire seven-foot stack. In seconds, the wall was gone, but as the line of bots moved quickly off among other piles, she could see the tops of the stacks wending their way down distant aisles like some strange caterpillar late for an appointment.

"In fact," thought Shanni, "this looks like a cross between one of those ancient puzzles, where you spend most of your effort moving a hole around among the squares, and some sort of a race." Quite some distance ahead, bots were dismantling two walls of crates like a parting curtain, giving her a view into the center of the cargo bay. And just as she was wondering how all this chaos could be juggled and coordinated, she saw her answer — there, standing on a crate surveying all about him, stood a man in white uniform, the very bosun-tech to whom she was instructed to report.

———————————————

"Bosun, sir, permission to report?" the bot asked, looking up at Daric.

Daric made the slightest signal with his little finger, and the bot waited patiently.

Like a symphony conductor in the middle of a demanding passage, Daric checked the progress of his various groups of bots, keeping them in synchronization and giving them new directions through a system of almost imperceptible hand signals. When all of his charges were sufficiently coordinated, he again signaled the bot before him.

"Bosun, sir, the trainee has arrived, and is waiting at the aft airlock."

"You may escort her to terminal station number two, and tell her that I'll be there shortly."

As the bot moved aft to fulfill its assignment Daric again scanned the cargo bay, carefully avoiding looking at any of the surveillance cameras overhead, and whenever a group of bots passed near his position he gave them new orders via the almost invisible hand signals.

Soon, only the most thorough analysis could have revealed that all of the bots' cargo shuffling activity throughout the vast bay had now become circular in nature, like moves in a chess game where both opponents are stalling. The squads of bots dispersed and formed as swiftly as before, urgently transferring cargo in a series of complex steps, but there was one slight difference — until Daric should change their orders, they didn't require the least bit of supervision.

He could have taken a nap.

Instead, he dismounted from his crate and walked amidships toward terminal station number two.

————————————————

Waiting at the terminal station, Shanni felt a little less in danger of being run over by the hectic activity in the cargo bay, partly because she was next to the inner wall of the immense room, and partly because no bots were charging back and forth through it balancing their heavy loads. One group was busily dismantling a wall of crates nearby, but to her relief even these headed off in another direction.

The bot that had escorted her was standing by, but Shanni had never felt comfortable making small talk with bots: their tendency to take everything literally — or to take a long time trying to puzzle out something that couldn't be taken literally — almost always left her frustrated.

She didn't have long to wait, however, before the young man in the white uniform came walking her way accompanied by a bot on either side. At a distance she saw that he had a nice slim figure, well revealed by his Mono-mol uniform. "An interesting young face, pleasant enough," she mused as he approached, adding when he came close enough, "and aren't those eyes intense."

The two bots stopped a pace back as he stepped forward to shake her hand. "Welcome aboard. I'm Bosun-Tech of the Reliant III."

"Trainee Shanni 8122-457-1415, Cluster 94960, Planet 15, reporting for duty."

He turned to the three bots. "You may return to your duties."

Shanni was alert enough to catch the bots glancing at his right hand before they wheeled around and strode quickly to join the group dismantling the last of the neighboring wall of boxes. She almost shivered as she saw that exactly three boxes remained, which they scooped up before joining the tail of the departing parade.

"The captain has assigned you to me," the bosun continued, "you've already signed Ship's Articles?"

Shanni turned back from the bots, trying to concentrate on his words. Barely pausing for her nod he went on. "I'll be responsible for your training throughout this voyage. Your first duty watch will begin at oh-six-hundred tomorrow, when a bot will arrive at your quarters."

She liked his voice, although his manner seemed overly stiff and formal, and she decided that she'd better be careful not to threaten his sense of authority for awhile. "I wish I knew more about ship's protocol," she thought.

"A bot will now take you to your quarters," he continued, and a bot walked up to them, as if by magic, "where you will find orientation materials that will help to familiarize you with the ship and your duties." Again, he shook her hand briskly, saying, "Glad to have you aboard."

Shanni barely had time to reply, "Thank you," and hastily add, "Bosun," before she was apparently dismissed — her bot-guide was opening a door-sized hatch in the wall and obviously waiting for her to step through. Nodding a wordless farewell to the white-suited young bosun, standing so erect and proper, she thought to herself, "I wonder if there's a man inside that machine."

She turned and ducked through the opening, followed by the bot who swung the heavy hatch shut, then spun a wheel that mechanically locked a dozen metal dogs.

The clanging of Shanni's footsteps down the narrow passageway was nothing compared to the bot's — in order to have several times the strength of a human, they also had to weigh three times as much.

To make her question heard over the clamoring echoes she almost had to shout, "What do his friends call him?"

As they continued down the corridor the bot looked at her momentarily, then walked head down for some time, looking for all the world like a metal philosopher considering some subtle ramification of her question. Turning toward her again it finally answered, "Since the crew is so few in number, he has no friends on board. His human name is Daric."

Chapter *28*

OBSERVING BOSUN-TECH — A ROBOT-MASTER

THE BRIDGE OF the Reliant III was spacious and grand.

In hallowed tradition handed down from spaceships of yore, rows of dimly lit consoles flickered with arrays of intensely colored brilliant pin-pricks. Whether located on big slanting tables, standing panels, or hanging from racks overhead, dazzling lines of tiny lights glowed, or moved, or crawled, or blinked, purporting to communicate the well-being of the ship.

Their real purpose, however, was evident in the extravagant beauty of their design: serried ranks of constellations overhead in every color of the spectrum, and great semicircles of intricate displays surrounding the luxurious swivel-chairs labeled "Captain", "First Mate", and "Second Mate".

For generations, no one had been able to shake the most fundamental religious belief of spaceship owners, builders, and captains alike: that the ships they loved should be grand, and that the bridge should be the grandest of the grand — the most awe inspiring and holy monument to technological triumph that the mind could conceive and the technician manifest. For generations, as each spaceship was finally completed and powered up for the first time, owners and builders and captains had lined up to sit in those swivel chairs, just to look around at all those glittering displays, sigh contentedly, and know deep in their hearts that something was right in the universe.

To say that the bridge of the Reliant III was average for a Core-freighter was to say it was grand, spectacular, beautiful and impressive in the extreme. It was also empty, since crew could only enter on direct orders from a ship's officer, and all three officers were in a small room just off the bridge, looking at the surveillance monitors.

Captain Volnath, First Mate Kegler, and Second Mate Stulmin were all watching Daric, who was again standing atop a crate, directing the busy bots stowing cargo in the aft port cargo bay.

Impressed, Stulmin muttered, "I don't know how he does it. Look at them move that cargo! It's like a chess game: pile some here, step aside, four bots here, eight there. I'm fried and basted if he hasn't got them shuffling around like a small army."

"And look how each group just gets out of the way before the next is marching through," added Kegler. "He sure can move cargo. Too bad..."

Kegler suddenly shut up under the withering glare of the captain. "He's too smart. I want both of you keeping a weather eye on him. Know where he is and what he's doing at all times. Anything fishy, tell me.

"What about the girl?" asked the first mate.

"I've assigned her to his watch — he's to train her," Captain Volnath growled. "Find him and you've found her. Remember, one of you knows what he's doing at all times."

With that the captain rose and left the room, motioning for Kegler to follow.

Still watching Daric on the surveillance monitor, Stulmin shook his head. "He sure can make those bots move cargo!"

———————————————

Chapter *29*

WHO IS THAT GIRL? — HACK HER RECORDS

IN THE CARGO bay, Daric was directing the bots from atop a crate placed just in front of the terminal station. Before him a bot looked up, asking, "Permission for a question?" Daric surveyed the situation around him, and gave several subtle hand signals.

Immediately, two groups of eight bots each began building two large stacks of crates that just happened to shield Daric and the terminal station from the view of the surveillance cameras in the ceiling. When the piles were complete, Daric stepped down from his podium and said to the bot, "Granted."

"When I can't see your hand am I allowed to infer signals from actions of others in my group?" the bot asked quietly.

"Yes," Daric replied, "and what is the classification of hand signals?"

"Code 7 Bosun-tech Daric only, most secure, bots only, rank override, no reference to other humans."

"That is correct. Resume your duties, propagate these answers to all ship's bots only." As the bot turned away, Daric moved quickly to the terminal, seating himself on a small bench he pulled out of the wall.

Working swiftly and smoothly, he was undetected as he breached layer after layer of the ship's security system. In half a minute he had established himself as auditor of the vessel's personnel records, and was carefully exploring the files when he suddenly found his own.

Some of the personal history he saw there displeased him, and he briefly considered taking it out. "Too easy to check," he decided, but then saw the notation that this was only his third voyage, and he began thinking about how much more impressive it would look if it were his sixth or seventh. Again, caution intervened, and he got back to the business at hand.

"There she is!" he whispered. Slipping a Crystal from the pouch in his uniform, he inserted it into the terminal and recorded the contents of both files. He only had time to glance at the contents of Shanni's before re-pocketing the Crystal and erasing his tracks from each level of the security system. Finally, he convinced the terminal station, too, that nothing had happened, then shoved the bench back in the wall and resumed his position atop the crate just as groups of bots began dismantling his privacy-piles.

"Damn," he thought, as he subtly conducted the symphony of robot activity before him, "I'm an inch taller, but she's six months older than I am."

––––––––––––––––

Chapter 30

[Rad:na] Questor's Interference
— From the missing Finders

"Wreckage ahead!" she called.

"Whereaway, Questor?" shouted First-Mate-Norr.

"Three points to starboard, as nearly as can be told," Joss called down from her newly finished navigator's platform. "I'm encountering interference."

Norr frowned at that. Anything affecting the Navigatrix's powers concerned him mightily. "Three points to starboard, beings!" he bellowed to the Rad:na deck-watch. "Lookouts aloft with a weather eye! Wreckage ahead somewhere! Who'll be the first to sight it?"

The violent gale had long since subsided and the Rad:na vessel was sailing though the blue CoreFires on a broad reach, so the minor course change was easily accomplished. Norr nodded with satisfaction as lookouts swarmed eagerly up the rigging among spark-wreathed masts and yards, ignoring the lightning bolts crackling across the surfaces of the mighty energy sails. When the tiny figures reached their crow's-nests atop the masts, the mate made his way to the foot of the navigator's platform. "Permission to ascend, Questor?"

"Granted, Mate-Norr."

As soon as his head rose through the hatchway in the floor the mate froze, silently watching his Navigatrix.

The Questor's slender body, clad in her form fitting space suit, looked more like a red-lacquered statue entitled "Concentration". Her back was slightly arched, her head tilted back, eyes closed, her gloved hands as usual clasping the Finders set in the railing. She was both motionless and seeking, and Norr waited, hardly breathing, while she probed with senses beyond his own. Finally, with a shake of her head she was clearly back in her body and the mate resumed climbing up onto the platform, asking about the interference.

Joss's eyes searched the luminous CoreFires ahead. "Aye, Norr. Somewhat frustrating, and most peculiar. Just now I was sensing wreckage ahead, but also receiving another obscure and conflicting sense of wreckage I can't locate."

As he arrived beside her, Norr's puzzled frown deepened. "Questor, is the platform unsatisfactory? Can you tell what's causing it?"

"It's not the platform," she assured him, looking down at the elaborately carved figure in each hand. "It's the Finders themselves."

"The Finders?" Norr was shocked.

"Odd, but true. For these past days I've been receiving a strange interfering ghost image, like hearing two comm channels at once, one much fainter than the other. Not serious, but definitely annoying."

Incredulous, Norr shook his head. "How is that possible?"

Her eyes probed the nebula ahead for any visual sign of the wreckage. "I can only guess," she said, "but as you know I was exceptionally attuned to the pair of Finders that were carried away with my platform. If they were still within range when I linked to the new ones, it's just possible that I could be sensing both pairs. That's why I had us return to the scene of our near disaster yesterday, to see if the missing ones were there."

"Ah. Without success I gather, since we didn't stop."

"If they'd been there before, they were gone by the time we arrived." The Questor's fingers roamed the familiar details of the carvings. "Still, if it is the missing Finders I'm sensing, they must be somewhere relatively nearby."

Norr brightened. "Then they might be caught in that wreckage ahead?"

"It's worth a try..." Joss raised a hand for silence as a cry came from high in the rigging.

"Wreckage, Ho!" the lookout called. "Dead ahead! Five thousand yards!"

Norr immediately climbed down through the hatch until only his head was showing above the platform. "Navigatrix?"

Gazing intently ahead through the occasional bursts of star-foam cast up by the bow, Joss discerned a gaunt dark shape amid the swirling CoreFires. She shook her head as if to clear away the annoying interference. "Make directly for it, dead slow as we come near. Maybe we can put end to this puzzle!"

"Aye, dead slow as we come near," said Norr's own head, just before it suddenly dropped from sight. Without even touching the steep stairs, the mate slid down the railings all the way to the deck below, landing with a mighty thump. "Avast there, beings," he bellowed, at least as nearly as his Rad:na words could be translated into a tongue of Humankind, a rich and ancient argot not heard since the days of ships that sailed upon the seas of MotherEarth. "Hands aloft! Furl the skysails and topgallants! Strike the spanker, the mizzen, and the main! Smartly now..."

On the platform, Joss twisted each finder a quarter turn, unlocking them from the railing in preparation for transferring to the conning station beyond the ship's prow.

————————————

Chapter *31*

[RAD:NA] CAPSIZED CATHEDRAL — MORE THAN COINCIDENCE?

STANDING BY AT their lines, some of the crew-members scattered about the deck watched Joss and Norr on the little conning platform, barely two yards square and perched halfway out the bowsprit. Most, however, were gazing intently at the dark U-shaped form that had emerged from the CoreFires's indigo turbulence — a section of a large ship's skeletal keel and a dozen ribs, now less than two hundred yards away.

Beside Joss in the conning station, Norr looked away from the wreck to check the rigging behind them. All sails were furled except for the reefed topsails on the foremast and the main, and even there the golden lightning was flickering only faintly. Peering over the side, he gauged the star-wake, now but a dozen yards wider than the hull. It was slipping aft so slowly that half of the blue-white embers had winked out before the stern passed by.

"Dead slow, Questor," he reported.

"Good. Stand by, Norr. We'll soon know."

Her hands were on the Finders, now remounted on the conning station rail, her senses probing for that peculiar faint echo. Dead ahead, the wreckage floated in mid-space.

"It's huge!" muttered the mate. "Like a ruined cathedral turned upside down!"

"Well spoken, Mate-Norr," Joss whispered with a shiver. "A gutted cathedral from another race, now capsized among our clouds of fire."

The near end of the burnt out hull section yawned ahead, fully twice as tall as the Rad:na vessel and several times as wide. Enormous blackened ribs reached upward like overturned Gothic arches, their torn off tops making a ragged silhouette against the nebula above. Each successive arch seemed more ghostly as it was veiled by intervening drifts of phosphorescent blue. Below, as straight as an aisle between tiny deserted pews, the metal keel still glowed red-hot amidst the surrounding gridwork.

"It's big enough," Norr murmured in awe, "that we could sail right through it!"

The Questor's eyes were bright, her gaze locked straight ahead. A slight smile played about her lips. "My first mate must be psychic. That's just what we're going to do."

"Navigatrix! You're joking!"

"Hardly, my faithful Norr."

"You've located the Finders then? They're here?"

"Not that I've detected, but I'm convinced that something for us lays within, if only we have the will to enter and the eyes to see it. Take us through, Norr, right down the middle. Alert the helm."

Norr bowed briefly, then squared his shoulders. "As my Navigatrix commands!"

The crew at their posts, whether watching the two in the conning station or the grim wreckage now only a hundred yards beyond, stood ready at their lines. With each passing second they awaited the call to change course and bear away from that looming derelict. At last, the mate turned toward them.

"All hands!" Norr called out. "Prepare to sail through the hulk!"

The comm channel was suddenly alive with muffled exclamations of surprise.

"Helmsman," barked Norr, "do you spy that lurid compass, that steel keel still glowing at red heat, fresh from the hellish fires of disaster? Set our course by that dire axis, and, mind you, align us true! Do not deviate as we enter those dread portals, lest our vessel meet its doom!"

"Aye," came the reply from the helm. "Within fifty yards it shall be so! I stake us all upon it!"

"Deckhands," Norr's voice rang out, "stand firm at your lines. Mind your sails, mind them well! We proceed at dead slow, so if fortune rides with us your task is easy. But should the chance gust arise, only your swift and sure actions can keep it from sending us into those grotesque columns!"

"We are aligned on the new course," the helm reported. "Thirty yards remain."

"Sailors, Questor-Joss fears not this gruesome monument from Humankind's side of the Gap-walls," the mate continued. "She bids us enter, the better to fulfill our ancient purpose. Are the Rad:na ready?"

"Aye! Ready. We are!" many replied.

"Then be vigilant! Keep her steady as she goes, beings," Norr called in a strong voice as he turned again to the iron skeleton awaiting them. "We enter! Steady as she goes!"

No matter how vigorous their reply, no matter how willing and dedicated the crew lining the rails, their voices grew hushed as the sailing ship glided between the uprights of that first gigantic rib.

Questor-Joss and Norr craned their necks to see the ragged steel tops towering so high above the Rad:na vessel's tallest mast. There, twisted shreds of smaller girders still adhered to those mammoth pillars like withered steel vines. Between the first massive rib and the second, the walls of the cathedral were mostly agape, with only a few beams and a sparse tangle of wreckage spanning the gap.

"Looks like she met a violent end," First-Mate-Norr said to his Navigatrix. "We're lucky this wasn't one of the pieces that came at us through the Gap-wall that night."

Still grasping the Finders, Joss leaned her head over the railing. "Look below, Norr. Your eyes will tell you why I'm not particularly expecting to locate the missing Finders here."

Puzzled, Norr also peered over the railing. Below, the hull was igniting a minimum of star-foam, and below that, the wrecked freighter's red-hot keel slid slowly astern. "Forgive me, Questor, my eyes are open, but I'm not seeing."

"That keel, Mate-Norr. Too hot by far to be part of the ship that almost destroyed us days ago. These are the remnants of a different vessel."

The second blackened rib glided silently by while Norr checked the energy winds aloft. Still calm, and their sails were drawing evenly, moving right down the cavernous center of the derelict. "Two ships wrecked in so short a time?" he mused. "Coincidence?"

"Perhaps not," Joss replied, steadily gazing ahead. "Something unusual could be unfolding in the Gap. We may have to be especially careful not to interfere while they work out their own destiny, if it's a matter of good versus evil among the Humankind."

The mate nodded. "You sensed evil nearby, just before you turned our ship aside."

For a moment, she observed the mate thoughtfully, then came to a decision. "Norr, I only made it by a hair's breadth, diving off that platform. There's something I must tell you, in case I don't survive." She was touched to see the pain in the first mate's eyes.

The Questor looked aft along the bowsprit to where the Rad:na crew were lining the railings, speaking in whispers as hushed as if the ruined cathedral were haunted by the spirits of sailors lost. She, too, lowered her voice.

"During the storm, without alerting it, I detected the presence of an Owd hiding somewhere in this galaxy! That means it must have been hidden before the seeding. And now, after millions of years of waiting, it's quietly becoming active!"

"Just as Humankind is nearing the core and the portal!" Norr exclaimed. "The Owd! But for the Rad:na, they'd have long since infected all the galaxies with their evil!"

"There's more. Its presence was revealed in a vision, a vision of levels of evil. At the highest level was the Owd's clawed hand. The form was as games of chess. It moved a pawn. On another level, that pawn was a player. On its board, as part of its own evil plan, it in turn pushed a pawn. On the next level, the next player therefore pushed a pawn, and so on." Involuntarily, Joss shivered and glanced over her shoulder. "The final level was here. I believe the final pawn was pushed toward us!"

Norr looked up at the wreckage of the third arch passing high above their heads. "As the only Rad:na ship in the region, that could give us a grave responsibility."

"And raise grave conflict between our two sacred directives — preserve the nurseries from interference, preserve the galaxies from the evil of the Owd. Consider this: The Rad:na fail as Keepers if we interfere while a developing species sorts out good and evil among their kind. But what if the Owd know we cannot interfere? What if the Owd have been manipulating some of the Humankind to achieve their ends?"

"The gateway!" Norr whispered. "If humans under the influence of the Owd reached the portal, winning free access to all the galaxies..." The troubled mate shook his head, then checked their progress — half way through the dead leviathan with a half dozen giant ribs remaining before them. Their course was still true. "Questor!" he exclaimed as he was struck by a sudden thought. "In terms of your vision, at a higher level, could our near catastrophe have been more than a coincidence?"

"Chaos!" she swore. "And I call myself a ninth generation Keeper!" Releasing the Finders she grasped his shoulders. "You, faithful Norr, have seen what I have missed! Yes! At a higher level, given the Owd's subtle powers, even such an unlikely coincidence could have been arranged if it were planned far enough ahead!" Her mind was racing.

"Could it even have been an attempt to destroy our ship?"

Her eyes roamed the massive ruin gliding by. The implications were mind boggling. She gasped as the pieces began falling into place. "I've been blind! Even my reactions could have been anticipated!" she whispered in awe. "Turning the ship aside — even the trajectory of that final piece could have been planned! What if my platform being carried away was no coincidence either?"

The mate's voice was outraged. "An attempt to kill my Navigatrix?"

Joss looked down the tunnel they must still traverse, her mind seeking something it had missed, something so big, so obvious — suddenly the final piece clicked into place! "The missing Finders!" she cried out. "The Owd itself couldn't use them, but if they fell into evil human hands..." Quickly she again grasped the Finders on the railing, probing, searching. "They're not here, Norr! Where they are I can't tell, somewhere not too far away, but they're definitely not here."

She shut her eyes, trying to follow that faint echo. Suddenly her eyes shot open, and her lips curved in a grim but triumphant smile. "But wherever they are, I can tell one thing — they are not yet in anyone's hands!" Her eyes blazed with determination. "Our course is clear, Norr! We must find them first!"

Unlocking the Finders from the railing, she began running down the bowsprit with the mate following. "Me to my platform and you to your deck!" she called as she ran. "Get the crew cracking! Unreef the topsails! Break out the topgallants and the spanker!"

Following her at a gallop down the narrow bowsprit, Norr protested, "Questor! There are still four ribs to go! The space is narrow!"

"We can do it, Norr!" she cried, leaping to the deck and sprinting toward her platform. "We must out-race time itself! Make us fly, Norr, make us fly!"

"Unreef the topsails!" the mate thundered as he ran across the deck. "Aloft, there! Are ye made of stone? Come alive! Moments count, my beings!" Catching up to the Navigatrix as she reached the base of her ladder he barked, "Watch your helm! Crowd the starboard wall as those sails take the wind. Leave room to port for the masts to heel over!"

"That's my Norr!" Joss exulted. "We're late, thanks to my blindness, but perhaps not too late, thanks to your vision. We entered this dark cathedral seeking enlightenment, and found it." Clambering up the ladder she called down, "Perhaps the Rad:na will not be so easily defeated! Make all the speed you can, First-Mate-Norr!"

"Aye, Questor!" he replied with a wave. "All hands! Set the topgallants! Man the spanker to keep our heading!"

Below, the hull spewed star-foam wide. Above, the sails bellied and caught the energy winds. Again the captive lightning leaped boldly across their taut surfaces. Crowding the windward pillars, the helmsman watched the top of the masts heeling hard alee. The third arch passed swiftly astern as the beautiful ship took the bit in her teeth.

"Come on, my beings," Norr bellowed. "There's yet more room alee! Are the Rad:na not sailors? Let's have more sail!"

By the time the ship burst through the final portal, she was under full sail, her masts hard over, their tops barely clearing the lee wall. Lightning thundered across her huge energy sails, and her star-foam wake surged far out, spilling beyond either side of the dark hulk she left behind. "That's the way, beings!" Norr called. "That's the way it's done!"

————————————

A few minutes later, Questor-Joss looked astern at the distant derelict wreckage, then checked the energy winds aloft. "They'll not soon sweep it back into the Gap," she mused, "and we may be returning this way as we search for those Finders. No sense in having an extra hazard to navigation." Leaning over the railing, she called down, "Mate-Norr, eliminate the wreckage."

"Aye, Questor," he acknowledged. "Ahoy aft. Eliminate the wreck."

"Aye," replied a deckhand from the stern. "Eliminating the wreck." The crew-member moved to the rail, unlocking one of several similar devices mounted there and swiveling it until it bore on the rapidly disappearing derelict. Apparently satisfied with its aim, he activated it, sending a narrow brilliant beam astern. The macabre iron skeleton that had so recently enclosed them erupted onto a thousand tumbling fragments, each ablaze with consuming fire until nothing remained but a faint gray cloud rapidly dispersing in the indigo CoreFires. The deck-hand then restowed the weapon.

"Wreckage cleared, Questor," Norr reported.

————————————

Chapter *32*

WE'RE ALIVE! — DRIFTING IN COREFIRE

WE'RE ALIVE!" Mutch shouted.

"We're alive! Marneen yelled back.

Two tiny figures still tied together by a length of line congratulated each other as they drifted through the CoreFires itself. They were shouting for joy — the howling in their ears had ceased the moment they penetrated the Gap-wall.

"Our suits survived!" Mutch called out from his end of the tether.

"We survived!" Marneen called from hers. "You were right! A kid in a bio-suit can survive in CoreFires!"

"We wouldn't have if we'd been close to that go-board — did you see that thing blow into a million pieces when it reached the Gap-wall? We'd have been table scraps!"

"Cooked table scraps!" she agreed. "And that was such a small motor, but it went off like a bomb! No wonder all the junk we've seen that's been in CoreFires is so torn up."

"Yeah, I'd hate to be near something big, like electrical things, and computers, and bots. Remember that burnt control room we played in at the Ring? Gross!"

"But we've got nothin', so we made it! Wow!" she exulted.

"Nothin' but each other, Marneen," he added. "We stuck together, didn't we?"

"We sure did, Gap boy! No matter what! You've been so fine, Mutch, and I know you wouldn't have gotten into this if it hadn't been for me."

"Hey, the same to you. We got into it because we're us! We might not get out of it, but at least we're flying like nobody else is. A while ago, when I was lookin' for you after that pilot's cruiser blew us away from the freighter? I wondered if we'd live to see Firedawn. Well, guess what!"

"What?"

"We did, 'cause here it comes." Mutch waved an arm in the direction they were flying.

The CoreFires plasma of glowing indigo was changing before their eyes, showing the first blushes of purple. A softly billowing cloudscape, it flowed toward them on a gently surging energy tide.

Through a deep cumulus canyon they flew, exclaiming as the clefts and crevices in the cloud-walls flooded with luminous purple, then violet.

"Oh, look!" Marneen said, pointing ahead to where a slowly roiling ridge looked like it was catching fire. As they skimmed low over the cloudtop, they looked down into strange whirlpools of dark velvet red. "It looks so hot," Marneen gasped. "I hope it doesn't burn us!"

"Nothing's hurt us so far," Mutch reminded her, giving her hand a reassuring squeeze. Then he looked up and saw that they were going to plunge right into a wall of glowing red. "Hang on!" he shouted.

In moments they were through the cloud, and Marneen couldn't resist the turn-about. Smiling broadly, she squeezed his hand, saying, "Don't be scared, Mutch, nothing's hurt us yet."

He laughed, turning to face her. "Yeah, I guess you're right. Nothing to be scared of, is there?"

The clouds passing behind her head were colored in brilliant reds and burnt oranges. The succession of soft warm colors swept across her face as she tried to smile. It was too much. The tears welled in the corners of her eyes, catching flecks of fire. A tender sadness over-whelmed her. "Mutch," she said, fighting back the tears, "What's to become of us?" She turned, looking ahead into the Firedawn. "We'll just drift on and on." She bit her lip. "We'll never get back to the village!"

Still holding her hand, he, too, turned to look ahead, searching for something he could say. Nothing came.

Silently clasping hands, the two watched as they passed on through nebulous sheets of flame. Mutch gave her hand an extra squeeze.

She returned it. Lost in thought they flew deeper and deeper into the CoreFires.

———————————————

Chapter *33*

[RAD:NA] HUMANKIND IN COREFIRE — TWO CHILDREN!

THE REDS OF Firedawn glinted off Questor-Joss's sleek red spacesuit, wrapping her slender, near-human figure in shining shards of flame. Within her helmet and its almost invisible bubble, her face was softly sculpted by the fire-light. Eyelids closed, she probed again for the missing Finders.

Beside her, Norr watched silently until her keen eyes opened again, rapidly scanning the CoreFires ahead. "Shall I change course again?" he asked.

"No, we'll keep this heading for awhile. I still can't get any sense of their direction, but their presence seems a little clearer than it was before. I hope they're not somewhere within the Gap."

"Questor! That hadn't occurred to me. And we can't venture into those voids!"

"It also might make them difficult to locate."

"How so?" the mate asked.

"I'm just guessing, since it's never happened before to my knowledge, but the Gap-walls might be a formidable barrier. Even with the Finders I can hardly sense anything within the Gaps, and we don't receive any of Humankind's comm chatter even when we're sailing right next to the Gap-walls. It might be enough to cloak their location." She checked the CoreFires ahead, now incandescent shades of orange. Seeing nothing requiring immediate attention, she again closed her eyes. "Wait while I try again."

So intently was she probing for that faint echo of the missing Finders that it was some time before she realized she'd been hearing something strange. She straightened, looking about.

"Norr," she asked, "do you hear something odd on the comm?"

Norr tilted his head as he listened. "No, except for a little static, kind of scratchy, and I can barely hear that at all."

"That's it, but it's not quite static. Listen."

Norr looked down for a long moment, then shook his head. "I can't tell, Questor. It's too faint."

Joss's eyes narrowed with concentration, apparently to no avail. She turned to Norr. "Have the crew be silent for awhile."

"All hands," the mate bellowed. "Pass the word, then belay all chatter. Total silence on the comm channel until further orders."

An instant cacophony arose as the crew-members advised their shipmates, then it quickly tapered down to the last few in the rigging and below decks getting the message. Soon, throughout the ship, all nonessential activity had ceased. Groups frozen in mid-conversation looked like nautical statuary, some leaning on the rail, some standing about the deck, and the helmsman silently watching the sails, occasionally shifting the spokes of the big wheel in response to subtle changes of the energy winds. Someone attempted to stifle a cough, then cleared his throat.

"Listen, Norr," whispered Questor-Joss.

It was something more than static, although so faint that the mate marveled at how she could have detected it. "What is it?" he asked, unable to make sense of what he was hearing, even though it was getting somewhat louder. The scratchiness occurred in strange unpredictable bursts, unlike anything he'd ever heard before.

"It's communication!" the Navigatrix exclaimed. "Not on our frequencies, but on a channel that slightly overlaps one of ours. Norr — it's an alien tongue! Humankind!"

Now the bizarre signal was loud enough for Norr to agree. "It must be. Does that sink your theory about the Gap-walls?"

"It's not from the Gap, it's somewhere nearby! Humankind within the CoreFires!"

"You're sure?"

Questor-Joss was back at the Finders, probing intently. "Yes! Somewhere close by!"

Norr's astonishment showed in his voice. "We knew it was bound to come, but so soon, and so suddenly! We can't interfere — we'll have to avoid their ship! Can you locate it?"

"I'm probing for it. Alert the crew, then resume silence."

"All hands stand ready to change course," the mate called out, "then maintain silence." After a brief flurry of activity on the deck the ship sailed into the Firedawn as silently as before. Norr could now easily hear the scratchy bursts of alien communication but their meaning remained a mystery. "Any luck?" he whispered uneasily, anxious to avoid the interlopers.

Joss's brow was furrowed with concentration. "Somewhere close," she murmured, "but where? I can't find their ship. Curse this interference!"

Taking a deep breath, she calmed herself for maximum effectiveness, ignoring the nagging static sounding ever louder in the comm. "Take your time," she told herself. "Don't fight it. Let the Finders do their part. Be open." Her head was back, her eyelids nearly closed in the golden light, her eyes unseeing. From the depths of her trance she tried to speak, her lips barely moving. "Falling... CoreFires..."

Norr leaned close to hear her words, so softly modulated upon her breath.

"Falling... two... two of them... no ship..."

Suddenly she was back. "Norr! There's no ship! Wait." She probed anew.

Suddenly she turned to the mate, eyes wide. "Norr! They're Humankind young. Two of them. Children!"

"Can you tell where?"

"Somewhere nearby!"

"Which direction?"

"I'll try again — before I was searching for a ship. Ahead! Close ahead!"

"We'll have to come about quickly and retreat to a safe distance, then circle around them. Too bad it'll delay our search for the missing Finders, but we have little choice. Shall I give the order?" When the Questor turned toward him, the mate was dismayed to see tears in her eyes.

"They have no ship, Norr! They're doomed unless we save them!"

He was astounded! "We have no choice! As Rad:na we can't interfere! At least there are only two of them."

"Two children!" She cried in horror. "Norr, they're children!" Her tears overflowed and coursed unnoticed down her cheeks. "Granted we can't interfere while the species sorts out good versus evil among themselves," she argued, "but these are children! They're neither good nor evil! They're innocent!"

"My Navigatrix," Norr replied, his inner torment plain upon his face, "you propose to save them? How? Where?"

"Wait," she said, pouring herself once again into the Finders, sending her senses forth, seeking the two lost children of Humankind.

"Goddess," she cried silently, "help me if I'm right, or help me to know if I'm wrong!" The golden light on her closed eyelids showed the movement of her pupils beneath, desperately searching right and left, high and low. "A Rad:na Keeper! Two innocent children of the nursery race! Goddess," she pleaded, "help me know what to do!" In her anguish she probed as never before. Something, on the edge of perception. "So alien.... so strange..." A little clearer, but still too faint.

"Norr," she gasped aloud, "I can almost sense something. Maybe a location... Faint. It's so hard!" She opened her eyes, looking into his. "Norr, can you support me in this?"

In agony he tried to interpret the sacred duty of the Rad:na. Looking into the eyes of his Navigatrix he found his answer. "Goddess, help me," he breathed silently, then spoke aloud. "Yes, Questor, I can. I do!"

"Then place your hands atop mine on the Finders. Support me, Norr, while I probe."

"Aye, Questor," he whispered, "I do."

Deep in her trance, Joss murmured, "Something... almost... perhaps a location... in the Gap... so faint... so strange..."

———————————

Still tied together, Marneen and Mutch drifted into a tall CoreFires chamber with walls of dark bronze just as the wavering auroral sheets at the far end began to stir and swirl. Mutch watched as the glowing curtains grew more agitated, twisting and writhing for a great distance up the cloud-wall. "If I could steer, I'd steer away from that!"

"Me too!" Marneen affirmed.

But they were headed right for it. A net of lightning spread upward, then golden fire. Out of the turmoil emerged ship of the Rad:na.

"Oh-boy-oh-boy," Mutch kept saying, over and over. "The Flying Dutchman! I'm not ready for this! I think I'm going to pass out."

"Don't you dare!" whispered Marneen, "or I'll kill you dead!"

"Go ahead! Maybe I'd rather skip this whole thing!"

"Not on your life! You think I'm going through this alone? No way, not today!" she hissed, poking him hard in the ribs.

As the Rad:na ship, or the Dutchman as they called it, emerged from the fire, they saw it was even more alien than tales described, with the lightning bolts flashing among its energy sails, its spark-wreathed masts, and its dark hull moving through freshly erupting showers of blue-white microscopic stars.

"It's coming right for us!" Mutch shouted.

"Do you think it sees us? Let's wave!"

Wildly waving arms and legs, Marneen and Mutch tried to make themselves as visible as possible, but the ship showed no sign of turning aside.

"What if it hits us!"

"Mutch! I think it's slowing down!"

"You're right! Wave some more!"

The billows of sparks around the hull were definitely diminishing, and the sails slackened although the lightning crawling over their surfaces seemed as active as ever. As they watched, the Dutchman slowed to a stop, with the sparks around the hull diminishing to fitful bursts here and there.

"It's stopped, but we're still moving toward it," Marneen whispered.

"Well, we've got no steering and no brakes, so I guess that's that."

"Look up there!" Marneen exclaimed.

The lightning in the Dutchman's rigging had changed to blue, and lines of star-embers started to wink into being, extending the axes of the masts far above the alien ship. New lines of blazing star-specks reached out from the spars, to give birth to others growing at new angles. In less than a minute, a complex glowing tracery several times the size of the Dutchman reached out into the fireclouds, and from them waves of brightness streamed back in toward the strange vessel.

As Marneen and Mutch drifted closer, the Flying Dutchman looked bigger and bigger. "If something doesn't stop us pretty soon, we're going to bump right into the front of that thing," Mutch said. Peering up at the rigging, he saw that the waves of energy from the strange sky-grid were wrapping the ends of the spars and masts in a deep blue glow, and from there it was working its way inward, and then down the masts. Just after it reached the hull, a glowing blue spot materialized halfway between the drifting pair and the mysterious ship. "Marneen, it's making something," he said.

"I sure wish I knew what it's doing," she replied.

Pulsing waves of blue light flowed from the CoreFires, down the masts, and into the rapidly growing spot, now swelling into a luminous sphere hovering dead ahead of Mutch and Marneen.

"It's getting bigger!" Mutch cried, wide eyed.

"We're going to bang into it!" Marneen gasped, shutting hers tight.

Suddenly it was quiet.

"We didn't!" Mutch whispered in awe.

Marneen opened her eyes to see Mutch pressing his hands against the blue glow. From the inside!

"We're inside it?" she exclaimed. "Inside the ball of blue light?"

"We're inside it!"

They could still see the ship,

"Look, Mutch. The sails are filling again. The ship's starting to move!"

"We are too! They're pushing us, Marneen! They made this ball for us, and they're pushing us in front of their ship!"

Marneen grabbed both of his arms. "Oh, Mutch! Could they have known we needed saving?"

Swallowing hard, he whispered, "We better cross all our fingers, Marneen, 'cause they're sure taking us somewhere."

Marneen, watching the clouds ahead breaking into brilliant gold, nodded.

_____

Chapter 34

RETURN FROM FIREDAWN
— BACK ON THE GANGWAY

MUTCH JERKED AWAKE as his hand slowly penetrated the bubble, encountering a textured metal surface.

Marneen, still asleep, rolled over and snuggled her back against him just as the glowing blue sphere dissolved away to nothing, depositing her — now rudely awakened — in the middle of a gangway. Sitting up, she went to rub her eyes but found she had her helmet on. "Look's like mid-morning," she mumbled, peering up at the CoreFires between yawns. "We didn't get much sleep last night, did we?" Suddenly it hit her. "Where are we?"

Mutch was looking around in open-mouthed disbelief. "Dutchman's. On the gangway. There's the POSH!"

"We can't be! Can we?" She looked for herself. "It is! Mutch, it can't have been a dream!"

"No way! When I woke up that big glowing bubble was almost all here, then it just sort of evaporated!"

Slightly benumbed, the pair stood up, looking at the familiar scene. No one was in sight. A short distance ahead, the doorway of the POSH beckoned.

"Why not?" Marneen asked.

"Yeah," Mutch replied. "Why not?"

They walked toward the open door, stretching the stiffness out of their legs.

———————————

Chapter 35

TAKING TURNS – OVER DRINKS

MUTCH SPOKE FIRST. "Hi, Li-Tharm. Boy, are we glad to see you!"

Then it was Marneen's turn. "Yeah, are we ever! Could we have a drink? We don't ask very often."

"Not too very often, anyways. We'd really like one 'cause we just got saved!"

Li-Tharm looked over Otitius, who nodded and began whipping up the kids favorite drink, a harmless and staggeringly sweet concoction that they found especially desirable because no adult would sip it without instantly spitting it out. "Saved from what?" she asked.

With a brief glance to see who's turn it was, Marneen jumped in. "We hitched a free ride to stowaway on that freighter, except an e-fog strike zapped the lines!"

"But we were almost there," Mutch continued, rapid fire, "way up there, so we'd have made it 'cept they did a running start and the pilot's vessel zipped in and caught us with the back blast!"

"It knocked us go-board over tea-kettles," Marneen giggled, "and we fell a long ways, but I figured out how to miss Dutchman's, otherwise we might've smashed right through the POSH roof!"

"Wait a minute," interrupted Li-Tharm, I'll get your drinks. When she set them down the two kids began sucking eagerly on the straws, rolling their eyes to show how good it was and what the adults were missing. "What happened then?"

"Well, we got slung into the CoreFires and the go-board blew to smithereens!" Marneen's hands flew wide, almost spilling the rest of her drink. "We were zipping in deeper and deeper, and we'd have been lost forever except for what happened next! Guess what came right at us through the CoreFires!"

They both looked expectantly at Li-Tharm. She leaned down toward the table and whispered, "What?"

Together they shouted, "The Flying Dutchman!"

Mutch was talking so fast his words were running together. "It was big and scary but we waved and it stopped, and it did some weird stuff up into the sky and made this bubble..."

"...and the Dutchman put up a zillion sails, and pushed us back the way we'd come. We fell asleep."

Mutch triumphantly finished the story. "We woke up on the gangway when the bubble popped, so we came in here, all rescued, and boy are we glad to see you!"

"Yeah! We really are!"

Li-Tharm straightened up, properly amazed, "What an adventure! Do you want another drink?"

Both Mutch and Marneen looked down and the syrupy sludge in the bottom of their glasses, then nodded eagerly.

"Can we take it upstairs?" Marneen asked. "We've got to run and tell Cirra."

"Don't forget to thank Otitius," Li-Tharm cautioned, and the two kids nodded and scampered over to the bar.

"Thanks, Otitius," Mutch said, in as deep a voice as he could manage.

"Me too," added Marneen.

"I'm glad you got rescued," offered Otitius, refilling their glasses, "but let me give you a little tip." He motioned them closer, and continued in a kindly but serious voice. "You might upset folks if you go around telling stories about that ship, the Steadfast. I guess you haven't heard, but if you'd stowed away on that ship you wouldn't be here to tell about it — Junker found the wreckage just past Littlebend, and the crew is missing, to a man. Folks are pretty shaken up, so you give them some slack, OK?"

The two kids were shaken up too. "OK, Otitius. Wow! We didn't know!" said Mutch in a quiet voice.

"Thanks, Otitius, we understand," a subdued Marneen added. "Gee, how awful!"

As the kids clambered up the steep stairs, Li-Tharm walked over to her customary leaning spot on the bar. "They're a little wild sometimes, but they're good kids," she said.

"Yeah, I think their hearts are in the right place," agreed Otitius. He polished a nonexistent spot off his two-ton bar until the upside-down Li-Tharm was perfect and clear. Looking up at the right-side-up version, he shook his head with a little smile. "What imaginations!" he mused.

——————————————

Chapter 36

Ship in a Bottle – The Bosun's Passion

SHANNI HAD GOTTEN used to clanging down echoing passageways, and, with a little trial and error, could now find her way around a good portion of the Reliant III. "It's got to be right here somewhere," she murmured. Turning a corner, she spied a half open door some distance ahead. "Promising," she thought, considering the short crew. The bosun-tech had told her that for every human they were short-handed, a ship on this run had to carry ten extra bots, and that the Reliant was right at the absolute minimum human count with only the three officers, the bosun, and her.

"Oh, well," she thought, "maybe that's what got me signed on with no experience. And it sure puts Daric in bot-heaven with all those extra bots to supervise."

Coming to the doorway, she tried to knock, but the metal hatch was so solid that she got smartly stinging knuckles for her effort, but little sound. "I won't try that again," she thought. Peeking in she saw Daric working at his small desk. "Am I intruding?" she asked.

Daric swiveled around in his chair, appearing quite odd in a pair of little granny-glasses with heavy rims. He didn't seem to see her at all until he had blinked a few times, after which a normal awareness showed in his eyes. "Oh, hello, uh..."

"Can I just be `Shanni' when we're off duty?"

Daric took off his glasses which were fastened to a cord, and set them on the desk. "Yes, of course. Why not? OK, Shanni it is. Come in."

Both Shanni and Daric were wearing their white Mono-mol uniforms without their helmets, as was customary on board whether on or off duty. "What's that?" she asked, indicating a glass object on the desk in front of Daric.

"It's a bottle."

"It looks positively ancient!"

"It's supposed to," he replied. "It's a replica of a museum specimen. I had it made on Space End during the last voyage. It was delivered just before we left port."

"It's beautiful," Shanni offered, "What's it for?"

"Well, it's part of an ancient tradition." Daric reddened. "I'm kind of a history nut, especially about Humankind's original world, MotherEarth."

To steady herself, she rested her hand lightly on Daric's shoulder as she leaned closer, examining the bottle. "Tell me more about the tradition."

Welcoming a subject dear to his heart, and hoping she wouldn't take her hand away too soon, Daric explained, "On MotherEarth, early humans sailed wind-powered ships on the surface of the seas, and the sailors used to carve miniature wooden models of their ships which they inserted into bottles.

"Fascinating. How'd they do it, then?"

"All the rigging had to unfold into place after the model was slipped into the bottle through the narrow neck. It was quite difficult."

Shanni's hand left his shoulder as she pointed at tiny bits of wood scattered about the table. "So you're building a model of the Reliant?"

"No, I'm building a model of one of those ancient wind-powered sailing ships, then I'll fold it open in the bottle."

"Amazing!" Her voice was quite sincere. "How do you know how to do it?"

With a sly expression of pride, Daric fished his Crystal from its pocket on his chest. "The information is right here! From archives around the system, I copied..." there was the slightest pause, and his face reddened again, "...I requested copies of ancient plans, specifications, treatises on how to sail, lots of stuff. Here, I'll show you."

Daric handed Shanni a pair of data glasses. Shanni quickly adjusted them and asked, "What next?"

Daric reached for a thin flexible cord, attaching one end to the glasses and the other end to the Crystal, which he then attempted to slip into the pocket on her uniform. As he fumbled at the pocket, Shanni didn't offer to help him out, but took great care to keep her smile to herself.

"Now blink at the little symbol in mid air to turn on the data glasses and then blink at the symbol that looks like an old ship. "What do you see?

"Oh! It's beautiful! It's like it's made of millions of glowing lines, right in the middle of the room. Is it an ancient ship?"

"It's the plan of one, and you're looking at the rigging. Now, do you see a symbol that's like a bird?"

"I see it. Oh, Daric, I'm flying around the ship! All I have to do is look where I want to go."

"Daric, I want to learn all about flying around like this. I'm already OK on looking to the side, and climbing and diving, and the ship is lovely. It's like I'm a little bird flying anywhere I want among the rigging!"

"And you don't even have to worry about hitting something, although it can be set that way, too. Do you want to see something else?"

"Only if you promise I can try this again sometime."

Daric laughed. "OK. Look for a symbol like a clock with an arrow beside it, pointing left."

When Shanni picked out the symbol, but was startled when the whole scene instantly shifted to something else. Involuntarily, she blinked, and the scene shifted, again. In a stuttering cycle, she was bombarded by series of unrelated instantaneous scenes, and it was several moments before she calmed her blinking reflex down, and the picture before her stabilized.

"What you're seeing is what I was working on just before you came in — the way the little masts will fold."

Unbeknownst to Daric, what Shanni was really seeing was a file Daric had saved several days before — she was looking at the copy of his personnel records from the Reliant's files. Only briefly torn between nosiness and respect for his privacy, she decided to take advantage of the opportunity that the fates had brought her. She learned the spelling of his name, quickly read most of the page of his employment history, and was mildly shocked to find out that he had been asked to leave his home planet. "Strange," she thought, "I've never heard of something like that." The page offered no further information, so she tried blinking at the other clock symbol to see if it would step forward rather than back. It did, and she was further surprised to find herself looking at her own records.

"Aha! He was curious about me!" she said to herself. "Maybe he's not such a machine, after all."

Chapter *37*

VOLNATH'S EMERGENCY
— TO THE ENGINE ROOM

ON THE BRIDGE of the Reliant III, Captain Volnath was standing at the helm like captains of old, hands turning the polished wooden spokes, steering his ship through a relatively wide passage that twisted along between the glowing CoreFires walls. As far as actually controlling the ship and keeping track of its many systems, the three big U-shaped consoles with their swivel chairs and many controls were superior, but, during easy stretches, he preferred standing at the big wheel with its associated footpedals and voice system. Taking his hands off the spokes, he said, "Reliant, two points up, five points starboard," and watched with secret satisfaction as the big wheel spun of its own accord, and the ship slowly swung to its new heading.

"Kegler," he said, fishing a Crystal out of his pocket, "put this into the Control Station, but don't start it yet. Tell me when you're ready." Over his shoulder he added, "Stulmin?"

"Aye, sir?" the second replied from the little surveillance room behind the bridge.

"Where are they?"

"Still the same, Captain, in his quarters."

"Crystal's ready, Captain," Kegler acknowledged.

"This looks like a good spot. Start the program, Kegler."

"Started, Captain." Various red lights and warning signals began to dot the consoles and displays.

Captain Volnath eyed the CoreFires walls ahead, gauging his free room, and trimmed the heading a little with the big wheel. When the ship steadied on course, he said, "Reliant, all ahead slow," and the ship's systems began to bring the big freighter's speed down to a crawl. "Reliant, give me a mike." Obedient to his command, a microphone lowered on a cord from the overhead. "Reliant, route to Bosun, give me a green light when live." Shortly a small green light showed on the mike, and the Captain spoke into the microphone.

"Captain Volnath to Bosun-tech. We are showing several engine warning lights on all three engines. I'll remind you that these are the new cross-linears, so the problem could be in any or all of them. Proceed to the engine room at once, and report when you've corrected the condition." The green light winked out.

"Bosun reporting. Aye, Captain. To the engine room at once," came the immediate reply over ship's comm.

"Reliant, mike up." The microphone line withdrew back into the over head as the captain continued over his shoulder, "Stulmin, are they both on their way?"

The voice from the surveillance room confirmed, "Both on a dead run, Captain."

"Watch them from the cameras along the route, and let me know when they reach the engine room."

"Aye, Captain. Will do."

———————————————

Daric considered himself in excellent shape physically, and he was surprised and pleased to find Shanni matching him stride for stride during the long run down the passageways leading to the engine room.

Undogging the only hatch, they entered and re-sealed it as per the regulations posted so prominently on the door.

"Wow," Shanni whispered as she saw the huge size of the room and the immense head-casings of the three engines intruding through the aft bulkhead — each over two stories high, and half again wider than they were tall. In front of each engine was a group of readout panels, at the moment fairly sprinkled with red lights, many flashing urgently. Daric wasted no time in going over to each panel in turn, and surveying the status.

"You know this stuff?" queried Shanni.

"Some of it," he replied. "Some I can guess, just because it stands to reason. For instance, all three sets of panels are showing exactly the same information."

Shanni was surprised, but on standing back and comparing them, she saw that, as far as she could tell, it was so.

"Unfortunately, with this type of engine," Daric continued, "you can't easily tell if one or all are causing the problem." She followed as he knelt down beside the panels for engine number one, and began pushing buttons and watching the corresponding changes in the displays. After some experimentation, he paused, looking at the displays, lost in thought. Although very curious, Shanni thought it better not to interrupt his concentration. Daric then pushed one more button, which didn't change the lights at all. Stroking his chin with his hand, he kept staring at the lights. "Hmmm," he said.

"Hmmm, what?" Shanni asked.

Still staring down at the lights in deep concentration, Daric murmured, "Like the doctor says, `Hmmm.'" Coming to some conclusion, he again spoke to Shanni. "You go to the number two engine and look at the group like this."

"OK, I'm looking at it."

"What's number four from the left?"

"Red."

"What is it when I do this?"

"Black. It went out."

"OK, Shanni, push the button under the left-most light, then go do the same on engine number three while I do this one."

As soon as she had finished with number two, Shanni hurried over to number three and repeated the operation, only to jump back, startled, as a loud klaxon went off and continued to fill the engine room with its raucous warning warble. She looked to Daric for guidance and he motioned her to come to him.

"What'd I do?" she shouted over the noise.

Daric motioned for her to kneel down beside him at the base of the number one readout panels. "You started the alarm," he said matter-of-factly as he pressed more buttons. Some of red lights now turned yellow, but many more now turned to red and started flashing.

"I know that, but what'd I do?"

Daric spoke in a low voice next to her. "I needed the alarm to cover our voices. Talk quietly. Something's wrong here, but it's not a typical engine problem. In fact, it's so improbable that it doesn't make much sense. It's even just possible that it doesn't exist, that somebody's playing games with us. But if this engine business were a false alarm, somebody would have to have gone to a lot of trouble to rig it. For the next step, I'm going to have to get behind that big panel. If somebody's playing games, it'll have to be without anyone seeing me."

"There's no one here but us!"

"Shanni, don't look around, but there's a surveillance camera in the ceiling, as there is in most places on this ship. Don't be frightened, but I'm going to have to put it out of commission."

Shanni fought the urge to look around. "What? Why? You could be in big trouble if you destroy a camera."

"Shhh! We could be in big trouble if I don't. It'll look like an accident. They'll still know we're in here, but they won't see me get behind that panel."

"How will they know we're in here?"

"They'll watch the passageway outside, and they can tell where our suits are."

"Our suits?" Shanni was shocked and puzzled. "What is all this cloak and dagger stuff?"

"Yes, they monitor the location of your suit and mine. I don't know why, but I found out that they do. Now go over to engine number three, and when I tell you, hold down the right-most button no matter what happens, and keep it down until I motion you to release it. I'll be doing the same here." He turned briefly to look into her eyes. "Trust me. Now go."

Shanni had her misgivings, but was willing to go with what she saw in his eyes. "Strangest man I've ever met, and things keep getting stranger," she thought. "Well, here goes." When she was ready, she looked to Daric and he nodded. She pushed the button firmly home and held it there, although the lights in the ceiling of the engine room started pulsing wildly, getting brighter and brighter. Squinting against the glare, she held the button down as the light flared brighter still, then blew out with a flash. She concentrated on keeping the button down, remembering Daric's words, as the brief blackout was relieved by a system of automatic red emergency lights. She could smell something electrical getting very toasty, and then there was a loud pop and a shower of sparks from the ceiling. Looking across at Daric in the dim red light, she saw him nod. Almost shaking, she took her thumb off the button.

———————————————

Chapter *38*

APHERON, LIKE CLOCKWORK
— THE CAMERA'S OUT

STULMIN SHOUTED FROM the surveillance room, "Captain, those bozoes fat-fingered the engine room utility power! The lights and camera blew!"

"Switch to the camera in the passageway outside," Captain Volnath shouted over his shoulder. "Do I have to do all the thinking myself? Kegler, check the suit monitor and put it up next to Stulmin's active display."

"Aye, Captain," Kegler replied. "They're still in there, trying to figure out what they screwed up, from the look of it. The suit monitor has them futzing around on the number one control panel. That should keep them busy for awhile."

"Stulmin, is the door still shut?" shouted the captain.

"Right."

"Good. Stulmin, you just keep an eye on that door and the suit monitor. Kegler, get out the optical link, and get it set up. Here he comes, right on schedule. You could set a clock by Major Apheron."

Kegler unfolded a tripod, then mounted the high-security optical transceiver on top of it, so called because it could only be detected by someone with a similar device right in the path of the beam. When the first mate had the optical link powered up and patched into the ship's comm, he reported, "Ready, Captain."

"And none to soon," muttered Captain Volnath. Looking out the panoramic windows of the bridge, he saw Apheron's high-powered

Patrol ship closing at customary full speed, followed by full braking, until it was station-keeping just off Reliant's starboard bow. Slowly Apheron's vessel swung broadside to Reliant's bridge, and then, at the window just above the insignia of the Core Patrol, a bright blue pinpoint spot appeared. "There it is. Have you got it?"

"Aye, Captain," Kegler replied, "it should be coming through momentarily."

"Volnath?" Apheron's smooth voice was unmistakable.

"Volnath here, go ahead Apheron."

The blue light in the window of the Core Patrol cruiser winked again. The optical transceiver did its magic, and the Reliant's ship's comm sounded again with Apheron's voice. "The meet has been changed. You'll rendezvous at the small dead end two hours this side of Two Forks. As soon as we're done with the voice-link, I'll send a data load for your nav system. Prepare for the cargo in the fore port cargo bay. Everything as planned?"

"Like clockwork," Volnath replied.

"You'll keep it that way, Volnath. Just like clockwork!" There was a sudden cold tone of menace in Apheron's words. "Apheron out, here's the data load."

Kegler glanced at Volnath's reddening face. The captain was glaring out the window like a bomb about ready to go off. Kegler hastily looked back at the indicators atop the tripod, and announced, "Transmission complete and verified, Captain," just before the blue light on the Patrol craft winked out, and the cruiser wheeled and sped away. Volnath, still staring at the rapidly diminishing Patrol ship, said nothing.

Kegler had barely finished stowing the optical link when the captain handed him another Crystal. "Put this in the control station, Kegler, and tell me when it's ready. Stulmin," he called loudly, "they still in there?"

"Aye, the door's still shut and the suit locator says they're just leaving the number one control panel."

"Perfect," said Volnath, with a thin smile on his face. "Kegler, you ready yet, man?"

Keglers fingers danced at the terminal. Expressionless, he replied,

"Ready now, Captain."

"Run the program, Mister Kegler, this should be amusing."

"Aye, Captain. Program running." On the many console displays, arrays of lights suddenly switched from red to green.

"Reliant," said Volnath, "Mike. Route engine room. Give me a green light when it's live." The mike spun rapidly down from the overhead, the light turning green even as the captain grabbed for it.

With some relish, Volnath placed the mike to his lips. "Captain to bosun. Very good, Bosun, whatever you did cleared up the problem." Volnath, smiling, looked at Kegler, who was grinning ear to ear. "You may stand down now, and return to your quarters. Captain clear."

The green light went dark, and the captain said, "Reliant, mike up." Then, louder, "Stulmin, they out of there? I don't want them nosing around."

"Aye, Captain," affirmed the voice from the surveillance room, "on their way back."

"Keep an eye on them, Stulmin."

"Captain," Kegler inquired with a snicker, "you going to dock their pay for the lights and camera?"

"A nice thought, Mister Kegler, but I think not," the captain replied. "I don't want them even thinking of the camera. Have the bots replace the lights as daily maintenance, and the camera, if there's another in spares."

Turning again to the wheel, Captain Volnath spoke to the voice system, "Reliant, all ahead full." Spinning the wheel to a new heading, he aligned his ship with the next bend in the channel. "Kegler, get the nav system working on that rendezvous data. We wouldn't want to disappoint the good Major Apheron."

———————————————————

Chapter *39*

DISCOVER A TALLEST MAN — THE LITTLE WAY

LUMINOUS GREEN, THE plasma streamed endlessly by, drifting and eddying like a phosphorescent fog. Sometimes thin and tenuous, it could suddenly turn thickly obscuring, swirling like a magician's cape and causing everything to vanish, before your very eyes. Glowmist, it was called, and it flowed perpetually through the twisting passage known to the villagers, and few others, as the Little Way.

Deadly CoreFires pressed close all along the sinuous tunnel, never more than a hundred feet in diameter. Winding all the way from the Firefall, source of its mists, to Foggy Hole, a small side chamber not far from Dutchman's, the narrow Gap was far too dangerous for supply ships or even the Core Patrol's speedy cruisers. Only the stubborn villagers of Dutchman's ventured here in their rough-and-ready style, relishing guiding their small motley craft through hazards daunting enough to bar the ever-watchful eyes and the long arm of the Core Patrol.

As the glowmists streamed round a bend deep within the Little Way, from the left there came a sound — or what became a sound when picked up by a bio-suit or a vessel's comm — the faint falling "ooooo-ah" broadcast from a foghorn. Instantly reflected and transformed by the Gap-walls, its ghostly echoes reverberated up and down the tunnel before dying away in the fog-shrouded distance. When thick mists hid the waiting CoreFires, listening to the changing timbre of those echoes was the only way the hardy villagers could detect the deadly walls and continue to navigate through twists and turns they could not see.

Hardly had the echoes ceased when a different call boomed faintly from the right, "aaaaaaah-yo", setting off another host of hollow echoes from all sides. "Yo... yo... yo...," they exclaimed in diminishing tones until the mists once again wafted in silence. Before long the first call repeated from the left, obviously closer, and again it was answered by another from the right.

Both sources remained invisible until a swirl of the magician's cape suddenly revealing a small open space-skiff coming from the left, heavily laden with a tottering pile of junk that almost overflowed the thwarts. As it rounded the bend, Otitius, the lone figure on board, decided that it was high time to pause and re-stack his cargo, where-upon he brought his vessel to a stop. "Don't tempt Fate," he told himself, "unless you're willing to get what you deserve."

Surveying the pyramid of mismatched lamps, bent chairs, and dented storage lockers, he concluded that anything short of a more carefully constructed foundation was indeed unduly tempting Fate, so he set about the task with a will, whistling a tune to himself that was periodically punctuated by the loud warning blasts of his skiff's fog-horn.

After a couple minutes of dismantling the top of the pile and temporarily stacking items in the few vacant crannies available, he straightened up with a different shaped lamp in each hand, looking for a place to set them down. Turning around awkwardly, wobbling slightly because his legs were disappearing into such a tiny hole amid pieces of junk, he realized that has feet occupied the only remaining place on the skiff, and the tottering junkpile amidships was barely diminished. His whistled tune died away.

"Now what?" he asked. "Otitius, my man," he told himself, "I do believe you've gotten yourself into a bit of a pickle. You're standing here in the middle of the Little Way looking like a fog-bound human lamppost," he gave the lamps a futile wave, still unable to find a spot to put them down, "with a skiff full of goodies and a complete shortage of holes to put them in."

The skiff's foghorn hooted sympathetically.

He tried setting one lamp back on the central pile, but hastily removed it as the whole lot began to tilt. "Steady, now, steady!" he admonished the pile as it rocked back and forth before settling once again into a precarious equilibrium. Wishing he could scratch his head in perplexity, Otitius the Human Lamppost twisted around in the vain hope that some overlooked cranny might be hiding behind his back. "No such luck," he muttered. "What I need," he decided, "is an expandable skiff. Now where am I going to get one of those?"

The foghorn hooted again, but if it was offering a solution, Otitius was unable to translate its reply. Then he heard an answering call from an approaching foghorn, and he knew from the sound that it must be somewhere close by. "Junker must be getting his fair share of visitors today," he thought, "I wonder who this is."

As he scanned the glowmists, Otitius was greeted by a strange sight — first to emerge was a great crested metal head with fierce eyes, half bird, half dragon, surmounting a tall thin neck three times the height of a man. As the craft glided forward, freeing itself from the enveloping mist, it was as though the ancient myths of Humankind's MotherEarth had been summoned forward through time to be melded and manifested here, given primal form in iron and steel at the hands of a slightly mad shipwright-sculptor.

The slender shape and high prow were from the ancient Vikings, and the two uplifted small platforms at the stern, spread like two tiny wings, spoke subtly of royal barges carrying semi-deities through their realm during the dawn of history on MotherEarth's Nile. Above all, the tall figurehead silently shrieked defiance across the ages. Surviving the hells of all the eras, reborn yet again in the present amidst the CoreFires, the fierce visage of the Phoenix triumphantly risen from the ashes was an image that struck a resonant chord in Gap dwellers, who by necessity turned each day into a small triumph of survival.

Somehow, the power of that ancient icon was augmented rather than diminished by the way it was sculpted from junk pieces of wrecked spaceships. The whole strange craft emerging from the glowing mists was similarly wrought, for it had been fashioned by Junker as a gift — some said a love offering — to Cirra.

Cirra herself was standing on the starboard wing-platform at the stern, guiding her vessel, and the smaller figures of Marneen and

Mutch were atop the port wing, pretending that it was they who were doing the piloting. Waving as they approached, all three burst into laughter at the sight of Otitius, standing amid his overflowing skiff, still holding a lamp in each hand.

Laughing good naturedly at the absurdity of his own situation, Otitius waved back with the lamps as Cirra's craft slowed and came alongside.

"Looks like you found a few new things for the POSH," Cirra called with a chuckle.

"New old things for the POSH," amended Otitius between blasts of the foghorns. "They'll fit right in. When I left Junker's Ring they fit into my skiff as well, but just now I made the mistake of trying to restack them. Now they've mutinied and taken over my vessel, and are threatening to throw me overboard. I'd just concluded that I needed an expandable skiff."

"Oh, I think the Phoenix will suffice," Cirra laughed. "There's loads of room on her deck and we're in no hurry. Go ahead and lay everything out however you like, then repack the skiff."

Scrambling down from the Phoenix's port wing, Marneen and Mutch ran along the deck, shouting, "Can we help, Otitius? Please? We could set the stuff around on the deck, and when you're ready we could bring you whichever pieces you wanted!"

"Looks like my problem is solved," Otitius replied with a broad smile. "Yes, you can help, and most welcome. But stand back, because you're going to like the first step. I'm going to tip this whole teetery pile right over into the Phoenix, and then you can pick up the pieces and lay them out so we can see what's what. Stand clear now!"

"Oh, boy!" Mutch shouted. "Wait 'til we're ready!"

"OK, I'm ready," Marneen called, squatting on the deck as close as she dared.

"Me, too!" Mutch added. "Let 'er tip!"

Cirra smiled as Otitius gave her a big wink and approached pile's summit with the two lamps in his hands. "Shall I do it?" he asked.

"Do it!" Marneen and Mutch replied in unison, clapping their hands as their bio-suits dutifully relayed the sound.

Using the lamps as pushers, Otitius nudged the top of the pile, which immediately tipped over and cascaded into the Phoenix with a satisfactory crash of upturned chairs and rolling lamps.

"Yay!" Mutch exclaimed. "We'll sort this, then get the rest that's still left in the skiff. Wow, what great stuff!"

Marneen was already pulling chairs along the deck, two at a time, and setting them up in a row.

As the pair scurried back and forth from the fallen pile, Cirra and Otitius stood talking quietly between foghorn hoots while the Phoenix's deck rapidly took on the appearance of a well organized swapmeet.

"I couldn't have asked for a better solution. Sure beats being a human lamppost," Otitius said, watching the kids at their work.

"Oh, I don't know," Cirra answered with a mischievous smile. "I thought you had a certain indefinable charm. Maybe the POSH could use you to add a little extra touch of class!"

"I'll leave that to Li-Tharm," he countered, "and stick to a job I know."

Most of the pile was gone when Marneen tipped a storage cabinet off an upside down swivel-chair. Mutch hauled the cabinet off to join the others of its kind while Marneen poked at an odd piece of junk jammed in the tilt-mechanism of the chair. Try as she might, she couldn't pull it free.

"This is stuck," she told Mutch as he returned.

"Let's both try it," he replied, sitting on the deck beside her, then bracing his feet against the chair and taking a firm hold on the object.

Doing likewise, Marneen said, "OK, pull!"

Both grunted with the effort, but there was no visible change.

"Again," Mutch said, "Pull!"

This time it came free, sending them rolling over on their backs with the object in their hands.

As they sat up Mutch exclaimed, "Look! It glows!"

"It's strange!" Marneen added, turning it around so they could examine it.

About a foot long and two to three inches thick, they saw an elaborate carving fitted with a locking mount at its base, as if it fit into something else.

"It's sort of like an extra skinny person," Marneen ventured, "and sort of not. What do you suppose it is?"

"I dunno. That lower part is all covered with those little bitty markings, and this sorta looks like a face. You think it's magic?" Mutch asked.

"Maybe. It's sure strange! Let's ask Otitius."

"If it's magic, let's ask Cirra."

Getting up, Marneen settled it. "We'll ask 'em both," she said, running over to where the adults were conversing.

"What've you got there?" asked Otitius as they approached.

"We thought you'd know," Marneen replied, holding up the sculpture. "It was jammed in the bottom of one of the chairs."

"I never saw it," Otitius answered. "Had no idea it was there. In fact, I've never seen anything like it."

"Us neither," Mutch affirmed.

"Cirra, you look," Marneen said, placing the mysterious figure in her hand.

"Is it magic?" Mutch asked. He was pleased that Cirra seemed to be taking his question seriously as she turned the faintly glowing object around, sometimes pausing to feel it with her eyes shut.

"It could be, but of a kind unknown to me. I, too, have never seen anything like it." She looked closely at the intricate carving. "Whoever created it fashioned it with the greatest of care, perhaps even reverence. Marneen, can you help me? I'd like to see if I can sense its presence."

"Sure. What do I do?"

"Here, you take it. Now, I'm going to shut my eyes. If you'll move it around, I'll try to point at it, wherever it is."

Marneen eagerly stepped back a few paces, holding the object at arms length. "Here we go!" she said, "I'm moving it," but, unmoving, she clutched it to her stomach while trying to suppress a giggle.

Eyes closed, Cirra pointed at Marneen's stomach.

"That's no test!" Mutch proclaimed. "She could hear you giggling! Try again."

This time Marneen held the object high, then low, then she tiptoed over to Mutch. Wherever her hand went, Cirra's finger followed.

Otitius gulped, feeling rather spooked by the way things were going. "She must be peeking!" Marneen shouted.

That somehow made Otitius feel a little better until Mutch went up close to Cirra's face, carefully checking her eyes. "No, she's not. Try one more!"

This time Marneen ran silently over behind Otitius who was standing with his hands clasped behind his back, and put the sculpture into his somewhat unwilling hands. Then she stepped quietly away, moving her empty hand up high, then low to the deck. Cirra's finger remained pointing at Otitius' stomach.

"That's sorta magic," Mutch said as Cirra opened her eyes, and Otitius brought the faintly glowing object out from behind his back and hastily offered it to her.

Again Cirra contemplated it. "Well, Mutch, it certainly has a powerful presence. I can feel its influence, which seems benign, but its purpose and who made it are a complete mystery to me. It almost feels like it's a Talisman from some unknown culture."

"Is that kinda magical, Cirra?"

"Yes, Mutch, that's kind of magical."

"Then, that's what it is for sure," Marneen chimed in with absolute conviction. "It's a Tallest Man from an unknown culture!"

"And the Tallest Man's kind of magical," Mutch added, eagerly, "and since he's away from his unknown culture, maybe he can look out for us!"

Marneen's voice was hopeful. "He looks kind, and I think he likes us."

"Maybe he can help us find the way to go when the glowmist is thick or we're lost!" Mutch turned to Otitius. "Could we keep the Tallest Man, Otitius, to help us find the way?"

"Please, Otitius," Marneen implored, "can we keep the Tallest Man?"

"It's fine with me," he replied. "You found him; I didn't even know he was there."

Mutch turned to Cirra. "Please, Cirra, can we keep him? He could look way far ahead, farther than the Phoenix bird can see, then he'd whisper which way to go to the Phoenix and we wouldn't get lost."

Marneen jumped right in. "When we get to the castle, we can ask Junker to fix the Phoenix head so the Tallest Man can watch from there, and whisper right in the Phoenix's ear! Please, oh please, Cirra, can we keep him? Please say yes!"

Cirra looked back and forth between the imploring faces, then looked up at the Phoenix head on the prow. Smiling, she handed the Talisman to Mutch and Marneen. "Looks like the Tallest Man has found a new home. Now if you want to ask Junker to fix a way to put him up on the Phoenix head, you'd better finish up helping Otitius or we'll never get to the castle."

Marneen and Mutch were practically beside themselves. Mutch held up the figure between their faces. "Tallest Man," he said hurriedly, "we don't know why you're away from your unknown culture..."

"Or how long you were stuck in that old chair..." Marneen interrupted.

"...but you're not stuck any more," Mutch continued. "You have a home with us now, and we'll ask Junker to fix it so you can ride the Phoenix!"

Marneen took the figure. "We're going to give you back to Cirra now so we can help Otitius as fast as we can, and you won't get lost in the junk again. You'll like her a lot; she'll take good care of you, and in a few minutes we'll head for the castle!" With that, she handed the Talisman to Cirra, and the two raced back to the junkpile.

Never had Otitius seen them work so swiftly and smoothly. In almost no time, they had the skiff empty and the last items laid out in orderly fashion on the deck of the Phoenix.

"We're ready," they announced proudly. "You just point to what you want and we'll bring it you."

"What service!" he exclaimed gladly. Turning to Cirra, he added, "I don't suppose you could go on meeting me this way every time I go out junking to the Ring?"

"Better make the most of it while it's here!" she laughed, holding up the glowing Talisman. "It was probably all the Tallest Man's doing!"

———————————

Chapter *40*

PAST THE FIREFALL — STEER CLOSER!

A HALF HOUR later, the turbulent glowmists were varying wildly, from an almost transparent haze to complete opacity. In preparation for their emergence from the Little Way, Cirra told the youngsters to take the foghorn off automatic, and gave them the task of sounding it only when the mist was especially thick. As the small tunnel widened, they tried to sound it not at all, for none of the Gap dwellers wanted to call attention to the inconspicuous end of their semi-secret passage as they were coming back into a chamber accessible to large spaceships. This time no big ships were visible. In fact, few ventured into this side chamber because of the extremely variable mists flowing from the Firefall, unless one included the hulks and wrecks Junker towed to his hideaway.

Once in mid-channel, Cirra bent their course to starboard, turning the face of the firebird directly into the gusting waves of glowmist. Mutch and Marneen were peering intently forward, holding the Tallest Man between them, anxious for their first glimpse of the Firefall.

It came without warning as a great rent opened in the seething curtain of mists, ushering the Viking-like vessel into the clear space that always surrounded the Firefall itself. Only a half mile across, this void aroused feelings of vertigo in all who entered when they looked down a good three miles to where it was lost in a swirling sea of mist, or upward a similar distance overhead to where it was capped by another roiling cloudmass. Piercing the gap vertically was the laser-bright green of the Firefall, a thin incandescent plasma column in constant motion, composed of a falling stream of ball-lightnings of all sizes numbering in the tens of thousands. The smallest floated down as slowly as burning snowflakes while the larger were constantly overtaking their tiny brethren. All descended serenely until, miles below, each radiant sphere burst into a cloud of glowmist.

"Go close, Cirra!" urged Mutch, his face eager in the brilliant green light.

"Real close!" added Marneen, not to be outdone.

Laughing, Cirra steered more towards the center of the Firefall. Once the maneuver had wrung hysterical shrieks from her young passengers she quickly bore off again, leaving their closest approach to the beautiful column no less than a respectful quarter mile. Even so, the passage was awe-inspiring. Whether craning their necks to see the stream of falling plasmas pouring out from the CoreFires so far above, or peering over the side, picking out individual fireballs to follow in their long descent until they burst in the glowing mists miles below, the travelers were enraptured by the grandeur they were witnessing. Even as the Firefall passed behind, they strained for last looks before a sudden swirl of magician mists again cloaked it from their view.

Junker himself had been the first to penetrate the mists behind the Firefall, and discover the four mile wide Glimmering Cavern, as it was called, where he had made his home. As the mists thinned to a softly luminous haze, Mutch was almost jumping up and down on starboard wing platform. "We're almost there," he shouted to Cirra.

Smiling, she called back, "How can you tell?"

"Well, you can see through the glowmist just like at Junker's, so we've gotta be getting close."

Cirra knew they were rounding the final bend, but feigned ignorance. When the cavern and Junker's Ring came into view, Mutch bounced like a jumping jack. "See! I told you so! There it is, just like I said!"

———————————————

Chapter *41*

JUNKER'S RING — SCRAP CASTLE

To MUTCH AND Marneen, and the villagers as well, Junker's Ring was an enormous trove of orbiting treasure. The Ring itself was two miles in diameter with the far side only dimly showing through the glowing green haze, a stately circular procession of countless pieces of junk and wreckage.

Its carousel parade of free floating ship-hulks and keels, hoists and cargoes, crates of this and containers of that was a vital resource to the Gap dwellers. To the Ring they came to rummage and prowl, to sort through What Once Was, seeking some combination of frammishes, do-dads, and thingamabobs that could link an urgent need to a make-do solution.

If the Ring was the fabled secret bone yard where space-hardware went to die, Lyard and Garms — Junker's first and second mates — did double duty as heavenly hardware salesmen. Roaming the Ring in their space-punts, they answered questions put by their scavenging customers and suggested other routes to the Holy Grail when no suitable frammish could be found. If a piece of junk got bumped into a more eccentric orbit, one of these two cheerful keepers of the graveyard would shepherd it back into place. Many a lucky villager had waited patiently while Lyard or Garms ransacked their voluminous memories, eventually coming up with a "Seems to me I recall seeing something about like that a few months ago. Let me take you..."

The Ring was held in orbit by the combined fields of an amazing collection of dead engines that Junker had massed in the center, and upon which he had built his junk-sculpture castle, known as

Junker's Keep.

Mutch and Marneen were ecstatic at the sight of the Ring, pointing and exclaiming to each other and the Tallest Man as they identified various pieces of wondrous debris. "Look," Marneen shouted, "look at that big old cargo hatch. If we could put a motor on it we could make a go-board as big as a house!"

"Yeah, and we'd both be captains, and everybody'd have to make way for us when we came by," Mutch added before they fell into a fit of giggles.

Their joy was compounded when Cirra told them to take the helm. "Hey," Marneen exclaimed, "we are captains now!"

Under Cirra's direction, they gleefully began the process of shedding excess momentum, and letting the pseudo-gravity of the castle spiral them in toward their destination. The only complication was guiding the Phoenix-prowed craft upward for awhile, in order to pass over — and closely observe — the fabulous Ring of orbiting junk, and then downward again to rejoin the plane of the two spiral shaped docks that girdled the engine-mound beneath the Keep. Cirra smiled at the kids enthusiasm. As long as they were steering, patience wasn't the slightest problem.

With the Ring left behind, the two young captains turned their attention toward the castle, their favorite place in the whole Gap. Around the base was clustered a small indecipherable forest of structural junk, a cacophony of beams and masts struggling to rise above a tangled Babel of prized scrap that Junker had sequestered away for his current and future personal projects.

Emerging above the more or less vertical mast-tops was the castle proper, tall and slender. Slotted with stained glass windows, its walls were festooned with fanciful gargoyles of junk, with frivolous parapets and minarets, each well known to Mutch and Marneen who loved to climb among them. The higher the castle rose, the wider it became, until about halfway up it had grown wide enough to sport two side towers capped by conical spires.

"The one on the left is mine," Marneen explained to the Tallest Man, "and the other one is Mutch's, but everybody can climb on each other's." Their towers were of unequal height but identical in another respect, each leaned outward several degrees, one to the right, one to the left, combining a sense of temporary balance with a certain air of suspense.

Between the two tipsy towers rose the Keep itself, eccentric, playful, yet undeniably grand, like a gifted child's highly ornate drip-castle made of steel instead of sand. A magnificent stained-glass window over forty feet tall was set into a great Gothic arch and nestled between whimsically decorated columns. Above that, "Higher than we can climb," as Mutch explained, the central spire rose another forty feet. Atop it perched a geodesic globe of steel and glass, from which sprouted Mutch and Marneen's most favorite thing of all, a large but incredibly delicate shimmering sphere of metal dandelion seeds. Their only regret was that they couldn't climb among the radiating stalks like a giant jungle gym.

It wasn't really a dandelion, of course — that ubiquitous plant that had come along with Humankind throughout all the suitable worlds — but it looked like one. Junker had mounted umbrella-ribbed antennas on twenty foot masts, poking directly out from sixty points on the geodesic sphere. Designed to receive plasma signals from every direction, the ghostly glow of their e-fields topped the highest spire of the castle with a flickering dandelion of green light, created so Junker could surround himself with the strange sounds of the CoreFires.

All of these wonders had taken their toll on the two youthful "captains" by the time Cirra's craft was approaching the castle; both Marneen and Mutch had cricks in their necks from looking up for so long. When Cirra offered to take back the helm, they readily agreed, then laid down on their backs so they could enjoy the best view as they glided in close beside Junker's towering abode.

Marneen held the Tallest Man on his back, so he could look up too. "This is it, Tallest Man," Mutch explained, "Junker's Keep!"

————————————

From somewhere in the highest reaches of the castle's central hall came the echoing sounds of strange music. Greenish gold light was streaming in through the great stained glass window, illuminating the four figures seated about a round table, and the one small sculpted figure standing on the table itself. Above their heads, a fanciful chandelier fashioned of junk in the shape of a magical merry-go-round circled to the odd music echoing from above. Its whimsical hardware steeds hung from tiny chains amid a dangling forest of spinning fractured crystal that seized the light from the window and sprayed it in colored fragments about the room.

Cirra's long hair was loosed, catching spectral glints from the beams that wandered through it, and she was again wearing her long white gossamer gown. If she resembled a goddess, Junker looked more like a monk, clad in a long robe of coarse material, the hood folded back behind his salt and pepper hair, his graying beard wreathing sensitive lips and the smile-lines that lurked beside them.

Marneen and Mutch were, as always, in their bio-suits and helmets, ready to go "out" and play on the parapets of the castle as soon as they had finished their tale.

"...So when Mutch and I got safely back to the POSH, we told Li-Tharm, and several other people, and they just kind of said `That's nice'", concluded Marneen. "I guess it took us a while to realize that nobody really believed us. Not about going up to stow-away on the ship, or falling into the CoreFires..."

"...and especially not about the Flying Dutchman," Mutch added. "They'd just start talking about somebody who thought they'd seen the Dutchman sometime..."

"It wasn't like they thought we were lying, exactly," Marneen clarified, "more like they thought we'd dreamed it up or something and forgot it wasn't real. But it was real, Junker, even though nobody'd believe us!"

"Except Cirra," offered Mutch, giving her a grateful look.

"And now me," added Junker, the gentle smile-lines leaping into action. "I thank you for coming and telling me everything that happened. Cirra thought it was important for me to know all about it. You know," Junker added, with a story-telling tone to his voice, "sometimes when there's some big change brewing deep in the CoreFires, or somewhere up and down the Gap, but everything's still all smooth and calm and ordinary here, Cirra'll get up and start listening and sniffing, like she's wondering what's out there. Sometimes gives me goose-bumps, just watching her." He gave a little shiver and gestured toward himself with his thumb. "When it happens, I, for one, get just a mite extra cautious, and keep my eyes peeled 'til I can find out what's going on."

Mutch glanced at Cirra with new-found appreciation, then, mimicking Junker, said, "I'm going to be a wee bit extra cautious, too!"

"Me too," chimed in Marneen.

"It's just a feeling I have," Cirra confided, "but maybe it's just as well that folks didn't take you seriously, and that it might be best for us to keep this to ourselves until we see what happens."

Junker made a motion like he was zipping his lip shut tight. "OK by me," His words were muffled by his closed lips.

With a giggle, Mutch repeated the gesture. "Me too!" he mumbled.

Marneen laughed outright, then did the same. "Anmmmd mmmme!", she said, although the words were hardly recognizable, her lips were shut so tight. "You, too, Cirra!"

Cirra completed the impromptu ceremony, and Mutch asked, "Can we go climb on the outside of the castle?"

"Only if you're extremely good at it," replied Junker. "Later Cirra and I will come out, too, and you can help me make a place on the Phoenix head for the Tallest Man."

As the kids rushed downstairs, Junker picked up the curious glowing figure from the table and walked arm in arm with Cirra toward the big couch set between four slender columns in the center of the room. "How about some music?" Junker asked.

Cirra, tightened her arm around his waist and watched her own sandaled feet stepping amongst the circling shards of colored light. "Sounds wonderful," she answered.

Seating themselves comfortably in the deep couch, they looked out through the stained glass window, and when Junker touched a switch, the couch began to rise like an elevator. Higher and higher they rose toward the strange music emanating from above. They settled back, watching the stained-glass designs slide down below them, looking through to the window to the panorama beyond with its slowly orbiting ring of what was junk to the out-worlders, but treasure to the Gap dwellers. Junker put his arm around Cirra. "Very strange," he murmured. "Some strange things have been happening in this Gap lately."

"And, my junkman," she whispered, snuggling into his shoulder. "getting stranger."

Leaving the top of the Gothic arch and the great window below, the couch continued to ascend the narrowing cone of the spire with only an occasional passing embrasure of red or blue to mark their passage. Soon they emerged into the glass and steel geodesic sphere atop the castle, where the elevator stopped in mid-air at the very center.

Junker and Cirra leaned back contentedly on the big couch, looking through the diamond-shaped windows all about them, and on through the shimmering green electrical fields of the dandelion antennas. Beyond was the ever-changing beauty of the CoreFires, softly visible through the light haze of glowmist. From all parts of the dome, Junker's antennas translated the nebula fields into sounds that converged on the suspended listeners, and as they gradually became attuned to the strange harmonies that corresponded to the slowly changing swirls and convolutions, it was almost like they were floating in the CoreFires itself. Almost.

"Wouldn't that be something," Junker murmured, absently turning the Talisman about in his hand, "if the kids really were surviving and drifting right in the midsts of the CoreFires?"

"I'm convinced they think they were," Cirra replied.

For awhile they leaned back quietly, giving themselves to the mysterious music from the galactic core, then Junker leaned his graying head on Cirra's soft shoulder. Looking up through the dome, lost in the fireforms above, he whispered again, "Wouldn't that be something?"

Cirra was looking up too, and, hearing his tone of voice, thought of the long line of sailors and explorers who had spoken similar words in all the human tongues. She leaned her head against his. "Yes," she agreed, "that would be something."

Nestled between them in Junker's hand, the Tallest Man from an unknown culture glowed silently.

Chapter *42*

[Rad:na] Uncharted Journey — Finder in Human Hands

In troubling times, much like Humankind, the darkest hours of the night sometimes summoned the Rad:na. So it was with Questor-Joss as she peered over the fantail railing, watching the glimmering wake trailing into the distance. In the near vacuum of the CoreFires, her suit-comm transformed the infinitely complex streaming plasma fields into the familiar sounds of their passage — the deep throated whisper of the energy winds encountering the rigging above, the surging sibilance from the swaths of star-foam being created below.

With a sigh, she turned from the phosphorescent trace of the Rad:na ship's passing. Making her way forward across the quarterdeck, she automatically scanned the huge sails aloft where yet another familiar sound originated, the muted rippling thunder from their captive lightning. Nicely trimmed, she noted, and drawing well in the light but steady energy winds sweeping through the rigging. If she was surprised to see the mate also prowling the deck at this unlikely hour, she gave no sign.

"Permission to join the Questor?"

"Granted, First-Mate-Norr, and welcome."

As they walked on, the flickering glow from the lightning aloft showed his expression to be as thoughtful as her own.

Coming upon the "helmsman" — in this case a woman — "manning" the big wheel, Joss told her, "I'll take the helm for awhile."

"Aye, Questor," she replied, relinquishing it with a courtly bow as she stepped aside. "Lookouts are posted — there have been some sudden patches of fog. Winds have been much as you see them." With another respectful bow, she was gone.

In the flickering darkness, Mate-Norr observed his Navigatrix at the helm, her eyes straight ahead. Rather than looking up, she seemed aware of the sails as a whole, for the slightest shiver in any one of them was immediately answered, or even anticipated, by her slender fingertips passing the spokes of the wheel smoothly to and fro. Beneath his feet he could feel the mass of the ship subtly moving like a thing alive, sliding to meet and harness each variation in the pressure of the winds aloft. All aboard were superb sailors, and those who manned the helm were the best of the best, but none could match Questor-Joss. Glancing aft, Norr could tell by their wake where she had taken the wheel. From there on, it was ruler-straight. He wished other aspects of their course seemed so simple.

"Strange events," he commented quietly. "Strange events seem to have overtaken us, these last days."

"Profound events," Joss replied softly as the tips of her fingers continued to converse intimately with the wheel, and, through it, with the ship itself. "They would surely have overtaken someone, perhaps even everyone, in time. We've been more fortunate than clever to stumble on their import while there's yet time to act."

"Permission to speak very boldly, Questor?"

"As always, Norr. Your every perception is of inestimable value to me."

"My Navigatrix, this Firedawn, Goddess help me if I did wrong...!"

"This Firedawn, faithful Norr, the Goddess helped you to do right," she replied emphatically. "There is no wrong in what you did. No wrong in your supporting me in what I did." As she spoke, traceries of reflected lightning from above glinted about her helmet and its field bubble, and momentary golden flashes revealed her expression, sensitive, yet resolute. "As Questor, it is given to me to choose the course, even if it lays where none have gone before," she continued. "As mate, it is given to you to make that course a reality, which, as always, you have done, well and truly."

"Fog coming!" called one of the lookouts.

"Aye, fog," Joss acknowledged. In moments they were enveloped in a thick streaming mist, made all the more disorienting by the diffuse golden flashes that now seemed to emanate from all around them. "If there was any wrong this Firedawn," Joss insisted quietly, "it was mine alone."

Norr stood, unable to speak, watching her eyes gazing into the flickering golden fog as if they could see to the far horizon. "Perhaps they can," he thought, longing to help lift part of her burden. "Alas, mine cannot." He saw her straighten slightly, even more resolute than before.

"I am Questor." she said. "I am Rad:na. And I have chosen. Who knows how the fate of galaxies may flow from two saved children of the Humankind? I do not, yet I chose." Turning for the first time toward the mate, she added, "It appears that the Owd have long planned and prepared for this encounter, while we've suddenly been overtaken by strange events, armed with little more than the simple way of the Goddess. My choice, this Firedawn, was an expression of Her simple way, as lived by this Questor, this Rad:na. I can only hope that there is some truth in this that can weigh against the clever evil of the Owd."

As suddenly as it had enveloped them, the fog swirled away over the side, leaving Norr a clear view astern. Their track was as straight as an arrow.

Joss spoke again. "It is well that you joined me on the deck in these early hours. There's something more I must tell you, something I learned but shortly ago."

She turned again to the CoreFires ahead, her eyes searching, her lips pausing, the words unspoken.

"Questor?" he asked.

"One of the missing Finders is now in human hands," she whispered.

"No!"

"Yes, without doubt. Benign hands, as nearly as I can tell, but human hands none-the-less. Events are unfolding rapidly. It's clear that, like it or not, we are embarked on an uncharted journey!"

—————————————

Chapter 43

RENDEZVOUS FOR TRANSFER — DILIGENCE

THE DARK CORE Patrol cruiser bored through the cavernous Gap near Two Forks at high speed, its curving course carrying it close to the blue CoreFires walls as it streaked around the bends. Through the control room windows, the red-lit figure of Major Apheron could be seen seated at the console, checking his instruments.

"Almost there," he muttered, retarding the throttles to half speed.

Around the next curve lay the mouth of a small side tunnel — a dead end passage — that Apheron peered at intently while he guided his cruiser on by, continuing down the main channel for another half dozen bends.

"All clear. Excellent!"

Slowing the Patrol ship further, he brought it very close to the fiery blue wall at the right-hand side of the chamber, then turned hard aport in a U-turn that barely cleared the CoreFires on the left-hand wall. Speeding up again, the cruiser doubled back on its tracks until it dove into the mouth of the dead end side tunnel.

Once in the narrow passageway its retros flared bright violet, slowing the ship for a sinuous section before it emerged into a large chamber surrounded on all sides by swirls of incandescent indigo. There it hovered like a hungry wasp.

This way and that it swiveled, planar field thrusters flaring with every move as the major surveyed the chamber. Although no ships were in sight, Apheron only intensified his search of the convoluted CoreFires walls, sending his craft darting into each glowing nook and cranny that could possibly hide even the tiniest of vessels. Twice he covered every surface of the chamber, until finally even he was convinced that nothing had been missed.

Finding no prey, the hovering wasp suddenly spun and sped back through the bends to the entrance.

"Perfect," Apheron said aloud, looking at the clock on his instrument panel." Ahead lay the main channel, and as his craft neared the mouth of the dead end, he slowed it to an inconspicuous drift in case a stray ship should be passing by. Again finding no one, he edged the cruiser out into the main Gap, then leaned back and smiled.

"So far, so good. Now for an update." He punched up a comm screen on one of the console displays, frowning in momentary frustration as it filled with static instead of the information he sought. Even this close to Two Forks, communication through the Gap was chancy at best. Easing the Patrol ship to mid-channel suddenly cleared the static and filled the screen with the latest Core Patrol report of current shipping.

Apheron smiled with the satisfaction of a chess master seeing the components of a long developing gambit assembling into a configuration of power. "Still the same," he murmured. "Unless one of these ships comes in ahead of schedule, this is going to be an unusually quiet neighborhood. Now, where's the Diligence?"

Another of the pieces on his board moved smoothly into place in the form of a medium sized supply ship coming into view from the direction of Two Forks. As it neared, it slowed markedly, and blinked its docking lights three times. The cruiser with the Core Patrol insignia flashed its lights in the same signal, then swung toward the side passage. The all black freighter also turned toward the dead end tunnel and began to follow the Patrol craft, carefully threading its way through the first bends.

———————————————

With both ships safely hovering facing each other in the glowing indigo chamber, the Patrol craft's lights blinked once more, to be answered by the docking lights of the supply ship.

"Diligence, Major Apheron — Core Patrol." The transmission was at lowest power. "Captain Pheerson, your cooperation in these security measures is appreciated. Please remember to set your ship's comm to lowest power before replying to my transmission."

"Captain Pheerson here. Happy to accommodate, Major. Have we satisfied the conditions of the Bonus Contract?"

"As soon as I verify the cargo, Captain. Please have your bosun open the cargo hatch." "Aye, Major. One moment."

Apheron swung his smaller vessel around toward the Diligence's forward starboard cargo hatch, which began to slide open, revealing seven large crates lined up in the otherwise empty cargo bay. Pulling a device shaped like a hand gun from its slot in the console, the major aimed it through the Patrol ship's window at each of the crates in turn, and watched a display screen of verification codes.

"Is all in order, Major?" asked Captain Pheerson as Apheron's Patrol craft moved again to a position in front of the Diligence's bridge.

"Quite in order, Captain. You've fulfilled your contract, and I so certify. My compliments to all hands. The transfer will be via your cargo hoist — the other ship will receive. Please hold station here until I return with the Reliant."

"We'll be ready, Major. Diligence clear."

"Core Patrol clear."

Leaving the Diligence behind, Apheron swung his cruiser once more toward the entrance. After navigating the bends smoothly, he again slowed his vessel before emerging from the tunnel mouth. The coast was still clear. "Now," he muttered, "where's Volnath?"

———————————

Chapter 44

VOLNATH'S LATE — A BIT OF FRICTION

Is everything proceeding like clockwork Mister Kegler?"

"We're running a little late, Captain."

Captain Volnath's eyes narrowed as he spun the wheel, guiding the Reliant along the main channel. "Let the high and mighty Major Clockwork wait a little," he muttered.

"Captain?" queried Kegler.

"Steady as she goes, Mister Kegler."

"Aye, Captain, steady as she goes." A buzzer sounded from the starboard wing of the bridge. "Crew requesting permission to enter, Captain," Kegler reported.

"What do you see, Stulmin?" called Volnath, over his shoulder.

From the surveillance room Stulmin replied, "It's both of them. Captain, the bosun and the trainee."

"Check the condition of the fore port cargo bay, Stulmin."

The second rapidly switched the view from camera to camera, then shouted back, "Empty and clean as a whistle, Captain. It's all ready and waiting."

"As you were, Stulmin, and shut the door. Let them in, Kegler."

Kegler hit a button, opening the door at the far end of the bridge, and Daric and Shanni entered. Shanni was clearly wide-eyed at what she was seeing. As they drew near, the first mate motioned them to stop. Waiting at attention, the pair took advantage of their rare visit to officer's country by looking around at the wonders of the bridge.

"Have them report, Mister Kegler," said the captain.

"Aye, Captain," acknowledged the first, then to Daric and Shanni,

"The captain will see you."

The pair stepped the few paces toward the captain and again stopped at attention. Daric did the talking. "Bosun-tech Daric and Trainee Shanni reporting to the bridge as ordered, Captain."

"Very good, Bosun. You may stand at ease. What is the condition of the fore port cargo bay, Bosun?"

"The bay is empty and in order, Captain."

"As it should be, Bosun. You'll be taking aboard some cargo. We've been informed that the docks at Two Forks are full, so the transfer will be taking place sooner than anticipated. As required by Article 14, I'm officially informing you both that this is a bonus cargo, and you will each receive shares if it's delivered safely and on schedule."

Daric and Shanni looked at each other in delighted surprise, then remembered that "at ease" was a relative term, and the closer to "attention" it came, the better. Quickly, they straightened, and looked back at the captain.

"In this case, due to security requirements, it also means you'll have no port leave or outside communications until we reach our final destination. Clear?"

Again the duo exchanged looks, although this time their expressions were more constrained. "Understood, Captain," Daric responded.

"Understood," Shanni added.

"Bosun," the captain continued, "go prepare that cargo bay to take on seven crates weighing 1.30 tons each, contents very fragile, very valuable. The other ship will hoist, we'll receive. Have the required bots at the ready. The cargo hatch will open when we're alongside the other ship. On the double, now. Dismissed."

With a quick duet of "Aye, Captain", Daric and Shanni hurried from the bridge to execute their orders.

"How are we doing, Kegler?" asked Volnath.

The first mate consulted the nav system. "Should be round the next bend, Captain."

As Volnath spun the wheel to set up his ship for the curve, he called out new orders to the voice system, "Reliant, all ahead half, and prepare to slow further." In response, the massive ship began to slow down, wringing flurries of creaks and squeals from the hull.

Apheron grimaced as he checked the clock. Fuming in mid-channel, he consulted his tenth update of the shipping list, the numbered seconds gnawing at him all the while as he wondered whether Volnath would arrive before some other ship came along. At last he saw the Reliant easing around the bend in the main channel. Seething, he flashed the lights of his cruiser three times, whereupon the Reliant acknowledged with its docking lights. "All the way to three," the major hissed. "Very good, Volnath, for someone who can't read a clock."

Additional minutes ticked by as the Reliant killed enough speed to make the turn. Apheron itched to upbraid Volnath, but his plan called for radio silence. When the Reliant was finally in position, Apheron's Patrol ship took the lead, guiding the freighter toward the forbiddingly small side passage in the CoreFires.

"Reliant III to Core Patrol. You want us to follow you into that?" It was Volnath's voice on the ship's comm, transmitted at normal power.

At first, Apheron was frozen in disbelief, then, for a moment he was overcome with rage. "He can't be that stupid! If that idiot is baiting me I'll have his hide!" Regaining control, he forced himself to an icy calm, and checked his own transmitter to be sure it was at minimum power. Using formal address in case they were overheard, the chess master resumed the game, making the best next move, considering the circumstances. "Core Patrol to Reliant III." His voice was neutral. "Transmit only at minimum power, and only within the side passage. There is sufficient clearance. Core Patrol, out."

"Acknowledge," replied Volnath's voice, at minimum power.

Just as he was congratulating himself on his handling of the situation, Apheron realized he had made a mistake — only a tiny mistake, probably insignificant, but a mistake never-the-less. He realized he'd acted too hastily. "I shouldn't have mentioned the side passage! Think first," he berated himself. "Always, always, think first."

———————————

Chapter 45

TWO SHIPS IN THE CHAMBER
— DILIGENCE AND RELIANT

APHERON, AT LONG last, had his two charges more or less side by side in the CoreFires chamber.

The Diligence, stationary, was hovering with her fore starboard cargo hatch open. The larger Reliant was attempting to come close enough alongside to bring her fore port cargo bay within reach of the Diligence's hoist. A freighter to freighter transfer in mid-space was tricky enough, but maneuvering the Reliant into position within the close confines of these fiery walls left little room for error.

Tense, brief messages flew back and forth between the two captains over the ship's comm channel, and they in turn communicated with their respective crews on internal comms to avoid confusion.

Apheron monitored the ship's channel and observed the whole operation closely from his Core Patrol cruiser, while the Reliant was jockeying carefully — very carefully — closer to the Diligence.

In his white bio-suit and helmet, Daric stood on the lip of the open cargo bay and peering aft between the two freighters, trying to judge their relative motion and alignment. "Stern's still out seventy yards and closing slowly. Bow's at fifty, but closing too fast," he called over the comm system to Second Mate Stulmin. "And the stern's still too low."

On the bridge of the Reliant all three officers were at their consoles, carefully coordinating the firing of the planar field attitude thrusters.

Meanwhile, in the Diligence's cargo bay, Daric's counterpart was seated in the hoist gantry, sighting along the nested sections of structural steel to be sure they would clear the hatch of the other ship when extended. He shook his head. "They're still low, Captain," he reported to Pheerson.

Shanni watched Daric from the back wall of the cargo bay, trying not to worry while he leaned over the edge of the deck, the ship shuddering and creaking with each thruster firing.

Apheron had positioned his cruiser ahead of the two freighters in line with the narrowing gap between them, and from his viewpoint it was becoming obvious that the maximum reach of the cargo hoist would leave precious little space between the ships. Fretting about the time, he forced himself to remain silent as the Reliant edged closer and closer to the Diligence. Now the distance was about right, but the stern of the Reliant was still too low.

Daric walked to the aft end of the open hatch, hung on, and leaned far out for a better look. "OK, slowly accelerate the stern upwards until I tell you to quit."

"It's going. Say when," Stulmin replied.

In the urgency of the task, neither was conscious that they had dropped all formality. "Now!" Daric called, looking along the flank of the Reliant. The massive ship slowly swung upward toward the plane of the Diligence. "Get ready to decelerate with about the same amount of thrust."

"Ready!" Stulmin shot back.

"Thrust!"

"Thrusting."

"Be ready to cut off... be ready... coming up... cut-off!"

"Thrust off!" Stulmin leaned back in his chair and took a deep breath.

"How are we, Pheerson?" Volnath queried on the ship's comm channel.

"Dead level and stationary, Reliant. A pretty piece of work. Let's transfer cargo."

"An excellent plan, Captain Pheerson," replied Volnath, taking a deep breath himself, "an excellent plan, indeed."

"Finally," muttered Apheron.

———————————————

Chapter 46

THE BOSUN TRAINING SHANNI
— CARGO HOISTING

IN THE CARGO bay, Daric signaled for Shanni to join him.

He allowed himself a few moments of pure enjoyment, watching her loping easily across the deck. Her bright expectant expression brought a warm smile to his own face. "A perfect opportunity to familiarize her with cargo handling," he had reasoned, but an increasing bodily warmth as she approached made him aware that business and pleasure were happily coinciding.

When Shanni was beside him, Daric pointed across the empty space separating the two freighters to where his opposite number, the bosun of the Diligence, was starting up the big hoist gantry. "The seven crates are all in a line, and we don't know which one he's going to pick up first, but it will probably be at one end or the other. I need to know where to position the bots, so watch which way he starts to move the hoist."

"I get it," Shanni nodded, "OK, it's starting aft."

Daric turned and gave a subtle hand signal, and from the ranks of robots waiting at the rear of the bay, a dozen stepped forward. "I'll place them opposite that aft-most crate, but we'll have to guess about how far the boom will reach into our cargo bay when the hoist is fully extended." He decided to test her a little. "Where would you guess, without knowing more about their hoist?"

A mischievous smile played about Shanni's lips as she recognized the challenge, and accepted it with relish. She looked Daric right in the eye as her mind went over what little she knew. "It took a long time to get the two ships lined up without colliding, and you were hanging your body way out into space to get the job done. So, I say it was tricky, and the ships aren't ten feet closer together than they need to be. That means the hoist is barely long enough and the crate will come down pretty close to the edge of the deck." She tilted her head in a way that sent a momentary shiver up Daric's spine, and her impish smile widened. "Am I right?"

Daric was delighted. "You may have a natural talent for bosuning," he laughed, "but even so, you can't have my job yet. As to your answer, I'd doff my hat," he said, indicating his helmet, "but I need it to breathe with."

Daric directed the bots to the estimated landing spot, and looked across the gap just in time to see the other bosun's approving nod. With one last look around the bay, Daric triggered his comm and reported, "We're ready in the cargo bay, Captain."

Chapter *47*

Commence Transfer — On the Bridge

On the bridge, Captain Volnath also checked his console one more time, then spoke into the ship's comm, "We're ready when you are, Pheerson."

"All set, Volnath," came Pheerson's reply, "we're going to pick up the first piece."

"You may commence transfer." said the voice of Apheron.

Killing ship's comm with a snort, Volnath turned to Kegler. "How kind of the major to give us permission!" Switching the comm back on, he turned back to the scene out the bridge windows. His eyes widened in disbelief as he saw Apheron's Patrol craft starting to move toward the Reliant and Diligence! "Where in Chaos is he going?" he exploded, shooting erect. The message was duly transmitted to the other two ships.

Pheerson's vocal eruption was as startled and outraged as his own. "I'm a bot's behind if I know! Is he trying to go between our vessels? Core Patrol, what's going on? Please reply immediately!"

"No cause for alarm, gentlemen," came Apheron's smooth voice. "There is adequate clearance, and I'm merely positioning my ship to supervise the transfer."

At this, Volnath rolled his eyes to the ceiling, slapped off the comm switch, and gave vent to a loud cry of rage and frustration. "Bot-bolts in a basket! That's all we need!" His boots rang as he stamped across the metal deck. "An amateur chef in the galley," he shouted, "while we're trying to transfer cargo in a CoreFires oven barely bigger than our ship!" Kegler kept his head lowered as Volnath passed by, growling incoherently. Still seething, the captain pounded his fists on the control room window sill, then raised his head and looked across the void to the bridge of the Diligence. Volnath laughed sardonically when he saw Pheerson's demeanor mirroring his own.

Peering down at the Core Patrol cruiser inching its way aft between the two freighters, Captain Pheerson gave it a final heartfelt shake of his fist before striding back to his console and reaching for the comm.

Volnath grunted as Pheerson's voice, icily calm, said, "Please take great care, Major Apheron, to stay well clear of the ships and my hoist gantry, lest you endanger us all. We are proceeding to transfer the first item."

————————————

Chapter 48

CRUISER BLOCKING TRANSFER — FIRST CRATE

IN THE CARGO bay, Daric and Shanni stood side by side near the edge of the deck, watching intently across the void as the Diligence's bosun positioned the gantry above the aft-most end of the line of crates.

While they waited, Shanni asked, "Daric, how do you know how many bots you'll need?"

"The captain said the crates weighed 1.30 tons each," he replied, "and they look to be about square. Twelve bots can handle more than three times that weight, leaving a healthy safety factor, and there'll be just enough room for one on each corner and another two on each side. Using any more could create a problem."

Across the way, the other bosun lowered the big cargo clamps smoothly into the fittings atop the crate, locked them home, and as swiftly began lifting the first piece of cargo clear of the deck.

"He's good! Did you see how perfectly he lined that up?" Daric said to Shanni. "We could have this transfer wrapped up in no time."

The heavy crate rose higher, until at about fifteen feet it leveled out and moved forward toward the open hatch. "He's not only keeping it high enough to clear our bots," Daric explained, "but allowing extra in case one of the ships should shift." Shanni nodded, watching the telescoped boom sections extend beyond the Diligence's cargo bay. Further and further the boom extended, a slender bridge reaching across the void, bringing the crate into the Reliant's open hatch.

The crate swung high overhead as the hoist reached the full extent of it's travel. Shanni's guess was so close that Daric only had to repositioned his bots by a couple of feet. Slowly the crate began to lower toward the upraised arms of the waiting bots, all optimally placed in a square to receive the heavy load.

Shanni watched breathlessly as the crate descended to just above head height, where the bots then took the full weight. She saw Daric give a hand signal to the bosun on the other ship, whereupon the locks swiveled, the clamps withdrew, and in a smooth motion the hoist rose again and began retracting across the gap, back into the cargo bay of the Diligence.

Meanwhile, the bots under Daric's direction carried the heavy crate some ten paces further in from the edge of the cargo bay, and carefully lowered it onto the deck. Four bots then leaned over in unison, each pulling a titanium bar out of one of the innumerable small holes in the floor, and reinserting the bar through a fitting in each the corner of the crate.

"What are those?" Shanni asked.

"They're called cargo pins," Daric replied, "They keep cargo from shifting by locking the corners of crates and pallets into the grid of holes in the deck."

"Some pins! What are they, about four feet long?"

"And an inch and a half in diameter. About twenty pounds, and much stronger than steel."

As soon as they had finished locking the pins with a final twist, Daric positioned the robots at the spot where the next crate would arrive.

"I'm sure impressed," Shanni observed. "This is incredibly efficient."

"Especially when people really know their jobs. Here comes crate number two already. That bosun is as quick as he is smooth."

High over their heads the second crate arrived, suspended from the end of the Diligence's extended hoist boom. Shanni, Daric, and the dozen bots were all watching the load slowly winching down toward their upraised hands, when suddenly it stopped, swinging in mid-space, still well above their heads.

Turning to see why the bosun on the other ship had stopped the hoist, Daric was astounded to find his view blocked by a portion of Apheron's cruiser.

Instantly Daric reported to the bridge, "Captain! This is the bosun in cargo bay. There's a Core Patrol spacecraft between the two ships, blocking our line of sight, and we've got cargo hanging in mid-space. How that craft got in between there I can't say — there can't be much room to spare. Please advise!"

———————————

Chapter 49

GIVE HIM WHAT HE WANTS
— TWENTY-FOUR BOTS

BARELY HAD VOLNATH received Daric's report, when Apheron's voice came in over ship's comm. "You want what?" exploded Volnath in reply.

With the exaggerated calm of someone talking to a child, Apheron repeated, "I want twice as many bots handling that load."

Doubly infuriated by Apheron's tone, Volnath snapped, "Stulmin, how many bots are receiving those loads?"

"Uh," Stulmin counted, "twelve, Captain."

Quickly running the figures through his head, Volnath fumed. "More than enough. Meddling fool!" Then into ship's comm, "There are twelve bots, Major, more than enough. Please ease your ship back carefully, being especially careful to avoid the cargo hoist, so we can resume the transfer."

"I'm quite capable of counting to twelve, Captain Volnath," came the immediate reply, "I can even read a clock. I repeat, I want twenty-four bots handling this delicate and expensive cargo." Apheron's tone hardened. "Twenty-four, Volnath. The last time I checked, that was the number of hours in a day."

Clenching his teeth, Volnath addressed Daric. "Bosun, Major Apheron wants twenty-four bots receiving each piece of cargo. Accommodate him."

"Anything you say, Captain, but there isn't room for that many bots — it could create a hazard. Begging your pardon, sir, but twelve is the right number."

"Of course it is," growled Volnath in a foul humor, "but do it anyway!"

"Aye, Captain, twenty-four it is."

———————————————

With considerable misgivings, Daric signalled another twelve bots to join them.

Shanni, who had been hearing the exchange on her bio-comm, turned questioningly to Daric, who tried to look reassuring in spite of a queasy feeling in the pit of his stomach. Taking a small liberty with his instructions to minimize the crowding, Daric directed four of the bots to position themselves just beyond the corners, standing by with cargo pins at the ready. Then he smiled again at Shanni, and directed the others to squeeze into the square of waiting bots, and all eyes were once again on the crate swinging high above their heads.

Apheron's ship slid back just far enough to permit the Diligence's bosun to again see his load, whereupon the hoist operator started to lower the crate toward the upraised fingertips of the bots. Just as the bots were taking the full weight of the crate, what Daric had feared came to pass — a minor chain-reaction of jostling among the overcrowded bots, and for a few seconds the crate tipped alarmingly.

Daric knew the crate was still safely attached to the hoist cable, but he had no way of anticipating Apheron's next reaction — the Core Patrol ship surged forward as if to intervene, catching the cargo hoist cable on its superstructure, thereby swiftly pulling the heavy load up several feet out of the bots' hands. As the cable freed itself of Apheron's vessel, Shanni, Daric, and the bots watched in frozen horror as the crate fell toward them, then stopped when the cable jerked taut!

"Will it snap?" thought Daric, in that agonizing slow-motion instant.

The cable held, but the impact dislodged the side-covers of the crate.

Seeing one of the covers falling toward Shanni, Daric felt like he was trapped in a dream where his body couldn't move fast enough. She was too far away he knew — he couldn't reach her in time. His mind raced. A hand signal. The bot next to her was looking his way. Quickly!

Even amid the illusion of slow motion, the bot's response was a blur. Driving its metal arm above Shanni's head like some kind of robotic black-belt, its fist met the falling panel, shattering it into several pieces, the largest deflected harmlessly away. One piece, however, struck Shanni's helmet, and to Daric's anguish, he watched her head recoiling from the blow, and saw her sinking limply to the deck.

Overhead, the suspended load swung back and forth, still supported by the crate frame and pallet, undamaged, but to Apheron's dismay, the contents were now visible for all to see — a twenty six-hundred-pound Crystal, large enough to contain two month's data for an entire planet.

Beneath it, all Daric could see was Shanni's inert form, crumpled on the deck. He rushed to her, checking first to see if her helmet was cracked, and her face bubble intact. "Unconscious, but breathing," he noted with relief.

The group of bots still stood in a square below the swaying Crystal, watching Daric lift Shanni's limp body into his arms and carry her tenderly to a safer area of the cargo bay where he laid her gently upon the deck. For some time, he looked down at her face, then stood erect, motionless. Even to the bots, Daric seemed to change before their eyes, although just how was beyond their understanding — something strange and human.

They watched attentively as Daric turned toward the immense Crystal swinging slowly above their heads, watched as he turned toward Apheron's spaceship, hovering just beyond the open Cargo bay door.

Daric's eyes narrowed, staring unblinkingly at the cockpit windows. His head lowered slightly, but his gaze never shifted from its target, and he started to walk.

Leaving Shanni's barely stirring form on the metal deck, he strode toward Apheron's ship. With the briefest glance toward the watchful bots, he gave a sign, and the four bots carrying the four-foot metal bars strode to join him. When one of the bots was beside him, Daric extended his hand, and the bot placed the heavy cargo pin in Daric's palm, and watched the human's fingers close over it.

Daric gave another sign, and a bot seventy feet distant swiftly pulled another pin from the deck, and hurled it end over end across the cargo bay to the bot at Daric's side. Without breaking stride, the robot raised its arm and caught the spinning bar in its metal hand with a ringing clang.

Side by side they walked, Daric in the center, two bots on each side. Something urgent, probably important, the bots inferred. Something human.

Side by side they strode, each swinging a four-foot metal bar stronger than steel, four metal beings and one of flesh and blood.

And, ironically, it was Daric's face that was devoid of human expression, Daric's eyes that were brighter, colder, harder than steel.

———————————————

Chapter *50*

TOO MANY BOTS — SHANNI HURT

SEATED AT HIS CONSOLE in the Reliant's bridge, Stulmin's eyes were wide and he was unaware that he was speaking. It was if he'd left his voice running, unattended, repeating a litany over and over. "Holy Mother of the Universe, Who gave birth to all before the birth of Good and Evil," he chanted, "Holy Mother of the Universe..." He paused, mouth agape, staring into one of the displays on his console, then, still unaware, resumed, "Oh, Mother of the Universe..."

"Knock it off and tend to your duties, Stulmin!" Volnath growled. "Things are bad enough without you mumbling your prayers like a child."

On the display before him, Stulmin was watching Daric and the four bots marching relentlessly toward the open hatch, and — just beyond — Apheron's ship. He saw the metal bars swinging from their hands. "Oh, Holy Mother..."

"Can it!" shouted Volnath.

Stulmin, suddenly aware of his captain but still almost incoherent, pointed to the screen in front of him. "Look, look, look..." he managed, "...cargo bay, look..."

Impatiently Volnath switched one of his own displays to a cargo bay camera, and swore under his breath as it showed him Shanni's body lying on the deck. "Apheron!" He reached for the camera controls to get a closer look. "That meddling fool!" Volnath found the zoom, focused the view on Shanni's face. "A member of my crew!" On the monitor, Shanni stirred. "At least she's not dead."

Volant leaned back, staring darkly at the monitor. "That interfering egomaniac has caused an injury to a member of my crew!" He swore again.

"No, look, look!" Stulmin grunted. "cargo bay..."

Puzzled, Volnath snapped the display to another camera, and now he, too, saw the scene that so benumbed Stulmin. "Oh, no! Not on my ship!" he whispered, filled with foreboding. Without taking his eyes off the display, he shouted, "Kegler, look at the docking bay monitors!" Then to himself, he swore again and shook his head. "The major has the temper of a viper, and that craft of his could wipe out a city, let alone the Reliant! And nobody challenges Apheron. Nobody!"

————————————

Chapter 51

LOOK AT THE MONITOR! — STULMIN'S PRAYERS

"INCOMPETENTS!" APHERON HAD exclaimed when he had seen the crate jerked up out of the robot's hands. "A planet's ransom in data, and it's juggled about by idiots! Do I have to do everything myself?" he complained, not yet aware that the incompetence was his own. Suddenly, however, he was in the midst of an emergency — his ship slowed, the nose tilted up, and when the snagged hoist cable slipped off the superstructure, his ship lurched forward again. Stealing a glance at the freighters so close at each side, he knew the situation was escalating dangerously.

In a cold sweat, he wondered why his trusted cruiser wasn't answering the controls properly, wondered whether his next efforts would make things worse. He knew he had almost no margin for error. "Got to keep from hitting anything," he cautioned himself grimly, "Remember the hoist just above, don't get tangled in it."

The nose was still coming up, but without knowing what was wrong, he was afraid to try to correct for it. "Think fast, you've only got seconds before you hit the hoist," he told himself, and then it dawned. "The hoist! I must have snagged the hoist." A blend of skill and desperation drove his hands as they darted from control to control. Slowly the nose started coming back down as he strove to inch his ship back out from under the cargo hoist, every moment fearing to hear the sound of a collision above.

No sound came. Finally, his instruments showed the cruiser was again safely at rest between the two supply ships' cargo bays. Apheron sagged back in his seat and wiped his forehead on his sleeve, only to sit bolt upright as he thought of the crate. "The hoist! I snagged the hoist. What happened to the crate?"

He looked into the Reliant's cargo bay to the end of the cargo boom. High above a group of bots his precious cargo was swinging, but it took him a moment to understand what had happened. He cursed as he saw the Crystal exposed for all to see, then saw the side panels of the crate lying on the deck. Again he scanned the Crystal swinging in mid-space. He could see no sign of damage. It seemed to be perfectly seated in its complex mount, and he could even see the delicate golden probes arching up the sides to contact the Crystal on its many faces — they appeared undisturbed.

Once again he sagged back in his seat. "That was close, far too close," he whispered, wiping his palms. "But," he consoled himself, "things could be worse."

————————————

Chapter 52

FOUR BOTS — TWELVE PACES

TWELVE PACES, NOW nine, now five, separated Daric and the four robots from the open cargo bay hatch and the brink of the void. As they reached the edge of the deck they stopped, and Daric looked long and hard at the dark form of the Major within his Patrol ship. As the bots watched, Daric hefted the metal bar in his right hand, drew back his arm, took aim at Apheron's window, and heaved the bar with all his strength. Immediately, he gave a sign and extended his hand. The bot on his right quickly replaced the bar with its own, then extended its arm high to catch a new spinning cargo pin hurled thirty yards across the cargo bay with perfect accuracy by one of the bots standing underneath the Crystal.

Apheron jumped, startled, as Daric's four-foot bar ricocheted off the window beside him. "Debris?" he thought. "What now?" If he was startled before, he was incredulous when he looked toward the Reliant's cargo bay and saw five figures, one a human, standing feet wide-spread on the brink of the deck, each lazily swinging a metal bar in one hand. Alert at once, his nostrils flared as he struggled to make any sense of what he was seeing. "Am I trapped in a nightmare?" he asked.

Daric raised the cargo pin in his hand, then pointed it toward his own face, then extended it toward Apheron, then back toward himself. Lowering it once more, he resumed swinging it easily, just above the deck.

"Has the Universe gone mad? He wants to talk?" With the click of a switch Apheron added a bio-comm frequency to his ship's comm. "What do you want?" he asked cautiously.

"You are Major Apheron?"

"Yes, of the Core Patrol."

"I am bosun of the Reliant. We need to have a little talk. I suggest you turn off your ship's frequency."

Apheron was instantly livid at the young whelp's audacity, at his impertinence! "I can hear you," he growled dangerously.

"You've made several mistakes during this cargo transfer," Daric said, still swinging the four-foot bar from his right hand. "Serious mistakes."

————————————

What's he saying?" shouted Kegler in frustration.

"He's switched off his comm, and his suit's out of range! I'm trying other cameras," Stulmin replied, "but they can't pick him up either."

"The fat's in the fire now! Our young bosun could get himself erased." offered Kegler as he switched among the surveillance systems.

"No skin off our nose either way," observed Stulmin.

"That's only true as long as the Major doesn't get over-excited and blow us all to atoms. Here, I've got him," Volnath shouted, "on ship's comm! You can hear him in the background on Apheron's comm."

Apheron's voice sounded low and deadly, "I can hear you. Go ahead."

As the Reliant's officers listened eagerly, Daric's reply was cut off.

"Damnation!" Volnath barked, "Apheron's turned off his ship's comm. I can't hear a thing."

"That kid's waked the tiger now!" Kegler shook his head fearfully. "I wouldn't want to be in his shoes."

"Help Stulmin pray, Kegler," Volnath warned, "this whole ship is his shoes!"

————————————

Your last mistake was one too many," continued Daric, "you injured my colleague."

Apheron now saw Shanni's figure laying some distance back on the deck. "He's lecturing me? This is madness!" he thought.

Daric extended the bar at arm's length, pointing directly at Apheron in his Patrol ship. "This is my deck — I'm responsible for the safety of *your* cargo and *my* crew." Daric's voice was coldly intense, deadly serious. "This is how it's going to be: each piece of cargo will be handled by twelve bots under my supervision, and that of my assistant. Observe if you wish, but transfer resumes only after you remove your vessel from between our ships and station it at a safe distance." Daric paused, emphasizing each word. "There will be *no — more — mistakes*."

Apheron's face was purple, his lips drawn back in a snarl, his eyes filled with loathing. He didn't even have to look at his console — the location of every button had long since become instinctual — and he struck like a snake. In answer, the turret above his head swiveled swiftly toward Daric, and Apheron's finger was poised to fire.

More swiftly still, Daric responded, signing to two of his bots, who hurled their bars as if they were shot from cannons. Twin blurs streaked instantly across the void, striking the swiveling turret with explosive force! Twin bars harder than steel drove deep into the mechanism, pinning it immobile before it was halfway turned toward Daric!

Reeling from the thunderous impact just over his head, Apheron could hardly believe his eyes when he saw two of the bots near the hanging Crystal instantly hurl a fresh pair of cargo pins thirty yards into the waiting metal hands of the bots at the lip of the deck.

"I said," Daric continued, "there will be no more mistakes." He shook his finger slowly, as if he were admonishing one of his bots. "If that weapon had fired, it would probably have triggered the destruction of this ship, and therefore the Diligence. Yours would have been caught in between. You'll have to agree, that would have been a serious mistake."

Consumed by rage, Apheron, surveyed the weapons at his disposal. Daric's words continued over the comm. "Of course, it would be terrible if there were any damage to your window." Apheron's eyes were glazed, and his eyelids twitched as he glanced fearfully through the window at those swinging metal bars, realizing he was not wearing his helmet. Back to his console they turned, looking for weapons fast enough to evade the robots but mild enough to avoid self destruction.

His hands shook with fury as he started to choose, then tried to think.

"Or, perhaps, damage to your precious cargo..."

Apheron made his choice, an evil grin on his dry lips. He turned toward Daric with an expression of triumph, his hand descending toward the console.

Daric signed again, and the bot at his side again hurled a bar.

Apheron watched in growing horror as it spun end over end, arcing unerringly toward the twenty-six-hundred-pound Crystal suspended from the hoist. "No!" he screamed, body and brain jolted as if by electric shock, suddenly seeing an image of his chess game shattered into a million pieces. *"No!"* he shouted into the comm.

The cargo pin struck perfectly, piercing the metal crate-frame, setting the load to swinging afresh, leaving the huge Crystal still unharmed.

Clockwise the massive load spun on the end of the cable, slowing with each revolution, the Crystal's facets glinting in the lights of the cargo bay. As it slowed and reversed in a counter-clockwise spin, the slender golden contact probes looked like flying buttresses rising to merge with a crystalline cathedral more complex than any human architecture.

Clockwise, counter-clockwise, always slowing, it swung as Apheron's staring eyes gazed hypnotically at the glinting facets, his mouth working soundlessly.

Gradually he exorcised the insane rage from his body, willing the chess board back into being. As a planet's worth of data circled to and then fro in front of his eyes, he sought to center himself again in the chess master's persona, to send his primal furies back to their underworlds, to once again fondle his favorite weapon — the sharpest, the deadliest of them all — reason.

"You're quite right, Bosun," Apheron said into the comm. "There will be no more mistakes. You may proceed with your plan and resume cargo transfer as soon as I've maneuvered my ship to a safer distance."

––––––––––––––––––

Shanni was sitting up, trying to rise.

"Here, let me help you."

There was something in Daric's voice, a new calmness perhaps, or perhaps a new depth, that brought a blush of life to Shanni's cheeks. "Thank you," she whispered as she stood, steadied by his hand. His eyes looked both firm and tender, she thought.

"Let's finish transferring that cargo," he said, and she nodded.

———————————————

Captain Volnath looked thunderstruck. Apheron's voice was coming through again on the ship's comm. "After consulting with your bosun, I've modified the cargo transfer procedure. We'll follow his recommendation of twelve bots, and I will observe from a safer distance. Cargo transfer will resume as soon as my ship is on station. Core Patrol clear."

"Acknowledge," came the voice of Captain Pheerson.

Volnath triggered his comm. "Understood. Ready when you are." Still open mouthed, the captain shut off the comm again, and looked across the consoles at Kegler and Stulmin. "That kid didn't have a bot's chance in CoreFires of coming out of that alive!" Volnath shook his head in amazement. "I'd give a year's pay to hear what it was he said to Apheron."

———————————————

With the seven crates pinned down safely in the Reliant's cargo bay, Apheron's Patrol craft led the two space-freighters through the CoreFires tunnel back toward the main passage. "Think first! Always, always," he told himself. His eyes were scanning the instruments before him, observing the slow turmoil of the CoreFires in the tunnel walls, checking whether there was sufficient clearance for the larger ships behind him. All the while, his mind's eye was surveying the chess board, modifying the gambit, adding certain new details that brought a cold smile to his face. "Reason," he hissed softly.

———————————————

Chapter 53

THROUGH THE GLOWMIST
— AND COMING FAST

LYARD, WILL YOU look at that!" exclaimed Garms, pointing up into the thin green glowmist. "I do believe it's the Contender, coming like a singed bat out of fire."

Lyard straightened up and peered along Garms arm. "I swear, Mr. Garms, through the years there's been occasions when I've become a mite aware that you've the Devil's own time seein' the nose in front of your face, but until this very moment it never dawned on me what was wrong. When they put you together, poor soul, they got your eyes out of the eagle box — it's a wonder you've got no wings." Squinting, he continued, "Aye, I can see a dot out there, and it's moving fast, but if glowmist had flies, I'd get out a swatter."

The pair were standing on the deck of the Aries, moored alongside the castle pier. Between their feet, half a pump lay on its side with various parts of the other half strewn for some distance about the deck. From a hole in the deck, a long skinny valve assembly began to emerge like an Indian rope trick, only to have the illusion spoiled when it was followed by a hand and Junker's muffled voice on the comm from below, saying, "Here's the rest of it. It'll take me a minute to undo the fittings." Garms laid the valve aside, and the hand snaked back into the hold.

"You think kinfolk of one of those girls at Grand Jetty got after Hup? He's sure pushing that ship fast for glowmist," Garms offered.

"Comin' fast, all right. Already I can make out it's the Contender.

Nowt else in the Gap so shiny and shipshape 'ceptin' the freighters," Lyard replied. "Sometimes that boy looks like an out-worlder. Think he's trying to set another of his records?"

"Never saw sense in it, myself — he holds them all, and he's the only one who pays any attention to them. Whatever spins his beanie, I guess. Looks like we'll know soon enough. If he's coming here, though, he's going to have to do some fancy back-pedaling, or go right on by."

The descent was spectacular. Retroing at maximum power, Hup was clearly trying to arrive at the dock at the earliest possible second. For awhile Lyard and Garms were convinced he wasn't going to be able to stop in time, but to their surprise, when the red and white Contender killed the last of its momentum, it was within a couple hundred feet of the pier.

"Pretty sharp, I got to admit," acknowledged Lyard. "Might be there's something to trying for records, after all."

As the Contender approached the pier opposite the Aries, the contrast between the two craft was striking. Junker's tug, with its whimsical junk-sculpture "J U N K" and huge engine, had an air of extreme competence while not taking itself at all seriously. The Contender, on the other hand, was a speedy pilot's cruiser that looked as if it had been recently purchased on one of the more well-to-do out-worlds. In reality, it was just as much fashioned from Gap scrap as Junker's vessel, and it's appearance was due only to single-minded dedication on Hup's part. As it came alongside the dock, Garms leaped to make it fast, and Hup came bounding out of the cabin.

"You've come to the wrong place," Garms joked, "we're fresh out of girls."

"Just as well," Hup shot back, "you probably forgot what to do with them, anyway. Where's Junker?"

"In the hold," Garms replied, gesturing toward the Aries.

"Tell him I need to talk to him," Hup called up to Lyard, who then spoke into the hole in the deck. "Tell him to hurry!" Hup added.

"What's up?" Junker asked as he jumped down to join the others on the pier.

"I came from Dutchman's as fast as I could. Something unusual's been happening with the CoreFires — it got really still and quiet, then started gusting out tendrils pretty much like glowmist only much faster. It blew out Salty's antenna again, and he says no way is he going to fix it until this dies down. So I headed for your place and beat it here, but it's spreading this way, fast. I thought maybe we could use your antennas to get some idea of what's going on."

"Sounds good to me, Hup," Junker replied, "but you'd better think twice before you choose to stay here — the Contender could be in danger, and you, too."

"In danger? How's that?"

"Well, it's OK at Dutchman's if the CoreFires field shifts: the whole village just shifts with it. Have you thought about what would happen here?"

"The same thing, right? The Keep would just move with the flux. What's dangerous about that?"

Junker pointed to the two-mile-wide ring of orbiting derelicts and flotsam. "Dutchman's isn't surrounded by that. If the castle got shifted, each piece of scrap circling around it'd be accelerated differently depending on where it was in its orbit. After a few thousand collisions, some of that stuff would be bound to fall in toward the Keep, and the Contender too."

Junker knocked on his helmet. "So far, so good. The flux has stayed stable all these years — that's why I chose this cavern. But who knows what'll happen if the CoreFires's doing something unusual? Hup, I know what you've put into that ship, and you've got to decide if you want to risk it in the middle of a few million tons of loose junk."

Hup looked wistfully at his gleaming red and white craft, and then at Junker's motley tug. "You're right," he said, shaking his head, "yours could sure take minor dings a lot better than mine, but, as far as the big stuff goes, we're both running the same risks. I'll stay. Let's go do it."

"You're on!" Junker replied, breaking into a dead run.

———————————————

Chapter 54

SHAKING THE TOWER — COREFIRES COMING

ALL FOUR SET off for the castle at a rapid pace. Once again the contrast was extreme, with Lyard and Garms in their typical cast-off Mono-mol suits, Hup in his spick-and-span red and white uniform that he had charmed a Grand Jetty girl into making him, and Junker in his unique bio-suit that looked like rags and tatters. Whatever the differences, all four dashed into the castle and up the stairs with common purpose. When they reached the main hall, Junker directed the others.

"Lyard, unlatch the other end of the sofa from the elevator. Garms, show Hup where the analyzer is, and both of you roll it over here." Meanwhile, Lyard and Junker had detached the sofa and rolled it aside. "OK, roll the analyzer onto the elevator, and lock it into those pockets. Now everyone stands inside the white lines."

Junker hit a switch and a safety railing rose around them, then the elevator began ascending rapidly. The acceleration was dizzying as they sped up past the big stained-glass window, and on up into the narrowing spire. As they rose into the geodesic globe, the platform slowed so quickly their stomachs were still climbing while their bodies came to rest.

"Look! It's already beginning," said Hup, pointing to the CoreFires. Clearly, the normal turmoil was gradually slowing down.

"I'll turn on the sound," Junker said, "Lyard, plug the analyzer into the antenna channels. Let's see what we get."

When the sound came on, the typical music of the CoreFires was already diminishing in volume and complexity. Looking out the dia-mond-shaped windows, they could see the fireforms and convolutions of the nebula were everywhere smoothing out. Within a couple of minutes, the sounds had faded away to silence, and the last hints of roiling swirls in the Gap-walls had disappeared.

The only variation in the scene was from the flickering green glow of the e-fields webbing between the ribs of Junker's dandelion antennas.

Now, as they shifted their weight, the occasional creaking of the platform was loud in the dome, and they unconsciously tried to keep from moving.

"Thanks, Hup, I'd have hated to have missed any of this," Junker whispered. "Since I got the antennas up, I've never heard it this quiet. It feels like the CoreFires's inhaling all that energy and holding its breath."

"Otitius said he'd heard about something like this happening long ago." Hup spoke quietly, but even so his voice echoed back from the facets of the geodesic sphere. "But what came of it, he didn't know."

"These eyes have never seen the like," Lyard muttered, uneasily scanning the Gap-walls for the slightest sign of change.

Junker checked the readings on the analyzer. "It says the antennas are working," he whispered in the silence. "and what we're hearing is what they're receiving — nothing, zero." Wherever they looked it was the same, the CoreFires was motionless, quiet.

Garms put his hands on the safety railing, and the elevator creaked again. "...All about them the sea grew quiet," he quoted softly from an ancient story, "and the cries of gulls were stilled. In the deeps, the Leviathan stirred..."

————————————————

Chapter 55

[RAD:NA] BRING THEM DOWN!
— SHE'S BLOWING OUT!

CLIMBING DOWN THE steep stairway from her platform, Questor-Joss made her way across the deck looking for First-Mate-Norr. The deck hands were scurrying about, trimming the yards this way and that, trying to wring some advantage from light but variable energy winds, but to little avail. Spying the mate, a dozen yards aft of the helm, she strode toward him.

"Who's best at whistling up a wind?" she joked, laying a hand on the helmsman's shoulder as she passed.

"I wish I knew, Questor," was his heartfelt reply. "We could use a whole whistling chorus this day!" Feeling the ship responding to a light gust from another quarter, he spun the wheel again, working hard to maintain their heading.

Norr was shading his eyes, looking aloft where the energy sails were barely pulling, their captive lightning anemic and fitful. He grunted in frustration as the mainsail above his head began to shiver, but it soon bellied properly again. Seeing Joss, he apologized, "Sorry, Questor, it's the best she'll do for now. We're carrying everything but stunsails with little to show for it. I know we're overdue for the next tack, but we're going to have to keep to this heading until the energy winds pick up."

"Understood, Norr," she replied, shading her eyes as well. At times the sails were nearly slack. "Not much you can do with this. I thought I'd bring you up to date with what I've learned so far."

"I'm all ears, Navigatrix."

The Questor dropped her voice so that the mate alone could hear. "I still can't sense the direction of the missing finders, but I'm learning something from the tactic we've been using — zigzagging while I try to tell if their presence is weaker or stronger. I only wish it weren't so slow."

"Aye, and all the slower for now!" Norr muttered, peering aloft. "But you have learned something?"

"I think so. I believe the two missing finders are now in two separate locations, and that one may be nearby."

"That's heartening!"

"Not so fast, my faithful Norr, because it's the one in human hands, and it's within the Gap."

The mate's expression fell as quickly as it had brightened. "Beyond our reach!"

Joss moved closer and further dropped her voice. "The news is not all that bad, Mate-Norr," she murmured. "The one Finder is still in benign hands, and, while the other is hidden from us, I've sensed that it is hidden from another as well. It would be well for now if that were true."

Norr glanced about, then spoke under his breath, "Ah, Questor! And if the scent had been lost..."

"...at the time of the collision...," Joss finished. "My thought as well — the Owd could presume the Finders destroyed. That could buy us some precious time, but we must be careful lest our actions give anything away."

Norr looked up at the first sounds of a great banging aloft followed by groans from some of the deckhands. The huge sails had been driven aback by an adverse gust of the energy winds, but no harm was done as it immediately subsided to a dead calm. When all sails continued to hang slack, Norr and Joss strode quickly to the port rail for a better look at the CoreFires.

Peering over the side, the mate reported, "No wake at all! We're stationary!"

"And no sign of a wind to port," Joss added. "Come on! Let's get a better look aloft!" Quick as a cat she climbed the ratlines, then swung over and dropped onto the huge spar atop the mainsail. Running past the mast, she continued out to the starboard tip, closely followed by Norr. There, far above the deck and far out beyond it as well, they had a magnificent view of the CoreFires to starboard.

Steadying himself with a line, Norr studied the glowing fireclouds as far as they could see. In every direction, even above and below, the story was the same. "Chaos!" he swore. "I've never seen it so quiet!"

"I have," the Questor replied in a grim voice. "A long time ago."

Norr gave her a puzzled look.

"It'd be incredibly unlikely, but if the Core winds continue to die away to nothing, I'm not going to take a chance — we're going to get every scrap of sail off her except maybe a reefed topsail. Then, if I'm wrong, we'll put it all up again."

"Wrong? About what?"

"A supernova in another galaxy, somewhere near its central portal. The portal shuts down, of course, triggering others to do likewise to protect their galaxies, but not without consequences."

She hung way out over the spar tip, checking the CoreFires far below the ship. "The outgoing matter stream is halted gradually, but the incoming has to be cut off instantly for protection — that generates a field shockwave that spreads through the core nebula. In most places it's harmless, even unnoticeable. But in others, it can focus to great intensity. I was training at the time, and our ship was sailing quite some distance from our central portal when it shut down."

She looked fore and aft, and shook her head. "The first sign was the energy winds falling to an absolute calm, like this, then the CoreFires brightened just before we were hit by a storm front with a wind you wouldn't believe. Under full sail the masts snapped instantly, carrying all our rigging away along with several hands. Many others were injured and that wind pounded us for hours. I'd a lot rather waste our effort striking the sails than risk being caught again."

The two figures standing on the tip of the spar took one last look around at the CoreFires.

"I've seen enough," Joss said. "Bare poles except the fore topsail! And quickly!"

"Aye, Questor!" the mate replied, then bellowed down from the rigging, "Avast, all hands! Turn to and listen up!"

———————————

Chapter 56

A Keening Wail — So Faint At First

Junker became aware of the sound of his heartbeat.

As often as he had watched the mysterious convolutions of the CoreFires from the tower, he'd never seen it so still.

"Spooky," said Lyard.

"There!" said Garms in a hushed whisper. He pointed to a region in the CoreFires that was showing a barely perceptible brightening.

Very faintly, from that direction, came a sound, a keening wail, as if from far away a chance wind had brought a cry of mourning. Junker could feel the goose-bumps rising on his arms. For a moment, it seemed but an illusion, but then the sound returned. "What could raise such a heartrending cry?" Junker thought.

Junker shivered as Garms' whisper seemed to answer his thoughts. "...and on the Day of Judgment, the sea shall give up her dead..." Garms' knuckles were white on the railing.

Again, the unearthly dirge sounded.

"And there!" added Hup, pointing to another quarter.

"And more, over there," Garms indicated.

The faint wail became a chorus, arising first from the direction of Dutchman's, but soon spreading about them on all sides. On the otherwise featureless CoreFires walls, glowing spots appeared in ever increasing numbers, and swiftly grew in size. Garms concentrated on watching only that first spot, straining to see any visible change. When it appeared, he almost stumbled backward into the analyzer, he was so surprised by the sudden jet of glowmist that was expelled from the nebula, penetrating the Gap-wall like a gout of flame. It was accompanied by a low peal of thunder that died as the fiery cloud slowed and dissipated, only to be followed by a more violent ejection of glowmist, a flaring tongue that streamed vigorously for several seconds, reaching out farther from the CoreFires walls.

Garms pointed, and called loudly to make himself heard over the wailing chorus and another timpani roll of thunder, "Hup, is that what you saw at Dutchman's?"

"Sort of, but this seems more violent."

Now the swelling crescendo of lamentation surged all around them, as if the Keep were some insignificant piece of scenery on the stage of an opera for giants. Within moments its inhabitants were caught up in the unfolding of some titanic libretto, and the geodesic dome was alight with the glare of many eruptions bursting from the CoreFires. As they grew, they united, giving rise to a gusting wind of glowmist that soon became a gale. Already, in the direction of Dutchman's, the CoreFires itself was obscured, hidden behind the streaming storm front of glowmist racing toward the castle.

Garms and Lyard watched warily as the first prominences reached the Ring, swallowing up a derelict hull and numerous smaller pieces of orbiting debris, but whether large or small, they all seemed to exit the turbulent clouds on the same circular course as when they had entered.

"I see it, but I'm afraid to believe it," said Garms.

Lyard replied, "Welcome news, for sure. At least it's not blowing the Ring apart before our eyes."

"Well, now it's our turn," Hup shouted, as the glowing squall-line was about to engulf the castle. "Brace yourself!"

It was well they did, for when the first blast hit, the dome shook, and the tower creaked and groaned. Instantly the geodesic globe was enveloped in a torrent of streaming luminous vapor, and the four within were gripped by the illusion that the facetted sphere was suddenly hurtling through the mists at great speed. Even looking down at the rest of the castle, or looking out to the dimly seen Ring didn't seem to help — with the elevator shaking and the sound half hurricane shriek, half thunder, Junker's entire domain seemed to be rushing headlong through the storm.

"Cap'n, look at the antennas," Lyard shouted.

Junker, who had been concentrating on the analyzer readings, looked up. Beyond the windows, the sixty dandelion antennas were trembling and shaking from the buffeting gusts of the plasma tempest. The ones most directly facing the furious onslaught were pressed towards the tower, their delicate ribs flexed to the extreme as the e-fields stretched and tautened under the pounding assault. Those in the lee of the dome were vibrating chaotically, but for the moment looked reasonably protected. It was the antennas that were taking the force from the side that were giving Junker the most concern — they appeared about as secure as an array of beach umbrellas in a blizzard. Between each rib, the e-fields looked like glowing electrical spinnakers in danger of snapping their masts, and the supporting stalks that anchored each antenna to the dome were bending alarmingly.

"I don't know how much more they can take, Lyard," Junker shouted. Once again he checked the readings on the analyzer. "And the force is still getting stronger. Some of these look like they're going to be carried away. It's probably just as well."

"I don't follow you, Cap'n," Lyard shouted back.

"I think it's the e-fields. They're what's shaking the tower. The hulks in the Ring, and even the small things are passing right through, so likewise the castle should be unaffected. But the antennas are bending, so it must be the e-fields that are transmitting the force to the tower."

"I'm with you now, Cap'n. You're thinkin' if the antennas transmit enough force to move the Keep, it could break up the Ring, so better that the antennas should be carried away."

"We have plenty of spares, Captain," offered Garms, "and it wouldn't be too much work to replace them after this is over."

"Garms, you watch this reading. If the Keep starts to move, cut the power to the antenna fields, but otherwise I want the analyzer to keep recording this. Lyard, watch the ribs on that antenna over there. I'm going to try to unhook its power. If it straightens back up, we'll know it's the e-fields."

"Cap'n, I don't think you'll want to do that, 'cause you'll have to..." Lyard replied, but too late. Junker had already swung over the railing, and was hanging on to a minor handhold and foothold underneath the elevator, a full eighty feet above the floor of the main hall below. Stealing a quick glance over the railing, Lyard muttered a prayer for the safety of his captain who was wrestling one-handed with the power cables. "Tend to your duties, you old mother hen," admonished Junker, smiling up at Lyard, who immediately concentrated on the antenna in question.

"Right on, Captain!" he reported loudly. "She straightened right up as soon as the e-field cut off!" And to himself he added, "Now will you please get back on deck like sane folks."

In moments, Junker vaulted back over the railing and questioned Garms, "How are we doing?"

"No problem yet, Captain, but the force is still climbing."

With a sudden clatter, one of the antennas on the "windward" side snapped loose and crashed into a window, giving Hup quite a start. "It's OK, Hup," Junker reassured him. "Those windows are diamond coated, cut to size from the bridge windows of freighters. They'll hold."

With a sheepish grin Hup nodded his thanks, and tried to look nonchalant as two more antennas were swept away. He hoped they weren't falling in the neighborhood of his vessel. "Is it still getting stronger?" he asked.

"Some, but not much. It looks like its reaching its peak," Junker shouted above the tumult. Another antenna support broke, and the resulting tangle of debris cut a swath through six others before the whole lot pulled loose and tumbled away into the raging turbulence.

———————————————

Chapter 57

FORE TOPSAIL — DOUBLY REEFED

IT'S TOO LATE, Questor!" Norr shouted over the roaring tempest. "I've got every hand we can spare up there, and they can't bring it in! That sail's like a wild thing! We've tried everything!"

"Then bring them down before it goes! We'll just have to hope the sail or the spar give way before the mast! Go, Norr! Bring them all down!"

Shouting over the ionic howling in their comms was hopeless — only by climbing up to his shipmates on the spar could Norr make his orders known. Questor-Joss uttered a prayer for his safety as he mounted the pitching ratlines, shaking violently as the foremast itself shuddered under the screaming energy winds.

All the sails had been struck in time, save the fore topsail, doubly reefed. They had planned to keep it set unless the wind proved too strong. It had. But now, thrashing in the teeth of the gale, it defied the crew's desperate efforts to bring it in. During any given second, not one square yard of it was spared from the countless lightning bolts writhing on its surface — the entire ship was lit as if by a giant welder's arc, and Joss had to shield her eyes as she tried to make out the mate's progress up the shrouds.

By the strobing light First-Mate-Norr made his arrival on the yard-arm known, motioning for all hands to descend. He remained — to Joss's distress, although she knew she'd have done the same — until the last weary crew-member was climbing down ahead of him.

To her relief, Norr soon rejoined the Questor on deck beside the helm, now manned by two of the strongest hands.

"She's unnaturally down by the head," the mate shouted. "That one sail is trying to drive her bow right through the planar field!"

"From the look of that mast, it won't for long! Should we take an axe to the topsail sheets and hope it wouldn't carry away the forestays?"

"I think the spar'd go for sure, and who knows what it'd take with it!"

The entire ship was pitching violently fore and aft, the topsail thundering taut each time she righted herself. One more time she pitched — one time too many! With a blinding flash the sail blew out leaving a few tattered shreds bent to the yardarm. The rest disappeared into the CoreFires gale.

Immediately the ship steadied, the remnants of the sail keeping her bow foremost.

"We're favored!" Joss exulted, hugging Norr. "We still have the mast and the spar as well!" Leaning close to the pair at the helm, she shouted, "Just keep her running before the wind! We'll ride it out and bend a new topsail when it lets up!"

Norr heaved a mighty sigh. "Questor, we again owe it all to you!"

"That once, long ago, was enough for me, Norr," she replied with a laugh. "And twice is for fools! May the Goddess help us to avoid the ways of fools!"

Norr slapped her on the back. "She already has!"

—————————————

Chapter 58

JUNKER RIDES IT OUT — ELEVATOR DOWN

OUTSIDE THE GEODESIC dome, several more of the dandelion antennas were carried away in the raging gale. "That's one way to get a little more peace and quiet!" Junker yelled, triggering a laugh from his companions.

During the next few minutes, most of the other antennas gave up the ghost, singly or in groups, until only a ragged few survived. While the savage roar was almost as intense, the diminishing number of sound sources in the dome had dropped the volume considerably, and Lyard only had to raise his voice a bit to make himself heard. "Looks like you called it again, Cap'n. How's she reading?"

"A little less, Lyard," Junker replied, "and dropping slowly. Looks like it will take a good long while yet to blow itself out. In a minute I'm going to have you and Garms go down and get the Aries ready to go if need be. Don't worry about that pump, she'll do fine on the auxiliary. I'll stay here and watch the Ring and the instruments, and try to warn you if we need to move fast. Hup, what do you want to do?"

"There's a way we can go down?"

"No problem."

"Then if you're recording all this, I'm going to see if I can get to Grand Jetty before this storm does. I might be able to ease the minds of some of the folks there."

"It's all going on Crystal," Junker laughed. "You can play it back later without missing a thing." Junker put his hands on the young Pilot's shoulders. "I know you'd love to get a certified speeding ticket from the Core Patrol, but don't wreck the paint on that ship of yours."

"Hey, Junker," Hup replied, "no new dents on your tub either!"

"All right, Lyard," Junker announced with a chuckle, "you heard Captain Hup. We have our orders — no new dents on the Aries. Let's get this analyzer chained up so you can take the elevator down to make her ready."

As Garms and Lyard made the analyzer fast to four chains hanging from the top of the dome, Hup asked, "How will you get down, Junker?"

"Well, if you forget to send the elevator back up, you'd better get out of range in a hurry, because I just might chuck something down to improve your memory! All secure?"

"Secure, Cap'n," Lyard answered.

In a lower tone of voice that didn't carry over the still strident sounds of the plasma-storm, Junker added a few last instructions to Lyard and Garms. "If I see the Ring breaking up, I'll flash the tower lights three times. Wait for me if you can, but if you see any of that junk orbiting in, get the blazes out and save the Aries. Clear?"

"I understand, Cap'n," Lyard responded

"Now hear this," Junker intoned in an official manner, "all ashore that's going ashore!" whereupon he straddled a small seat on the side of the analyzer, and saluted very formally. "You may lower away, Mr. Garms."

Hup, Lyard, and Garms all stood stiffly at attention, and returned the salute. "Thanks for having us aboard, Captain," said Hup, unable to repress a smirk, and Garms ceremoniously pressed the "down" button, leaving Junker and the analyzer hanging in mid-air and mid-dome as the trio, still saluting, descended.

Suddenly there was a clink as a small bolt bounced off the elevator floor. "Don't forget to send that platform back up," Junker called from far above, "unless you want some more reminders."

———————————————

Chapter 59

ROUGH SEAS MAKE FINE SHIPMATES — BEDRAGGLED DANDELION

LYARD AND GARMS stood in the pilot house of the Aries, watching Hup's craft streaking away into the storm until it disappeared.

Garms looked thoughtfully at his companion, then looked out the window at the castle, still wrapped in the swiftly streaming eddies of glow-mist. Atop the Keep, the geodesic globe now sported only a few tattered antennas, a bedraggled dandelion after the Titan's child had poofed its seeds to the far heavens. Garms could picture his captain there, listening still to the music of the CoreFires, reluctant to miss a note no matter how fierce the passage. "He'd be right in there," he thought, "sailing with the gods, if he could."

Garms turned to Lyard, saying, "If things get bad, I don't give two nuts and a bolt what comes orbiting in, I don't care if it's violating orders, I don't care if it's endangering the Aries — I say we just keep dodging debris until he's on board or dead. That's what I say. You with me?"

Lyard smiled quietly, and for a long minute they both looked up at the sphere atop the tower, still looking as if it were hurtling through the mists at great speed. "Was there ever any question, you misassembled son of an eagle?"

Garms face crinkled up in a smile. "An old man once told me, `Rough seas make fine shipmates.'"

"Aye, to that!" answered Lyard.

––––––––––––––––––––

Chapter 60

SOMETHING SMOLDERING
— CHECKING RELIANT'S CARGO

SOMETHING WAS SMOLDERING. Shanni was sure of that. But whether in was her spirit, her body, or her mind, she couldn't say.

"It reminds me of waking up in the middle of a wild night back on Space End," she thought, "seeing clouds streaming past the full moons and feeling as if the wind were roaring right through me."

Her body was on autopilot, nearing completion of the evening inspection round in the Reliant's cargo bay, dutifully walking the orderly right-angle aisles between perfectly vertical stacks of crates and boxes.

But all the while her restive spirit was prowling the night forest of her own emotions, casting about among the scents for one that might reveal a trail, any trail.

"Or how I felt when I looked past the moons to the CoreFires high in the sky," she mused, "longing to go up there so bad I didn't even feel my bed or the covers, only the longing."

Row upon row, her mind automatically checked the lashings that kept the piled crates anchored firmly to their proper places on the deck. She sighed. Internally, nothing seemed in its proper place. Waking in the night had become the rule, not the exception. Sometimes by the hour, or even by the minute. For the past three nights she had been slipping back and forth across the border between dream and daydream, between sleep and wakefulness. "Everything's topsy-turvy.

My dreams are so real, and reality feels like a dream."

Shanni's body had been acting up as well, her thermostat varying wildly, giving rise to sudden chills and flushes. And a tingling that came and went — not the sharp pin-prickles of a re-awakening limb that's gone to sleep, but a subtle, sensual, barely perceptible feather-light tingling. It kept ambushing her unpredictably. "In fact, that's what everything's been like," she realized, "it's like the whole world's been tingling."

Shanni briefly considered the recent blow to her head as a factor, but rejected it. "Admit it," she told herself, "you know exactly what's causing it."

The cause was walking five paces in front of her, and even the sight of him quickened her emotions. Daric's long hair was stirring slightly with each stride — neither of them was wearing a helmet now that the cargo bays were again filled with air — and her eye followed the soft curve down to his shoulder. His back looked trim and fit within the sleek white Mono-mol uniform, and his movements seemed more sure and graceful than she remembered from "before", as if he had tapped into some new part of himself. It seemed to suit him very well.

She smiled at her thoughts. "Can he have changed so much, or is it me?"

Remembering the tense events separating "before" from "after", she was caught between another sudden shiver and a flush upon her cheeks.

As he walked along, Daric methodically scanned each stack of boxes and checked the tension of the tie-down straps. "She's been lagging behind and hasn't said a word for several minutes."

In his mind, he played back their sparse conversation, and pictured her body language to see if he might have said something that offended her. "She seems more distracted than anything; it could be from the blow to her head. Maybe I should slow down, but what if she just wants to be alone with her thoughts?"

His concern evaporated as Shanni suddenly pirouetted past him, dancing several paces ahead and setting him alight with unnamed desires.

With the stage presence of a mime, she turned to the left and began parodying his inspection of a tiedown strap. Shading her eyes she sternly scanned the lashing from high above her head down to the deck, bending slowly forward from the waist, legs straight, until she looked like a cross between a pixie and the number "7".

Spellbound, Daric watched.

Quickly the "7" swiveled around to examine the strap on the other side of the aisle. This time her gaze traveled upward as she straighted again into a "1". Having checked the very top, she signed an OK with a circle of her fingers, and disappeared around the corner.

Daric was still standing there with a grin on his face, pixie-be-witched, when a hand reappeared around the last tower of boxes and a finger beckoned him onwards. With an explosive laugh, he complied.

Bounding round the corner, he saw they were beginning the last row, and, to his regret, she was again a little distance ahead.

"Daric, Bosun, sir, why do we check the cargo every night?" she asked, spinning around in the aisle. "Nothing ever needs fixing."

Daric started to answer, then laughed incredulously. "Are you playing games with me?"

Shanni lowered her eyes demurely. "Me? Would I play games with you?" Then, puzzled, she added, "What games?"

"There, down at the far end of the aisle, the only thing that's needed fixing in the entire bay."

"What? I don't see anything."

"I'll show you. Third pile from the end."

When they arrived, it was Shanni's turn to be surprised: the top half of the stack of crates was shifted to the side, less than an inch. "You saw that?" she asked.

"Only after you pointed it out, as it were. And it wasn't that way last time."

"How can you be sure it wasn't stacked that way?"

"Not by bots. Never happen. No, it's shifted, so the strap must be too loose. As you said, that's what we're here for. I'll call for bots." Stepping to a comm-station in the wall, Daric pressed a few buttons and said, "Reliant, this is Bosun Daric. I need two bots at the Aft Port Cargo Bay near E-37."

Shanni leaned against the wall, watching Daric supervise the bots for the few minutes it took them to accomplish their task. "I hardly know him," she whispered aloud, thinking of his odd rapport with the robots, "or much of anything about him. I certainly don't understand him." Thoughtfully she watched him dismiss the robots who disappeared down the aisle, and tilted her head as he walked toward her. "A little more sure, somehow. I don't think it's just me, I think he's really changed. Grown, maybe."

Daric smiled as he approached. "Only one more bay to check, the quickie," he said, motioning with his head toward the airlock to her right.

As they proceeded toward the lock, her spirit, her mind, and her body all felt newly entwined with the man at her side by the powerful events that had taken place so recently beyond that door.

When she reached the door, labeled tersely "Fore Port", Shanni reached out to spin the wheel that controlled the locking pins, but Daric stopped her with a light hand on her shoulder. Turning her more toward himself, he smiled gently, and with his other hand brushed a strand of her hair away from her face. "You're not wearing your helmet." he said quietly. "Always check for air, Trainee Shanni, when you're not wearing a helmet. Even if they seldom make a mistake like that, the bots could have been in there, and air's not much of a concern to them."

Shanni looked into his eyes for a moment, and blushed. Turning back to the door, she moved her shoulder out from under his hand and almost whispered, "Thank you, Bosun, I'll remember that," immediately wishing that she had her voice under better control. She checked the indicators to the right of the door, saw that both the lock and the bay showed air, and glanced at Daric with a little smile. "It says it's safe to proceed." One corner of her mouth curled up a little more. Almost inaudibly she added, "Sounds like a fortune cookie." She spun the wheel and opened door.

Daric heard the words, standing perfectly still and holding his breath, freshly bewitched while watching her open the second door, then followed her into the last cargo bay.

———————————————

Chapter 61

WANT OF A HORSHOE NAIL
— THE WAY PEOPLE WORK

THE BAY WAS VAST, dark, almost empty. Their steps echoed in the cavernous space, and their eyes gradually adjusted to the dim red night-vision lights that speckled the almost endless ceiling. Far ahead, their goal was the row of seven dark cubes, the only cargo crates secured in the entire bay.

Shanni shivered.

Daric, who was walking beside her, had been watching her out of the corner of his eye. "Is your suit set too cold?"

"It's just that so much has happened here," she replied.

"Would you like the lights on bright?"

"No, this is much nicer. I like it this way."

Again, they lapsed into silence, two figures dwarfed by the gigantic room, the sounds of their footsteps spreading like rings in a quiet lake, only to wash back as hollow echoes returned from their myriad reflections against the distant metal walls.

From time to time, Shanni stole a glance at Daric, and eventually came to a decision, turning toward him and speaking in a low voice. "Daric, I saw some of what happened here, what you did here." She looked ahead, toward the seven identical crates, the one surrounding the fateful Crystal having been fully repaired. "I came to, I couldn't get up or speak," she continued softly, "but I saw."

"You had quite a blow on the head. Maybe you were just seeing things while you were regaining consciousness."

Shanni stopped, and for the first time that evening looked long and deeply into his eyes. Daric couldn't have moved for all the tea in China. Very quietly, she spoke. "I saw. I saw what you did."

Daric looked at her, even more, he saw her. He dropped his gaze, not daring to believe what he might have seen in her eyes. "I guess I lost my head," he mumbled. His eyes were still cast down toward the deck as his memory took him back to re-live that first moment, that awful slow-motion moment. He felt again the engulfing wave of torment, and the words were wrenched from him in a guttural whisper, "Shanni, I couldn't reach you in time, part of the crate was falling toward your head! You were too far away!"

He raised his eyes toward hers, and she caught her breath at the expression of despair etched on his face in the dim red light.

"I had a bot deflect it, but it shattered, and one piece..." He paused, tried to continue, "...then I saw you go down." He looked away across the deck. He choked out the words, "I thought you'd been..."

Shanni reached a hand toward him, her fingertips touching his chin, and gently turned his face toward her again. As his cheek came in view, a glint of red revealed the track of a tear.

"Your helmet wasn't cracked, your bubble was intact, but you were so still. I carried you to a safer place." His words came out in a rush. "You were so limp, so fragile. I laid you on the deck, and at last you stirred." He remembered that tears had so obscured his vision that he could hardly see her face, that face that might have been lost to him, and he had suddenly known how much he wanted her to be part of his world. His tears threatened to well again, and with an effort he forced them back.

He looked across the cargo bay toward the seven crates. "All that stupidity. You hurt. More stupidity on the way. It was like the world had started rolling down the wrong path. It was just too much. I had to change it."

A strange expression came over his face, reflecting some major shift within. His eyes seemed focussed on some far horizon, confronting what he saw there.

"No matter what," he reiterated, "it was wrong, and I had to change it."

As he spoke, she remembered what she had seen, his manner, that will of cold-forged steel.

"It was like I became a bot, had bot strength, even thought like a bot. The whole world became just one thing."

"No, it's not the same expression I saw then," Shanni thought. It had the same power and determination, but now there was also such a great human warmth.

"I just couldn't let them do that to you," he finished, squaring his shoulders and taking a deep breath. Slowly, he came back to the present. "I guess I went a little crazy."

Even in the dim red light, her eyes were bright. "You did that for me." It was more statement than question.

He glanced at the deck, then back into her eyes. "Yes."

They resumed walking again toward the row of dark cubes.

"It seemed very dangerous," Shanni said.

"Maybe. Who knows. But that crate coming down toward your head was more than dangerous," he said, picturing the robot's black-belt blow that saved her. "We were very lucky."

"I hope we continue to be lucky," she added fervently. "You could have been in a lot of trouble, maybe. I'd hate to see you suffer because of me."

"You bring me only happiness. It's probably all been forgotten."

Shanni took another look at his face, then turned her attention to the massive cube they had approached, the first in the row. Up close she could well believe that it weighed over a ton. She wandered down to the next one, so newly repaired, but hard as she looked, she could see no sign of their misadventures, detect no flaw on the featureless surface of the crate.

Looking up, she placed one hand on the shiny smoothness of the cover, and asked Daric, "Why do we check these so many times a day? How could they shift when they're pinned down like this?"

"They couldn't," he agreed. "Probably it's because they're so valuable."

"Are big Crystals so hard to make?" She stretched both hands up as high as she could reach, as if her palms could absorb some emanations through the shell of the crate.

"It's what's in them," he laughed.

"In them?" She turned, leaning her back on the crate that had almost cost her life.

The vision of her leaning there made Daric speechless for a second, then, with a tiny shake of his head, he turned and looked up and down the row of crates. "These seven Crystals probably hold all the data for running an entire planet for a year."

Pacing down the line, he looked at each cube as if he could see the intricate Crystals within. "Without them, everything would come to a screeching halt. Everything!" At the end of the line he turned, walking toward her again, waving his arms. "People could starve, chaos could spread, a whole world could be shut down. You remember the old tale, `The kingdom was lost, all for the want of a horse-shoe nail?'"

He stopped in front of her, torn between trying to communicate the seriousness of the situation and simply wanting to look at her upturned face. "In these crates are the whereabouts of all the nails in the kingdom for the coming year. If time runs out, the kingdom is in dire straits. That's why we'll get a bonus as long as they're delivered on time."

Shanni stood erect as suddenly as if her weight against the crate might be endangering the kingdom. Slowly she walked down the row, looking up at each cube in turn. There was awe in her voice as she said, "I had no idea!" Then she stopped, and turned toward him. "Daric, how do you know all that you do? I mean about the bots, the old ships, these giant Crystals?"

He, with a pride that came from long dedication, replied, "All my life I've been interested in how things work."

They both resumed walking beside the enigmatic dark blocks so perfectly aligned in the dim red light. A few steps behind, Daric watched Shanni's back moving in the soft red light. She seemed to be turning his answer over in her mind, examining at it from every side, as if it were a new idea. He thought of the excitement the questing had given him over the years, just the pure joy in learning, as unconscious and natural to him as the joy of running was to a cheetah.

"How things work," Shanni repeated to herself, looking back briefly over her shoulder. "All my life, I've been interested in how people work."

She walked on, while he was suddenly rooted to the spot, thunderstruck by the difference that had never occurred to him. How people work! While his feet were hurrying to catch up, his mind was reeling with the magnitude of the territory that lay behind that simple statement. Near the end cube she stopped, looking up at the smooth surface.

"A Crystal for an entire planet," she whispered thoughtfully. Turning, she asked, "Daric, may I ask you something?"

"Sure."

"Something very personal?"

It was Daric's turn to blush, which didn't show in the red light, but there was no mistaking his expression — he had been aching to be more personal. "Yes..."

"Why did you leave your home planet?"

————————————————

Chapter 62

DARIC'S SHAME — CRYSTALS WITHIN THE CUBES

DARIC FELT HIMSELF dashed from the highest heights to the deepest pit imaginable. His face flooded with the hot blood of shame, and his spirit was beset by panic.

Seeing his expression, Shanni continued hurriedly, "I saw it on your personnel record when you were showing me the data-glasses. I saw my records too. I didn't mean to, but something went wrong and there it was."

Daric had thought he couldn't be more embarrassed, but now he realized that she had known all this time about his spying on her files.

"I was flattered that you were interested enough to have looked up mine," she added.

He looked up, meeting her eyes with some difficulty. "Thanks for saying that," he said. Engulfed in a fresh wave of shame and fear now that his skeleton was out of his closet, he nevertheless forced himself to blurt out, "I was asked to leave."

"Why, Daric?"

"Because I'd been poking around in the information systems, actually on several planets."

"What's wrong with that?" she asked.

"I was poking around where people weren't supposed to. It could be dangerous if someone did the wrong thing."

She looked up at the crate, picturing the Crystal within, the slender golden probes arching to contact its translucent facets. "So, if someone goofed, it might lose some horseshoe nails?"

"Exactly. Or a lot of horseshoe nails. They're very strict because the consequences could be enormous."

"But you knew how things worked, so you could get into forbidden areas?"

Daric reddened, invisibly, thinking of the personnel records. "Yeah. And the more I used the system, the more I learned. I was very good at it, and I had the resources of entire worlds at my disposal."

"Did you ever goof?"

"No! Of course not!" His voice was indignant. "At least," he added more honestly, "I don't think I ever did. I knew more about the system than most of the people who maintain it and improve it."

"But they found out, anyway?"

Chastened, he lowered his eyes, "Yes."

Again Shanni raised her hand, as if trying to sense what lay within the huge Crystal. "Did you ever change anything?"

Daric thought of all the things he had routed to himself, all the services he had used, the countless times he had covered his tracks, even here, on the Reliant. Even the materials for his unfinished ship in a bottle. "Yes. Often."

Softly, almost tenderly, she asked one last question. "So, if you'd been them, would you have had plenty of reason to ask Daric to leave the planet?"

He looked past her to the dark cube, and the six other cubes behind it pinned so securely to the metal deck, picturing the massive Crystals within, and the data they contained. Beyond them, he pictured the well-being of a planet, and pictured someone entrusted with guarding that well-being. "They didn't even know the half of it," he admitted with a sigh. "Yes, if I had been safeguarding the planet, I would at least have sent me away."

She couldn't see the vision in his mind, but the long-held secret sadness in his eyes was apparent. "I guess that's the way things work," she said. Then she smiled and poked a finger on his nose. "But I'd have done something different."

Daric was startled out of his pit of shame. "Different?"

"It's the way people work," she countered, tweaking his nose and wrinkling up her own with an impish grin. "I'd have given you the job of safeguarding the planet! But then, I'd have cut off my nose to spite my face."

"How do you mean?"

"Think, silly. You'd still be working on that planet, and I wouldn't have met you here!"

Daric, overcome with relief, planted a quick peck on the tip of her nose, and she, just as quickly pushed him away, spun in a circle, and sauntered toward the edge of the deck where Daric had faced down Apheron. There, she stood thoughtfully looking at the closed cargo hatch, her hands clasped behind her back. Daric came to her side, and she turned to him, saying, "That was very brave, what you did here."

"I had to," he whispered, for her face was very near. "I didn't decide to. I just had to." He was drawn to her lips, but lost in her eyes. Returning his gaze all the while, her lids slowly, so slowly covered her eyes, and her face moved the tiniest bit closer. Daric wasn't quite sure how it happened, or how long it had been going on, but he knew he was kissing her with all his heart, and his heart had so much it needed to say.

How long is a kiss? How can time be counted when time has stopped? Eventually, time resumed its heartbeat, and, breathless, they slowly withdrew. Shanni's wondering eyes roamed his face, his mouth, and returned again to his eyes. Inch by inch, they drew back, until they had returned to arms length. Still looking into Daric's eyes, Shanni raised her right hand toward his face, and with a touch that wouldn't have disturbed a feather, place one finger on his lips. Even in the dim red light, she could see his lips answer with a gentle kiss to her fingertip.

Neither spoke or looked at the other on the long walk back toward the entry lock. Their footsteps loosed bat-flights of sound that fled to the farthest reaches of the metal cavern and returned in ringing chitterings that they didn't hear. Their steps passed innumerable cargo pin holes in the floor that they didn't see. The seven dark cubes behind them could have been on another world.

They themselves appeared to be suspended between two worlds, the shiny metal deck mirroring the red dotted ceiling above into a reflected ceiling below, their inverted doubles walking beneath them, meeting shoe sole to shoe sole at every step. Half way to the lock door, the couple below and the couple above simultaneously joined hands without breaking stride.

At the doorway, Daric and Shanni paused, looking back to the cargo bay, empty except for the seven cubes arrayed like some neolithic monument.

"We're done checking cargo," Daric said quietly. "Would you come to my quarters tonight?"

Shanni turned toward him, each hand taking one of his, and she gave him a long look before replying. "Daric, I'm feeling very shy with you right now, and it's not because I don't care. It's because I do. It's like making tea. The leaves are in the pot, and I need to let them steep. Trust me."

As she released his hands, Daric couldn't quite figure out why he felt a great surge of hope instead of disappointment. He looked again across the cargo bay to the seven cubes, picturing the planet Crystals within. He was surprised to find that his shame and guilt somehow seemed less planet-sized, to find his mind abuzz and his body electric, and his spirit with an awakening appetite for tomorrow.

Neither spoke, but each could feel the presence of the other. Each felt the strong stirring of emotions long untouched, the swirling currents of new ideas, the first hints of a rich new aroma. Each felt the anticipation of watching the circling tea leaves beginning to settle and wondering what the configuration would foretell.

Shanni squeezed his hand, and they turned and walked out. The echoes of their footsteps flew back and forth about the metal cavern until the last had found crannies to nest in and silence reigned. Beneath a speckled firmament of red, locked in alignment on the metallic plane, the seven perfect cubes sat alone like some absurd Cargo-henge, wordlessly demanding suitable sacrifice. The only sound was the occasional creaking of the hull as the ship wended its way.

———————————————

Chapter 63

APHERON'S ARRIVAL — LUBBERS WATCH

CALM. PURPLE. DEEPEST purple, slowly stirring like velvet fur over the ripple of feline muscles, the CoreFires moved as if it had almost wakened, then stretched, sighed, and slipped again into the magic warmth of panther-dreams. For mile after mile the gently curving cavern wound through the sleeping CoreFires, wrapped in the soft, slowly undulating folds of dark purple. Occasionally a more luminous violet upwelling suffused the surface with its glow before subsiding once more into the somnolent CoreFires night.

Far down the tunnel, so broad and easy that it had come to be called Lubber's Watch, a group of tiny man-made lights proclaimed its repetitive announcement — Ship here...Ship here...Ship here — as blatant an intrusion amid the majestic beauty of the CoreFires as a loud cheap clock ticktocking its way into a symphony hall.

Even though the ship was maintaining a good pace, it was some minutes before it had approached near enough to reveal itself as a freighter, and another minute or two before it became apparent that it was the Reliant III. Through the windows, the wide expanse of the bridge was empty, except for a lone figure standing at the wheel.

In this case, the designated "lubber" was Second Mate Stulmin, his form lit from above by dim red lights that preserved his night vision. Occasionally, he checked the array of consoles, with their miniature landscapes of orderly colored lights. Most of the time, however, his eyes were scanning the cavern ahead, his practiced fingers slowly passing the spokes of the wheel from hand to hand in response to the gentle bends of the CoreFires walls. For a moment he thought he saw a flash of blue, way ahead, but when he blinked his eyes it was gone. At least another minute passed before he realized that his eyes hadn't been playing tricks on him — much stronger this time, a blue point of light in the distance blipped in the triple strobe pattern reserved for the Core Patrol.

"Reliant, mike," Stulmin called to the voice response system, which lowered the comm mike from the ceiling above his head. The Patrol ship was approaching very rapidly, and as it neared it blinked its lights twice, and twice again. "Reliant, blink docking lights three times. Route mike to captain." As the Patrol craft matched speed just off the Reliant's port bow, Stulmin took the mike in hand. "Sorry to wake you, Captain, but Apheron's arrived."

"Be right there," came the muffled reply.

In a few moments a doorway opened in the aft wall of the bridge, and Captain Volnath emerged, still tying his robe. Even with his years of practice at waking instantly, he was hard put to get his body moving during the wee hours when the human organism is at its lowest ebb. With a frown and an audible wheeze he approached the wheel, slippers slapping on the deck. "I'll take her, Stulmin," he said, clearing his throat and squinting toward the windows. "You set up the optical link." Soon his vision cleared, and he assessed himself as more or less fully operational. "Leave it to Apheron," he grumbled, "to be flapping about during the hours of werewolves and vampires."

Stulmin fetched the high-security transceiver from a locker, and before long had it set up on its tripod. Aiming it at the pin-point of blue light in Apheron's window, he was rewarded by a "Signal Acquired" readout. "It's patched through to comm, Captain."

Bringing the mike to his mouth, the captain spoke. "Volnath here. Good to see you so bright and early!"

Apheron's unmistakable voice replied over the ship's comm, "Good morning, Captain Volnath. Some business is best consummated in private, so I took the liberty of having the head-waiter seat us in a less crowded part of the restaurant. I have excellent news."

"I'm all ears," Volnath replied.

"Events have conspired to provide me with a rare opportunity to assure that we'll be uninterrupted during our long-awaited harvesting. There was a strong glowmist storm near Dutchman's Gorge."

Volnath was immediately concerned. "Is it headed this way?"

"Ease your mind, my dear Captain, it blew itself out a little past Grand Jetty. And to ease your mind further, it is the key to my being able to reserve the grand ballroom, as it were, exclusively for our private use."

Carefully turning the mike off, Volnath growled to Stulmin, "Curse his hide, he gives me the creeps when he talks like that, petting himself about how clever he is. Sometime I'd like to see him left standing at the dock after his ship departed, while he was still getting around to the point." Turning the mike back on, he continued, "I don't follow you, Apheron."

"Oh, but you will, my esteemed Captain, and you'll find that you have been well provided for. Here is how my plan unfolds. Today, after dawn, I will spread word that the CoreFires is showing signs of another instability in Grand Caverns, so for safety reasons, the Core Patrol is prohibiting travel there for twenty four hours. Inbound traffic will be held at Grand Jetty, and outbound at Dutchman's."

"What about the Gappers? This section's crawling with them."

"Quite right, Captain. In this instance we are most concerned for their safety as well, so Grand Caverns is forbidden to all. Anyone found between Grand Jetty and the Maze will be subject to arrest, and moreover, while in custody, their vessels would probably have to undergo a safety inspection and re-certification at Two Forks. Regrettably, a most time consuming process."

"That ought to hit them where they live," Volnath agreed with an evil chuckle. "You do know your business, Apheron."

"Never forget that, my trustworthy colleague, and we shall get along famously. The next phase is simple: you will proceed on schedule toward Grand Caverns, and when you reach Grand Jetty, they will of course inform you of the travel prohibition. You will reply that you have a top-priority cargo, and are exempt, giving them my authorization number, which will be A377.

"A377," Volnath repeated.

"Correct. Once past Grand Jetty, you will maintain absolute comm silence — I emphasize absolute silence, Volnath."

Volnath reddened, and a vein stood out prominently on his neck. "I heard you, Apheron."

"Good." Apheron's tone was once again oily. "You'll proceed to the far end of Grand Caverns, a little before the Maze. I'll send you the coordinates now."

Stulmin checked the top of the optical link. "Got 'em, Captain."

"Verified," said Volnath.

"Excellent. It's that simple! You'll stop at that location, and we'll begin the transfer."

"Not until Kegler and I are on board your ship!" Volnath interrupted. "That was our agreement! Nothing moves until Kegler and I are on board! Then Stulmin transfers cargo, and we bring Stulmin across."

"Captain, Captain, calm yourself. A mere omission on my part, I assure you, a slight verbal simplification. That of course is our agreement, and I wouldn't dream of beginning transfer before you and Mate Kegler were safely on board."

Volnath killed the mike again, and looked at Stulmin, putting his hands together in a pious gesture. "Wouldn't have occurred to him in a thousand years I'll bet. After just telling us never to forget how well he knows his business? He must take me for a fool!"

"When our little party's over," Apheron continued, "we depart with our baubles though the Maze. From here on, everything runs like clockwork." Volnath winced at the phrase. "After I leave here, we'll have no further communication until you see me at Grand Caverns."

"What if you're late?"

"You'll wait — I'll have insured that there will be no intruders. But, as you know, Volnath," Apheron's voice became more intimate, and Volnath could picture him leaning closer to the mike, "I'm never late."

"The Reliant will be on time," Volnath replied to the implication, "you have my word on it."

"And I respect your word, my good Captain Volnath, as I would respect the word of an honest man. Honor among thieves, eh? Then all is in readiness, is it not?"

"The plan is simple enough, Apheron; we'll do our part."

"I'm sure you will. There is one other thing you can do for me, Captain." Volnath winced as he pictured Apheron's mouth so close to the microphone, for that amplified breathy whisper seemed to fill the hundred foot width of the Reliant's bridge as it poured from the ceiling speakers. "A little favor, a persssonal matter." The word hissed as if from a large snake coiling around the ship — Apheron's lips must have been almost brushing the mike.

Volnath sorely wished he could somehow turn down the ceiling speakers, "And what might that be?"

Could you arrange for the bosun and the girl to be in the engine room?"

"Easily," Volnath replied, "In fact, that's where we kept them out of the way during the last time we talked to you."

"Excellent," the echoing voice gloated. "Then, do so! When we drive the Reliant into the CoreFires, I'll savor the sight of the engines being pulled right out of that engine room."

With a shudder, Volnath pulled the robe more tightly about him. "Unless your cruiser's developed a sudden immunity to CoreFires, you could share their fate."

"Admittedly a delicate balance, being just close enough to see everything, but not so close as to become part of the festivities. I'll be sure to reserve the best seat. Is all agreed, then?"

"I'm sure you meant to say `we'", corrected Volnath sardonically. "Yes, everything's clear."

"Until we meet again."

"Until Day's End. Volnath out."

Stulmin dismantled and stowed the optical link, and resumed his post at the wheel.

Volnath took a deep breath, stretched, yawned, and padded back toward the door to his quarters. Over his shoulder he called, "Steady as she goes, Stulmin," before closing the door.

Stulmin peered ahead at the rapidly diminishing flare of the Patrol cruiser's engines until they disappeared around a far bend. Once again his fingers automatically passed the familiar wooden spokes of the big wheel from hand to hand as he threaded the Reliant along the tunnel through the dark purple CoreFires. "Steady as she goes," he repeated softly to himself, then added grimly, "the things we do to make a living."

———————————

In the Gap-walls about Dutchman's the CoreFires dawn was exceptionally exquisite, exceptionally bold. Unfolding in a sweeping display of contrasts, it took the breath away. Night colors had only partially relinquished the field this morning, still charging across great areas in stampeding masses of blacks and steely greys, like the dark armies that maneuver within the undersides of thunderheads on the move. Arrayed against their might, the newly risen colors of Firedawn blazed forth in a defiant progression of reds and oranges augmented by reinforcements of incandescent gold. Double back as they might, the marauding hordes of grey failed to vanquish the gold-clad forces from the battleground, for as soon as a fiery outpost was overwhelmed fresh conflagrations arose behind them, turning pursuer into pursued. And so the galloping armies continued to surge and sally across the face of the CoreFires, providing a morning of unusual beauty and contrast.

Silhouetted against this swirling background of gold and grey, the village of Dutchman's was like a dew-bejeweled spiderweb somehow floating in mid-sky. The thread-thin gangways strung between the motley scattering of metal buildings flashed like strands of spun gold, and the scrap-fashioned abodes this morning appeared to be decorated with sparkling rubies and sapphires set by the genius of a Gap dwelling Cellinni bent on creating the ultimate offering for his prince and patron.

Along the spidery walkways there were many villagers up and about, and many of those had paused to watch the magnificent Firedawn. From some of the more distant junk-hovels-turned-jewels that floated about Dutchman's like a constellation, residents coming in aboard their skiffs also paused to enjoy the grandeur of the morning. Whether on skiffs or gangways, whenever they resumed their way, the villagers were converging on that dilapidated inn, the POSH.

———————————

Chapter 64

MORNING TALES — ABOVE THE POSH

THE COREFIRES LIGHT streaming through the window of a small room in the back of the POSH melted from gray to gold. The soothing music coming from a Crystal player contrasted sharply with a sudden intake of breath and a suppressed gasp of pain from a woman leaning forward in her chair with her bio-suit pulled down around her waist. The woman standing over her was Cirra, dressed in her purple and red Mono-mol.

"Stings, doesn't it," said Cirra sympathetically as she daubed a healing solution on some cuts and abrasions scattered on the woman's back. "But they'll heal quickly and completely. There. It's done, Felicita."

"I was so stupid, Cirra! I store things in the loft, and for months I've known that ladder was on its last legs."

Cirra moved to help her get the suit closed up without aggravating the woman's more serious injury. "Your wrist will take longer to heal. It's just a sprain, but it'll be pretty sore for a few days, and then it'll take a while for the stiffness to go away. You did everything right." Cirra finished closing the suit and patted Felicita on the shoulder.

"Except getting injured in the first place, but I'm sure lucky my wrist wasn't broken. That would've really slowed me down." Felicita gathered up her things while Cirra turned off the Crystal player. "Thanks, Cirra, I don't know what we'd do without you. You'd better get on upstairs now. You've spent more than enough time on me, and it must be getting close to time to light the Firesphere."

"I've still got plenty of time, thanks." Cirra held the door open as they emerged into the main room of the POSH. "Come back day after tomorrow, and I'll make sure everything's going as it should."

A group of a dozen villagers was milling around the tavern, "hello"ing and "what's new"ing, and every minute or so a few more came in through the front door, doffing their helmets, replacing those wandering off to climb the steep stairs at the side of the hall. Felicita joined the group, replying to a flurry of inquiries about her wrist with cautions not to slap her on the back.

Meanwhile, Cirra went over to the comm shack, calling, "OK, Salty, it'll be just a few minutes. I'm going up now."

"Thanks, Cirra," he replied, putting his headset down on the table. From a locker beneath his desk, he removed a wad of cables and small metal boxes that looked even more makeshift than the rest of the equipment in the room. Untangling lines as he went, he connected them to various pieces of equipment until the space above his desk was fairly festooned with a tangle of wires. When he was down to one last cable to connect, he stood up on his chair trying to push the jack on the end into a tiny hole in the ceiling, but try as he might, the cable wouldn't quite reach.

"Here, I've got it," came the welcome voice of Otitius from below. "This part's just caught under the corner of your desk. There! Try it again."

Again on tiptoes, Salty tried to make the last connection. "Perfect! Thanks, Otitius. I have to patch it through," he explained, getting down off the chair, "because there's at least a couple of ships due this morning." Salty picked up his headset, took a sign from a drawer, and as they were leaving the room hung it from one of the cables swinging over his desk.

"I'M UPSTAIRS," it announced succinctly.

When they returned to the main room, everyone had left except for a few late-comers who went straight from the front door to the stairway after calling out a brief, "Mornin', Salty. Mornin', Otitius."

The latter quickly completed his last chores behind the two-ton bar, gave its beloved surface one last wipe, then placed a sign on it that showed how verbose and loquacious Salty's had been, covering all the key concepts with half as many words — to wit: "UPSTAIRS".

"After you," said Salty to his friend at the foot of the stairs.

Topping the stairs was like stepping into another world. The scent of warm spices filled the air. A symphony of worldly sounds was heard over the low babble of quiet conversation — bird calls and animal cries, the susurration of winds through trees and the tumbling surfs of seas.

The Hall of Tales was as large as the tavern below, but seemed limitless, as no walls could be seen. Instead, the space was enclosed by ephemeral waves of wafting color, billowing veils of shifting iridescent rainbow hues.

Had an emperor of old ever seen Lumiveil, as it had come to be called, he'd have ceded a province for a few yards of the magical material. Had it been created for its beauty alone, it would have graced the architecture of planets throughout the Galaxy. But its molecular mesh, a sieve of precisely spaced holes, had been designed for the most lowly of utilitarian functions — it was folded in hundred acre lots in the filters that recycled biological wastes in large spaceships — an association far too organic for the refined esthetics of the starry worlds.

Here in the Gaps, however, retrieved from the scrap pile, its other qualities reigned in stunning display: transparent due to the holes, liquidly supple and almost weightless as only materials of molecular thickness can be (although Lumiveil was technically grown as one giant molecule), colored with the purity of a sun-bending dewdrop. In essence, the precisely spaced holes created diffraction grating by the acre, so the pure spectral colors of the prism flashed and rippled endlessly through its surface in moving moire patterns. When hung in dozens of layers, as in this case, the layers interacted, stereoscopically sending the colors flowing off into the distance or bringing them streaming back.

Stepping into the Hall of Tales, then, was like stepping into a world where the perimeter of the human meeting ground was encircled by a host of rainbow colored auroras, sometimes dancing slowly in place, sometimes gathering their moire robes about them to wander afar on their own business, only to think better of it and waft their willowy way back to be near the humans lest they miss something interesting, or possibly even magical.

Close by the top of the stairs, Li-Tharm was presiding over the source of the rich incense-like bouquet that permeated the air, a hemisphere filled with the ubiquitous hot Earthtea so beloved by Gap dwellers. No matter how scarce any other resource might become, somehow there always seemed to be solace readily available to one and all in this drink that had become a symbol of hospitality. As each villager topped the stairs, Li-Tharm handed her or him a cup, then dipped her ladle into the steaming brew and poured a fragrant stream into the waiting vessel.

When it was Salty's turn, he tucked the headset under his arm, and inhaled deeply as the cup began to warm his hands. The floor was covered with cushions, many with backrests for the convenience of those so inclined, and most of the cushions were now covered by people. Salty made his way to the back of the hall, where a cushion was reserved for him beside a small outlet mounted in the floor. Settling himself, he fished a couple of small boxes out of his pocket, connected them to the headset, and jacked his cable into the floor. A quick check of the equipment confirmed that he could now attend to any communication duties with the quietest whispers and not disrupt the Morning Tales. His responsibilities attended to, Salty sipped his Earthtea with a contented sigh, and quietly conversed with his neighbors.

Li-Tharm, having no new customers, hooked the ladle over the edge of the big cauldron for anyone wishing to help themselves, and found her own place on the floor. At this, the low hubbub of conversation quickly subsided, and Otitius stepped to the front of the hall where the Lumiveils hung in deep profusion.

Standing beside a four foot glass globe perched on three junk-sculpture lion's feet, he spoke. "Welcome to Morning Tales. During intermission this morning, Esslon will share a way she has found to use an E4 reflex starter as a two way converter. For those interested, she'll be near the top of the stairs. And following tales, Saima and Williger from Grand Jetty will conduct a workshop in Mono-mol." The lights in the hall began to dim as Otitius concluded, "Today's Old Tale will be `The Overlord's Three Lessons.' The New Tale is `Morley and the

Maze.'" The illusion of an immense space grew overpowering as the lights dimmed to deep blue, and the wavering auroras shimmered in turquoise and violet, swaying in otherworldly rhythms. Otitius placed his hand on the top of the glass sphere, and at its bottom a single ember began to glow. "Welcome to Morning Tales," he repeated, then he, too, found a cushion on the floor.

"We welcome the spirits of our past, and the spirits of our future," a rich voice began, and the figure of the woman emerged from the veils, still dark behind the flaring brilliance of the Firesphere. "We ask them to join us here in council, that we may learn our history, and what history we would write for those to come." She stepped forward placing her hands over the Orb of Fire. Her hair was long and loose, her robes of gossamer white, her voice resonant and musical. It was Cirra and it wasn't, for now she was village Storyteller. The flames within the glass globe lit the beauty of her form and face, and rippled on upward as two tall incandescent wraiths flanking her on either side. "We would learn to see ourselves, who we've been, and who we would become. Wisdom, Grace, and Beauty are all about us. Join us here, spirits, that we may learn to see. And learn to be."

———————————————

Chapter 65

WHERE IS EVERYBODY?
— APPOINTMENT IN THE GORGE

DOWNSTAIRS, APHERON STRODE through the front door of the POSH. Glaring about the deserted tavern he growled, "Where is everybody?"

From the shadows behind the bar, a helmeted duo emerged — the hulking form of Ulnar followed by the diminutive figure of Cribble. Ulnar put a finger to his lips and pointed toward the ceiling, while Cribble whined, "You're late."

"Everyone's late this morning," Apheron fumed, "and everything is taking longer than it should. Those fools at Grand Jetty dawdle like they're senile."

Again, Ulnar put his finger to his lips. "Everybody's upstairs."

"We're missing Morning Tales," Cribble complained.

"Let's be quick, then," Apheron said, this time more quietly. "Ulnar, you and Cribble will leave here in separate vessels taking different routes, and meet me at the small cul-de-sac in the CoreFires near this end of Dutchman's Gorge — I'll be there in two hours on my way back from Littlebend."

"We got to leave soon to make it," warned Ulnar.

"We'd miss all of Morning Tales!" bemoaned Cribble.

Ignoring Cribble, Apheron continued, "Cribble's to bring a comm record Crystal from Dutchman's comm shack..."

"Which one?" interrupted Cribble.

Taking a deep breath, Apheron silently counted to three. "Any one."

Cribble nodded rapidly with a sudden expression of comprehension, and left the group, scuttling into Salty's comm shack. In moments he returned, handing Apheron a Crystal, saying, "Now we don't have to miss the story telling!"

"For the love of…" Apheron exploded in a hoarse whisper, trying to give Cribble back the Crystal, which Cribble was adamantly refusing to accept, jamming his hands in his pockets. At the sound of hurried footsteps approaching on the gangway outside, Apheron thrust the Crystal at Ulnar, who quickly hid it in a pocket. Ulnar then pulled the other two back into the shadows behind the bar, where they tensely watched a latecomer dash in through the front door and up the stairs without so much as a glance at the rest of the room.

"Sorry, boss," whispered Ulnar, releasing Apheron's arm, "he'd have seen us."

"Quite all right, Ulnar," the major whispered, unconsciously brushing off his Core Patrol uniform. "This has continued far too long, and it would be far too awkward if we were seen together. We meet in two hours. If Cribble isn't there you lose your share."

"We'll be there," whispered Ulnar, grabbing Cribble by the collar and quick-marching him toward the back door. On the way, he fetched the comm shack Crystal from his pocket, shook it in front of Cribble's face, and then jammed it into Cribble's pocket. At the back door, Ulnar released the smaller man, turned back toward Apheron with an "everything's under control" expression, then placed a big boot on Cribble's backside and shoved him out the door.

"Why idiots? Why must I always work with idiots?" In frustration Apheron pounded his fist on the bar, which he immediately knew was a mistake — he might just as effectively have pounded his fist on two tons of concrete. Flexing his stinging hand, he glared at the one-word sign, and strode quickly toward the stairs.

————————————

Chapter 66

HALL OF TALES — INTERRUPTED

UPSTAIRS, IN THE Hall of Tales, the rapt audience was no longer above the POSH, or even in the village — Cirra's skills had carried them far away in time, space, and imagination, into the Court of the Overlord.

And it was no longer Cirra performing before them, or even the TaleTeller — it was the fearsome Overlord himself they saw pacing across the throne room in a fury.

Whirling suddenly, the figure sent billows of spectral scarlet surging up the Lumiveils. Hair flying, her gossamer robes trailing behind like a silken banner, Cirra strode across the "stage", her manner at once imperious, petulant, threatening, every inch the ruler, captive of his own excessive power. Wheeling again she stopped behind the Firesphere, placing both hands on the glass globe.

Slowly her hands caressed the glass surface, slowly one hand began to creep forward spider-like, and her audience cringed, feeling what it was like to be subject to that unrestrained and terrible power. Even more slowly, she leaned forward, bringing her face close over the hot light of the fire within the sphere. "You what!" she demanded.

Wheeling again, she instantly became another character in the tale, the cowering Chamberlain, shrinking before the wrath of his master, fearing to answer, compelled to answer, but the Chamberlain's reply was lost in a fast-growing confusion spreading from the top of the stairs. It was Apheron.

Apheron had pictured himself striding commandingly up to the Firesphere and taking charge of the meeting, but instead found himself struggling to maintain his balance, tripping and lurching among the closely packed villagers seated on the floor.

Leaving a wake of indignation, he staggered to the front of the group amid a rising grumble of surprisingly intense hostility, and momentarily felt a primal fear of falling down among the jostling bodies at his feet.

Cirra stepped forward, and to his mortification, offered him a steadying hand.

Quieting the assembly with a gesture, she motioned for the lights to be brought up. "Major Apheron. I'm sure the Core Patrol wouldn't have interrupted our Morning Tales unless it were something vitally important. What do you have to tell us?"

Still facing Cirra as he emerged from the press of the crowd, he felt subtly out-maneuvered without knowing on what front. Glowering in his discomfiture, he permitted himself what he hoped was a humiliatingly lascivious look at her body before answering, "The Core Patrol needs to notify everyone of a matter vitally concerning their safety."

Cirra ignored the insult as beneath her contempt. "What a welcome change, Major, to have the Core Patrol concerning itself with the likes of us." Turning to the crowd, she announced, "Major Apheron has something to tell us concerning our safety. Please give him your attention."

"The CoreFires in Grand Caverns is showing signs of instability reminiscent of the recent storm in this region," Apheron began, "so in the interest of everyone's safety, the Core Patrol is placing Grand Caverns off limits to everyone for twenty-four hours. Is your comm-operator present?"

"I'm here," called Salty from the back of the room.

"Good. Inbound traffic is being held at Grand Jetty, and that includes the two ships you were expecting this morning. Outbound ships will wait here at Dutchman's, unless of course they decide to heave to at Littlebend before coming through the Gorge. This ban also applies to all small craft and local traffic. This means everyone."

The general mutter of resentment was growing loud enough that Cirra motioned again for quiet.

Apheron also had pictured himself as the smooth diplomatic voice of authority, concealing the Core Patrol's iron fist of power within the extended silken glove, but as he looked at this ragtag sea of rebellious faces, his chess-master persona was suddenly drowned in his flooding frustrations.

"To enforce this ban," he continued, "anyone found between Grand Jetty and the Maze will be taken in custody, and their vessels will undergo a safety inspection and lengthy re-certification at Two Forks." Scanning the unruly faces as if daring someone to challenge his proclamation, he concluded, "The ban expires at daybreak tomorrow."

Knowing it had gone badly, knowing he had violated his own plan, Apheron gave a curt nod to Cirra and turned toward the stairs. Head down, cheeks burning, he marched quickly as people moved aside to give him a clear path. Even so, in passing he bumped the hemisphere of Earthtea, flipping the ladle out which clattered onto the floor as he quickly descended the stairs.

Li-Tharm rose to steady the sloshing cauldron, and Otitius handed her the ladle, which she held on high for all to see.

"We'll take a short break," Cirra announced. "I'm sure many of us could use a refreshing cup of Earthtea. If it's agreeable to Esslon...?" Cirra paused until she saw a verifying nod in the audience, "...she'll be at the top of the stairs with her "how to" tips. I promise you all that this interruption won't become a permanent addition to the Overlord's Tale. We'll continue in a few minutes."

The ensuing laughter broke some of the tension, and many folks rose to join a line that was swiftly turning empty cups into fragrant hand – and throat-warming sources of satisfaction. From person to person, reactions and opinions were received, examined, and passed on, gradually taking on the sensual smoothness of well fingered coins.

One idea seemed to be universally affirmed — any event was much improved when accompanied by a good hearty cup of Earthtea.

————————————

Chapter 67

IN HALLS OF RELIANT — WHICH WAY?

DARIC PAUSED AT the intersection of two metal passageways deep within the Reliant. It was early morning, although everything in sight, of course, looked exactly as it did at any other time of day. Except maybe today.

To Daric, with Shanni at his side, nothing looked familiar this morning, as if somebody had snuck in during the middle of the night and subtly rearranged everything in his world. Navigating the maze of passageways throughout the ship had become second nature to him, and yet, facing the choices before him, he felt like whoever had been playing with the corridors last night had forgotten to put them back.

Smiling at the memory of her own encounter with the frightening intersection during her first few minutes on board, Shanni asked, "Lost? You?" The echoes of her voice returned from the four directions, augmented by the usual pops and creaks of a space freighter in motion.

Daric looked down the different passages, only subtly differing in the masses of orderly metal pipes and tubes running in the space above their heads. "For a moment, everything looked different," he said, a little wonder in his voice. "It's like when you occasionally get turned around, and the scene is the same but your expectations are off by ninety degrees. Shanni, I think you've spun my compass!"

She laughed, and the trill multiplied metallically. "I'm honored," she replied with a curtsy.

A little sheepishly, Daric admitted, "I'm actually not sure where we are."

"Well, I'm no help," she responded, "I haven't been watching where we're going, I've just been watching you."

Daric's breath stopped for a moment at that thought, and he could feel his ears turning pink. "I don't know if we turn at this one or the next one. What's your guess?"

"It's only an intuition, but I'd say the next one."

"The next one it is," he replied, "or at least it's the next one that we'll try." They walked on, the clanging of their footsteps preceding them. Daric was mindlessly watching the pipes changing lanes overhead as they went, no more attending to navigation than before. The rest of his mind was busy buzzing from thought to thought, memory to memory, sipping nectar from something Shanni had said this morning, or something else they did yesterday. He stole a quick glance, and his mind flew back and forth between the shape of her nose and the arch of her eyebrow.

"Here we are," she laughed as he started to walk right on by the next intersection.

He saw that her intuition had been correct. "I'm glad one of us still knows her way around."

Shanni dropped her eyes, and said shyly, "I'm not too sure it's me."

Daric tried to focus his mind on business. They had just met to start the "dawn round", the first inspection tour of the day, and he was keeper of the itinerary. "First, our most precious cargo, then you'll check the manifest for the opposite bay. There are no stops today, but there might be a drop-off scheduled for tomorrow. If that's the case, we should split out that cargo and make it ready for unloading."

They had arrived at the lock labeled "Fore Port", and Shanni pointedly checked the readouts for air before spinning the wheels that opened the doors. With a tiny smile, she said, "It still says it's safe to proceed."

Safe? Maybe. But to Daric and Shanni the big cargo bay was charged with emotion. Every step of their long walk across the deck seemed newly daring, and both were studiously formal and silent, but intensely aware of each other. Suddenly Daric paused in mid-stride, for just a split second, but the discontinuity jolted Shanni. She glanced at his face, and was surprised to see something in his expression that cautioned her to keep moving as if nothing had happened.

A little bit later she again looked his direction, and Daric in turn glanced ever so briefly at the ceiling to his right.

Puzzled, Shanni watched the deck ahead of her feet, and then the answer hit her. She waited a bit more before confirming her suspicion — Daric had glanced at one of the surveillance cameras, and the camera was tracking their progress.

She shivered at the intrusion into the mood of her morning, but also felt even closer to Daric, in a kind of "us" and "them" way. The implied eye behind the camera felt to her a little ominous, but, she thought, what was that compared to the abdominal butterflies of "us" that were already making this day unique in her life?

She continued walking, and with a momentary sidelong glance assured him silently that she had seen and understood.

When they reached the first cube she asked, "Daric, how do we know that the Crystal is still inside?"

He laughed. "Apart from the difficulty of moving it, and the question of where you'd move it to, the pallet that's pinning it into the deck is actually the mount for the Crystal itself. It would take a small army of skilled technicians a couple of months to separate them."

They progressed down the line, seeing no change in the precious cargo, nor did they expect to see any. Shanni noticed that the camera was still following their progress. When they reached the last cube, Shanni was preparing to turn back when Daric froze as if stunned.

"What?" she asked, genuinely concerned.

"That's strange!" he exclaimed. "Very strange. Someone's moved the cargo hoist!"

Shanni looked down to the far end of the huge cargo bay. The big gantry containing the telescoping sections of the cargo hoist was parked a short distance from the far wall. "It's moved?"

"Since we checked last night. It's supposed to be parked against the wall. Let's have a closer look." As they walked toward the far end of the bay, beyond the range of the surveillance camera, Daric noted that a new camera took up the job of tracking their movements.

The closer they got to the cargo hoist, the larger Shanni realized it really was. Extending almost the full width of the cargo bay, it also reached almost to the ceiling. Massive wheels allowed it to travel fore and aft along the length of the bay, and true to Daric's words, it was parked a short distance, some thirty feet, from the wall.

"Who, and why?" Daric was thinking as he directed their path toward a ladder hung from a small semi-open cabin at the inboard portion of the device. He glanced at a terminal station on the wall of the cargo bay. "I could find out by breaking into the Reliant's data system but without the bots and boxes around the terminal I'd be in plain sight." Just as they reached the base of the ladder he knew what to do.

"I'll teach you how to properly park a cargo hoist," he said cheerily, placing both hands around her waist from behind, and his head close to her ear. Quickly he whispered, "When we get in the cab talk normally, but we'll whisper in short bursts," then he lifted her so she could reach the first rungs of the iron ladder. His hands were tingling from the feeling of holding her slender waist as he jumped up to catch the first rungs and follow her up the ladder.

Shanni was impressed with the view from the control cab high above the deck. Just overhead the structural gridwork of the telescoping hoist sections stretched forward across the width of the cargo bay, like a collapsible bridge obviously capable of supporting great weight. The gantry supporting the hoist was even more massive, looking like bridge piers mounted on many wheels. She marveled that all of this could be controlled by one person from the few control panels in the cab. "Did it roll during the night?" Shanni asked as Daric joined her.

"That's supposed to be impossible," he answered. "Here, sit down," he said, doing the same, "and I'll show you what's what. Once I've logged in, don't touch anything on that panel to your right under any circumstances, OK?"

"Right."

"First I'll log in, don't worry about the details. Ooops. I must have done something wrong. I'll have to start over." He gave her a disarming grin, but his eyes directed hers to a small readout as he pushed buttons in rapid combinations. "Last Command," it said, then, "Logout Stulmin," then, "Shutdown Motors".

Shanni understood that he was somehow stepping backwards through a list of previous commands, which were now coming too fast to make any sense to her. For additional cover, she gestured toward the forbidden panel, bringing her fingers close to the controls, and asking with a twinkle, "Don't touch these?"

Daric had to laugh in spite of himself. "Right! You learn fast." He himself had been learning fast, having stepped through the entire previous session. He whispered, "It was Stulmin. He just got in and checked that it was working, then shut it down. He forgot to re-park it." Aloud he said, "OK, I'm logged in. This is the transverse lever. Put your hand on it."

Shanni whispered, "Was he trying to move a Crystal?" and, aloud, she asked, "This one?"

"That's it." Quietly he added, "No, he didn't have the hoist pick up anything. He just tried it out and left." Daric placed his hand over hers and moved the lever a little to the side. In answer, the entire gantry moved five feet to the left and stopped. Daric turned to her in spite of everything, giving in to the feeling of his hand covering hers. His eyes closed as with infinite tenderness he clasped her hand tighter.

Shanni's eyes closed too, as she felt herself completely carried away by the simple pressure of his hand enclosing hers, and for a long minute neither spoke. Then Shanni felt the brush of his lips on her eyelids, first one, then the other, and she thought she might faint. Inadvertently, her hand moved the lever sightly to the right, and a hundred tons of structural steel moved and stopped, bringing her wide-eyed back to reality. "Wow!" she exclaimed. "Talk about hazardous working conditions!"

Both leaned back in the relief of laughter.

"Think you can park it against the wall?" Daric asked.

"I can try!" she answered, adding in a whisper, "Why Stulmin? I thought that was your job."

"OK, it's all yours. I'll just sit back and watch." He leaned back, and added under his breath, "It is."

Shanni felt a cold chill of unknown menace, and for just a moment met his eyes with an expression of care and concern.

Daric briefly squeezed her hand. His eyes answered hers, but his voice just said, "It's OK, Go ahead. I dare you to show me that you know how to park."

Shanni sat up straight in her chair, rubbed her palms together, placed one hand on the lever, and looked down off the edge judging the distance between the massive machine and the end of the cargo bay. Then, with a crooked little responding-to-a-challenge grin crinkling the corners of her eyes, in one smooth motion she parked a hundred tons of gantry less than a yard from the wall. Daric leaned back and laughed.

————————————————

Chapter 68

GANTRY PARKING — OVER SEEN

STULMIN, SLEEPILY WATCHING the surveillance monitor, shot awake and almost fell over backwards at the boldness of Shanni's maneuver. He glanced over his shoulder at the back of Captain Volnath standing at the wheel, silhouetted against the grey and gold CoreFires, and unconcernedly passing the spokes from hand to hand. Looking back at the monitor, Stulmin was slack-jawed with a combination of disbelief at Shanni's skill, and relief at her success.

"They up to anything, Stulmin?" Volnath queried over his shoulder.

"If you only knew!" thought Stulmin, but he also thought of the chewing out he would get if the captain found out he had forgotten to park the cargo hoist. "Nothing, Captain," he called out, "except the usual. Checking the cargo and a little smooching."

"Keep an eye on them, Stulmin," the captain growled.

Stulmin dutifully turned back to the monitor, propping his head up with his hands and manfully trying to keep his eyelids above half-mast. "Aye, Captain," he replied.

————————————

Chapter 69

CREATING AN ALIBI — IN DUTCHMAN'S GORGE

YOU CHEATED. YOU disobeyed orders!" Cribble complained.

"You just keep that punt moving," Ulnar grunted, accelerating his own open space-skiff enough to bump Cribble's smaller craft from behind.

"Hey!" Cribble waved his arms wildly, trying to keep his balance. "What'd you do that for? I'm moving, I'm moving," he complained. However, when he got his hand back on the tiller, he did surreptitiously advance the throttle a notch. "You're the one who disobeyed orders; the major said take two separate vessels..."

"We're in two separate vessels," Ulnar countered.

"...on two different routes. You followed me!"

"We left the POSH separately; that's two separate routes," Ulnar proclaimed, "and you better keep your mouth shut about it if you know what's good for you. What I did afterwards was see you got here and didn't sneak back for Morning Tales, that's what."

"I wasn't going to sneak back!"

"Then how come you was turning around when I caught you?"

"I wasn't turning around. Why would I turn around? I was just... I just dozed off for a minute and got off course."

"Yeah! So I come along to keep you awake!" Ulnar sped up his skiff and bumped Cribble's craft again. "You think you can stay awake now?"

"I'm awake!"

"Well, if you're so awake, here's where we turn. I'm damned if I know why the major risks taking his fancy Core Patrol ship into such a narrow hole just to talk to us. Get a move on, Cribble. We'd better be in there when he shows up!"

High up, and on the outside of a bend, the side cavern in the Core-Fires was small in comparison to Dutchman's Gorge. Coming as it did in the midst of a particularly twisty section, it was normally inconspic-uous, and today almost invisible among the wildly contrasting swirls of gold and grey that were racing along the surface of the nebula. Ulnar was right that the opening would be a dangerously snug fit for Apheron's cruiser, however it still dwarfed the two open spacecraft and their space-suited occupants.

"Gloomy as a crypt," grumbled Ulnar, as they turned into the side tunnel just as the surrounding CoreFires changed to a dark steely grey. "Come on, Cribble, get that thing moving! If the major comes around the bend while we're in this narrow entrance he's likely to bump us right into the Gap-wall! You ever thought of that?"

Apparently he hadn't, because Cribble's punt suddenly almost dou-bled its speed. "You slippery runt, you been holding out on me! I ought to pound some respect into you," Ulnar shouted, unable to carry out his threat since the other craft now proved to be faster than his own. "Just wait'll I catch you; you can't stay out of reach forever!"

Cribble, however, simply ignored the stream of imprecations behind him, and kept increasing the distance between the two small vessels as they made their hasty way through the danger zone. Moreover, once he had reached the relative safety of the wider inner chamber, he simply turned his craft around and waited for the big man to catch up. From long experience he knew that Ulnar's volcanic temper seldom erupted for long, and that the threatened pounding had probably diminished to a shaking at worst.

He was spared even that, as it turned out. Just as the big man's hand was lifting Cribble by the scruff of the neck, Apheron's Patrol Cruiser came whipping around the bend and spun to a stop but a short distance away. Ulnar's expression immediately changed to that of a solicitous head waiter, and he actually made the gesture of dusting off the shoulder of Cribble's spacesuit before setting his diminutive partner back down in his punt.

For a long moment Cribble stood looking down at his shoulder, totally mystified by the idea that he had been the victim of dust in space.

"Cribble, you ain't got the sense of a brand new bot," Ulnar fumed, "just forget it and get your punt next to the major's ship or you'll have worries you can't imagine. Move!" Suiting action to his words, Ulnar quickly brought his skiff alongside the big Cruiser, followed by Cribble, who kept sneaking glances at his shoulder as if it held some miraculous residue that might reveal the true meaning of life which seemed somehow to have eluded him up to now.

Major Apheron, dressed as always in his dark Core Patrol suit and helmet, waited for the readout that told him all the air in his control cabin had been withdrawn and stored in the rest of his ship, then pushed a button that slid the window beside him open. Extending his hand through te open window, he asked Cribble, "You have the stolen Crystal?"

Cribble brought his punt to the window, and fished the Crystal out of a narrow pocket on his space suit. "You mean the Crystal you had me get from the POSH comm shack? The one I tried to give you this morning? I didn't steal it! You told me to take it. Why would I steal it?"

"So I can confiscate it. Give it to me."

Cribble was looking a little bit cornered, and turned to Ulnar, appealing, "I only took it because he told me to. Why would I steal it?"

"Just give the major the Crystal, and don't worry about it," Ulnar replied.

Reluctantly, Cribble placed the Crystal in Apheron's dark glove.

"Thank you, Cribble." There was an edge of icy sarcasm in the major's voice. "This place is as good as any; do you both have time pieces?" At their nods, he continued. "Ulnar, this evening you will leave somewhere, not the POSH, in time to come to this place at the sixth hour. Cribble, you will leave the POSH in time to also arrive here at the sixth hour."

"What for?"

Apheron's patience was wearing thin. "To give Ulnar the Crystal which I will confiscate as possible contraband, stolen property."

Cribble looked back and forth between the other two faces, and even down toward his shoulder, seeking enlightenment. When none came, totally confused but willing, he said, "OK, give it back to me and I'll give it back to you tonight."

Apheron clenched his fist around the Crystal as Cribble tried to grab it. "No, you..." clenching his jaw, the major swallowed the word "idiot" and substituted "fail to understand".

Carefully, he explained, "You and Ulnar will meet here at sixth hour. My Core Patrol log will show that I found you exchanging possible stolen property, which I will confiscate for investigation. I, however, won't be here, so I'm taking it now. Therefore, I'll even have the contraband in my possession as further evidence that we were all here." To forestall any further attempts on Cribble's part, Apheron quickly withdrew his arm back inside the window.

Cribble brightened. "We come here tonight and you won't be here?"

"Exactly!" The major glanced above as if all his prayers had been answered, and breathed a sigh of relief.

Cribble, for once, was seeing happier faces about him, and continued eagerly, "Then we won't have to come, either! We can just say we were here." He paused, and added conspiratorially, "There's a good card game tonight at the POSH." Cribble's puppy-dog smile slowly faded as he looked from face to face, seeing only the usual mounting exasperation. He even looked down at his shoulder for some faint sign of consolation, then decided that the Universe was beyond his comprehension and that silence was probably his best chance for survival.

"Why do I have to work with simpletons?" Apheron implored the silent heavens. "I pay well, I offer opportunities for advancement, and still I'm cursed by idiots!" Glaring at Cribble, he growled, "That is exactly why you have to be here tonight! Ulnar, you understand?"

"Yeah, Major. Sixth hour tonight, him from the POSH, he and I meet here, you already have the Crystal, and you're somewhere else but your Core Patrol log shows you caught us exchanging something stolen. Right?"

"Correct, Ulnar. The heavens are generous."

"Boss?"

"Never mind, Ulnar, you have the important part. See that it unfolds as planned."

"Right, boss. No problem."

As the window began to slide shut, Cribble panicked, jumping forward and sticking his arm in through the window, groping wildly for the Crystal. Fortunately for his arm, Apheron stopped the window mechanism in time. "I didn't steal it! I don't want to be arrested! I gave it to you — you told me to!"

Apheron tried to push Cribble's flailing arm out of the cockpit, and failing that, tried reason. "Cribble, listen to me. Cribble, you fool, you're not being arrested, I'm just investigating."

Slightly mollified, Cribble stopped grabbing blindly, but refused to take his arm out of the window without further reassurance.

"Mr. Ulnar," Apheron fumed, "do you understand the plan in its entirety?"

The worried Ulnar immediately replied, "Yes, Major. Sure do! Yes sir!"

"Then will you please explain it to your partner sometime at your leisure, and in the meantime, please remove your friend from the interior of my ship. I have urgent business elsewhere, and if both your vessels haven't withdrawn to a safe distance, they will be caught in the backblast as I start my engines. One other thing, Ulnar."

Ulnar wrapped his hands around Cribble's waist, and pulled him back from the cabin window. "Yes, Major?"

"If Cribble should fail to satisfactorily fulfill his portion of the plan, I'll arrest you! I'll count to ten before I start the engines." With that, the window slid shut.

Ulnar heaved Cribble into his punt, then leaped to start the engine on his own skiff. Looking in the window at Apheron he saw the major holding up one finger, then two. Both Ulnar and Cribble got the point, and Ulnar kept calling out, "Yessir, Major! We're going right now, see? Fast as we can! Anything you say, Major!" while urging his skiff forward at its top speed. Once again he was condemned to watching Cribble's craft outdistancing his own as they raced to safety.

Inexorably the fingers announced 7, 8, and 9. Apheron permitted himself a cold smile at their mad scramble, then flashed all ten at the window and gunned his ship at maximum acceleration out the narrow defile in a masterful display of his piloting prowess.

Cribble's punt was now also exiting the chamber, steadily drawing further ahead of the pursuing Ulnar.

"Come back here, you runt!" the big man railed, futilely pounding on the throttle of his space-skiff. "You could of got us killed for sure!"

As they headed out into Dutchman's Gorge again, there wasn't the slightest sign that the ever-diminishing Cribble was paying the any attention whatsoever to Ulnar's bellicose rantings. The big man stood up in his skiff, shaking his giant fist and shouting, "Wait for me, I got to explain the plan!"

Cribble kept on going.

Grumbling, Ulnar sat back down and poked the throttle one more time to see that it was truly at maximum. Following his distant partner back toward Dutchman's he rumbled, "You can't stay out of reach forever."

———————————

Chapter *70*

HUP LEAVE THE GAPS?
— THOUGHTS AT THE FIREFALL

THE TWO SHIPS hovered side by side in mid-space, facing the Firefall — Junker's disreputable space-tug, the Aries, and Hup's spotless cruiser, the Contender. Hup and Junker stood on the decks of their respective craft, making fast a couple of mooring lines so that the vessels wouldn't drift apart while they talked.

Junker finished tying the stern line, gave it a mighty pull to test it, then walked forward to join Hup who had leaped across from his own ship and now stood on the bow of the tug. As Junker approached Hup didn't turn around, but kept looking out at the majesty of the laser-green Firefall.

"Take your time," Junker thought, seeing the tension in Hup's body and the young man's fist rhythmically clenching at his side. "When it's ripe, it'll drop." Leaning back against the wall of the cockeyed pilot house, Junker let his mind loose among the slowly falling cascade of ball-lightnings.

After a couple minutes, Hup's back straightened and he stretched, the brilliant green light playing across his spic-and-span red and white spacesuit. "Thanks, Junker," he said, still without turning around, "you're a real friend. I'm glad I happened to catch you; I need to talk to someone."

Junker watched Hup's silhouette against the brilliance of the Firefall. "All this would be nothing without our friends," he observed.

"Yeah, it's pretty amazing," Hup continued while tilting his head far back, looking up to where the never-ending fall of light emerged from the swirling glowmists miles above their heads, "but I've got to get out of the Gaps."

"Leave the Gaps, Hup? This has been your whole life. It's what we know." Junker could see Hup's body tense like a drawn bowstring.

"They think we're dirt, Junker! They treat us like the dregs of the galaxy!"

Junker's eye roamed the junk-sculpture embellishments to his ship, saw the random reflected shards of the Firefall in the many panes of the stained glass windows he had so painstakingly crafted. He watched the slowly wavering shadow that young Hup cast on the deck, a deck Junker had begun building before Hup was born. "Who does, Hup?"

Hup turned his back to the Firefall, facing Junker with an expression half anger, half anguish. "The out-worlders. The crew-members."

"Yes," Junker replied, "The only out-worlders we know are the crew-members."

"We're scum to them, Junker, flotsam without a world!"

"The crew-members," Junker went on thoughtfully, "scared, fish out of water..."

"How's that?"

"I was just thinking," Junker answered, "the only out-worlders we see are the crew-members, scared, like fish out of water."

"Them? Scared? They're unbelievably rich! On one voyage they make more than we do in a lifetime! Their home worlds have everything! They retire when they're young! They're respected, Junker. They live among the stars! Their worlds are lands of plenty!"

"You're right, Hup. And what do we have?"

"Slim and none! As next to nothing as they can keep it! We risk our lives and they call us dirt!"

Junker leaned over the side and looked far down to where each plasmaball of the Firefall was bursting into a cloud of glowmist. Hup came to stand beside him, silently watching the stately stream of light. Junker spoke. "When'd it happen, Hup?"

"When, what? What do you mean?"

"When did a crew-member say something that got to you?"

"Well, I guess I did hear something at dawn, this morning, over at

Littlebend. At Pop's Place. He wasn't talking to me, I just overheard him."

"What'd he say, Hup?"

"Nothing worth repeating."

Junker's straightened up and his eyes were blazing. "Cut the bot-crap, Hup, we're better friends than that. Now tell me what he said that got to you."

Hup lowered his eyes, took a breath, and answered, "One was just talking to the other — both crew-members — just talking between themselves, but kinda loud, you know?"

"I know. And what'd he say?"

"He said, `You know what you need on board?'" Hup stopped, looking out at the Firefall.

"Then?"

Hup's back was turned, and Junker couldn't see the shame on Hup's face, but he could hear it in his voice. "The other guy replied, `No, what?'" Hup was quiet for a moment, his hands gripping the rail, then he spun around, facing Junker. "The first guy says, `You need a Gapper.' and the second guy says, `Why? We've got plenty of bots.' and the first guy laughs and says, `Yeah, but there's some things a bot just won't do!' and they laughed and laughed. I wanted to fight or to say something, but I couldn't think of anything to say. I didn't even really want to fight. I just left."

Junker leaned his head back against the wall of the Pilot House. "Fish out of water," he murmured.

"The crew-members?" asked Hup.

"Hup, they're scared! It's only bravado."

"Scared? What of? They've got everything!"

"Scared of CoreFires. Scared of Death. Scared of Life. Scared of not having everything! Scared of being with people who have to make do — afraid it might be contagious and they might catch it. Even scared of freedom."

"Who'd be scared of freedom?"

"Hup, if you came from one of the starry worlds where your whole future was laid out and everything was provided for, if you had to venture into a place where a touch of CoreFires meant your ship was destroyed, where your fellow man could stab you in the back if he chose, where your very life relied on cooperation from folks who lived without supervision, learned without education, loved without rules, grew anyway they chose, wouldn't you be a fish out of water?"

Hup was silent and looked glum.

"What is it, Hup? There's something else. Spit it out."

"On the way back I passed a Core Patrol ship coming the other way. He was barreling down the middle of the channel like he was late for the last ship to Paradise. I gave him plenty of room, but he kept coming on and edging over to my side of the tunnel. I swear he was forcing me closer to the wall just to throw his weight around."

"In your mood, it's lucky you didn't tangle with him. You gave way and slowed down?"

Hup reddened. "Well, sort of." With a sheepish smile he admitted, "I didn't actually slow down, and I guess when his path kept crowding me to the wall I finally just set a straight course and kept on it."

"Close to his course?"

Hup actually grinned, and nodded. "Not too close. It was my right-of-way."

Junker shook his head. "You could've been dead right! Did he give way?"

"Not much."

"Bot-brain!" Junker laughed. "I suppose you're smart enough to know how dumb that was. Mr. Young Hothead Gapper gets pissed off at a stupid remark in a tavern, so he sets things right by going head to head with a Core Patrol cruiser. Real swift! You got anything against having birthdays? So you missed each other and the Contender still has all its parts, as near as I can see. Didn't he come back and get you? He could have tied you up for weeks!"

Hup still looked sheepish, but he was still grinning. "We weren't that close. Anyway, he kept on going, just as fast as ever. It was just the last straw, Junker! The Core Patrol is always looking out for the ships of the out-worlders, and never cares about us, unless it's to throw their weight around to remind us that Gappers are just botcrap and to keep us in line!"

"Did you just notice that?" Junker shook his head as if Hup were an example of what the Gaps were coming to nowadays. "The starry worlds fund the Core Patrol — we sure don't — and they get what they pay for. If we service the supply ships and stay out of their way, they leave us alone. They know Gappers are too independent to stay under their thumb, so they keep letting us know who's boss. You challenge the Patrol, Hup, and they're either going to make you eat it, or they'll just gobble you up to set an example. That was probably Major Apheron, and you'd better hope he didn't recognize your ship," Junker waved his hand at the shiny Contender, "although there's not much chance of that."

"It's not fair, Junker. We're people just like them. They think we're the junk of the Universe, as useless as that ring of stuff orbiting your patched-up castle!"

"Well, maybe we are! On their worlds, their future's been laid out to the tiniest detail, part of a grand scheme that will continue forever, and we're nothing more than what we can make out of whatever we've got, and that's blasted little! If you're on a world that can make anything that's needed, what's orbiting in the Ring is scrap, worthless. Here, it's treasure — raw materials to make whatever your mind can dream up, like the Contender. You're a young man, Hup, and a good one. You might even make a good older one, if you learn to stop daring the Core Patrol to bounce you into the CoreFires. You've got to find out where you want to be."

"Thanks, Junker," Hup shrugged his shoulders, "I've just got to get out of the Gaps."

"If that's what you want to do, Hup, but the starry worlds are set In concrete. I don't think they have what you're searching for. They're starving for freedom, and you're hooked on it in big daily doses."

"Where else is there, Junker?"

Junker looked at the Firefall, then at his own craft and then Hup's shiny imitation of an out-world ship. "I wish I knew. Here — eating crow when the Core Patrol wants to see me eat it — is the best I've been able to find so far," Junker laughed, a touch ironically. "Mind,

I'm not much fonder of crow than you are, Hup. If I find someplace better, I'll sure let you know! We'd make one hell of a crew!"

Hup embraced the older man, tears in his eyes.

Lit by the Firefall, the younger man in his slick red and white space suit leaped across the gap onto the deck of his own ship, cast off the lines, and as the two ships began to drift apart he looked back at the elder in his elaborately wrought tatters. "If you ever find that some-where else, old man, let me know, even if I'm on one of the starry worlds. I don't care if your ship is straight out of the scrapyard; I'll sign on and we'll sail to places no one's ever seen. You have my hand on it!" Hup leaned way out over the railing.

Junker stretched out and took Hup's hand in a solemn shake, then both laughed and let go just before they'd have been pulled overboard into the void.

"I'm going to Grand Jetty," Hup called across the widening space between the ships. "About sixth hour tonight I'll be back at Grand Caverns to fulfill a pilot's contract with a supply ship called the Reliant III. I'll be bringing her through the Maze to Dutchman's, or maybe even on through the Gorge to Littlebend. You might go on out to Grand Jetty yourself, today. There's rumors of a couple more ships in the afternoon."

"Thanks for the tip. It's a generous whippersnapper who shares with his seniors."

"That's OK, you old buzzard, I think I get more than I give, on average. Call me when you set sail for that special place."

"Sounds good to me, you misfit. Don't let the Core Patrol catch your butt and dispose of you before I sign you on!"

"OK, I won't be looking for any trouble." The words were almost lost in static on the comm channel as Hup's ship swung away from the Aries. Junker couldn't be sure, but he thought he made out one phrase more, something like, "Keep the faith, old man, we'll fly or die!"

The smile lines crinkled beside Junker's eyes and beard as he looked at the glory of the Firefall and breathed a prayer for Youth and Hope. "You're steering too much by the way things ought to be. Could be I'm steering too much by the way things are," he mused.

"Maybe somewhere in between there's a course we can set that'll let us fly without having to die trying. Myself, I'd much rather specialize in living. Dying comes along soon enough anyway."

As he finished dressing the mooring lines, Junker made out a faint light blinking in the distant glowmist. Soon it was followed by the sight of Cirra's Phoenix-craft emerging from the swirling fog. She was alone, and as soon as she saw the Aries near the Firefall she waved and brought the helm hard over.

"Now, there's a good reason to specialize in living!" Junker chuckled, returning her wave.

————————————————

Chapter 71

[Rad:na] Coming About
— Two Finders in One Place

Within the CoreFires the energy winds were fresh, and the sails of the Rad:na vessel — including the new topsail — drawing evenly. Her wake of temporary stars was not as long as it might be, for she was close-hauled on the starboard tack, trading off speed to sail as close toward the wind as she was able.

Questor-Joss's boots were planted wide on the slanting deck as she stood abaft of the helm, conversing with her first mate.

"Well done, Norr," she said quietly, "this next tack should take us above the Gap near the missing Finders without arousing suspicion. Even if the Owd is aware of our movements, it'll appear to be just one more tack to regain our position when the nova-gale overtook us."

"Both Finders are now in the same place?"

"I can't tell for sure. They're both definitely in the Gap, somewhere near where we'll be crossing. We'll stay a good distance above, but I should be able to learn more as we pass. Then we'll stay clear of the territory for awhile."

"Aye. Coming up on the course change, Questor."

"Then bring her about, Norr. I'll be on my platform."

With that she made her way forward while the mate began barking orders to the hands.

The Rad:na were magnificent sailors, however, as befitting a famed Navigatrix, Joss expected her crew to excel. Her keen eyes missed nothing as she crossed the deck, and when Norr gave the command to come about, she started silently counting seconds.

As she passed the helmsman, she saw from the fingertip touch he was using to bring the wheel over, a spoke at a time, that her ship was so admirably "suited" — that she was feeling almost no drag from the rudder — and the gradually curving wake was preserving her momentum as well. With the maneuver begun, Norr was now silent and the deckhands were moving in swift synchronism, knowing well the multitude of steps necessary to head her up into the wind without losing way.

"Fifteen, sixteen...," Joss counted to herself.

As the energy sails above their heads began to shiver and shake, the mate cried out "Helm's alee, beings!" Instantly the sheets for the forward sails were let go so those aft would help bring her around. The canted deck was coming level beneath Joss's feet while she continued to walk forward, ignoring the thunderous clatter above as the wind now pressed the huge square sails aback against the masts.

"Twenty five, twenty six..."

"Off tacks and sheets!" Norr bellowed, then shortly, "Mainsail haul!"

Critically Joss watched the intricate sequence unfold, the deck hands flying from task to task without wasted motion. Freed at the proper moment, the after yards nearly flew around of themselves, then the lightning abated in the aft sails as they were becalmed by the head ones, setting off a flurry of activity during the brief moments they were slack and easy to handle.

"Thirty nine, forty..." With the deck now canting to the opposite side, the Questor reached the bottom of her ladder-like stairs just as the mate called out the final command, "Let go and haul, my beings!" By the time she reached the top, the last of the yards had been braced sharp up and the deckhands dispersed, their vessel already pulling well on the new tack.

"Fifty four seconds. Now, that's the way it should be done," Joss said with a satisfied glance back at their wake. Grasping the finders, she began probing ahead.

———————————————

Chapter *72*

A TIMELY MEETING — GRAND CAVERNS CLOSED

As her craft came along side, Cirra called up to Junker. "On your way out from the Keep? Looks like I barely caught you." She heaved the bow-line up to the tug's deck where Junker made it fast to a bitt.

"Too true! And you wouldn't have if Hup hadn't caught me too! A double case of good timing as it turned out. I thought you were doing Morning Tales today. Did you come out just to catch me?"

Cirra nodded as she tossed up the stern-line. "A strange warning at Morning Tales! I left immediately after." She clambered up on deck and motioned with her head toward the pilot house. Junker didn't need a second invitation.

———————————

When there was sufficient air in the cabin, Cirra's face bubble turned itself off with a soft pop and she quickly removed her helmet. Junker also started to take his off, but his hands stopped in mid-task while he watched Cirra shaking out her waist length hair. When she had finished, she threw her head back and looked at him with a megawatt smile.

His hands finally remembered what they had been doing, but before they could resume their assignment Cirra stepped forward and her own hands swept his aside, lifting Junker's helmet above his grizzled head and hanging it on the cabin wall. Her flashing eyes were close in his face before they closed, and she attacked him with a long hard kiss, full of warmth and urgency.

Junker didn't know why he was getting such a passionate onslaught from her lips and teeth and tongue, but he knew he could reply with a heart-felt fervor. For a long time there was only the kiss, then the mutual embrace, then a couple of minutes of heavenly itchy tickles as she nestled her head on his chest with his cheek and nose buried in the cloud of her hair. Still holding him tight, she whispered something he couldn't hear.

Tilting his head back enough to free his ears, he asked, "What was that?"

She stepped back and took a healthy handful of his beard from each side of his face. "My junkman," she said tenderly, "you're still here. I thought I might not catch you."

"You very nearly didn't. You came from Dutchman's through the Little Way?"

"Yes, right after I finished giving Morning Tales. I thought you might be headed for Grand Caverns."

"I am, as a matter of fact. I was just starting out for Grand Jetty, which either means going through the Caverns or straight through the CoreFires, and the Aries would never forgive me if I took her into the CoreFires."

"Nor would I," she laughed. "Besides, most of that scrap she's built out of probably has bad memories of a past life that suddenly ended that way." Her expression became more serious. "That's why I came, in a way. They say Grand Caverns isn't safe! Something about an instability in the CoreFires that might get worse."

"That's a surprise." Junker peered out the various windows of the pilot house to see if he could discern any changes in the glowmist, but all appeared normal, including the Firefall as it continued its stately perpetual cascade. "Too bad we can't warn Hup!"

"Hup?"

"He just left for Grand Jetty minutes before you arrived, but there's no way we can tell him. He was out of comm range before you showed up, and the way he travels, I'd never be able to catch up with him. He was planning to come back from Grand Jetty to the Caverns at sixth hour tonight to take a contract ship, Reliant III, through the Maze, and maybe through the Gorge as well."

"Maybe he'll see the instability and turn back. Or if it's not too bad yet, he'd just go on through it to Grand Jetty and they'll warn him there. They'll be holding the Reliant there anyway."

"Holding the ship? It must be serious. They seldom hold traffic for any reason."

"They said it's something like what preceded that storm that blew out Salty's antenna at Dutchman's and carried away most of yours at the Keep. They've closed the Caverns until tomorrow dawn."

"That one sure reduced visibility," Junker mused, "but otherwise it wasn't actually dangerous to a spacecraft. Hup's ship didn't have any problem, and we were ready to move the Aries if we had to. They're discouraging supply ships from going through 'til then? Who's `they'?"

"Not discouraging, prohibiting. `They' is the Core Patrol, and they're prohibiting all travel through Grand Caverns. All outbound traffic is being stopped at Dutchman's or Littlebend, and all inbound at Grand Jetty, so that'll include Hup's contract ship. And not just the supply ships — everybody. They'll hold Hup there, too."

"Gappers too?" Now Junker was really puzzled.

"The Core Patrol interrupted right in the middle of Morning Tales at the POSH to make the announcement. The Patrolman was pretty heavy-handed when he threatened any Gapper's craft found in the forbidden zone with inspection and re-certification or worse; he got off on the wrong foot and everybody was pretty upset. In the end, he just stormed out and set off full blast for Littlebend. I'd better tell you what happened."

As Cirra recounted the events at the POSH that dawn, Junker kept stroking his beard in a thoughtful way. "Strange things unfolding in the Gaps lately," he observed when she had finished. "At least we'll be safe at the Keep, although I wish we'd been able to warn Hup."

Cirra looked around the cabin where a hundred little images of the Firefall were refracted in the small stained-glass sections that surrounded the big windows. "The Core Patrol should be on its way back from Littlebend by now. I guessed they'd stop at the Ring to notify you, but I didn't want to chance their missing you. I'm sure glad now that I trusted my intuition. You'd have been long gone." Cirra gave him a quick hug, and went to the window where she could see her vessel tied alongside the tug. "After stopping at the Ring, the Core Patrol will probably continue all the way back to Grand Jetty to clear the area of any stragglers, so they might catch up with Hup before he gets to the Caverns."

"I hope so. Although I don't see anything unusual in the glowmist, we might as well get under cover at the Keep if the CoreFires's acting up again. I'll follow you and the Phoenix from here to the castle."

After they had kissed and donned their helmets, Junker hit the air button, and they waited for the evacuation to complete.

"How many were there from the Core Patrol?" he asked.

"Just one. Major Apheron."

"Our local version of the Overlord!" Junker exclaimed. "I knew he was in the territory and I should have put two and two together!"

"What is it, Junker? Is it serious?"

"Only for Hup. Now I really wish I could warn him. Hup's been leading a charmed life for years — snuggling up to CoreFires at top speed — but it could be serious if Apheron catches that hotshot in the forbidden zone."

"Why? I'm sure if Hup couldn't have known about it, he'd just get a warning."

"Ordinarily. But Hup had a little bit of a run in with the Core Patrol between Dutchman's Gorge and Littlebend. If it was Apheron, that youngster could get himself in big trouble: Apheron's at least as quick tempered as Hup. And if anyone can catch up with Hup before he gets out of the Caverns, it's Apheron!"

"Maybe we can delay Apheron a few minutes at the Ring," Cirra answered, "and give Hup a little extra margin, although I don't know — even with all you say about him and Apheron, it might be better if he got the warning. What do you think?"

"I wish I knew! We'd better get under way in any event. OK," he said, as an indicator light came on. "The air's stowed; let's go." Junker hit the latch that opened the cabin door.

241

Cirra rapidly descended the ladder to the deck, then clambered over the side and dropped down to the stern platform of her Viking-craft.

————————————

Bow's loose," Junker called from the deck, and her vessel's tall prow, three times the height of a person, began swinging out from the flank of the Aries. While he was walking aft to deal with the stern-line, he watched the vertical shadow of the prow cross the gunwale and align with Cirra, shading her in a band of darker green.

When she saw the fierce metal Phoenix-head silhouetted against the brilliance of the Firefall, Cirra changed the helm to hold it there. Something in that image reverberated through her being, something about the iron bird facing... what?

Before Junker could cast loose the remaining line, she called, "Wait a minute, Junker."

Junker, kneeling on the deck of the tug, looked over the rail and felt the chill of the supernatural. Cirra was standing in the wavering vertical shadow band of darker green with her eyes closed, her arms before her, palms up, and an expression of intent listening on her face. Again she opened her eyes, contemplating the dark Phoenix-head eclipsing the descending stream of lightning-spheres as if she were looking for something more. She seemed to come to a decision.

"Junker, would the Aries be stable here if we left her unattended for a while?"

"Surely, if it weren't for too long."

"Just now I had the faintest hint of a vision, just momentarily, in the Firefall. Nothing I can explain, but something compelling, important. If you could come aboard and take the helm, you might be able to help me see more."

By way of answer, Junker loosed the stern line and jumped down on board, whereupon Cirra gave him the helm. "I'll direct you from the prow," she said, making her way forward.

Junker hadn't realized how literally she meant the words until she began climbing the tall neck that supported the Phoenix sculpture, her feet engaging the tiny foot-holds set in the back and her hands reaching around the sides of the metal neck. Soon she reached the top and straddled the fierce dragon-bird's head, her legs clasping it's cheeks, as at home as any young girl on a pony ride. Again she extended her arms forward and resumed her concentration. When she spoke, instead of having to call out as Junker had expected, her voice sounded disconcertingly close in his ear.

"Take me toward the Firefall. The feeling is strongest in that direction."

Junker complied, and occasionally she directed their course to one side or the other, as if casting for an elusive scent.

"It could be from the Firefall, or from the other side. Try circling in toward the fall."

Junker brought the helm over, then steadied it on the new course. From miles above to miles below the flowing fall of lightning-drops descended in a steady stream, like slow-motion sands in the CoreFires's hourglass, timing forever. Closer and closer the Viking-like spacecraft orbited the incandescent column in mid-void, with Cirra astraddle the high prow and Junker piloting from one of the stern wings.

Never had they been so close to the Firefall. Now there was a sound in their ears, like a faint chorus of a thousand independent angelic voices, each choosing a different pitch, but with all the pitches slowly descending in a never-ending "Aaaaaaaah."

When Junker looked up the view was awesome. He tried looking down, and quickly thought better of it. "Better concentrate on steering," he told himself, "too much gawking might be a bad idea."

Cirra was turning this way and that up on the Phoenix-head when she slipped slightly to the side and steadied herself by grasping the Talisman figure so favored by Mutch and Marneen. It was strongly mounted and welcome support, but more importantly, she instantly felt more receptive and attuned to the energies she was seeking. "Why, thank you, Tallest Man," she acknowledged silently, "I need all the help I can get."

With one hand around the faintly glowing sculpture, she closed her eyes and opened her spirit wide, becoming empty that she might be filled. Then she gasped. For a brief moment she had glimpsed some sort of dark silhouette, not against the green Firefall, against a column of blood red. It filled her with foreboding.

Her voice whispered again in Junker's ear, "I almost saw something. I know I need to see more. The feeling is always strongest in the direction of the Firefall itself. Junker, turn us toward the Firefall."

Junker looked up at the height of the column and swallowed his objection. Putting the helm over again, he swung the ship directly toward the Firefall. The angelic chorus swelled in their ears.

"It's right, Junker. Keep going. The Talisman helps me to focus. Is there any way I can remove it to hold it in my hands?"

"Easily," he replied. "Just grasp it firmly and twist it a quarter turn; it'll come right out of its socket." Junker watched Cirra on the prow, now dwarfed by the descending fireballs before her. She tilted her head back and raised her arms, holding the Talisman in her hands. Junker looked to the sides, and to his consternation, tiny motes of lightning were drifting down even now about the ship. Close ahead, glowing globes up to the size of houses were falling in profusion. The angel chorus seemed to be all around them.

"I can't see it yet, Junker, but I know what we have to do."

Junker's hand on the tiller held the course true for the middle of the Firefall, although sweat was trickling down his forehead in spite of his bio-suit's best efforts. "Hard over!" his mind kept saying, "Come about while there's still time!" Swallowing hard, he took a deep breath. Aloud, he said, "What should we do, Cirra?"

Amidst the angel choir in his ears, her voice sounded totally calm, absolutely certain, as she whispered, "We have to go into the Firefall, Junker. Take us right through the middle and on out the other side."

Junker choked back a protest. He looked up the column, the plasma fall now almost over their heads. While his rational mind was cowering in fear, trying to control his hand on the tiller, he threw into the balance his love for Cirra and his profound respect for that in her which was beyond understanding. "Chalk one up for blind faith," he thought, keeping the course as it lay.

The brilliant green of the Firefall glistened off his face, now bathed in sweat within his helmet. His attention was locked on Cirra, although the ball-lightning all about her was blindingly bright. Glancing up, Junker was suddenly sure they were about to enter the plasma stream, and with a pounding heart he realized Cirra, in the front of the long craft, was going to enter first.

She, however, seemed serene, straddling the metal Phoenix-head, arms upraised, hands clasping the Talisman as if she were welcoming the coming immersion. The first globes enveloped her, and the entire metal craft was clothed in plasma-glow, including the tiller in his hand. In moments she was swallowed in that falling wall of searing luminescence, and foot by foot the rest of the ship was following. Junker held his breath as he, too, was engulfed.

————————————

Chapter 73

AN ANGEL CHORUS
— CIRRA AND TALLEST MAN

NOW THEY WERE deep within the thousand descending voices of the angel chorus. The falling spheres of light were so brilliant and numerous as to overwhelm the mind, leaving only a sensation that the ship instead was rising steadily through some incomprehensible host of light-beings.

Cirra brought the Talisman to her heart and closed her eyes. So bright was the luminance without, that the world within her lids was also a world of light, except that instead of the green of the falling orbs, it was the red of the blood in her eyelids, pulsing to her heartbeat.

"Help me, Tallest Man," she thought. "Help me to see."

Red. The sense of foreboding returned, redoubled. As it had wafted through the myths of a thousand worlds she recognized a stench of evil. But what was the form she had glimpsed? That momentary silhouette, black against fiery red? Pressing the Talisman to her heart, she let the Phoenix carry her forward, searching, seeking.

Now the sense of evil was overwhelming, but still she pressed on with eyes closed. "Help me to see, Tallest Man."

A swirl of blazing red, then gone. Red fire on black metal, then gone. A minute crystal ball, up is down, down is up, momentary scraps, instantly gone.

"Open yourself," she thought. "Be open, receive it all." Her pulse beat in the red of her eyelids, her heart pounded against the Talisman. "Help me, Tallest Man."

But as she opened herself to see, she opened herself to evil as well. She could have been in the steel halls of the Overlord as a vast laugh echoed everywhere, immensely sadistic and powerful. She felt that she was being delivered, naked and defenseless, into its suffocating presence.

Filled with fear and revulsion, still her spirit persisted. From somewhere ahead it heard a faint heartrending cry of love and anguish. When she moved toward it, her spirit was staggered by the monstrous answering laugh, cruel and triumphant. On and on it echoed as she reeled through metal halls turning to flame.

"Tallest Man!" she called, "Help me!"

Then she felt something envelope her, something other than the descending luminous spheres. She felt lifted and sustained, as if she had merged with an ancient unbroken line long dedicated to defying evil. Newly armored against that evil presence, she let the Phoenix carry her forward, breathing, "I thank you, Tallest Man. Let's find the image we've sought."

She knew with certainty where it lay. She had only to follow that forlorn cry of love and anguish, so small amid the gloating echo. There she saw again the tiny crystal sphere, and within it an inverted image of a column of fire! Looking beyond the small sphere, she saw the source of the image, a huge pillar of twisting CoreFires, blood-red!

And there also was the silhouette she'd been seeking. It was a freighter, silhouetted against the incandescent column, the dark metal of her sides reflecting the swirling red fires she was approaching. Her engines were flaring bright violet, accelerating her onward.

Clutching the Talisman, Cirra cried out in horror as they drove the exploding ship into the CoreFires!

———————————————

Chapter 74

[RAD:NA] SHARING MINDS — WHAT IS THIS!

BEYOND THE GAP, high above, Questor-Joss of the Rad:na struggled desperately to escape the vision she was sharing with an alien mind!

Tearing her hands away from the Finders she staggered back, open mouthed, gasping for breath, her feet barely missing the unseen hatchway gaping in the middle of her platform. Her spine bumped against the aft railing and her hands clutched it for support while the images of destruction slowly faded from her horror-filled eyes.

"Goddess help me," she whispered, chest heaving. "What is this?"

————————————

Chapter 75

CIRRA'S CRY — KEEP GOING!

HEARING CIRRA'S CRY, Junker was agonized, torn between running forward to help her and remaining at his post at the tiller. He could see nothing amid the endless cascade of fiery green. He heard nothing but the cries of angels. "Cirra!" he called in desperation.

He rose to grope his way forward, but as soon as his hand released the tiller it started to swing aside, and his years of experience took hold. Grasping it again, he brought it amidships and held the course, hoping that his lapse hadn't endangered her. Sweat dripped into his squinting eyes and the salt and pepper strands of his beard. "Cirra!" he cried again.

Faintly, from the midst of the angel voices she replied, "Junker! I'm all right! Keep going."

Helm in hand, Junker exhaled. His grizzled beard curved into a relieved smile.

It seemed an eternity, there among the falling fire-spheres, and only long practiced discipline enabled Junker to keep the course in spite of the overwhelming illusion that the ship was rising steadily, destined to be swallowed forever in whatever mystery lay above in the source of the Firefall. Finally, eternity was over as Junker began to discern the prow again among the thinning plasmas, with Cirra safely seated on the Phoenix head, the Talisman still in her hand.

"Thank you, Tallest Man," she acknowledged in a weary whisper as she carefully locked the figure in its socket.

Chapter 76

EMERGENCE — IN GLOWING GREEN

BEFORE LONG THEY emerged from the Firefall, only now the entire ship, and Junker and Cirra as well, were wrapped in a shimmering glow of brilliant green. When they were at a safe distance, Junker went forward to help Cirra descend shakily from her perch. With a strong arm about her, he accompanied her back to the stern platform and gently seated her beside the helm. Then, seating himself, he took the helm in hand and pointed to where the Aries hovered against the Firefall-lit glowmist a good half mile away.

Cirra nodded, taking a long deep breath as Junker put his arm around her. Both remained silent as he brought the Phoenix about to a new heading, making steadily for the tug. Slowly the strange green glow enveloping them faded away.

Reaching an arm around Junker, Cirra pulled him closer and leaned her head on his shoulder. In a quiet voice, she said, "I saw it, Junker. The vision. It was hard to look at." His arm held her tighter. "It was a ship going into CoreFires, exploding and all."

"Hup's ship?"

"No, it wasn't Hup's ship. A big ship. A supply ship. It went into a column of fire in Grand Caverns. It was awful, and it seemed to take forever. And even though it wasn't Hup, somehow he was in danger, too!"

"Grand Caverns," Junker echoed.

"We have to go there, Junker."

"And the Core Patrol will try to stop us."

"I've been thinking about that." Cirra raised her head and looked at the Aries, still over a quarter mile distant. "Major Apheron is on his way to the Ring and will be here shortly. If we leave for Grand Caverns he'll surely catch up with us long before we get there, and he'll send us back. But there is another way. We could get Lyard and Garms, and I think we'll need them."

"They're at the POSH. If I show up with the Aries, they'll have to hold me at Dutchman's, or the Core Patrol will stop me in the main channel. I don't see another way."

"The Little Way. We tie a line from the Phoenix to the Aries, and I lead you through the Little Way. I leave you hiding in the mists at Foggy Hole while I go get Lyard and Garms with the Phoenix and bring them back to the Aries. That'll put us behind Apheron, and we can proceed to Grand Caverns without anyone at Dutchman's being the wiser."

"Hold on, hold on," Junker exclaimed, "you mean for us to take a ship the size of the Aries through the Little Way!"

"Like a dog on a leash. Is the Little Way big enough?"

"Barely. One mistake and phhhht!"

"I'd lead, and you'd follow the Phoenix. When the mists get really thick, you just follow the leash; I'm bound to be on the other end of it. Do you and the Aries know how to heel?"

"Well, I suppose it's theoretically possible, but one mistake would put the Aries into the CoreFires, and you'd be history, too."

Cirra looked ahead to where the tug was waiting for them. "Junker, after seeing the vision of that ship going into the CoreFires, I'd say we have to go to Grand Caverns. Somehow, Hup's in danger, too. I'm willing to try it, under the circumstances. Are you?"

Junker brought the Viking-craft in a smooth arc toward the space-tug. "I hope the Aries will forgive me, but she and I will follow you. We'll have to be quick about it to get into the Little Way before Major Apheron gets here." She nodded, taking the helm from Junker and bringing the Phoenix alongside the tug without slowing down.

Chapter 77

ALL IN THE LITTLE WAY
— THE SCENT OF FOREVER

JUNKER LEAPED ONTO the deck of the larger vessel, calling out, "Keep going! I'll catch up with you before the Little Way." As he climbed the ladder to the pilot house, he added. "Compared to following you into the Firefall, this should be a piece of cake!"

Waving from the stern of the departing Phoenix, Cirra called, "Come on! You've often said you'd follow me anywhere!" She made the motion of blowing him a kiss through her helmet.

"You know," he laughed as he hung out the door, "my life might be a lot simpler if your perfume didn't smell so much like Forever!" Then he shut the door and rushed through the process of getting the Aries underway.

Just before the Viking-craft craft went into the billowing glowmists, the tiny figure of Cirra waved again.

Junker fired the engines, peered out the stained-glass window, and waved in reply. As the Aries started to move, Junker patted the wheel. "Stick with me, old girl," he said to his faithful tug. "We've seen a lot of good times together, and some tough ones too. I'm going to take you through a real squeaker; if we don't make it, we'll check out together — if we do, it'll be quite an adventure, and it might be important. You just keep answering the helm, and I promise I'll give it my very best."

Once again the grizzled captain and his battered space-tug became one with a grace polished by the miles of half a lifetime. Once again in answer to the throttle the purple glow bloomed behind the mighty engine, and the spokes of the wheel passed from hand to hand. The immortal fall of fiery green cast its wavering light on the tug as she wheeled away to follow Cirra's course.

If he was feeling a tad more mortal than usual, Junker didn't let it show in his voice as he encouraged his ship. "That's the way," he said. "Let's go do it!"

Soon, the Aries disappeared into the swirling glowmists.

————————————————

Chapter 78

[Rad:na] Atop the Mast
— Breaching Time Itself

From the highest crow's-nest Questor-Joss looked out at the Core-Fires, so deep in thought she didn't hear Mate-Norr's approach, even when he cleared his throat.

"Pardon the interruption, Navigatrix, but we've completed three more legs. Do you still want avoid that area of the Gap?"

"No pardon necessary." Bracing herself against the sway, she turned. "Yes, now more than ever we'll not want to draw any attention there. Keep tacking 'til we gain the position where the nova-storm hit us, then change to the heading we'd been following then. We'll keep our distance for awhile."

"Aye, Questor. It's not my place to ask what happened back there."

The quiet exhaustion was plain on her face, but her lips twisted in a gentle smile at the way he'd phrased the non-question. "It is your place, Norr, and it always shall be. I'd have told you sooner, but even now all is not clear."

Turning her face to the CoreFires, she continued in a quiet voice. "I now know more of the missing Finders — one was somewhere nearby, and the other was in use by an alien, a female of the Humankind!"

"In use!"

"In a manner of speaking. Apparently she was seeking, at grave personal risk, some sort of important vision while grasping the Finder." Joss paused, placing her hand on the railing to stop its trembling. She forced herself to continue. "I, of course, was probing with our Finders, and somehow merged consciousness with the alien." She turned back to the mate with stricken eyes. "I merged with the Humankind woman!"

Speechless, he nodded.

"While we were merged she found the vision she sought. I shared that vision, Norr, the culmination of some sort of evil plan, human, but reeking of Owd influence." She lived it again as she spoke in a guttural whisper. "Within the Gap, a large ship, deliberately driven to destruction in the CoreFires. It shall haunt my dreams."

"My Navigatrix," he said, "this is strange indeed! It may be that nothing like this has ever happened before."

"A Finder in use by an individual of a nursery species? Cross species contact through Finders? A Rad:na merging with an alien?" She laughed, grimly. "No, I imagine this is quite a first! I believe among the Rad:na I stand alone!"

"Never!" he replied earnestly, "If none else, I stand with you..."

"My faithful Norr!" she interrupted. "There's yet one thing more you should know before choosing so rash a course! One thing more about the possible extent of my transgression, about this strange momentary union between a Rad:na Questor and the vision-seeking woman."

As the mate looked into the Questor's eyes, he saw both pain and wonder there.

"I'm positive the vision we shared has not yet come to pass. It's possible," she continued in awe, "that we breached time itself! If events truly unfold according to that vision, then I have interfered beyond what the mind can comprehend. For when we merged, the sum of our two species reached ahead in time, possibly perceiving some sort of crucial interplay between good and evil among the Humankind, possibly even perceiving the influence of the Owd! And she now carries that image, which will guide her actions."

From the swaying crow's-nest high atop the ship, her gaze again searched the CoreFires ahead. "Goddess help me, the alien and I may have reached through time to a moment in our future, and even now be paradoxically reshaping our paths leading us to that moment!"

If she saw no answers in the CoreFires, she at least found a strange peace and acceptance there. Or perhaps it was within herself.

"Now we must all live out the consequences of what I've done. Go below and tend to our course, First-Mate-Norr. For better or worse you've sailed a unique voyage with Questor-Joss of the Rad:na, and she honors and respects everything you've done."

Silent, he bowed low.

"I'll remain up here for awhile with my thoughts."

Soon she heard his voice calling to the crew far below, "Stand ready to bring her about!"

As the mast leaned over to the other side she found herself counting silently, "…Fifty four, Fifty five!"

She looked astern at the curve in their fading star-wake, shaking her head and chuckling to herself.

"So quick!" she mused. "Less than a minute passes by, and suddenly we're all on a completely new heading!"

————————————

Chapter 79

PICTURING THE CAVERNS
— NORMAL MORNING ROUND

ABOARD THE RELIANT III, Daric was trying to be businesslike. "Everything normal so far," he said.

Shanni, walking beside him, stifled a giggle. "Perfectly normal!" Her straight face lasted all of fifteen seconds before it helplessly dissolved into another fit of giggles.

They'd completed half of their second tour of inspection for the day, the "mid-morning round", although in this instance the "high-voltage round" would have been far more accurate.

Time and again the inflection of a voice had triggered dreamy scenarios, the thought of a touch had aroused spiritual hopes and carnal desires. Daric couldn't concentrate. Shanni's body kept ambushing her mind. "Or is it the other way round?" she thought. Whichever, each corridor was charged with emotion, each cargo bay became a surreal stage wherein commonplace events couldn't have been further from commonplace.

They had inspected, if one could use that term in their present states of mind, the port side bays, finding the hoist exactly where Shanni had parked it and the seven cubes containing the planet-sized Crystals undisturbed. Now, clanging their way forward along the final portside passageway, the two were headed for the very bow of the Reliant. Although somewhat aware of the ever watchful cameras following their progress, for the most part they ignored them.

"No intersections. At least I can't get lost here," laughed Daric, looking ahead where the corridor continued without deviation for another hundred yards.

"Looks like half a whale's gullet," Shanni observed, "what are all the big ribs to the left for?"

Daric touched one of the massive metal ribs as they walked by. "It's the hull, holding our air in. This is the edge of the ship. On the other side of this wall is empty space. If it had portholes, you'd see the Gap-walls going by. We're forward of the cargo bays, in that long skinny section just behind the bow. Up ahead, the bridge and all the control rooms will be above us, although there's no way up from here."

"You could get lost if one of these were unlocked..." Shanni mused mischievously, pulling on a big padlock. On her side of the passage they were passing a long series of identical doors, each conspicuously locked. Her smile hinted they might get lost together. "What's in there, separating the port and starboard corridors?"

"Those would be rec rooms, recreational facilities. Maybe they're locked because we have such a small crew, or maybe Captain Volnath just disapproves of recreation. The ships aren't required to provide them. Probably it's just to keep me on the straight and narrow."

Shanni flashed him a quick smile. They were approaching the end of the passageway where they'd be forced to take a turn to the right when Shanni frowned, saying, "Daric, this can't be the very front of the ship! If there are big ribs to the side, and this passage just ends in that..." she searched for a word, "...sort of wall..."

"Bulkhead," Daric supplied.

"...bulkhead without ribs, there has to be another section in front of the bulkhead."

Daric smiled. "You're exactly right." As they followed the corridor's turn to the right, Daric put his hand on the heavy metal bulkhead. "There's actually one more room in front of this wall. Here, I'll show you." He walked a few yards farther on, then stopped, pointing down to the metal deck. "See this big welded seam? We're standing exactly on the middle of the ship. They actually make this part in two halves and weld them together."

Shanni noticed some details in the bulkhead that had escaped her on previous inspection tours. Set into it were what almost appeared to be two wide steel double doors aligned with the middle of the ship. Shoulder high, centered in the middle of each door — if doors they were — was a large iron ring hanging from a swivel mounting, looking for all the world like an ancient castle door-knocker.

"They are doors!" she exclaimed as she saw a latch further to each side that would have engaged the rings when the doors were open. She paused in sudden perplexity as her eyes took in a detail that invalidated her theory: a welded seam running all the way around each supposed door. She ran her finger up the center seam as if doubting its existence, then turned to Daric, mystified. "I don't understand. I thought..." Her voice trailed away in confusion.

"You were right," Daric answered. "They were doors, and they've been welded shut. There's one more room forward of this bulkhead, and the ribs make a circle enclosing the room. Observation windows are set between the ribs."

"Observation windows?"

"Yes, it would be the observation room for the crew whenever they were off duty."

"You mean we could see out?" Shanni cried, running her hand up the offending welded seam.

"Yes, I used to watch all the time. I couldn't get enough of it! That was on my first voyage, on another ship. It seemed strange to me, but most of the crew never came to watch. They just stayed in the rec rooms and played games, watched Crystal — things like that. So I just sat in there alone. There was so much to see, and so much of it was incredibly beautiful! I don't think I'd ever get tired of it!"

"Oh, I wish I could see it too!" Shanni pressed herself against the sealed doors. "Why're they welded shut?"

"I don't know. They were that way when I first came aboard. I sure was disappointed. Now I'm doubly disappointed."

Shanni grabbed one of the metal rings in each hand, and lunged back as if she could pull the massive doors out of the bulkhead by brute force. "I guess I'm not strong enough," she sighed. "Why doubly disappointed?"

Daric's voice was suddenly quiet, and tender. "Because I'd like to be able to show it to you."

Shanni gave up trying to pull the doors down, and turned around to face Daric with an expression that would have melted an iceberg. "You would?" she whispered.

He was standing several feet from her, but somehow he couldn't move closer. Her face was tilted to one side, her expression soft. "Especially today," he continued with effort, then lapsed into stillness, looking at her.

She looked down at the seam in the deck, touched it with a toe, then carefully placed one foot to starboard of it, and the other an equal distance to port. When she leaned back against the sealed doors, she wriggled her back until she could feel the middle weld centered under her backbone, aligning herself with the exact center of the ship. Almost indolently she turned her head far to her left, stretched her arm out, and grasped the metal ring in her fingers of her left hand. Slowly she turned, and mirrored the action, reaching out with her right hand.

Her innate sense of ritual had Daric hypnotized, as stunned as if he'd blundered into a room where some magical rite was about to be performed. His mouth was dry.

Closing her eyes, Shanni tilted her head back against the metal and rocked it back and forth until she could feel the welded seam precisely in the middle of the back of her head, completing the picture of perfect symmetry. She pulled on the unyielding iron rings as though the ship owed her something, and hadn't yet realized its obligation. Then she opened her eyes, finding his, holding them.

Chapter 80

DARIC AGAPE — BREATHLESS

DARIC'S MOUTH WAS open, totally speechless. It was as if she had given herself to some thought or gesture, and had somehow drawn him in with her, leaving the world behind.

"Why especially today, Daric?" she asked quietly, and her voice seemed deeper than he had ever heard it. Her head raised just a fraction of a degree, and he found her eyes provocative beyond measure, yet he didn't dare believe it was more than a wishful reflection of his own desire. Her eyes flicked back and forth, searching his, drawing him through the looking-glass, gently but inexorably teasing him into accepting a more immediate and overwhelming reality than the steel ship surrounding them.

"You said, `especially today', Daric. Why today?"

"We're coming to something very beautiful," he said, and his mind turned the words around this way and that as he looked at her beauty before him. His voice, too, was almost a throaty whisper. "I wish I could show it to you," gesturing with his eyes to the impenetrable barrier of the steel bulkhead behind her, contrasting so strangely with the warm aliveness of her body, the downy soft line of her cheek, the glints in her hair.

Her eyes were half shut, and he dared to think her lips were swollen. Her white-clad figure contrasted sharply with the dark bulkhead. She said, "It's only a wall, Daric. It's only steel."

"Only a wall!" His voice was silent, but his shout rang echoing through the corridors of his reeling mind. "Of course, it's only a wall! It's only steel!"

"The doors are welded shut, Daric. Can you take me through the doors?" She held him with her eyes. "Show me!"

"It's only steel! It's so obvious!" he thought in triumph, then, aloud, he said, "Yes, I'll show you, Shanni," and there was liberating joy in his voice.

———————————————

"What I wanted to show, no, what I will show you is called Grand Caverns. The ship is due there about sixth hour tonight — if we had windows to see through, we'd see it at Day's End, usually all colors of reds and oranges before the CoreFires turns dim and dark. But I'll have to show it to you the only way I've ever seen it, when I was on my first voyage."

As he spoke softly, the vision became real while the ship faded away. "Pretend we we're both there, together. Pretend it's in the middle of the CoreFires night, and everything's deep blue. Picture us in the observation room. It's built like a half sphere, with the ribs extending from the South Pole below us to the North Pole above us like longitude lines. In between the ribs are diamond coated windows so we can see everything. Imagine we're snuggling on a couch in the middle of the sphere, and the ship is rounding the last bend before Grand Caverns."

"Hmmmm, I can't wait," Shanni murmured.

"The caverns were named for the natural caves called the Grand Caverns back on the planet of Space End..."

"I've visited them," Shanni added.

"...then you remember the chambers with hundreds of stalactites hanging from the ceiling and stalagmites reaching up from the floor?"

"Yes. They were magnificent," she replied in a purring voice, as if she were leaning her head on his shoulder.

"As we get our first view of the CoreFires's Grand Caverns, we know what magnificence really is! Vast, two miles tall and up to a dozen miles wide, a long series of chambers populated with thousands of moving stalagmites and stalactites! Picture the floor covered with the usual host of CoreFires whirlpools, then grab hold of the center of a whirlpool and pull it up until the whole thing sticks up from the floor like a spiraling cone of CoreFires."

"Sort of like a twisting pine tree made of CoreFires?"

"Exactly! Now do the same for all the others."

"The whole floor is a forest of spiraling CoreFires cones?"

"Some reaching higher than the ship. And the same for the ceiling. Reaching down like thousands of very slowly spiraling glowing tornados. Sometimes, the lower ones and the upper ones have joined into giant spiraling columns of blue. It's an amazing view when we first get to look into the chamber, but as we enter the Caverns, we slowly thread our way among the cones and columns. It's breath-taking! And... Shanni, I forgot to mention the lightning."

"There's lightning?" she whispered.

"Great bolts of lightning! Every once in a while, from the hanging tip of a stalactite to the tip top of some stalagmite below. Sometimes a bolt flashes sideways, reaching across miles of the Caverns. Several times a minute there's a big flash, often far away, sometimes very near."

"Is it dangerous?"

"More exciting than dangerous. Now, use your imagination. Everything is in shades of luminous blue. Pretend our ship is well into the first chamber, and beginning to pick out a path between spiraling indigo columns laced with blue-white fire. We pass between two and you can look way up their sides. When we're this close you can tell how huge they really are! Far below, hundreds of baby spirals are growing, far too short to reach our ship."

"Seedlings?" she asked with a laugh.

Daric laughed, too, his heart soaring. "It's only steel!" he thought again, before answering her question. "Yes, seedlings. Next year's crop. Ahead three columns seem to be moving too close together, and the captain decides to turn aside rather than risk taking us between them..."

There, in the exact center of the ship, but not there at all, Shanni and Daric laughed and voyaged. She, looking up as if watching the lightning, swinging from the rings fastened to the welded steel doors now impotent as a barrier; he, but three paces away, arms flailing as he described the wonders. Freed, freeing each other, they laughed in joy at the imagined marvels all about them.

———————————————

Chapter 81

CAN'T SEE 'EM — NO CAMERA COVERAGE

ONE LEVEL ABOVE their heads, Kegler asked the cursing Stulmin, "What's your problem?"

Stulmin kept switching from camera to camera. "It's those kids! Since we welded the doors shut I've got no coverage from the observation room camera, and they've been stopped for a long time just outside the doors. The side corridor cameras won't reach, and I can't hear a word they're saying!" Once again he made another useless round of alternate cameras.

"Too bad, Stulmin!" laughed Kegler. "I could care less! They can't do us any harm from there! But if you're getting too frustrated..." Kegler reached into a drawer set in his own console and fetched a Crystal that he inserted into Stulmin's reader. A lurid romance video began playing on the screen next to the surveillance monitor. With a snicker Kegler slapped Stulmin on the back. "...this should keep you happy!"

"Bah!" Stulmin growled, wiping his mouth as Kegler's raucous laugh wandered into the other room. Again, Stulmin tried fruitlessly to find another camera, then gradually began checking the surveillance monitor less and less often as he was drawn into the action unfolding on the other screen.

Chapter 82

JUNKING IN THE RING
— THE SECOND TALLEST MAN

HERE'S ONE!" SHOUTED Mutch, looking like a spacesuited prairie dog as he popped out of a hole in a scrapped ship hulk orbiting Junker's castle. "And it's the right size," he added excitedly, waving the complex part above his head.

Marneen popped out of another hole, calling, "You found another one?"

Mutch held the part up proudly, "Sure did! It's a 140-T, too!" He turned toward a spacesuited woman who was waiting in a skiff tied up to the hulk. "Felicita, here's another one! Can you tell if it's the half you need?"

Felicita climbed onto the derelict, calling out as she approached, "That's great! I'm sure glad you came with me today. 'Til my wrist is better I'm no good trying to paw through this scrap. What with Lyard and Garms gone, I wouldn't have found a one if it weren't for you kids! Here, let's see what you've got."

Mutch handed her the part, and she examined it for a moment before exclaiming in disgust, "Another left half! Is that our fifth?"

Mutch and Marneen both agreed.

"The fifth left half," Felicita said, "and not one right half!" She looked at the kids. "Do you know what that means?"

Both shook their heads, puzzled.

Felicita leaned down and told them, "That means that this Farnham Anti-backflow Recovery Filter was junk when it was new!" She looked at Mutch. "Crappy design!" she pronounced. Mutch's eyes grew big. She turned to Marneen. "Fatal flaw!" Marneen's mouth made a little "o".

"How do you know?" Marneen asked.

Felicita put an arm around each child. "When you come out here junking, it's 'cause something has failed, given out, right?"

"Right!" they agreed.

"And we've found five left halves and no rights."

"Right."

"Which half failed on my filter back at Dutchman's?"

"The right half," Marneen answered.

"I get it!" Mutch exclaimed. "We're not finding any right halfs because other villagers already found them! Everybody's filters are failing the same way, so they all have to replace the same half!"

Marneen thought Mutch was pretty clever. "Crappy design!" she affirmed with a vigorous nod. "What's the fatal flaw?"

"I'm not sure," Felicita answered, "but a good guess would be..." She stopped as her audience had suddenly disappeared without explanation, popping down one of the holes leading into the interior of the hulk. Moments later a Core Patrol ship swooped low overhead on its way to the castle in the middle of the junk ring.

Felicita stood up and watched as it circled Junker's Keep, checking both spiral docks but finding them vacant. Then it flew on to the far side of the Ring and began to work its way around, flying slowly over the orbiting junk, obviously looking for something. As it finally approached the hulk she was standing on, Felicita waved, and the ship immediately slowed down until it was hovering only a few yards away.

A voice sounded over her bio-comm. "Core Patrol, Major Apheron. Are you in charge here?"

"Good morning," Felicita answered, then tilted her head thinking about it. Was it still morning? Early afternoon? Surely it was still late morning she concluded. "Yes, good morning," she said positively.

"Then you will be responsible for warning the others, " the voice announced.

"What? No, not me," Felicita countered, then continued, "Yes, it's morning. No, I'm not in charge, anywhere!"

Apheron was having his usual luck communicating with Gappers. "You are not in charge here?"

She shook her head. "No sir. Not here. Not anywhere."

"I need to issue an urgent warning," persisted Apheron, feeling like he was wading into a familiar swamp. "Is there anyone else here?"

Felicita looked up at the spacecraft and shrugged her shoulders. "Only Mutch and Marneen."

"Aaah!" The voice representing the authority of the starry worlds of the galaxy spoke as if addressing a backward child, obviously pleased at having made some progress at last. "Then I must speak with this Mutch and Marneen." The hovering Core Patrol ship shifted its position a little, as if anxious to move on. The voice continued, "Can you direct me to them?"

"They're right here. I can call them."

"Excellent. Please do so immediately."

"If you say so," Felicita replied with grave doubts, then poked her head into a hole and called for Mutch and Marneen to come out. Turning back to the hovering spaceship, she asked, "What's the warning?"

"It's an urgent warning concerning everyone's safety. I'll explain it to this Mutch and Marneen as soon as they join us. They'll be the ones responsible for warning the others."

Felicita was now even more dubious, shaking her head at the strange ways of bureaucracies in general and the Core Patrol in particular. Reluctantly, Mutch and Marneen reemerged from separate holes in the derelict hull to stand expectantly beside Felicita.

Apheron's groan sounded in their ears. "You, I take it, are Mutch and Marneen, and are not in charge either."

Mutch shook his head negatively while Marneen nodded vigorously, and Apheron cautioned himself to shape his questions more precisely. "Gappers and bots," he thought, "why can't they ever answer what you meant, instead of what you said?"

Much to the major's surprise, Marneen volunteered some information. "No one's here," she said. "I mean, we're the only ones here; no one in charge is here."

Then Felicita added, "We won't be able to warn the others 'cause we're leaving as soon as we can find the right half of a Farnham Anti-backflow Recovery Filter."

Mutch started to point to castle with a piece of junk in his hand but quickly hid it again behind his back. With the junk safely in his other hand, he again pointed in the direction of the castle. "If you want to leave a warning for the others, there's a sign everybody checks at the end of the pier. Right now it says, `Take what you need, we'll settle up later.' and it's signed, `Junker'."

"The heavens are kind beyond belief," the major thought as he looked toward the castle pier, "we've just dispensed with at least an hour's worth of misunderstandings." To the trio standing on the hulk, he broadcast, "If you are leaving, you need to be warned as well. The Grand Caverns is off limits to all travel until tomorrow dawn due to a dangerous condition in the CoreFires. This applies to all craft, including yours."

Felicita gestured resignedly toward her waiting vessel. "We're going back to Dutchman's. My skiff couldn't make it to Grand Caverns if it had a tow."

"Then you'll be safe," Apheron concluded. "If others should return before you depart, be sure they read the notice I shall post on the pier." With that, the Core Patrol Cruiser sped off toward the castle.

"You two saw him coming, didn't you?" Felicita said in a reproving tone.

"There wasn't time to warn you," said Marneen, looking a little guilty.

"And, besides," added Mutch, "you're an adult. If you're a kid you're always in trouble."

"Well, next time, warn me too, OK?"

"We're sorry," Mutch replied. "We will. Do you want to wait in the skiff? We have a little more stuff to check in this one."

When Felicita nodded and started off to the skiff, Marneen and Mutch quickly ducked back into the gloomy interior with its tangle of ruptured piping and overturned machinery.

"What have you got?" whispered Marneen, trying to get a look behind Mutch's back.

"You won't believe it!"

"What? What?" Marneen was torn between trying to be quiet and wanting to jump up and down. "What is it?"

"Do you have room in your pack for this?" Mutch held out a glowing object.

"Oh, wow!" Marneen breathed in an awe-struck whisper. "Wow!" Cautiously she took it in her hand, examining it in wonder. "It's another Tallest Man!"

"Yeah. I found it under a big pile of stuff. I almost didn't, but just when I was going to turn away, I saw a little bit of a glow peeking out from way underneath, and there it was!"

"There are two of them," she whispered, turning the glowing sculpture over in her hand, then holding it up in front of her face. "Poor Tallest Man," she said gently, "lost all that time underneath the junk! We'll take you to Junker and Cirra, and maybe you can ride the big fire-bird head with your friend, and you won't have to be lonely any more."

Mutch's face was also lit by the softly glowing figure as he bent close. "Don't you worry, Tallest Man," he added, "we'll take care of you. You aren't lost now, you can stay with us."

Marneen was concerned. "We'll put him in my pack, but how can we give him to Junker and Cirra? She left the POSH right after Morning Tales, and Junker isn't here."

"We'll ask Felicita to let us stop at the castle for a minute on the way back. I'm sure she'll say OK. But where could we leave the Tallest Man so somebody else wouldn't see him but Junker'd be sure to find him?"

Marneen thought for a minute, then whispered, "I know! I know! Oh, it's so perfect! We put him in the couch, and send it up into the geedizzic dome at the top of the tower! The Tallest Man can be watching out over everything, and only Junker or Cirra would think of the couch not being there. And when they bring it down, there'll be the Tallest Man sitting on the couch as a surprise. Don't you think it's perfect?"

"It's perfect," agreed Mutch. "Let's ask the Tallest Man."

"OK!" Marneen held up the glowing figure. "Tallest Man," she asked solemnly, "do you think it's perfect?" Then with her hand, she made the whole figure nod or bow several times to Mutch, and several times to her. "We do too," she explained. "Now we're going to hide you in my pack. It'll be dark except for your glow, but you'll be safe, so don't be afraid." Her hand swiveled the figure back and forth like the figure was shaking its head. "You won't be lost and alone anymore."

The figure nodded again to Mutch, and then to Marneen, to show that it understood, then they carefully hid it deep in Marneen's day pack.

"OK," Mutch whispered. "Let's go!"

Marneen nodded, then added a quick whisper to her pack, "We're on our way. What a lucky day!"

———————————————

Chapter 83

FOGHORNS HOOTING — AND WELL MET

WRAPPED IN GUSTING glowmists, Junker stood peering intently forward from the prow of the Aries. The echoing hoot of the Phoenix's foghorn sounded close ahead, but the vessel remained invisible.

"Port Junker, about thirty degrees, wide and gentle, I think." It was Cirra's voice on the comm, obviously very close.

"Almost too close," thought Junker, backing off the throttle one notch toward "Dead Slow", even though the line tied to the bow didn't appear slack. "Good guess!" Junker exclaimed as his ship over-ran a loop in the line. "I don't want fifty tons of space-tug climbing over your lovely backside," he muttered. Still no sign of the Phoenix — the line joining the two vessels just disappeared into the fog.

Standing behind a temporary conning station he had built for tricky salvage jobs, Junker began to crank the tiny wheel several turns to port, watching both the binnacle and the line which was now angling off to the left. "Glad I set it up down here," Junker thought, stealing a quick glance back at the pilot house where the stained-glass windows barely showed through the green mists. "Half the time I wouldn't have been able to see the deck, let alone the bow!"

"Now straighten out," came Cirra's voice, then another hoot of her foghorn. "We're almost to the end at Foggy Hole, but it's really thick ahead."

"I've slowed one notch on the throttle," Junker reported as he spun the wheel to straighten his course, "and I just over-ran a loop in the line. Shall I go slower?"

After another echoing hoot she replied, "Go to dead slow. I'll feel the line with my hand and adjust accordingly. If we can get through this we should be OK."

"Dead slow," acknowledged Junker.

After a minute she replied, "Our speeds are matched. I'm steering by the echo here, so I won't talk unless I have to."

"Right."

Junker, too lifted the line in one hand, the better to feel what was happening in the fog ahead.

"Stop, Junker! Dead stop, quick! Someone's coming and there's no room!"

"Stopping!" Then after a frantic few moments, "Aries is stationary, Cirra. Now I hear it, too."

A rather feeble toot sounded from someplace nearby.

Cirra sounded her foghorn three times in quick succession. Junker prepared to sound the Aries' horn in an emergency, but held off because he and Cirra had found it simply sent the Little Way into endless reverberations far too loud to be useful in picking out their way.

Once again Cirra sounded the emergency triplet, and this time there was a faint hoot-hoot-hoot in reply.

Suddenly Junker could see a good bit more of the line. Looking aft, most of the Aries was visible and the glowmist overtaking the ship was thinning markedly. "We're getting a break, Cirra," he reported, "there's a clear patch coming behind us."

Soon he could see the stern of the Phoenix, with Cirra at the helm on the starboard stern wing, and soon after that a disreputable punt rounding the bend ahead, giving another toot on its meager horn.

"It's Lyard and Garms!" Cirra exclaimed. "How far to Foggy Hole?" she asked as they approached.

"M'lady, you be but three bends away," answered Garms as he saw the Phoenix, but he was totally nonplussed when he saw the immense bulk of the Aries close behind. "Are ye mad? Or am I?" Garms exploded. "My eyes discern the Aries, but they've also told me I'm in the Little Way. All these years they've been faithful to me and I've come to rely upon them so! Now that they've gone awry, it'll be such a change to have to heed the counsel of these underdeveloped ears and a tapping cane!"

Lyard was equally dumfounded. "No, you old son of an eagle, either your eyes deceive you not, or, if you're mad, you've sucked me into the maelstrom of the mind to keep you company, for I also see the Aries, looking like she's emerging from the length of the narrowest of passages, the Little Way.

Junker leaned back, hands on hips, and roared out a peel of laughter and continued, "This gap in the fog can get us the rest of the way out of this CoreFires drainpipe if you two will just belay the palaver and turn to! We'll talk while we work! Garms, pull that excuse for a skiff into the Phoenix. Lyard, jump to the line and help Cirra pull the Phoenix back to the Aries. I want the Phoenix on the Aries' deck and lashed down within one minute. What brought you here? We thought Cirra was going to have to shanghai you two out of the POSH."

"It was Mr. Garms," Lyard called, as he joined Cirra in pulling the line in. "He got an incurable itch in his premonition, and there was nothing for it but we had to borrow this decrepit vessel from the POSH and make for the Ring. We surely didn't expect to find you two here!"

"You're both well met, you old sea-hogs!" Junker laughed, as the Phoenix came alongside the Aries. "Mind the hook, I'm going winch her up."

"Aye, Cap'n," acknowledged Lyard. "I thought ye were daft, Mr. Garms," he continued, "but I'm sorry I doubted ye. It were our captain who's daft!"

"We're all daft!" Cirra countered.

As the trio was riding their Viking elevator, Lyard with his hand on the cable, Junker called from the pilot house, "If you're with me, we're about to set course for something the Core Patrol prohibits, venturing into an unknown danger where the CoreFires is acting up, chasing after a hotshot kid that's been tweaking a Core Patrol major's nose, all on the say-so of a storyteller whose crazy enough to sail through the middle of the Firefall! What about it?"

Garms and Lyard jumped out of the Phoenix and began pulling her over to a set of tie-downs.

Lashing his end, Lyard called on the comm, "Sounds reasonable to me, Cap'n, I don't care if you get your orders from a bot that's found religion!"

Garms finished his lashing with a flourish, and as the trio on deck raced to the pilot house ladder, he continued, "Some old sailors once told me that a woman's compass can point towards a direction you never heard of." He gave a big wink at Cirra, waving her forward toward the bottom of the ladder. "Be that as it may," he concluded, "I keeps my eye on my duties, and leaves my captain to keep his eye on the horizon!"

As Cirra slammed the pilot house door closed, she added to the hubbub, "Here comes some more glowmist! You've got two more vessels on board. If you don't get out of the Little Way during this gap in the fog, two other captains are going to be chewing on your behind."

Junker fired the mighty engine. "All right, all right," he replied, manning the wheel. "I'm outgunned." He spun the wheel as they rounded the first bend, and the end of the tunnel was in sight. "We're on our way to Grand Caverns, and if the Core Patrol catches sight of us we're prison bait. Maybe Hup needs us, and maybe we're a bunch of loonies! Everyone on the right ship? All ashore that's going ashore!"

"Aye, Cap'n, all present and accounted for. Steady as she goes."

For her answer, Cirra just gave Junker a big hug from the back.

———————————

Chapter 84

DEAD SLOW IN GLOWMIST
— ARIES THREADS LITTLE WAY

I'M GOING CRAZY. I'm absolutely going crazy." Shanni was alone, walking aft along a starboard-side passageway. "This is not sane behavior." Her expression was stern. "Girl," she told herself, "if you don't want to get yourself kicked off this freighter you'd better get a hold of yourself! A pubescent teenager would look mature compared to you!"

She had been walking slower and slower. Her cheeks were flushed. A hardcopy labeled "Tomorrow's Manifest" dangled forgotten in her hand.

She looked up into the tangle of piping overhead, not even noticing the surveillance camera she was approaching. As she passed beneath it, lecturing herself, it didn't swivel to follow her progress.

"Your body's a vat of chemical chaos, your mind's a sea of hormones, only a month ago you swore off love for a year. What happened to logic? You're here for adventure and a ticket to other worlds, not romance. Straighten up!"

Shanni took a deep breath, and walked briskly for at least a minute before the paper dropped unnoticed from her hand. She continued to walk on a dozen paces, then slowed, sagging against a pillar, thinking of Daric's eyes.

Leaning her cheek against the cool steel wall of the passageway, she whispered, "Why me?"

She pictured his face, and how he always seemed to be holding hands with her mind, grabbing onto some stray thought of hers and holding it up to the sun as if it were the sparkliest wonder he'd ever seen. How he could suddenly stop in mid-word, overcome by tenderness. How he couldn't speak when he was looking into her eyes.

Shanni rubbed the cold steel wall with her cheek, feeling wordless. Suddenly her fist clenched. "It better be me!" she growled.

As changeable as a breeze, she was suddenly pensive again, looking down at her feet and noticing — without the fear of her first minutes on board the Reliant — that she was again standing on a grating a good four stories above the massive machinery so far below the soles of her boots.

"I can't stand it," she muttered. "I can't last the day." Her eyes opened wider. "I'll never last the night!" Again her voice grew stern. "This is crazy! You signed Ship's Articles, this is a tour of duty. Are you out of your mind?"

Shanni sighed. "I'm out of my mind. I'm going absolutely crazy."

Far below she heard a clang, clang, clang, and soon a robot came walking down the aisle between the huge machines. Her eyes shut for a moment as she savored the coolness of the metal wall against the hot flush of her cheek, and her mind absently listened to the clanging progress of the bot below. When the sound changed, she opened her eyes again. The bot was now almost directly beneath her, and steadily, tirelessly ascending a ladder.

Unable to shake off her mood, she pushed herself away from the wall of the passageway as the bot emerged a few paces away through a hatch in the grating.

"Are you all right?" it asked while it leaned over to close the hatchway.

"Fine, thanks," said Shanni, as distracted as ever, forgetting that the query was not from a human.

"Can I be of any assistance?" the bot asked.

"No, thank you," she replied, but on second thought added, "Yes, you can. Bosun Daric. Can you tell me his whereabouts?"

"Yes, Trainee Shanni, I can. He is beside the starboard aft evac station, between the starboard aft cargo bay and the engine room."

"Thank you," Shanni answered, then added a bit sheepishly, "one more thing."

"Yes?"

"Which way is aft?"

Without the faintest hint of sarcasm the robot pointed out the direction. "That way."

"Thanks again," Shanni said as she started aft and passed the bot which was now clanging its way forward.

The rhythm of its footsteps halted as the robot's vision system identified the piece of paper abandoned on the grating and sorted out the its spatial relationship to the machinery below. That accomplished, it picked up the manifest and analyzed its contents. Weighing the various probabilities, it called after Shanni, "Pardon me, Trainee, did you drop this?"

Shanni loped back and took the paper. "Yes, thank you. I'd probably have forgotten my own head if it weren't screwed on!" Then she ran lightly back down the corridor.

The bot found itself unable to continue its journey forward — even unable to retract it's arm from the position it held when it offered the paper to Shanni — due to a total preemption of its processing powers. In fact, it was to remain in that same position rooted to the spot for the better part of an hour while it contemplated the ramifications of human crew-member Shanni's statement that she probably would have forgotten her own head if it weren't screwed on.

Hand outstretched, face slightly tilted, it thought on, trying to picture her head, unscrewed.

"Fascinating," it muttered.

———————————————

Chapter 85

ROBOTIC AEROBICS — DARIC'S CRAZY IDEA

I'M GOING CRAZY." In his mind, Daric was berating himself. "If I get caught, it could mean big trouble!"

His voice, however, was calling briskly, "Hup, hup, hup, hup! One, two, three, four! Back, forth, back, forth! Hup, hup, three, four…"

Daric was standing on a box in the middle of the corridor where it widened out beside the evac station, barking cadence to two rows of eight robots each, lined up along the left and right walls of the passageway.

"Hup, two, three, four…" Clapping time with his hands, he watched critically as a packing crate went flying back and forth between the ranks of bots, snapped with amazing precision from bot to bot in time to Daric's chant.

"Too, slow, three, four! Faster, three four!" he barked like an aerobic drill-master. Daric stepped down, picking up the box he'd been standing on, and beat it like a drum, increasing the tempo. "Hup-hup-hup-hup, one-two-three-four…"

"Boom-boom-boom-boom," went the crate as it flashed back and forth across the corridor, caught and flung from bot to bot in a dizzying display of coordination. Fearlessly, Daric advanced, still beating his "drum", walking steadily between the two rows of bots oblivious to the rocketing crate that was often missing his head by inches.

About a dozen yards forward, a surveillance camera mounted just below the forest of pipes in the ceiling was panning back and forth to the same rhythm, looking as ludicrous as a spectator at a tennis match. Occasionally, it would stop and the next camera, about an equal distance aft of the action, would begin to wag its lens to the same compelling beat.

Reaching the aft end of his bot brigade, Daric turned and, still standing between the rows, tossed the box from his hands to the nearest bot. "Two-box-es-now! Hup-hup..." Steadily he marched forward down the ranks as both boxes crisscrossed in mid air, inches in front of his unflinching face.

Exactly half way down the line, which happened to be exactly halfway between the two surveillance cameras and just out of sight from both, Daric stole a quick glance at a robot flattened against the edge of the passageway with another bot standing on its shoulders. The upper bot was welding a small cable winch over a hole through the wall of one of the big evac tubes where it disappeared into the forest of piping above.

Daric smiled as he saw that they were nearly finished.

Back and forth the boxes flew in front of his face, the wind of their passage blowing his hair right, then left. "Let's-pick-it-up! Onetwo-threefour, onetwothreefour..."

Just as Daric the Dare-Devil emerged unscathed from the end of the rows, he saw Shanni standing a few yards away in mid-corridor, mouth seriously agape. He bowed, making the slightest signal with a finger behind his back, and the flying boxes went one-two-CRASH, colliding in mid-air behind him.

Daric turned and gave the bots a stern look before saying, "OK, let's try it again until we get it right! Hup-hup-hup-hup...", then he walked over to join Shanni.

"Are you out of your mind?!?" she admonished. "It looked like you could have been killed! And what are..."

Daric held up a finger, interrupting loudly, "Four boxes, hup-hup-hup-hup!" Now four crates were crisscrossing in mid-air. When he was satisfied with the rhythm, Daric called out, "Sound off! Count it out. Let me hear you!"

Sixteen bots chanted in unison, "One-two-three-four, Hup-hup-hup-hup..."

"I can't hear you!" Daric shouted.

"ONE-TWO-THREE-FOUR! HUP-HUP-HUP-HUP!" the bots roared out, filling the passageway with their echoing chant.

Daric turned to Shanni, speaking very quietly, "Don't look at the two bots against the wall. They're just out of range of the surveillance cameras."

"What's going on?"

"Shanni, I've figured out a way we might get to see Grand Caverns if we're very, very lucky."

Shanni's voice was tender. "Daric, you've already showed me the Caverns, and it was so special to me I'll never forget it."

"I mean really, to really show you when we get there this evening, and not just through a window. Do you know about the evac system?"

"No, just that this is called the evac station, and it has a bunch of steel doors." She blushed. "I didn't really do all my homework with the orientation literature, and I just skipped that part — if we'd had to evacuate the ship I'd probably have died trying to find the right page of the manual!"

Daric turned briefly to the bots again, shouting, "Eight boxes! Let me hear it!"

"ONE-TWO-THREE-FOUR!" rang up and down the passageway.

Quietly, he said to Shanni, "Each of those tubes running up the left side of the passageway has a transparent cylinder in it, a life-pod that can evacuate two people and supply life support for an hour without suits, or indefinitely if they're wearing their suits and helmets."

Checking the bots briefly, he continued, "Of course, it would be incredible if we could watch Day's End in Grand Caverns from one of those pods. It's like a glass cylinder with metal ends, so we'd be able to see everything, and since they have to keep from getting drawn back into a disaster, they're built to counter the ship's field. That means we'd be weightless, too."

"Could we do that?" Shanni whispered.

"Even if we could, I'm sure they wouldn't let us, not if they've welded the observation room doors shut. Besides that, three things prevent it. First, it would set off an alarm. Second, the life-pods are only for evacuation — they can leave the ship, but then they'd just float free and be left behind, 'cause once they're out they don't have any way to get back in. Third, the ship has to be stopped or the pod gets cooked by the engines."

Daric turned again toward the bots. The one against the wall was still tirelessly supporting the other atop his shoulders, and the last weld was nearly done. "Backwards! Let's finish it up, smartly now, four-three-two-one..."

"FOUR-THREE-TWO-ONE!"

"So what are you up to here?" Shanni murmured.

"Well, if we had a break in duties at the right time, and if we could get here unobserved, I've got two out of three covered and the pilot could take care of the third."

"You have? How?"

"That one evac tube is just out of range of both cameras, and I had a bot disconnect the alarm. Don't look at them, but the bot on the other one's shoulders is just finishing welding a small winch to the outside of the evac tube with a cable connected to the cylinder inside like a leash. The life-pod could wind its way back inside the ship. Problem number three would toast us to a crisp unless the ship happens to stop at the right time, but that's where the pilot comes in. We can't leave Grand Caverns until a licensed pilot comes aboard to steer us safely through a tricky section called the Maze. If he's late, the ship would have to stop for awhile waiting for him."

"Oh, Daric," she captured him in a squeeze, and planted a big kiss on his cheek, barely remembering to keep her voice down. "You crazy man! It's totally insane, and far too risky, but what a wonderful thought! I'll be day-dreaming about what it would be like to be up there, floating in the middle of all that, watching it with you. You're sweet, and nutty, and I love you for it." She gave him a tiny peck, then pulled back, blushing.

Daric was twice as red. The welding was done, and the bot with the portable torch handed it down to its metal buddy, then climbed down, being careful to stay close to the wall. The torch disappeared into one of the boxes straightaway.

Still counting loudly, the bots watched Daric. "OK, people," he said, ironically, "four-three-two-one, stop! Very good! Once more, same time tomorrow, same place." The two welding bots blended in with the others as they dispersed.

Shanni giggled, saying in a quiet voice, "You are the brashest looney I've ever met. I can't believe anyone would be fooled. Bots don't need practice, and don't think I was taken in by those boxes colliding, either! You're amazing."

Daric, suddenly shy, looked down at the deck. "Time for the afternoon inspection round. We'd better get going."

"Oh, I forgot," Shanni said, holding up the paper in her hand, "you'd better check this out first. Maybe I did it wrong."

Daric looked at the manifest listing the cargo to be sorted and moved from bay to bay for the next day. It looked pretty routine; nothing dropped off or coming on board since no stops were scheduled. "Here, let's check it," Daric said, stopping at a Terminal Station set into the wall of the passageway. He pulled the bench out all the way so they both could sit at the display. "Show me what you did."

Shanni's hands flew over the terminal, and what came up on the screen matched the hardcopy she'd been carrying.

"That was perfect," Daric complimented her. "No problem."

"Except this," she said, pointing to the screen. "No matter what I do, it doesn't show the planet-Crystals anymore. Not anywhere! They just don't exist."

"I didn't notice. Let me check it; I'll search forward to when they're off-loaded. Hmmm, nothing. It looks like somebody just forgot to extend them through the rest of the voyage. It's a funny mistake 'cause the system really ought to catch things like that, but you did it exactly right. It doesn't call for us to move them or anything, and there's no change in their status; it's just that their listing disappears. You did it right — there's just a mistake in the manifest." He closed down the terminal and slid the bench back in the wall.

As they walked down the corridor, Shanni said, "That was very sweet of you Daric, back there," she was speaking very quietly because of the cameras overhead. "With the bots and all, I mean. But the officers would probably see that we'd never ship out again if they caught us.

Either that, or they'd just cut the leash and leave us there!"

They turned a corner, walking down one of the smaller cross-passages. "The wonderful thing is that you wanted to give it to me," she continued. Gesturing up to the ceiling, she was picturing something much grander than the grey pipes and tubing. "I'll think of us up there, snuggling together..." She giggled, wrinkling her nose, "We'd have to hold onto each other because of the weightlessness. It would be like drifting free in Grand Caverns without a ship. Just the two of us, and all that beauty. You'd have to reassure me if I got scared by the lightning. It'd be so romantic."

She sighed, and reached for his hand, swinging his arm back and forth as they walked along. "Thank you, Daric," she said, pausing to look into his eyes. "It was a very romantic gift." Then she gave him a squeeze, and resumed walking. "If they cut our leash," she whispered, "we could just float there and have the grandest view in the Universe until another ship came along and saved us. It might be worth getting thrown in the clink for."

"Not unless another ship came by within an hour," Daric laughed. "Otherwise, the clink wouldn't concern us at all!"

"No, we'd take our helmets. Didn't you say `indefinitely'?" Shanni asked, leaning her head against his arm.

Daric began to stammer, "We'd... They monitor... We'd have to..." His face was beet red.

"We'd watch the colors fade," Shanni continued dreamily, "you'd keep your arms around me so I wouldn't float away. Maybe the next ship could come within three hours so we could take our helmets off part of the time for an occasional kiss."

"Uhhh, Shanni, Uh," Daric mumbled. "I, that is, there's a..." Gently he lifted her face away from his arm, and with a finger under her chin, turned her toward him. "There's something I didn't mention."

Looking into his eyes, she thought, "It would be so heavenly, just the two of us. He's so warm and tender, and so loving and vulnerable when he's embarrassed." She touched his lips with a fingertip. "What is it, bot-master?" she whispered.

"I have a confession to make."

Her voice was mostly sigh. "Confess, crazy man."

"There was a fourth thing I didn't mention about our going up in the pod." He cleared his throat, took a deep breath, and plunged on, "And it's been making me very crazy. I'm sorry, and I'm not. It's all very mixed up, but I've been scared to mention it."

She was leaning very close. "What's been making you crazy?"

"Well, they, I... They know where we are. They monitor the position of our suits!"

"So?"

"Well," he stammered, "to get to the pod undetected, they'd have to think we were someplace we were supposed to be." The words came tumbling out. "We'd have to leave the suits behind and get into the pod without them. When I've been picturing us in the life-pod, we've been, well... I was able to sneak one blanket into the pod, that's all. I know I've been a little crazy, a lot crazy. That's why we'd only have an hour, you see... I'm not making any sense."

She looked, and saw the yearning in his eyes. Moving back, she put a hand on each of his shoulders, looking him right in the eye. "Daric, let me get this straight." He nodded. "You risked your job rigging the life-pod..." He nodded. "To show me Grand Caverns for real..." He nodded. "But we'd have to leave our suits behind..." Red faced, he nodded. "...and get in the pod together..." His nod was microscopic. "...to float weightless in space, watching Day's End in nothing but a blanket?"

His eyebrows went up in a sad expression at the same time a winsome smile played faintly about his lips. "That's about it," he agreed.

Shanni felt like she'd been dipped in electricity. Stepping back, she poked him hard, right in the heart. "Young man," she said fervently, slowly shaking her head, "when you come up with a daydream, you don't stop half way!" Her voice was a husky whisper, her breath was short. "I've been a little crazy, myself, lately..." She made it sound like an understatement, and her eyes grew very intense. "...maybe you'd better hope this ship doesn't stop this evening, and I don't have to decide what I think about this."

When she leaned forward to kiss his lips her hand grabbed the back of his hair. The kiss was half bite, and as quickly as she had pulled him forward she pushed him back, then turned and started walking on down the passageway.

Daric licked his lower lip, then hastened to catch up.

Side by side they walked, saying nothing, their minds bubbling with crazy thoughts, their bodies awash in electricity.

After a minute she reached for his hand, and he squeezed hers in return. As they rounded a corner, she began swinging his arm backwards and forwards in time to their footsteps.

—————————————

Chapter 86

MEDUSA'S CHOICE
— SWEET-TALKING GAP-JOCKEY

COME ON, MEDUSA, nothing else makes sense!"

"Get ready for a two page message, Hup. Page one: `N'. That's `N' as in `Number'. Page two: `O'! That's `O' as in `One'! Put 'em together sweetie-pie! That makes `no' as in `no way'! When the Core Patrol tells me they're going to dice and freeze-dry Number One if I so much as let a bot-flea come into Grand Caverns from Grand Jetty, the answer is N, O, as in `Forget it, Hot-stuff'! Read me?"

Hup's shiny craft was hovering before the window of a ramshackle comm shack also known as Grand Jetty's Port Authority, hard alee of the Flotsam and Jetsum Inn.

"Medusa," Hup replied over the ship's comm, "I must be getting a lot of static. It can't be your sweet voice. I'll try again later." The sleek red and white cruiser spun like a hummingbird smelling nectar, and streaked toward the "outbound" edge of the Gap village.

There, rather than putting in at any of the dilapidated dwellings floating in space, Hup wheeled the Contender around to try again.

As soon as he was back, hovering before the comm shack, Medusa's voice was back in his ears. "What's the matter, young buck? She wasn't at home?"

"Come on, Medusa, you know my heart beats only for you!"

"Sure, darlin'. One beat for me, one beat for Delcy, one for Nadine..."

"Rumors! Wild tales! Fallacious fabrications fostered by frustrated females. Surely you don't believe..."

"Honey, I wasn't born yesterday, and I've got all these mouths to feed." Hup could picture her shaking the snake-like multiple braids that had become her trademark. "A sparks hears everything once, but if she hears it twice, it's her own fault. They don't call me Goldilocks for nothing. Turn to stone, sailor! The answer in no!"

"Oh, oooh, I can feel it happening now! I'm cursed! Your words are coming true, below the waist! Oh, save me..."

"That's your clodhopping feet, you son of a farmer!" Still, Medusa laughed in spite of herself.

"Turned to stone at my tender age, by a woman with a heart of..."

"Watch yourself, shiny-ship!"

"...such compassion, such warmth, such understanding! Who'd have thought it? Cruel fate!"

"A laugh a minute, cradle bait. Climb a mountain! Ask the guru! The answer is NO!"

Hup backed his ship off, still facing the comm shack windows. He began dancing it from side to side. "I'll be your love-slave."

"No!"

"I'll be faithful to you for ever and ever and honor you above all others and we'll live happily ever after!" The spaceship waggled its behind.

"No!"

"I'll wash your windows!"

"N... Talk to me. Ply me with fairy tales. Maybe you could get lucky."

"Medusa," he pleaded, "light of my young life, goddess of my desire..."

"Don't over do it, or you're history!"

"...reptilian coif of my dreams..."

"Good recovery!"

"It's the only thing that makes sense! All contracts are registered with the Core Patrol. Agreed?"

"Correct, you sneaky whippersnapper. You could charm the bio-suit off a stuffed mummy, but I warn you, not off of me!"

"Ma chêre, but of course! It is but a matter of Honor that I must squander my karma in a futile attempt at so Olympian a goal!"

"Go on."

"The Reliant is my contract ship. Agreed?"

"Agreed."

"And my contract, a copy of which resides in the files within your impressive office..."

"Low blow."

"...affirms that I am the pilot of record obligated to take the Reliant safely from Grand Caverns, through the Maze, thence to Dutchman's, and perchance beyond. True?"

"True. Now I want to hear a sweet tone in your voice."

"And," Hup continued sweetly, "The Reliant III has a special clearance, signed by a Core Patrol major, to zip through here with a `Howdy do, thank you ma'am' on its way to Grand Caverns and Dutchman's."

"I wasn't supposed to tell you that, and you'd better not tell anybody else! Be that as it may, I love the way you grovel. Go on."

Hup spun his ship coyly, then once again waggled its rear end. "So, what do you think this Major..."

"Apheron."

"...Apheron wants the ship to do when it gets to the end of Grand Caverns? Disappear? Unlikely! Become a permanent tourist attraction? No tourists! Perhaps he wants it to proceed through the Maze to Dutchman's, maybe even to Littlebend."

"Your logic is impeccable, and you have a nice voice and dimples."

"Would Major Apheron want the Reliant to be hung up..."

"Your words, not mine."

"...unable to proceed through the Maze without her pilot, due to an easily correctable misunderstanding between this unworthy but earnest youth, and the rightfully respected and notoriously lovely queen of the Grand Jetty Port Authority?" The red and white ship sidled back and forth seductively.

"Nice. A bit wordy. Perhaps overlong."

"Your word," Hup shot back, "not mine."

"The answer is still no."

"Medusa, how can you say that?"

"It's easy. Watch my lips. No."

"You're softening, I can tell. Still, you hesitate. Where have I gone wrong?"

"Hup, Major Apheron told me that all traffic was to be held, with only one exception, the Reliant. It has some cargo aboard so urgently needed that it alone has a top priority emergency clearance. There's even a code. He said nothing about you. You got no code, darlin'."

"Medusa, that's it! That says it all! Code or no, you have to let me go through since it's an emergency cargo — otherwise it's stuck at the Maze while somebody comes back to Grand Jetty to get the forgotten pilot. What a goof that'd be! They'd probably be mad, too. Maybe so mad they'd downsize your office."

Medusa snorted. "A high-priced sorcerer couldn't downsize my office!"

"One simple word, Medusa. It makes sense."

"All, right. Yes! But if any of this comes back to get me, you'd better bury the Core Patrol under a pile of explanations!"

"How can people bad-mouth snakes, Man's best friend? As for the Core Patrol, they love me so much you'd probably be better off to say you've never seen me before."

"I'm so reassured I think you'd better take off before I change my mind. Remember, you still have to do my windows."

"And I'm still turned to stone — what time do you get off?"

"Watch your innuendos, or I'll turn you in. At the speeds you travel, you could get back from Littlebend just about when I'm getting off, unless you got distracted along the way."

"Why am I wasting time?" Hup spun his ship in a full circle, then paused, again facing the dilapidated comm shack. "Medusa, you're pretty great, no matter what the others say."

"And you're a wise-ass, Hup. Too bad for us girls you're so good at it."

"Consider me gone, Medusa. I'll kiss you when I return, and don't get off early."

"I'll believe it when I see it, Gap jockey. Safe journey — swift return."

One last time the sleek red and white cruiser waggled its behind, then zipped off in the direction of Grand Caverns.

Inside the comm shack Medusa looked out the window, absently pivoting her swivel chair back and forth. In an unconscious gesture, the index finger of her left hand slowly wound a braid into a coil which she pressed against her cheek. "You're pretty, you're young, you're bursting with life, Hup."

Her finger freed the braid and she leaned way back in the chair, well into that delicious zone just this side of going over, and her long braids hung free over the chairback. "Remember to come back and see me," she whispered.

———————————————

Chapter 87

ARIES INTO THE MAZE
— A VIRTUOSO PERFORMANCE

THE ARIES WAS proceeding at speed down a broad tunnel through the CoreFires, a good three hours travel from where it had left the glow-mists behind at Foggy Hole. All four aboard were in the pilot house, helmets off, and Junker was at the wheel.

"Nowt but CoreFires astern, Cap'n," reported Lyard, standing at the small round windows looking aft over the Aries' huge winch and cable spools. "Neither hide nor hair of the Core Patrol in sight."

"Same for'ard, Captain," added Garms.

"M'lady," asked Lyard, "are you pretty sure they're more likely to be ahead of us than behind?"

"That's my guess," answered Cirra, "but I'll ask everyone a question in return — have any of you seen a Core Patrol ship in the last few days other than Major Apheron's, or heard of anyone else seeing one?"

Junker thought a bit. "Not for well over a week."

"Same here," replied Garms, intently scanning the tunnel ahead.

"I believe I can say the same but I'd not like to stake our fair ship on my memory of it," said Lyard, "and I haven't checked the log."

Junker, standing at the wheel, had been pushing some buttons on the panel at his side. "I just did," he said. "Only Apheron's ship. Lately, you can even identify it at a distance: It's top turret is always turned the same — way over to the side — like it got jammed."

"Then I'll stick with my guess," concluded Cirra. "If there's only one Core Patrol ship, it's now much more likely to be in front of us."

Lyard kept a careful watch on the scene out the aft-facing windows. "In that case, we've got the lookout with the eagle-eyes at the right station. At least we might spot that sourpuss Major Apheron before he sees us. He could've well been right to interrupt Morning Tales if he was running late in passing the warning, I'll give him that. But he acted like a third-rate Overlord when he was threatening the Gappers with confiscating their ships! Still sets me to aboil! I confess I scrunched up my willpower to a fair-thee-well trying to guide that ladle-full of Earthtea onto those steep stair treads just before his boots arrived!"

"Why, Mr. Lyard," Junker laughed, "and you, such a gentle fellow!"

"There's some as don't seem to learn from gentle, Cap'n. He's one seems as he could learn more from a fall. Maybe a stint in the cellar, although given our present position, he's more likely to send us there. Still nothing showing aft, Cap'n."

"Nor for'ard," added Garms.

"If he spotted us here, he'd have us for sure," Junker observed. "I haven't seen a cranny we could hide in for the last five minutes."

"How much longer 'til we be entering the Maze?"

"Just a couple more minutes, Garms. Keep your fingers crossed."

"Aye, and my toes as well."

"But not your eyes!" interjected Lyard. "They're on duty!"

"As you say," laughed Garms. "I never thought I'd be so anxious to enter the Maze. Those twisty passages warp my mind. I swear, Captain, every time we go through, somewhere just a few minutes into it I think I've got it solved and know exactly where we are. Then we go around one more bend and I know we aren't where I thought we were at all. Spooks me proper, try as I might! No wonder the supply ships need a pilot. Yet you take us through every time so slick and easy! The first mate is a hundred times better than I."

"I thank ye for the compliment, but it's not true," Lyard replied. "Don't put yourself down so. You're coming along just fine. And our cap'n doesn't make it any easier by going through a different way every time."

Junker laughed. "Keeps me on my toes and avoids the Core Patrol at the same time. Lyard's right though, you're better than you think. One day it'll all come together. About one minute to go. If Apheron doesn't catch us here we should be OK 'til just before Grand Caverns. The Maze has so many routes, his chance of coming across us gets pretty low once we duck into those tunnels."

"Maze ahead, Captain! I can just make out Dutchman's Holey Moley." Garms chuckled, thinking about the name. The far end of the Maze, where the wide space of Grand Caverns abruptly ended in a wall pierced by a multitude of tunnel entrances was known as the Grand Holey Moley. The Dutchman's end of the Maze was a pocket riddled with two dozen tunnel mouths called, of course, the Dutchman's Holey Moley. Garms, thinking that they had more than their share of excitement on this voyage, continued, "It's Holey Moley for sure, today! Not my preference for a steady diet, Captain. Still no Core Patrol. We're almost close enough to make a run for it in any event."

"Keep a sharp watch Mr. Garms. Making a run for it wouldn't do us any good at all. I'm sure I could lose Aphron in the Maze, but if he gets one glimpse of the word `JUNK' before we're into those tunnels, he'll have the Aries within a day. There's no place in the Gaps that's not his domain." Without taking his eyes off the CoreFires ahead, Junker called over his shoulder, "Cirra, what's your sense of the urgency in our getting to Grand Caverns?"

Cirra shook her head, sending her long hair swirling in waves. "It feels like something's hanging by a thread, Junker, and getting worse, moment by moment."

"That settles it then, I'm going to take us through the Maze at the fastest speed I can manage. Lyard, come take the wheel for a few moments. We need to get ready."

"Aye, Cap'n. Be right there."

Handing off to Lyard, Junker stepped back, quickly kissed Cirra, then began stretching like a gymnast doing one last warm-up before competing in his event. "Garms, are those two vessels on board chained down securely enough?"

"Aye, Captain, They're snug no matter what the Aries throws at 'em."

"Cirra, flip down those jump seats. I'll take her now Lyard. We all need to be seated, side by side, looking forward, everyone belted in.

You'll all be on lookout. If you so much as think you see another ship, sing out. Don't stop to verify, we'd rather have some false alarms than be too late in a collision. Lyard, you here, on my right. I'm setting the wheel to maximum sensitivity. Should you have to take it, it'll be five spokes lock to lock."

"Aye, Cap'n, port or starboard, two and a half's hard over."

"As fast as we can go, it'll still take us an hour through the Maze, and it's going to be a tough hour for all of us." Junker fastened his belt and flexed his shoulders. "I'm going to be sliding this tug through every bend and intersection. By the time we get to Grand Caverns that big engine will be hot enough to warm the POSH for a week." One hand at a time, Junker limbered up his fingers. "Everybody ready?"

Everybody was.

Still at speed, the big tug with its jaunty junk-sculpture letters "J-U-N-K" rapidly approached the Dutchman's Holy Moley marking the end of the wide main tunnel.

"Which one do you fancy Mr. Garms?" asked Junker as the two dozen tunnel mouths gaped just ahead.

"Captain, I'm in the mood for that small sort of heart-shaped one up and to the left."

"Still no Core Patrol?"

"All clear, Captain."

Junker's beard jutted out in a broad smile. "Then give a cheer, crew, for we've made it to the Maze. Hang on!" Junker kicked the Aries' stern out wide to starboard and jerked the bow up high, slewing the heavy ship sideways for several seconds. When he straightened out the skidding slew, the heart-shaped opening was yawning dead ahead, and coming fast. "Here we go!"

Suddenly the CoreFires was streaming past, close on all sides. Junker seemed to anticipate the bends before the others could even detect them, his hands setting up those skidding turns so that the mighty engine was already clawing hard to counter the centrifugal force pushing them into the Gap-walls on the outside of the bends.

Before an intersection was even visible Junker would've made his choice, driving the Aries toward a CoreFires wall that looked certain to consume them, only to have it open into a new tunnel branch waiting to receive them. Curve blended into curve, branches and intersections flew by. The grizzled captain and his ship became one entity of pure immediacy and motion.

In a particularly tricky section a bead of sweat slowly rolled down Junker's brow until Cirra reached across to wipe it away. From there on she kept a hand on the middle of his back to give him energy, and felt the grateful acknowledgment in the slight pressure back against her palm.

Lyard, watching the bends rocketing toward them, watching his captain's hands on the wheel, admonished himself in wonder, "Pay attention m'lad, live each moment of this as if it be your last — e'en though it might well be — for your eyes are privileged to be seeing a master as comes along once in a few generations, and you're sitting on the bench beside him as he's giving the performance of a lifetime!"

Garms's eyes were wide as the CoreFires sped by. "There's many a ship in the Gap faster than the Aries," he thought, "but not a one near as fast through the Maze as what we're seeing today!"

While the crew scanned the Maze, Cirra's intuition was ranging ahead, sniffing the winds beyond the senses, smelling danger and perhaps evil, and a strange scent of destiny that seemed to emanate from Grand Caverns.

"It seems so long ago," she mused as the Aries thundered on at full throttle, "and yet, wasn't it only this morning that Junker said something about the smell of Forever?"

————————————

Chapter 88

A MATTER OF STYLE
— RELIANT AT GRAND JETTY

GRAND JETTY AROUND the next bend, Captain," reported First Mate Kegler of the Reliant III.

Volnath was at the wheel. "Keep the engines at full speed, Kegler."

Kegler raised his eyebrows. "Captain?"

"If you're hard of hearing, Mr. Kegler, I can have Mr. Stulmin assume your duties."

Stulmin looked up from his console hopefully.

Volnath continued, "We're going by Grand Jetty at full speed. We have a top priority clearance, and everyone's going to know it."

"Ah, Captain," Kegler said with a smirk, "you do have your style. This ought to be quite a show!"

Stulmin, too, was now smiling broadly at the thought. As the Reliant rounded the bend he whistled and exclaimed, "Well, look at that! Three supply ships hove to in mid-channel and a bunch of Gap craft waiting off to the side. Looks like the major gets plenty of respect in these parts!"

"Still top speed, Captain?" asked Kegler with a gleam in his eye.

"Top speed," answered Volnath with relish.

"How about going right through the middle of that swarm of Gap flies?" asked Stulmin.

"You're too eager, Stulmin," Volnath warned. "They don't count anyway. It's the captains of those three freighters that are going to be eating their hearts out until tomorrow's dawn after watching us zip on by. I'd buy a few rounds just to hear them cursing us while they're stuck in that two-bit tavern tonight."

"Port Authority's calling, Captain," reported Stulmin.

"Don't answer, Stulmin." Volnath altered his course toward the three stationary supply ships, not so close as to be dangerous, but close enough to command their attention. "Don't answer, just send the code `A377`."

"Aye, `A377`."

Like a massive projectile, the Reliant was rapidly bearing down on the three freighters. Many of the small craft waiting at the side were swinging around to watch.

Stulmin looked up from his console. "They're calling repeatedly, Captain, I think they really want to talk."

"Just send the code once more, then shut off the comm. You won't want to miss a moment of this."

Stulmin, enjoying every bit of it, sent the code and switched off the ship's comm, then joined Kegler, who was standing next to the bridge windows anticipating the flyover.

Carefully Volnath lined up his low pass, and the sterns of the other ships loomed rapidly ahead.

"Whoooo heeee!" crowed Kegler.

"Eat our exhaust, swabbies!" Volnath shouted as the three stationary ships held by Apheron's orders swept by beneath the Reliant and were left behind.

"Hee, hee, hee, hee," laughed Stulmin, clapping his hands in glee. "Let's go back and do it again."

"Sorry, Stulmin, we've got better paying business awaiting us in Grand Caverns," Volnath chortled, "and as for the Reliant, there's no coming back to do it again!"

"Ten points for style, Captain!" said Kegler.

Stulmin stood at the windows as if watching a replay, still laughing and clapping his hands.

———————————

Chapter 89

HUP'S FIREDANCE — FLYING A MUSIC-SPACE

EVEN A BOT COULD figure that one out!" Hup muttered. "A supply ship can't go through the Maze without a pilot, and this one's hauling cargo so urgent it's got a clearance!"

Hup was deep in Grand Caverns, and deep in a one-sided conversation with his red and white spaceship.

"So the Core Patrol forgot, it doesn't change anything. Bot-brained bureaucracies! The whole point is the urgent cargo — the rest follows like the wag on a dog."

Hup steered his speedy craft in a swift S-curve between two columns of slowly spiraling CoreFires. Ever the perfect listener during Hup's soliloquies, his ship never disagreed and never interrupted.

"Mind you, it wasn't Medusa's fault," he continued. "She had her orders, and they told her if she didn't follow them, they'd dismantle her for scrap. If she hadn't seen the light, we'd still be back there waiting with everybody else instead of on our way to our contract. I don't know whether she was being clear-headed or soft-hearted, but either way we owe her. You be sure to get me back here tonight. Before she get's off, too, you hear?"

Almost automatically Hup's eyes roamed ahead of the ship, picking out a path between the two – to four-thousand foot tall cones of twisting CoreFires reaching down from the cavern roof like a forest of immense icicles etched in glowing golds and greys.

"Damn, I'm tired of being put down! Junker's right, I was crazy to challenge that Core Patrol cruiser, but if one more knows-it-all, has-it-all, tells me I'm lower than a bot's instep I'll explode as sure as

Firedawn! I'd better get out of the Gaps before that Major Apheron decides to give you a little nudge at the wrong time. Yeah, you can come with me. As long as it took to build you, sweet bird, I'd hate to leave you behind. I couldn't just park you down on the surface either, down in the bottom of some planet's gravity well — you have to be up and flying. We need a `how', and we need it soon."

Hup guided the beautiful ship in a high-speed arc around the narrower bend separating two of the immense caverns.

"The only way out of the Gaps is on board one of the supply ships," Hup explained, "and there's only two situations where I even get to talk to them, let alone sign on. One is meeting crew-members at a tavern. I'd have to keep from punching some loud-mouth's lights out, but that'd be worth it. Trouble is, the crew ain't going to sign nobody on, no how, especially a Gapper. The only one who can do that is the captain."

Hup's hands could have flown the sleek vessel on instinct, and were pretty close to doing it. "How about this for a `how'? The captain of the Reliant is pretty happy to see us waiting at the Grand Holey Moley. He takes us on board, and he sees how spiffy you are, and he's amazed when he finds out I built you. While I'm taking the freighter through the Maze I let drop the story of how we saved him a heap of time with his urgent cargo, and he's so grateful he signs us on, me as crew, you as the slickest ship's launch he's ever seen. And we live happily ever after! OK?"

A wistful note crept into Hup's voice. "Chance: half slim, half none, so don't get your hopes too high, sweet bird. I'll try, but I've never heard of them signing on anyone from the Gaps. If only there were some other way out of the Gaps besides all those civilized worlds, some other way out from under the thumb of the Core Patrol and the measly contracts we get for piloting. I'm real tired of having someone kicking me off the bottom rung of the ladder. I'll bet you there's nobody guarding the back side of that sucker! Man, I'd shinny up the back side of that ladder like greased lightning if I could just figure out how and where to start! If they blinked twice they'd miss it, wondering what stirred up such an updraft!"

The next cavern was resplendent in bronze and gold, and everywhere the bronze was melting moment by moment into a fiery orange. "Sometimes I'd give anything to find a way to leave. Sometimes I'd give anything to stay. Just look at that! It's so beautiful it'd bring tears to a bot's eyes. Looks like the beginning of Day's End, and a pretty one."

Hup checked their position and the time. "We're about a half hour to forty-five minutes early. We'll be waiting for them at the Grand Holey Moley with plenty of time to spare. Let's slow down and smell the roses."

Hup eased the throttles back from their customary full speed, and let the grandeur before him soak in.

"They're pretty smug in the out-worlds, considering they've got nothing like this. How can CoreFires be so beautiful and so deadly at the same time? Yeah, if that plasma gets one lick on your engines, you're fireworks! That's why Hup takes such good care to keep you out of kissing distance. But, Mother of the Universe, is it ever beautiful! If I were giving tours of Paradise, this would have to be close to the last stop."

Most of the Gap vessels were Spartan in the extreme, but in his quest for the perfect imitation of a luxury out-world ship, Hup had built every accessory imaginable into the Contender, no matter what he'd had to trade to acquire some of the components or how long it had taken him to obtain the final parts. He made use of one of them now, a sound-scape player. Selecting a Crystal from a small drawer in the console, he inserted it into the player, and after a short search found one of his favorites, a haunting and transcendent music-space by a Gap group called the Derelicts.

As with any sound-scape, the choice of a path through the music was up to the listener. Oft-times Hup explored the composition by trying a new random path, then saving it under a descriptive name if he enjoyed it. At other times, he'd follow a path he liked partway through the music, then branch off to find something new. With a finger on the button, he scrolled through the names of his favorite paths, comparing their mood with the beauty before him.

"Let's do this one together, brand new, as we fly," he told his ship as his fingers selected Music and No Visuals. "Whatever path we fly through the cavern will be our path through the music," he explained, choosing Copy Ship Path Realtime.

Through the cockpit windows he took in the magnificent scene. "OK! What a partnership! All the pinnacles of Grand Caverns to play with, the shape of the music to guide us, and our flight path in turn will sculpt the music we hear!" On the console, he tapped Begin Now. "Let's go, sweet bird; we'll do what we do best. It's aerial ballet time in Grand Caverns!"

As the music began, Hup turned the wheel and pushed it forward. In answer the ship rolled over on its starboard flank and stooped like an eagle with folded wings, dropping a mile while the music accompanied its descent with deepening arpeggios carving their way to the mother of all bass notes. With a "Pow powpowpow POW pow, NOW!" the Contender was enveloped in a driving percussive beat as she leveled out at the very floor of the CoreFires cavern, swerving among the skirts of the half-mile high swirling plasma cones.

Hup was no longer conscious of throttle, wheel, or hands as his mind flew and danced to the music, and his ship flew and danced to his mind. Musical phrase and arcing motion became one in a spaceship ballet beyond the gravity-bound dancer's wildest dream.

The deadly CoreFires was the beautiful partner in this incredible pas de deux, wrapped in rippling flame, a kiss away from death, but Hup's skill was sure, his ship superb. Again and again he flirted with the kiss only to roll his ship away in a magical arabesque, racing along the curving contours of the fiery surfaces, just out of reach.

Ahead, a lightning strike atop a particularly tall spire drew his eye. As he bent the ship's winding course in the new direction the music transmigrated through new keys and raised soaring harmonic structures of ethereal timbres. Upward he climbed, circling the CoreFires spire, the ship an extension of himself as it pirouetted, curve on curve, the music weaving new melodies to the shape of the motion.

Closer and closer to the tip of the spire the Contender danced. Tighter and tighter she wound around the apex where the flame of molten gold spun upon itself like a delirious ice-skater, until a great lightning strike quenched the spinning fire and Hup wheeled the ship away in a series of aerobatic maneuvers as graceful as calligraphy in space, and the music followed.

Looping, diving, carving space among the spires as a swallow carves the air among the trees, she — as all ships have ever been she — shaped the music that in turn shaped her flight, a dance in three dimensions in space, and many more in sound. Rolling over and over in joyous abandon, weaving among five merging incandescent columns, climbing, winding her way to the very top of the fiery vault festooned with its giant glowing icicles, she flew and danced.

Flowing, gliding, tumbling she descended, sometimes as playful as a falling leaf, at others as poised as a hawk wheeling on the breath of a thermal.

As the compositional structure forged its way toward a climax, Hup saw two great CoreFires cones, one from above, one from below, spinning in opposite directions, the tips growing toward one another and about to touch. Letting the music be his guide, he choreographed one final calligraphic sweep that brought the Contender up to the swirling points just as they merged, fused, unraveled into a net of lightning, and dissipated leaving only a soft golden haze as the last majestic notes echoed their way to infinity.

Chapter *90*

Aboard His Beloved Contender
— Arcing Among The CoreFires

RENEWED, HUP TOOK a deep breath.

The next song was as serene as his mood, and to Hup, the Contender also seemed content to soar evenly and wordlessly onward amid the deepening golds of Day's End.

For the moment, at least, all seemed right with the Gaps.